The CHRISTIAN DETECTIVE

The CHRISTIAN DETECTIVE

ROBERT ROGERS

THE CHRISTIAN DETECTIVE

iUniverse books may be ordered through booksellers or by contacting:

iUniverse
1663 Liberty Drive
Bloomington, IN 47403
www.iuniverse.com
1-800-Authors (1-800-288-4677)

ISBN: 978-1-4917-4803-9 (sc)
ISBN: 978-1-4917-4802-2 (e)

Library of Congress Control Number: 2015903304

Print information available on the last page.

iUniverse rev. date: 03/13/2015

Also by Robert G. Rogers:

Murder in the Pine Belt, 2010, Dirtdauberbooks.com;

A Killing in Oil, 2013, Whiskey Creek Press;

The Mississippi Campaign, 2014, Dirtdauberbooks.com;

The Pinebelt Chicken War, 2014, Dirtdauberbooks.com

Jennifer's Dream, 2013, Uncial Press,

La Jolla Shores Murders, Archway Publishing, 2014; all Bishop Bone Murder Mysteries.

Historical drama: Jodie Mae, 11/23/13, Create Space

Pre-teen Adventure story: Lost Indian Gold, 2012, Astraea Press

A teen Adventure: Taylor's Wish, Amazon.com

Suspense/Thriller: Runt Wade, 2013, Musa Publishing

Children's Picture book: Fancy Fairy, 2013, Dirtdauberbooks

Dedication

My thanks to all those who have read and commented on the book including Kathy who edited it, Ben who gave me a good read, Eva, Yarka, Nadine and many others including Reverend Scott whose sermons and wisdom were the inspiration for the story. And, a special thanks to Lucy who always has a helping hand for those in need. And, to my late wife, Carolyn, who saw good in everyone.

Most of all, I want to thank all the people around the world who have turned to the Bible for the strength to free themselves from whatever dark cloud had been hovering over them. This book is for you.

Prologue

It was Halloween night on a street in Mission Hills, San Diego, California, but no children roamed the street and none would. Only gated condo buildings faced it. No doors to knock on for candy treats.

A heavy-set man in a brown, well-worn leather jacket passed through the gate of his multi-storied condo, unique for its hint of Mediterranean styling. A soft breeze stirred the warm air. At the sidewalk, he turned right. In the dim light, his rugged face showed. The street was used mostly by the inhabitants of the condo complexes; there was little traffic. One street light was out and those that were lit cast the man in dim twilight. He hitched at his belt, a nervous habit, and began a slow walk to his ultimate destination, a McDonald's a few blocks away.

Approaching him was an odd figure dressed in a black witch's costume, complete with mask and pointed hat. Its right hand held a black, miniature baseball bat. The figure, somewhat shorter than the heavier man, walked with a kind of ambling swagger, letting the bat swing back and forth.

Along the sidewalk some distance away, a man and woman walked toward them with a casual, non-hurried, stride. They talked and laughed.

The witch bumped into the man from the condo, deliberately it seemed. The two exchanged words and the man pushed at the witch and gestured with his arm as if angry. The couple witnessed the encounter, but were too far away to hear anything except that the witch might have been singing.

The witch stepped past the man who glanced over his shoulder and paused to shove a clinched fist at the witch, before resuming his walk. The couple said his face showed anger and he said something but they couldn't hear what it was.

The witch took one step, stopped, suddenly turned and swung the bat at the taller man's head. It struck with such force that the bat broke. The man crumbled to his knees and fell face down.

The witch said something the couple could not make out and took off running in the opposite direction, hard, hanging onto the remaining part of the bat. The witch's black cape flowed behind.

After being momentarily stunned, the man and woman ran to where the man in the leather jacket lay on the sidewalk. The man knelt beside the man's inert figure and shouted, "Sir, are you okay?" There was no response.

By that time, the witch had rounded the corner out of sight.

"Check his pulse," the woman said.

"Nothing. He's dead," the man looked at her and said. "Call the police."

The witch was never found.

Chapter

1

Jake Carson trudged, face down, along the sidewalk in the Bird Rock area of La Jolla, California. He wore a light-weight surfer's jacket found on the beach, frayed khaki pants and shirt. His hair, uncombed, was light brown with premature graying at the temples, eyes a piercing, emerald green. His face showed the lines of hard living and the ruddy color of someone heavy into drink. The brown paper bag dangling from his hand gave testament to that. In it was a quart bottle of beer purchased with the last money he had.

Just ahead, on the opposite side of the street, he saw Minnie Sue, a tall, heavy-set woman wearing a blue uniform. She was talking with another woman. Both were well into their sixties. Minnie Sue served as night matron in the halfway house where Jake was headed. To take away the stigma associated with it, it had been named the Sunrise House.

She interrupted her conversation and motioned with her head in his direction. "That's Jake Carson. He's one of mine."

"He looks depressed," Minnie Sue's companion said, loud enough for him to hear. She was dressed in the uniform of a maid. La Jolla was a wealthy suburb a few miles north of San Diego in southern California so uniformed maids and servants were a common sight.

Jake only shaved and put on fresh clothes when he had work. And he only took jobs when he'd spent whatever he'd been paid for the last job.

"Well, I imagine he is." Minnie Sue lowered her voice to a whisper as Jake passed. He still heard most of what she was saying, but didn't give any indication that he even knew they were there. "From what I've heard, he was considered a pretty good lawyer at one time. Not even fifty and he's washed up. It's a crying shame what some people do to themselves." She shook her head back and forth with "tsks" to show her feelings of disgust.

She gossiped to her friend about the drinking problem that had landed Jake in the Sunrise House.

The file that came with his assignment said the judge had ordered Jake there until he could show he'd overcome the problem. That came after Jake had repeatedly appeared drunk and disorderly in court. It was either that or a minimum security facility but in consideration for Jake's past record as a lawyer, the judge sent him to the less harsh Sunrise House.

"In my opinion, he hasn't changed much," Minnie Sue said. "And, I don't think he wants to. Look at that paper bag. I'd bet my social security check there's a bottle of beer in it."

A noise caused Jake to turn his face briefly toward the Pacific where waves rolled lazily onto the white sands, some getting so far as to slap white froth against the sides of the giant rock outcroppings that broke the beach into separate play areas. The mid-afternoon sun, already in its descent in the western sky, had turned the clouds into streaks of orange edged in purple.

It was Sunday, mid-December. The cool breeze brought by the waves encouraged visitors to gather their towels, pets and children for an early end to their day of carefree frolic on the sand. Wet suited surfers, not yet willing to admit the day was over, continued to paddle out far enough to catch such waves as there were. Others, already out there, waited to catch a respectable blue curl for a ride in, then to do it again until finally forced to admit there'd be other days and other curls to catch.

Jake remembered the three unanswered calls posted on the house's bulletin board. With no money left for essentials, like beer, he'd have to answer one. The thought sent a shudder over his body. He didn't mind the work, as menial as it was. What he minded was being humbled before other lawyers, most of whom he felt superior to, with good reason. He was, or had been.

"How have you been doing?" They'd ask, code for "Are you going to stay sober long enough to do this job?"

His response, forcing a smile, "Haven't felt better in years. Enjoying the hell out of my, what shall I call it, retirement at no pay?"

So far that had satisfied the askers. They didn't press for details. Jake had had a temper at one time and standing a shade over six feet with a weight approaching two hundred pounds, no one wanted to stir it.

No alcoholic beverages were permitted in Sunrise House, but he drank anyway. On the sly, in the evenings, sitting on the edge of his cot, staring mindlessly at the wall-mounted television. Tuned to a channel one of the other occupants in the room preferred, usually nothing he'd have selected.

Only Jake thought it was on the sly. Minnie Sue, the keen-eyed matron who managed the house in the evenings, noticed everything and reported his indiscretions regularly to the court administrator. He didn't much care. Depressed as he was, his hope was that one day he'd simply die in his sleep. He'd lost everything but his life and that didn't seem worth getting up for every day.

Ahead, from a speaker, a male voice filtered through the beach noises and drew his attention. Light applause filled a pause. That was followed by what sounded like the gentle strumming of a guitar.

Across the street Jake saw a paneled van bearing the name of a local television station, complete with a satellite dish. Beside it stood a number of men and women in street clothes, some talking to each other, half paying attention to what was happening on the other side of the street.

A few feet away from the van, a man with a camera on his shoulder and a woman in a dark gray suit interviewed a man with dark, short hair, wearing a perfectly fitted black suit. He was holding what appeared to be a brochure which he periodically referred to during the interview. His face bore a serious look but he otherwise seemed comfortable.

Must be a news event, Jake surmised.

By then the speaker's deep, melodious voice was clear enough for him to pick up the words. From the softening of the tone, it appeared the message had entered a transitional belly. Then, the pace of it picked up. "I imagine the Lord's watching us. Wondering just what the heck we're doing. We're supposed to be keeping His commandants. Goodness me, don't we come right out and say we're a nation under God?"

Jake drew close enough to see the speaker, a tall, stately man, a little on the heavy side. He was dressed in white, right down to his shoes and gray-haired with a neatly trimmed snow-white beard and a mustache that stretched from sideburn to sideburn. A fair sized roll pushed at his belt. A microphone was strapped around his neck and positioned to catch the words he spoke. A battered old guitar hung around his neck and rested under his arm. He stood on an elevated wooden platform below the sidewalk, and had to look up to speak to those who had gathered along the rail to listen.

A young man with one arm around a surfboard and the other around a long haired young girl laughed and interrupted him with a shout. "Make love not war, preacher man!"

The speaker sought out the young man with his eyes, waved a hand in his direction, smiled and said, "In the book of James, the Lord tells us, 'If you know what's right and you do wrong, you're going to make me mad.' I pray you don't make the Lord mad."

The young girl slapped the back of the young man's head lightly and whispered something that Jake couldn't pick up.

"Thank you sir," the young man promptly replied.

A few yards from where Jake weaved his way through, four young people in green and white, two women and two men, all clean cut and smiling, faced the crowd from a space they'd carved out in front of the rail. As the man in white strummed his guitar, they clapped and hummed and sang.

Ah, glory be, Jake thought with a cynicism that had dominated his thoughts for some time. *They're filled with the Spirit.*

The words of Benjamin Franklin were more what he believed in. "The Lord helps those who help themselves." To Jake that meant you were on your own. Franklin's bit of wisdom had always been enough religion for him.

The man stopped strumming, held his arms out as though dispensing spiritual blessings then spoke in a soft voice that the microphone had no trouble picking up. "Jesus told this story to his disciples. A rich man in fine linen robes, stuffed himself with the best of everything. Outside his window, in plain sight, was an emaciated man, dressed in rags and covered with sores. Lazarus was his name. Anyone paying attention could hear the starving man begging for the crumbs that fell from the rich man's table. 'Just the crumbs, sir. A few morsels.' The rich man was appalled by the sight. So, what did he do? Well, he pulled his shades shut so he wouldn't have to see it! There's a lesson for us in that."

One of the four apostles called out, "Bless you, Brother Rasmussen."

So, Brother Rasmussen's giving the sermon today, Jake mumbled "excuse me" and pushed into the crowd.

The man in white smiled with a nod and continued. "Lazarus died and went to heaven. The rich man also died but he was sent to hell, to burn for eternity in its fires. I can just about hear him calling the Lord. 'Can you help me Lord?' And I can just about hear the Lord's answer. 'Lazarus called for help and you did not answer. What you have sown, you will now reap.'"

By then, Jake had pushed past the four apostles in green and white to break into open space. He was shocked to hear the speaker call out, "Sir! You with the bottle!"

What! Is he calling me? Jake reluctantly turned to face him.

"When Satan took Jesus to the high mountain and promised him the world if he'd serve him, Jesus said, 'Get thee behind me Satan. I will only serve God.' You sir, cannot serve God if your thoughts are clouded by alcohol. You will serve Satan. God has said that an alcoholic drink bites like a serpent and stings like an adder. I pray that you do not fall under that spell."

Jake grimaced and waved him off. A fresh breeze swept in from the ocean as if to push him on his way. It did not come fast enough however.

"Sister Rachel!" Rasmussen called out to one of the young women Jake had just passed. "Give that sinner a Bible. Sir, you will not find the answers to your problems in a bottle, but you will surely find them in the Bible. Remember, the Lord loves you."

The young woman shoved a Bible, bound in black, at Jake. He was about to push it away, but something about the way she smiled make him hesitate. By then, the Bible was in his hand.

Across the street, the cameraman broke away from the interview to film the exchange. The man being interviewed had patted him on the back to send him on his way. The woman in the gray suit followed and directed the cameraman's actions. One of the other men from the van held out a microphone to catch the exchanges between Rasmussen and Jake.

Don't waste your time. I'm already yesterday's news, Jake thought and trudged on without stopping.

Behind him, the man in white resumed. "I apologize for stopping like that, but that man was in need of God's grace." He gave his guitar strings a couple of strums. Taking their cue, his four disciples hummed and clapped their hands.

Rasmussen began to speak to the crowd, slowly, deliberately. "That parable I was telling you about, Lazarus and the rich man ... strikes me like ... well, I think it's knocking at our door. Our tables are overflowing while children around the world are begging for our leftovers. What are we doing about it?"

He panned the onlookers from one end to the other. "We're sending bullets and bombs." Frowning, he added. "Bullets and bombs don't feed anybody! Bullets and bombs kill mamas and papas! Dead mamas and papas leave even more children hungry! Does that sound like what a Nation under God should be doing?"

His voice dropped to a whisper and he glanced from side to side as if searching for something. "I just wonder if that spirit the Lord sent to hell, Satan by name, is telling us what to do. All the time, he's lettin' us believe we're doing the Lord's work!" He raised his voice to shouting levels. "It's time we stopped doing the Devil's work and started doing the Lord's work!"

The cameraman moved to the rail to film Rasmussen's remarks and kept his finger on the red button. It'd be edited later for the late night news. The woman and the guy with the microphone stayed close. The dark haired man they had been interviewing drifted to the rail to watch.

Rasmussen said, "Some years ago, I was in Omaha, Nebraska pushing pills for a drug company. Staying in a fleabag motel. A voice woke me from a deep sleep. It might have been a dream. I can't swear it wasn't. But, it sounded real. I sat up and looked around. Wouldn't you? It was July and hot, but that room was cool and I saw a white swirl at the foot of my bed. I heard the voice again. It said, 'Brother Rasmussen, It is time for a new age of Christians to take My message to the poor and downtrodden of the world. You must let them know that to be born poor does not mean they were born without hope. My word will be the source of their hope and you will be my messenger.'"

Jake stopped his rush to escape and turned to listen. *Did he say the Lord spoke to him?*

Rasmussen paused to let his words sink in. As he did, his four apostles resumed their rhythmic clapping and humming.

Jake recognized that one. They were humming the old Beetles tune, *Come Together*. He smiled, but didn't move. He was curious to hear what the man in white was going to say next.

A man who'd been leaning against the paneled truck, strode purposefully across the street to shout, "Preacher, are you sure you weren't taking those pills you were pushing. Do you expect us to believe that crap?"

Rasmussen stared at the man, no smile on his face, and said, "The apostle Thomas doubted that Jesus had arisen until Jesus showed him the wounds where he'd been nailed to the cross. Thomas became a believer. Don't wait too long to believe, my son. Look at me and listen to my story."

The man did.

And, the man in white said, "I told the voice—he didn't say he was the Lord, but I believed he was—that I was happy the way I was. I didn't want to be his messenger. I didn't know how. I'd only been inside a church one time in my whole life. The voice said I was not to fear, he'd show me the way. And, that was the end of that."

He stopped talking to reach down for a bottle of water beside him on the platform. After taking a long drink and wiping his mouth, he continued. "As you can imagine, I didn't go back to sleep that night. I reached into the drawer of my bedside table and pulled out the Gideon Bible and I began to read. Yes sir, I began to read that Bible. I'd never before had one in my hand, but I read that Bible. When I'd finished, I called my boss and told him I was quitting to do the Lord's work. He laughed at me."

Jake had spent his professional career "reading" the faces of witnesses, listening to their testimony searching for any indication that they were lying. He had to admit that Rasmussen sounded like he believed the Lord had spoken to him.

The guy who'd challenged Rasmussen, backed away, shaking his head without words.

All the time, the apostles continued to hum the Beatles' song, smiling and clapping their hands like they had no doubt that Rasmussen was indeed, a true messenger of God.

Rasmussen described how he preached anywhere he could, street corners, parks, anyplace where more than five people were gathered. He preached out of that Gideon Bible, He was laughed at, scorned, even attacked, but he stayed with it moving from city to city, living like a homeless man on what people gave him, sleeping in his old car. Finally, he got on his knees and prayed to be released from God's ministry.

"I told him I couldn't do it anymore. He needed a stronger man. That night He spoke to me again. He said my ministry for Him was in Africa. Somehow, I got there. South Africa. Worked my way through the Theological Institute of Johannesburg. Did missionary work up and down Africa carrying God's message. The Gideon Bible was my strength."

He picked up a tattered Bible from a small table beside him. "Without this, the Lord's words, I could not have survived. People beat me, ridiculed my words, chased me out of towns. I came to believe that I had failed and prayed to the Lord to be released. I couldn't do it anymore. I couldn't take it."

Intrigued, Jake came back to hear the rest of what the man was saying. The men and women who had come in the paneled van to cover the event quit filming to listen. And those crowding the rail seemed fixed in place, spellbound by the man's recitation. An eerie quiet lay over the area.

"The Lord didn't speak to me that night. Nor the next night. I thought He'd released me. I began looking for a way home and finally got a berth on a boat, working as one of the crew. One night, two weeks from port, He spoke to me again. 'I didn't tell you it would be easy. My son, Jesus, was crucified. Have you suffered more than my son?' Well, no, I told him but I have failed you. He said, 'You only fail when you quit trying. You must try again.' I did try again. And, sure I failed time after time, but I didn't give up and now, I'm doing His work. We're doing His work. We're the New Age Christians. AND, right now we're ministering for Him in Africa!"

Their current mission, he explained, was to build churches in Africa. Train local people to deliver the Lord's message to the children and use the churches as meeting places and schools. He explained that instead of teaching young people to sing hymns and learn English, they teach useful skills such as farming, carpentry, electricity and plumbing. Of course they brought food because nobody could learn if they were hungry.

"That's God's ministry in Africa. We don't tell them the blessings come from America. THEY KNOW IT COMES FROM AMERICA. We're building a bond with the people from the ground up. They love us because we love them. We don't send bombs or bullets, we send love! That's what God told us to do! Proverbs 8:17."

The people looking down at Rasmussen from the sidewalk broke out in spontaneous applause. Jake didn't join in but thought with his habitual cynicism. *Gotta hand it to the guy. He can lay it on. Probably crooked as a snake.*

Jake walked away as the four apostles began passing hats through the crowd. Rasmussen strummed his guitar and sang a hymn, but Jake was too far away to hear the words clearly.

Chapter

2

The late afternoon shade had begun to creep over La Jolla by the time Jake reached Sunrise House. Patches of fog had invaded the street in white misty waves and softened the ranch-styled home to an artistic charm it totally lacked in the stark light of day.

Built in the fifties, the old house had a covered porch across the front complete with cushioned chairs, gifts from patrons. Off white stucco covered the exterior walls, splotched and bleached by the sun and cracked in places, It had a front yard with patches of green and yellow grass. Flowering shrubs lined the borders though Jake had not seen a bloom on one since he'd been there.

The "Sunrise House" sign, in the middle of the yard, had been touched up. The sun was again bright orange with nice yellow rays over a white background. Sunrise House, in bold black letters, stretched across the width of the sign. *The dawning of our new day,* Jake thought cynically with a glance at it.

Bessie, the day matron came at seven and left at five. Her replacement, Minnie Sue, came at five. Usually, a different crew took weekends; all middle aged women, all on the beefy side, hair cut short, like they came from the same mold. All neurotic and all hated men, as far as Jake was concerned. *Probably for a good reason.* None ever wasted a smile, unless forced to in the presence of a benefactor. After all, donations were solicited.

The garage had been converted into two bedrooms for a total of five in the house. Two bathrooms and a powder room provided the necessary facilities. They slept two cots to a room except for one room. It had to accommodate three cots to provide a separate room for the matrons. Jake, the last to arrive, was in the room with three cots.

He felt a sense of dread as he mounted the wooden steps to the porch, like a cloud of death waited for him inside. Music played during the day, bouncy stuff designed to keep the mood of the inhabitants upbeat so they wouldn't kill each other. Jake heard it as a dirge. Something for their funerals even though the deaths of the inmates were still pending.

Since he'd been there, none of the inmates—Jake's characterization of the ten men assigned to the house—had been killed, but there had been fights. Usually over nothing. "Hard cases," those who wouldn't conform, were removed though most were given warnings and second chances.

Jake had one fight right after he'd moved in. An older guy, bristling with nervous tension, claimed Jake was holding up the coffee line one morning and elbowed him to move. It was the second time. The first, Jake let pass. Not so the second. He saw it as a test. The guy ended up on the floor with half a cup of coffee covering his shirt. "The color suits you," Jake told him. Nobody bothered Jake after that.

Both received warnings.

Half were in drug rehab and Jake wasn't sure all of them had broken the habit or even wanted to. Some acted scary to start the day, thin skinned with chips on their shoulders, daring to be jostled. By evenings though they seemed mellowed out enough so Jake could turn his back without fear of getting hit from behind.

A few, like Jake, were trying to beat a drinking habit. Unlike Jake, two men, first offenders, were on probation from doing something under the influence that might otherwise have resulted in jail time. None smiled. A smile could easily be viewed as a condescending slight or something equally sinister, both killing offenses to an incorrigible few, mainly the repeaters. Some of the repeaters, like one of the guys in Jake's room, talked to themselves and to the television and they weren't keen on being interrupted.

Most men looked for work during the day. All were supposed to work if they could find it. A few did. Some just wandered around La Jolla, begging for money or food or both with a sign at selected medians.

When he was broke and needed money, Jake served papers for the law firm where he had been a partner. He had a car but only used it when he was working and had money for gas. The jobs his firm gave him were in the nature of favors. Now and then, they trusted him with a research assignment, but rarely anything of importance. And, there was always some hesitancy when such jobs were handed out. He could see it on their faces, but he took the jobs anyway. Somehow, he managed to stay sober when he worked and had cut down the number of times he got "falling down drunk." Admittedly, it was attributable more to a lack of funds than a lack of desire.

He drank beer when he had money—hard liquor cost more and couldn't be safely secured in the house— until the cloaking cloud of quasi-intoxication took over his senses and swept away his responsibilities.

Jake threw the Bible the girl had given him on the small table beside his cot. Ordinarily, anything of value left out for more than an hour would vanish. He doubted the Bible would. Even clothes weren't safe. Although none of the inmates could wear them without physical repercussions, they did have street value. Like most, he locked the ones he wasn't wearing in a cabinet.

* * * *

After dinner, he sat on the edge of his cot, opened the bottle of beer he'd bought and sneaked swigs between footfalls of Minnie Sue who was moonlighting that weekend. Like his roommate, he stared at the television but his thoughts were on Rasmussen's sermon.

The man seemed convinced that the Lord actually talked to him. *Or he's a damn good actor.* As a lawyer, Jake had learned to be skeptical of what anybody said and specifically anybody selling anything or asking for something, as was Rasmussen. Selling religion and asking for money. Yet, as far as he could tell, the man appeared to be telling the truth. And, he had apparently started a ministry.

He heard Minnie Sue's heavy footsteps in the hall and slid the bottle under his cot, behind his legs until she passed. When he heard the door to her room close, he reached for the bottle and once more lifted it to his lips.

By chance, he saw the man on the other cot staring at him like a starving animal hoping the alpha male would leave something for him. His hungry stare made Jake feel greedy, as well as guilty.

Rasmussen's words about alcohol—*clouds the senses and stings like an adder*—made him feel even guiltier.

"Get thee behind me, Satan." Rasumssen's admonition popped into his thoughts. He wanted to laugh about them, but couldn't. *If only it were that easy,* he thought.

Without conscious thought, his eyes caught sight of the Bible the young woman had thrust into his hand at the beach. Rasmussen's Gideon Bible had supposedly given him the strength to survive the abuse that had been heaped upon him while he tried to spread the Word.

With some effort, he lowered the bottle. *Maybe I ought to think about quitting. Tomorrow. I'll think about it tomorrow.*

He lifted the bottle again, and finished it without stopping. Afterwards, he dropped the empty bottle, bag and all, in the trash bucket against the wall. It was his job to empty it so nobody would know. With a glance at his neighbor, he'd witnessed the man's shoulders slump when he realized that he would get no beer that night.

He picked up the Bible and bounced it in his hand as if somehow to measure its value. But, no value came to mind, so he dropped it on his table and got ready for bed. He had been reading a paperback book from the house's library. Contributors regularly dumped bags of things, including books, on the front porch.

He pulled the covers over his shoulders to get such sleep as was possible with all the noises in the house. Men got up at all hours. Sometimes it was a bathroom call. At other times, they argued with their demons, with their roommates, even the matron. He'd heard a few sit against the hallway wall and cry.

About six thirty the next morning, the sound of sirens woke them. It seemed as if every police car and ambulance in San Diego drove in front of the place. They'd heard sirens before—lots of older people called La Jolla home and cardiac arrest was not uncommon—but those sirens were nothing like the ones that morning. For some reason, a quip one of his law school professors used popped into his thoughts. After having one of the students recite the facts of a tort case, she'd look at the class and say, with a grin, "Gotta be a lawsuit in there someplace."

Jake put the interruption aside and dozed until Bessie, the day matron, made the wake-up round.

Bessie's voice woke him. "Time to get up. Carson, you've got table duty. Off your lazy behind. Get to it." Table duty required putting out plates, coffee mugs and flatware on a table next to the buffet line in the room where they ate.

"That's Johnson's duty. It's posted," Jake said.

"Not anymore. He got released yesterday. It's yours now." She didn't hang around for an answer.

He finished his kitchen assignment and picked up the morning paper to read with coffee. The headline that caught his eye was "The New Religion." Brother Rasmussen in his white finery with guitar accessory was the headline photo.

The story quoted the group's administrator, Alan Stern, about their mission—the building of churches in undeveloped countries. "Stern quipped that Brother Rasmussen delivers the spiritual messages and I make them financially possible."

The dark haired guy the woman was interviewing, Jake thought, *He counts the money. Probably arranged for the television coverage. Free advertising for the cause ... and the donations.*

The story recited how Rasmussen interrupting his message to pray for a man with a beer bottle. *That'd be me.* The closing paragraph listed half a dozen local churches where Rasmussen would be giving special services to talk about their mission.

The other inmates began to arrive and complain about the food. It was oatmeal day with toast. Most didn't like it. Sliced apples and peeled oranges on the side. Hardly anybody bothered with the fruit. It was left for the matrons to eat.

While they were eating, one of the younger men asked, "Where's Sister Brigit?"

Sister Brigit, a nun from the parish church, always came on Monday mornings to lead a devotional. She'd read from the Bible, answer questions and pray before leaving. Anyone asking could speak to her in private after breakfast.

Bessie hearing the question, answered loudly, "She's not coming! Somebody in her church got killed this morning."

The young man who'd asked said he was sorry. An older guy at the table next to Jake's mumbled. "Who cares? Mos' like better off dead."

Bessie corrected him. "Show a little respect! I don't want to hear that kind of talk in my dining room!" She touched the silver cross that hung around her neck.

The man scoffed.

Jake imagined most in the room felt the same way, at least the older guys. That's how he felt. Death would come as a blessing, an end to the disgrace he had to face each time he looked in a mirror; his failure as a human being.

He had ruined his life and disappointed all those who had been his friends and especially his family. His wife had divorced him long before he'd hit bottom. She moved back to New Mexico to start life over and had remarried. Their two children were married and beginning careers. They ignored his downfall and gave no indication that they cared what happened to him.

With breakfast over, he brushed his teeth, shaved, put on a clean outfit, not a suit. Serving papers, his usual assignment, did not require a suit and tie. Khakis or jeans worked fine. He kept his surfer jacket out in case the day turned cool. Southern California winters were generally mild, but now and then, they could turn cool.

* * * *

He retrieved his car from a side street and drove into San Diego for the assignment promised him by the law firm's office manager. The meter showed less than a quarter of a tank of gas. He'd ask for a twenty dollar advance for gas so he could serve papers. It was a humiliation he could barely stand; having to take menial work from a guy who'd flunked the law exam three times before giving up.

"Are you sure you're up to it, Carson?" the guy asked each time and always with a smirk. "No stopping for liquid refreshment, now."

Jake let the man's condescending attitude slide off his back. *What choice do I have?* It was the highest paying job available to him and he was broke.

Having picked up the papers he was to serve, he hurried away, not wishing to stay long enough to have to face his former partners. En route, he passed his old office, but didn't look inside. It was too painful.

"Jake," he heard his name called. *Walter Hoffman.* He'd moved into Jake's old office, the best on the floor with its grand harbor view.

Jake stifling the urge to ignore it, stopped and turned. "Hi, Walter," he said, forcing a smile.

"Come in, if you've got a minute?"

Jake laughed to himself. *Like I have to be in court.*

He walked in and sat down in a chair he'd bought for *HIS* office. "What's happening, Walter?"

"Did you hear? Oh, would you like coffee or anything? We bought a new espresso machine. Makes great coffee."

"No, thanks." What he wanted was a drink, something to make him forget being there.

"Sure. Anyway, I don't know if you heard, but the McGuires were killed this morning. Early."

What! Nate and Jeanette McGuire, his old clients before he screwed up and had an affair with Jeanette. He called her Jen. Nate was doing to her what he had done to his wife, before she'd divorced him. He was ignoring her and Jake took advantage. She was older, but with a woman like that a birth certificate wasn't a condition. Her charm dominated everyone she met. Jake was no exception.

Sister Brigit had missed the halfway house visit because somebody in her church was killed. *The McGuires? Jen wore a cross around her neck but it never registered that she was Catholic.*

He remembered one of the last times they were together; remembered her words as if she had just said them. "I love you Jake. I'll get a divorce." Being Catholic was probably why she didn't.

Jake's emotions were so scattered at that time, he wasn't thinking of "love." He was actually searching for a way to break it off when Nate somehow got wind of it or maybe she let it slip.

Nate stormed into Walter's office and shouted, "If Carson so much as touches anything having to do with my legal affairs, I'll move my representation to another firm. I should anyway, but I don't have to time to break in a new firm."

That was three years ago.

Nate was in real estate development, upscale condos, office buildings, but shopping centers primarily. Jen handled the leasing and selling. Jake had handled all their real estate work, transactions and trials when negotiations failed.

He had gotten to know Jen during a trial to force the owner of a piece of prime real estate to go ahead with the deal. After Jake had negotiated the contract, the man got a better offer and tried to back out. Jake sued for specific performance and won. Jen was Jake's key witness. It would have been impossible for him not to like her. Given his attitude of wanting to conquer everything that came his way, there was no way he would have passed up the opportunity to have an affair with her.

He thought of her often, her innocence and lack of guile. That she loved him was without doubt; that he had never fully reciprocated was equally so.

Jake had begun to drink heavily by then to counteract the pressure he was under. Working sixteen hour days was nothing to him. He had an active portfolio of clients and all had problems only he could handle. At least that was what he thought. Drinking was his first outlet for the pressure. Sleeping with women, married or otherwise, was his second. By that time, his wife had taken her divorce settlement proceeds and left town. He knew it was his fault and hadn't contested it.

"How'd it happen?" Jake asked. "I heard sirens this morning. I had no idea they were for the McGuires."

"We heard it too," he said. Walter and his wife had a condo in La Jolla. "Apparently, they went out for their morning run—they always jogged to the beach and back before breakfast."

Jake nodded. The McGuires lived in the Muirlands, an area southeast of the La Jolla downtown in a glassy, contemporary home with terrific views of La Jolla and the Pacific.

Walter continued, "You know that street winds around. Well, apparently, they jogged around a bend and must have drifted out into the lane. How much traffic would there be that time of morning? Apparently a car came around the bend and hit them in the back. From the report I got, they were killed instantly. The police have no idea who did it."

Jake shook his head in disbelief. If any two people had the world in their hands, it was Nate and Jen. They had two children, Amy, a doctor in La Jolla, and Phillip, who had been studying to become a chef in Colorado the last time Jake heard.

Walter said, "Amy was crushed. She let me know after the police called her. Phillip was apparently camping someplace with friends. She left word for him. Amy is named as executrix in the will. I guess you know that since you did the estate plan."

Jake acknowledged with a nod. Nate and Jen considered naming Phillip as co-executor with Amy, but felt he was still a bit immature. He was only a couple of years younger than Amy but for some reason had not "found himself." Those were Nate's words.

"She told me she had let Phillip know."

Jake had met both at a number of McGuire functions when he was their attorney.

"Thanks for letting me know." Jake left to serve the papers he'd been given but his thoughts were on Jen. He remembered her smile, the first time he saw her, her blue eyes and innocent look had swept through his mind like a gentle wind. And, the memory was still there.

Recalling Rasmussen words from the Bible, reaping what you sow. *I sowed disappointments and hurts. Now I'm reaping regrets.*

Chapter

3

He finished serving the papers without incident but instead of going back to Sunrise House to do whatever chores had been assigned to him, detoured to the Muirlands to see where the McGuires had been run-down. Actually, he wanted to see where Jen was killed. For some reason, he felt he owed her that much. *I owe her more than that.* She was an unfinished chapter in his life; the best thing that was happening to him at the time and he'd been so dislocated from life, he hadn't seen it.

The San Diego police crime scene squad was still on site; four officers dressed in blue. The portion of the street where it happened was roped in yellow ribbon.

Jake parked and walked to the scene. He didn't see anyone he recognized. That was a relief. His law practice had included the occasional criminal defense. To win, he often had to show the police witnesses were at least incompetent and at worse, corrupt. As a result, he didn't have many friends in the ranks of those dedicated to protecting and serving.

An officer spotted him and moved to intercept. *Authoritatively so,* Jake thought. *Coming to warn me off.*

Jake came up with a story and began walking with a confidence he didn't have, but remembered enough to make it look like he did. "Morning, officer," he said, also authoritatively, as he drew close.

"Sir, this is a crime scene. You're not allowed to be here," the officer replied.

"I understand, sir." He tactfully acknowledged the officer's authority, hopefully to disarm him. "I'm with the Hoffman firm. We're handling the McGuires' legal affairs." Jake reached into his shirt pocket and handed him Walter Hoffman's card. It had come with the papers he was given to serve in case he ran into a problem.

"'You Mr. Hoffman?"

Jake chuckled and said, "Don't I wish. I don't eat that high on the hog. I'm a lowly investigator for the firm, Jake. Just started. No cards yet. Mr. Hoffman sent me out to get a report for our file. What can you tell me?"

The officer shouted to another guy standing some yards away. "Ralph. Got an investigator from the Hoffman firm. Says they're handling the McGuires' legal work. Can I tell him anything?"

Jake was relieved the guy didn't recognize him. Maybe the fact that he wasn't wearing a suit and tie threw him off. Change costumes and change the person wearing them.

The guy glanced at Jake and gave the officer a nod.

"Have to get permission to go to the bathroom these days," he told Jake.

"Same with me," Jake said. "So, what happened? We were told it was a hit-and-run early this morning."

"That's about it. Based on what we have so far, it looks like the McGuires were running and a car or truck came up behind them and hit 'em so hard it drove them into that." He pointed to a jagged rock sticking out from the embankment. Below the rock on the asphalt somebody had drawn chalk marks where the bodies were when found. "Nobody saw anything and the car didn't hang around."

Something about that didn't ring exactly true to Jake, but he couldn't focus on it. It had been a long time since he had been forced to focus on anything.

Jake pointed to the while stripe along the side of the street.

"The car ... or truck must have been hugging the curve to hit them like it did."

"Yeah. That's what we figure. Somebody in a hurry to get someplace. Came around the bend and smack! We've checked every vehicle on the street. Not one with a smashed front end. We found glass." He pointed his hand toward an area that had already been cleaned. It was on the right hand side of the white bike lane stripe.

"Maybe somebody got lost. Might not live on the street."

"Yeah. Could have been a kid from another part of town, joy riding up here. Doesn't make much sense though. Kids I know don't get up this early."

"Unless they were out all night. Too high on drugs to go home."
He agreed with a grimace.

"Were they dead when you got here?" Jake asked.

"Might as well have been, but legally they died on the operating table. Both of them. I saw them right after the accident and no way were they going to survive for very long. Too mangled up."

"Damn shame. And the guy, or whoever, didn't have the guts to stop."

"Panicked, most likely."

Jake asked him to send a copy of their report to Walter Hoffman and left Hoffman's card with his name on the back. No last name. He hoped the guy didn't call Walter and ask for him since he was there without authority.

The officer handed him one of his cards which Jake shoved into his shirt pocket. "James Demarco" the card read.

Only when Jake was away from the scene did he remember what had bothered him. *Why were they running on that side of the street... with the traffic?*

Once at a dinner party, Nate was holding court with another couple, also morning joggers, pontificating about jogging protocol. "I always jog against traffic. That way, I see them and get out of their way. The same goes for bicyclists. They hog the bike lanes and claim the right of way. Jeanette and I stay out of their way."

So, why were they jogging on the wrong side of the street?

He recalled the testimony of an expert witness who was asked something along the same line. One of the parties to the law suit had departed from his usual habit of doing things. When asked to explain that abnormality, he had said, "Just because a human has been doing the same thing, the same way, year after year, does not mean he'll continue. It's the nature of man to change."

The jury didn't buy it.

Jake dismissed the question. It wasn't his problem after all. His interest stemmed from the affair he'd had with Jen and the guilt he was feeling. Not just about her, but about all the things he'd done wrong. It never seemed to let up. Usually, he used it as an excuse to pop the cap of a beer bottle and drink half without stopping.

To that end, he stopped by the supermarket and bought a six pack. He kept all but one in the trunk of his car. He could easily conceal one inside his coat. Once inside the house, he'd slide it under the thin mattress they put on the cots. It was a few minutes after five.

He changed into his "homeless" clothes, the ones he wore when he wasn't working and checked the chore roster on the front hall wall. His job was vacuuming and mopping. The whole house always smelled musty to him, no matter how many times it was vacuumed and mopped.

First though, he opened his bottle for a quick swig or two, afterwards hiding it behind his bedside table. None of his roommates were around. Actually he only had a single roommate since one guy had been assigned to another room.

The Bible on top of his table caught his eye. It was right where he'd left it. It reminded him that he had promised to quit drinking.

I didn't say I would quit, just think about it. Even so, he did cut short his second swig. That was in part due to another thought that had popped into his head, like a bright light. He let it go and went in search of the vacuum cleaner.

When those chores were done, he was asked to help in the kitchen. The guy assigned kitchen duty was out someplace, a frequent occurrence. So, Jake washed the potatoes and put them in a pot of water to boil as asked. He also put out the plates, glasses and utensils. A benefactor had donated juice so juice was on the week's menu. Most of the inmates would have preferred something stronger. Some did take coffee, a pot let over from noon when the day matron fixed a pot for herself and for the guys who'd spent the day inside. A few, evidently fearful of the outside from the way they furtively peaked out the windows from time to time, did hang around inside the house.

As dinner was coming to an end, an old motor home pulled up in front of the house. In faded letters, the words, "New Age Christians" showed on its side. Sister Brigit came around the motor home followed by none other than Brother Rasmussen. His Gideon Bible was clutched in his hand.

Bessie saw them and announced to the men still in the dining room, "Sister Brigit asked if she could give a special service to us since she missed this morning. Can we all meet in the parlor?" It wasn't a request. The parlor was the new name for the old living room.

"Bring chairs."

"This is Reverend Rasmussen," Sister Brigit said after we were all assembled in the room. Rasmussen let his hand stroke his white beard as he looked into the eyes of each of the men in the room with a smiling nod; his way of an introduction. "I'm so proud that Sister Brigit asked me to hold this special service. I want to do the same thing for every Sunrise House in La Jolla. I can almost see the new day's sun rising over each of your lives. Thank you Lord. I'm so proud of the work Bessie and all the administrators are doing to get you men back on your feet. And … able to serve God."

"Amen," Bessie said. Sister Brigit bowed her head. Her lips moved, presumably in a silent prayer.

"Two dear friends of the Church, Nate and Jeanette McGuire, were killed this morning," Sister Brigit said. "I prayed for them all day." She turned to Rasmussen. "Courtesy of Father Posey, the Reverend will have a special service in the parish hall Saturday afternoon. All of you are invited."

She turned to Rasmussen and said, "Reverend Rasmussen, will you lead us in a devotional for Brother Nate and Sister Jeanette?"

"Thank you, Sister. I am honored." He cleared his throat and said, "The McGuires have graciously blessed our mission with their support. Truly wonderful people. I have prayed with Sister Brigit that their souls be received in Heaven to sit with God and to know his wisdom." He concluded with a lengthy prayer.

Sister Brigit clutched the cross that hung around her neck and said, "Amen."

I can't see Nate blessing anybody but himself, Jake thought and chided himself for being cynical of the dead. *Still…*

Rasmussen read first from the Book of John about what Jesus had done during his life; how he was crucified and had arisen. He then closed the Bible and said, "What I am about to say is for all of us. We are all sinners. You see, God made man as he made animals, with instincts and urges. However, unlike animals He gave us the will to know what is right and what is wrong. When he saw that man wasn't using that willpower to do right, He sent his only son, Jesus, to tell us we must obey His commandments and live without sin."

"That's a crock," the man Jake had knocked down muttered.

Sister Brigit frowned at the man, as did Bessie. However, Rasmussen smiled at him and said, "Sinners doubt to justify their sins, sir. All of you know that Jesus was crucified. I think you know that He died on the cross for our sins. And, just so mankind would know God had sent him for that purpose, He was resurrected and walked with his disciples until he ascended into heaven."

The man who had just muttered scoffed and said, "How could he die for my sins? I wasn't born then."

"God set no time limit on the forgiveness, sir. God knew we'd sin long after his Son was crucified, as all of you here have done or you wouldn't be here, and He wanted us to know we could be forgiven for those sins until the time Jesus returns. *You* can be forgiven now. Jesus died for *you*. Hopefully you will become stronger each time you sin until finally you can resist the urge to violate God's commandments. Think on this: if you know right and you do wrong, you are committing a sin. If you know right and you do right, you'll be doing God's work and … not living in a halfway house. Thank you. Let's pray. Sister." He gestured toward Sister Brigit and bowed his head.

Sister Brigit ended the devotional with the prayer from Matthew, the Lord's Prayer.

Afterward, Bessie said, "We thank you Reverend Rasmussen and Sister Brigit for taking the time to visit with us. We appreciate it, don't we fellows?" She motioned for them to rise.

Taking her cue, most of them mumbled the expected, "Thank you."

Rasmussen said, "I thank each of you for letting me into your lives. And, you sir." He singled out Jake. "I remember you from Sunday. I pray that you have put your sinful ways behind you."

Jake said, "Count on it."

After a knowing smile and nod, Rasmussen invited everyone to the special service on Saturday afternoon at the Catholic Church. "Food courtesy of many volunteers."

Sister Brigit gave directions.

One man held out a dollar bill. Brother Rasmussen took it. "The widow's mite," he said. "The Lord blesses you, sir. I pray for you."

When they were gone and the motor home was down the street, Jake went to his room and retrieved the bottle of beer from its hiding place. It had been on his mind all through dinner and during Rasmussen's devotional.

He twisted off the cap and lifted it to his lips. As he did, his eyes caught sight of the Bible on his table. It seemed to gleam like a beacon. Rasmussen's sermon sounded in his thoughts as well. Man was given the willpower to do the right thing.

Damn. He lowered the beer to the floor. Jen's face came into his thoughts, her innocent face. Her tender words, before they agreed to end it. "I love you, Jake."

I could have loved her. Maybe I did. I should have told her. Tears formed in his eyes.

He reached for the bottle again but saw the guy on the next cot staring at him like he had the night before. *Get a life. Better than that, get your own beer. Am I that weak? Ruled by a beer!*

He knew he was. If he didn't have a beer to drink, he might very well be the one staring. *I'm the one who needs a life.* He pushed the cap back on the bottle and sat it on the floor. Later when he returned from a final trip to the bathroom, the bottle was empty. He didn't make a fuss.

He remembered all the things he'd done wrong the past few years; how he'd wasted his life.

"It's coming home to roost," his grandmother used to say about one of her sons, his uncle. She could have been talking about him. He reached for the Bible on the table next to his bed. It opened to the Book of Matthew with words that talked about doing good for those in need. He read a few paragraphs before falling asleep wrestling with his guilt. That was a blessing in itself. Usually he fell asleep thinking about his next drink.

Around three, he awoke thinking about tomorrow, a new day. One he hadn't messed up yet. The thought he'd had during the day crept back into his mind. He pushed it aside at first, but it kept coming back. And, it was still there when he got out of his cot the next morning. He laughed. *Maybe it's a sign.*

After breakfast, he dressed in the only presentable clothes he owned, and drove into San Diego to see Walter Hoffman, his old law partner.

* * * *

"Come in, Jake," Walter said when he saw him outside his office. "I didn't expect to see you today."

Jake took his offer of coffee and made small talk about the Chargers, San Diego's pro football team, while they enjoyed a cup. The team was having a decent year. Jake had scanned the sports section at breakfast. Otherwise, he wouldn't have known anything about them. However, he knew Walter followed football closely and wanted something favorable to talk about.

"Listen Walter, you're probably wondering why I'm here."

"I suppose I am."

Jake looked at him and said, "I want to work on the McGuire estate, Walter."

"Whaaat? No way! You know Nate was adamant. Besides, you … well, you know, you can't do legal work anymore."

"I can't represent clients, Walter. I can do leg work. And, there'll be some leg work in the McGuire estate. Amy is busy with her practice. Nobody here knows the asset structure of the McGuires better than I do. I want to do it!"

Walter was already shaking his head no. "I'd like to Jake. I know what you did for this firm, you built it. But … I don't know. Letting you get involved even at that level might not be considered prudent. You mess up and we spend the rest of our careers defending malpractice suits. Phillip would be all over us. Let me speak frankly. You have a drinking problem. It's one thing to stay sober long enough to serve papers, but could you stay sober long enough to handle the investigation required for an estate as large as the McGuires?"

Jake held his hand out. "Look. I haven't had a drink in over a week." It was a lie, but miraculously his hand didn't shake. He hoped he was sitting far enough away for Walter not to see the red rings of his eyes from the lack of sleep. He would assume Jake had been on a binge.

His old partner stared at him. "Jake, I considered you a friend, still do. That's why we're giving you our dog work. But, you're asking a lot now, old buddy. A lot."

"I was the best damned lawyer in this town Walter. I—"

"*Was, Jake. Was.* That was before you burned out and let booze and women take over."

"Damnit to hell, Walter. I'm past that now. I'll work for nothing and if anybody complains about anything, I'll walk away. If I show up with beer breath, kick me out. Whatever conditions you want to impose, I'll accept. I want to do something meaningful again."

"Why? You said you never wanted to see another legal problem. You were tired of everything, including life. You remember that conversation? You were drunk then."

Jake turned his face toward the window. He remembered. And, he was drunk and depressed.

"Yeah, I remember, but I'm not drunk now, Walter. I owe the McGuires. Truthfully, I owe Jen. I was a bastard to her. It gnaws at me. I want to do something to balance my books with her, even if it's just putting together a list of their assets and liabilities. All you have to pay are my expenses. If I could do even that much, ..." He choked up, unable to complete what he wanted to say. *Perhaps some of the guilt I've been carrying around will go away.*

"Listen Jake, there's not going to be much to do. Nate had put all his assets in the trust and when he decided to settle up and retire, six months or so ago, he made the thing irrevocable. He was afraid something or somebody would come out of the woodwork and tie up his assets in litigation. Amy's the trustee with sole powers to administer the estate. Nate and Jeanette would get all the income they needed, but legally, the trust had a life of its own and no creditors could touch it. An accounting firm prepared checks for him, paid his bills, that sort of thing."

Must have been a comfort to have so much money you didn't even have to write your own checks.

Jake said, "Then, there won't be much for me to do. What harm can I do? There may be the odd asset lying around that needs to be accounted for. Unpaid claims. Also, what about the accident? The estate might benefit if we could find out who did that."

"Hmm. Yeah. Could be a wrongful death by Amy and Phillip and maybe a survivor action by the estate against whoever did it, if you could find out that. I expect we could get a decent judgment for punitive damages, considering the viciousness of the act."

Walter made it clear that Jake would only handle such investigations as he assigned *and* only if Amy agreed. If she didn't want him working on the estate, he was out. If he worked, he'd be paid the usual hourly fee for investigators.

Jake was so happy he wanted to twist off the cap on one of his beers and drink it down without stopping. The thought made him aware that he had a habit that would be hard to break. And, what would happen when the pressure hit?

There won't be any pressure putting together the few assets and liabilities belonging to the estate, he told himself.

He couldn't have been more wrong.

Chapter

Humiliating in itself, Walter gave him a six hundred dollar advance which he used to buy a decent suit and pair of shoes at a discount store. He had money left over.

He vowed never to put himself in that position again. Then he scoffed at his vow. *What good is a vow from a man one step away from being homeless?*

He tried to recall the Bible verses he'd read the night before, about giving. It helped him focus on his mission, doing something for Jen, the last person who really cared for him. That night, he read the Bible again; Galatians about not giving up. *I won't.*

The next day, he called Amy's office from the phone at Sunrise House and set up an appointment to see her. Actually, he didn't talk to her, only her receptionist so he wasn't sure she knew he was coming in or the reason.

He was early but the waiting room was already filled. Something by Mendelsohn played over the speakers. *His Violin Concerto,* Jake thought, proud to have remembered. It had been a long time since he'd listened to anything classical.

The receptionist called his name and walked him back to a treatment room. A few minutes later, Amy McGuire, in her white lab jacket, strolled in holding a folder with his vitals in it. To avoid explaining to the receptionist why he was there, he'd filed in the medical forms like any other patient.

He saw that she was a lot like her mother, light brown hair, cut shorter than Jen's, same blue eyes, kind of shy, innocent face, a pleasing oval and she moved with an easy, gliding walk. *The soul of femininity, Jake thought. Must be in her late thirties.*

"Mr. ..." she appeared shocked. "I'll be. It's Jake Carson! What are you doing here?"

"Didn't Walter call you?"

"He did, but I haven't returned it. I've been swamped. It's the flu season. You should get a flu shot."

Jake agreed to get one while he was there.

"I assume you're here because Mom and Dad were killed." She choked up; stopped to dab at her eyes. "Sorry. I'm still dealing with it. God, I almost fainted when the police called me. I couldn't believe it. Still can't. I was just talking to them. It's not fair. They were so young. They hadn't reached sixty." She shook her head in disbelief. "They had rest of their lives to enjoy. The funeral is tomorrow. I think Mom and Dad should be at some function, seeing and being seen."

Jake agreed. "It has to be tough."

She nodded. Dabbed at her eyes again and asked, "Okay, okay, it'll pass. It has to doesn't it? So … why are you here? Dad said he never wanted to see or hear from you again." She looked hard at him. "I have to ask. Did you sleep with Mom? Dad said you did."

That question caught Jake by surprise. *I'm slipping. I should have anticipated it.* What was worse was how to answer it.

He looked at her, holding it for a second to give himself time to think of something. Finally, he hedged and asked, "What do you think?"

Without showing anything on her face, she said, "I think you probably did. Knowing your reputation. What I'd heard about it anyway, and knowing how Dad was neglecting Mom, I figured you had. Mom denied it, but Dad didn't believe her."

"There was a kind of magic about her I couldn't resist," he said, admitting his indiscretion by inference.

"She liked you. She told me."

"I liked her. That's the main reason I asked Walter to let me work on the estate. Maybe I can settle my accounts with her."

"And, since I'm the executrix, you need my approval?"

Jake nodded.

"I don't mind. Actually, I'm glad. I always liked you when you came to dinner. You had a certain excitement about you. Big trial lawyer. Dad said the other lawyers were afraid of you. I wasn't surprised to hear about you and Mom. Well, what Dad said."

"That was before I went to hell."

"That's also what I heard. Dad said you were a drunk and had lost your edge."

"He was probably right. For some stupid reason, I got the notion I could work twenty-four hours a day and take on all problems. Walk on water. I found out I couldn't."

She looked him in the eye and bobbed her head. He assumed she was agreeing.

"People make mistakes, Jake. Smart people admit them, make adjustments, and move on. Is it okay if I call you Jake?"

It was.

A commotion in the hall got their attention. "I don't care," a man's voice said. "I want to see my sister."

Ah, Phillip, Jake thought.

The door practically flew open. A slightly overweight man with a fleshy face in jeans stood in the door, pointed at Amy with an angry scowl on his face and said, "You changed the locks and the security code! I have just as much right to be in the house as you do!" He pushed an unruly shock of brown hair out of his face. He and Amy were about the same height, on the high end of five and a half feet tall.

"I'm with a patient," she said frowning, with a gesture toward Jake. "We can discuss this later, Phillip!"

"I'm discussing it now! I don't care who—" He looked at Jake, hesitated a bit and said, "Hey, I ... know you! You're that guy Dad was talking about. The lawyer who was sleeping with Mom. I've seen you at the house! You'd better not be involved. Dad said he didn't want you to set foot in his house again."

"Jake Carson," Jake said without offering his hand. He decided discretion was the way to play Phillip. "I was only your mother's attorney. You dad was mistaken."

"Bull. Dad said you were and I believe him!" He turned back to Amy. "It's my house as much as yours."

"Mom and Dad put me in charge of the estate and the trust. I'm not having you sell everything you can haul off. You'll get what's coming to you when the estate is wrapped up. Not before."

He scoffed. "You in charge! Ridiculous. What do you know about anything? You're just a pill-pusher. Dad wanted me to be in charge. He said so ... was going to."

"He didn't change the will or the trust."

"I said he was going to! We were patching things up. He knew I could handle tough jobs. He wouldn't approve of this two-bit jerk." He swung his arm in Jake's direction.

Jake bristled at the insult, but kept silent.

"The last I heard, he'd turned down your hair-brained idea to open a cooking store in La Jolla. I don't think you patched anything up."

"Things changed."

"Nobody told me. So, I'm in charge and you're not getting into the house until I say so. Now, get out of my office or I'll call the police."

"*Bitch!*" he said to her, gave Jake the finger and slammed the door as he stalked out.

"Wow," Jake said. "He was not a happy camper. Last I heard, he was in Colorado."

"He's been back awhile. He's staying with friends. Phillip usually sided with Dad on everything so he might complain that you're involved. However, as long as I'm the executrix and the trustee under the trust, I'll make the decisions."

"He could go to court, but I don't think it'll affect your appointment so all he'll do is waste his money."

"He won't do that. He's as stingy as Scrooge. He never throws anything away. Dad told me to give him on an allowance of a thousand dollars a week for doing nothing."

"Not bad." Jake said and smiled. Amy had Jen's confidence. That was another thing he had liked about her, her confidence. He hoped he had told her all those things, but was afraid he had not.

"Tell Mr. Hoffman I'm okay with you. I assume you can control your ... shall I call it your primitive urge to drink. I don't mean to be blunt, but there it is. I don't want to give Phillip any more ammunition than he has."

"Right. Well, I promise to keep my urges under control."

"Why don't we meet at the house tonight? I'll show you Dad's office and where Mom kept her stuff."

He got a flu shot on the way out.

* * * *

In the afternoon he called Walter to tell him what Amy had said but Walter interrupted to say, "Phillip McGuire just left, Jake. He was practically screaming. He wanted access to the house to get his personal things. I told him to make a list and I'd pass it on to Amy. He wanted Amy removed as executrix and trustee because she would not give him access and because, against his Dad's wishes, she was using you."

"What'd you tell him?"

"I told him I had no authority to tell her to do anything. If he went to court, the judge would most likely refuse to allow him to go through the house until an inventory of anything not already in the trust has been completed and filed with the court. I also told him that his Dad's directions to us had only to do with your status as an attorney. You were working for Amy and the firm as an investigator."

"Did that shut him up?"

"No. He was just getting warmed up. He said Amy's so-called fiancé was a free loader out to get her money. Nate didn't like him and had told him so. He hinted that Nate was going to do something to make sure the guy wouldn't get anything out of the estate."

"The trust was irrevocable. I doubt the fiancé was included in any of it and there may be nothing in the estate to probate. So, it's not likely the fiancé will get anything unless Amy gives it to him, which she'll have a right to do."

"I didn't get into that with him. It wasn't a legal matter. I told him that Amy's personal life was not a legal matter."

"Did he hit you?"

"I thought he might. He was about one rant short of me having Joe throw him out." Joe was the 6' 4" three hundred pound maintenance man for the building.

"I take it he left voluntarily."

"Well, he stormed out. I guess it was voluntary. He was mad as hell from the look on his face. I don't know if he'll see an attorney or not. He said that Nate was going to change his will and appoint him as executor. As you just said, that wouldn't have done him any good since it's unlikely there'll be anything in the estate to probate."

"In any case, I assume he had no proof that Nate was going to do anything."

"It was an understanding, he said. Nate hadn't called me so I have no reason to do anything. I'm assuming Amy did not object to your assignment as an investigator."

Jake told him that was right. "I'm meeting with her tonight at the house to get a feel for things."

Walter said he'd met with the other two senior partners and none shared his confidence that he could stay sober long enough to do much of anything.

"I had to assume complete responsibility for you."

Jake opened his mouth to speak, but Walter waved him off and said, "I think you can make it, Jake, but just so you know, if you don't, I'll be the one who has to answer for you."

Nothing like a little pressure. Jake cursed himself for his next thought—a cold beer, his crutch—and heard his thoughts say, "Get thee behind me Satan." It almost made him laugh, but his thoughts about a beer subsided a bit.

"Don't worry Walter, I won't fumble this chance." He said it with a confidence he didn't feel, but knew Walter wanted to hear it.

"Come by the office. I'll give you a phone. Also access to a computer which you can use here. No key to the offices. The others wouldn't agree on that. However, you can come in during office hours and use whatever you need."

"Thanks."

* * * *

Amy buzzed him through the gate at the street into the McGuire estate a little before dark. Her car, a Prius, was out front.

Anticipating his arrival, the front door was unlocked. She met him in the entry hall and greeted him with a perfunctory hug. She was still in her office clothes, a gray, light wool suit. The pleasant hint of her perfume brought back memories of Jen's … and Jen. He had to fight off a sudden push toward depression. *I may not be strong enough to do this.*

He followed her to into the living room. Its sweeping views of the Pacific and downtown La Jolla at twilight still impressed him. For the most part, most buildings in the wealthy La Jolla community were one or two stories though most condominium complexes were higher. Lights were just coming on to give the Village a Christmas tree look.

"Phillip stormed into Walter's offices with a list of demands," he told her.

"I'm not surprised. He left me a message saying how sorry he was to have made such a fuss and offered to stay in the house as a caretaker to keep watch over it."

"Likely paid an attorney to tell him how much it would cost to hear a judge say what Walter had already told him."

"I guess. I called back and told him we'd discuss it after you'd finished what you had to do. He immediately became obnoxious."

"It figures."

"So, what were his demands?" she asked.

"He wanted you replaced as executrix for using me against Nate's wishes. He said Nate was going to change his will anyway to appoint him."

"That shows how stupid he is. Practically everything is in the trust. Changing the will wouldn't have done anything. When Phillip came back from Colorado he asked Dad to bankroll a cooking store in La Jolla with enough money to blow competitors out of the water with promotions. Do you know what I'm talking about?"

He did. They were stores where people, women usually, signed up to learn how to cook healthy foods and to buy from the store what they needed to do it; trendy and fashionable and located in affluent areas.

"Dad kind of laughed at him. He told him to learn the business first working for somebody else. Then find a town that didn't already have more cooking stores than it needed. Mom said she'd help and got him a job as an assistant chef someplace. Phillip was upset that Dad wouldn't write him a check, but Dad hadn't changed his mind as far as I know."

"He *is* doing what Nate suggested." *And, Phillip seemed pretty positive Nate was going to change his mind at least about giving him some control over the estate!*

"Dad would have told me if he'd changed his mind. That amount of money would have had to come from the trust."

If Nate had had time to tell her before being run over?

"Phillip was also adamant about getting his personal things out of the house."

"He told me that as well. I told him I'd meet him here with the security people so he could pick them up. That's when he started getting obnoxious."

"And, he thinks your fiancé is a freeloader."

"Ha! I guess Dad did talk to him. Dad didn't like Warren. Warren Meyer's his name. He's a very charming man. That attracted me to him. Anyway, he tried his charm on Dad … and Mom. Well, Mom liked him. You know Mom. Like most women, she liked being flattered and Warren is a good-looking man. Dad liked him at first, but after a few dinners, he changed his mind."

"I'm not too surprised. That sounds like something Nate would say. He was the epitome of no nonsense. Anything not directly relevant to whatever problem was at hand was a waste of time. Charm without substance fell into that category."

She laughed. "A few months ago, Dad told Warren if he had thoughts about marrying me, he could forget it until he had enough income to support the both of us. I walked in when Dad was saying, 'Part time work, even coated in that bull you spread around, Warren, won't get it.' Dad saw me and said, 'Amy, I was just telling Warren he won't get our blessings to marry you until he gets serious about his profession.'"

Jake smiled.

"What does he do … for a living?" Jake asked.

"He's a doctor, like me. Internal medicine. What irks dad, irked him anyway, is that Warren doesn't have an office. He's a kind of substitute doctor. *Locum tenens,* it's called. He was subscribed to a service which doctors could call to arrange a substitute. Now though, it's pretty much word of mouth. If a doctor wants a week in Hawaii or something, they'll call. He stays busy."

"So, he has none of the problems associated with employees, malpractice or overhead, just collects money and sleeps well."

"Dad told me that Warren was like the grasshopper in the fairy tale. Live for today. To hell with tomorrow. He wanted Warren to be more like the ant."

"How did Warren take the putdown?"

"He smiled nicely and said, 'Mr. McGuire, I like a man who speaks his mind the way you do. I appreciate your advice and you can bet I'll follow it. I love Amy and I can make her happy.'"

"Did Nate scoff?"

"I think he did. But it didn't faze Warren. Nothing does. He's about as laid back as any man I've ever met. Not like Dad. So, why was I attracted to him? Maybe I needed somebody and he was there, smiling and charming. I love him and I think he loves me, regardless of what Phillip says."

"Love conquers all," Jake said to move past it.

Amy showed him the office where Nate and Jen worked. In it were their desks, a laptop computer, other equipment and file cabinets.

"You won't find many files in the cabinets. Dad was afraid someone would break in and find all his secrets." She laughed. "He was very careful so he kept his business-related files at the accountant's office. I have some in my office. Most, since the trust was made irrevocable."

"A good idea. Since you're the trustee, you need to be in control."

"I haven't had time to understand it all just yet, but I think I will over time. I'm still coming to grips with the fact that Dad isn't handling things."

"I understand."

"I'll give you keys to the house and the file cabinets, and the security code so you will have access to the place." She gave him a hard look which he interpreted as a request to reassure her.

"Don't worry. I'll stay out of the liquor cabinet." He wished he felt as confident as he tried to sound.

"Good. Mr. Hoffman told me both of us might have to shoulder the responsibility for anything you do wrong. I think he was trying to scare me into rejecting you." She laughed. She called the security company which regularly patrolled past the house to alert them of Jake's authorized entry into the house.

He understood their concerns. He had some himself.

"I don't think I'll take your time getting into anything tonight. I'll come back in the morning and start putting together my lists of things."

"What will you be looking for?"

"Mostly claims against Nate and or Jen, any assets not assigned to the trust, any claims they might have had against anybody. For example, their estate has a claim against the person who ran them down. You and Phillip have claims as well for the wrongful deaths of your parents."

"If we ever find out who did it," she said.

"Right. That's the big question. The household furnishings, as I recall, were included in the house when it was transferred to the trust, but there might be a few items of value I can look at."

"Well, call if you run into anything I can answer." She gave him her email address and told him that was the best way to make contact with her since she was often tied up with patient problems during the day and tried to relax at night.

She told him if she didn't answer right away, it was probably because she and Warren were out. "We go out a lot. We have a lot of medical conferences. And, as busy as we are, we eat out a lot. We play tennis when we can. Warren's very good."

Jake once played regularly but hadn't hit a ball in anger in years. He had the beginnings of a spare tire to show for it.

"I did want to ask one thing," Jake said. "Nate once said that he and Jen always jogged facing traffic for safety reasons. The vehicle that killed them hit them in the back. Not only that, it hit them hard, like it was driving fast. Odd for the narrow street."

Tears came into her eyes.

"If you'd rather not …"

She waved her hand to suggest that it was okay. She breathed deeply and said, "The times I jogged with them, we always jogged facing traffic. I have to say that we never saw any traffic. Most of the people on this street are wealthy and don't go anyplace early. Why do you ask? Are you saying … *it* might not have been an accident?"

"It just struck me as odd that all of a sudden they would have been jogging on the other side of the road. Has anybody made threats?"

She stared thoughtfully before answering. "None that they talked about in front of me. Warren and I often ate dinner with them on Sunday nights."

They lived together in her condo in La Jolla, she told him. He had a condo in a downtown high rise which he'd leased out after he moved in with her.

Jake asked how they met.

"He was working in the hospital where I was doing my residency in Los Angeles, seven years ago, now. He charmed me off my feet when I needed someone. We've been together off and on ever since, seriously since we moved in together."

"How long have you been in private practice?"

"A little over five years. Dad loaned me the money to get started. He never cashed the checks I gave him to repay the loan. He gave Phillip the same amount to go to cooking school and for support. Dad and Mom always tried to treat us equally. How'd I get off on that? What did you ask me?"

"About threats?"

"Oh yes. I remember. I don't know of any specifically. However, Dad did have a fling with a woman at his office, Cynthia Berger. She was upset when he broke it off. I heard about it when Dad and I were playing tennis. She was shouting in the phone so he had to explain. I'd met her at his office. She was glamorous and Dad could never say no to a pretty face."

He doubted ending the affair would have been motivation enough for her to run down the McGuires but he'd try to track her down. She might have a claim against the estate for wrongful termination or sexual harassment she'd been waiting to file.

Wrapping up the meeting, she said, "I've let the maid go so the house will be empty. The security company has the outside lights coming on at dusk and turning off at first light." She gestured toward the outside patio where the lights had turned on to illuminate the wide expanse of its stone pavers.

She looked at her watch. "I haven't had dinner. Would you join me? Is pizza okay?"

He'd skipped dinner at Sunrise House to meet her so pizza sounded good.

"I'll see if Warren can join us. Do you mind?"

"Not at all."

Chapter
5

As Amy got out of her car, another car pulled in beside her. A blond-haired man in a warm-up jacket got out of a steel gray BMW sports car and hurried around to hug her. As if overjoyed, he hugged her again, adding a kiss.

Warren, Jake surmised. He'd parked a couple of spaces away.

"Jake," she said as they walked close. "This is my fiancé. Warren Meyer."

"Ah yes, Warren. Jake Carson. Glad to meet you."

Warren shoved out his hand with a big smile that showed a full set of perfectly capped teeth. His handshake was firm and he looked Jake squarely in the eyes when he spoke and always showed a smile. He was an inch or so taller than Jake, had a surfer's lean build, with sky blue eyes.

Jake guessed his age at somewhere in the middle to late forties, about his age, really. It was difficult because the guy's face didn't show a wrinkle and he was in excellent shape. He trailed along with them, wishing he hadn't come. He felt like an extra thumb.

Inside the restaurant, Amy and Warren ordered beer. Jake reluctantly asked for a cup of decaf. A beer sounded good— too good—but he knew one would not satisfy his thirst. They ordered a veggi pizza to share and made small talk until the drinks arrived with Warren doing most of the talking.

"A vegetable pizza is healthier," Amy said when the conversation drifted to dinner.

Jake accepted that without argument. She was buying after all but as far as he was concerned, the only pizza worth eating was pepperoni pizza.

Warren said, "Amy says you'll be working on the estate. I understand you are an expert in these matters. I know she wants to get it resolved as soon as possible."

She probably told him I was a washed out drunk and disbarred lawyer.

He Ping-Ponged the comment saying, "I will be doing my best to make it quick." Then, to get the conversation off him, he said, "Amy says you're an internal medicine doctor."

"Yes. We figure out what's wrong and if we can't cure it, we know specialists who can. Amy is the best." He rubbed her back, adding a broad smile. She returned the smile. Hers came easily. *Like Jen's.*

Jake said, "A doctor's doctor, in a manner of speaking. Impressive."

"Thank you."

Jake wanted to ask where he'd gone to med school, but knew that was a social no-no. People can volunteer where they went to school, but in some circles it was considered rude to ask, as if checking their bona fides.

"Have you set a date yet?" Jake asked, looking at both. "To get married?"

Warren answered. "Not yet. Nate had some great suggestions about that when I discussed it with him. Now, this tragedy. I can hardly believe it. The man was so vital and Jeannette was such a wonderful mother and woman. Both were heroes in my book. I adored them. I'm so sorry Amy has to deal with it."

I bet he considered Nate's suggestions as great.

He touched her hand and clasped it in his for a gentle squeeze. "I'm so sorry, sweetheart."

She smiled faintly. "Thank you, Warren. Your support right now means a lot to me."

Their beers and Jake's coffee arrived. Amy poured half a glass and shoved the bottle toward him.

"Take the rest, Jake. I can't finish a whole beer. I should have shared a bottle with Warren."

"No, thanks," Jake said, shaking his head.

"It's okay. I'm not going to say anything," she said, showing a faint smile.

Warren said. "You can have half of mine as well. I don't need the extra calories."

Jake's first reactions were *half a beer isn't going to hurt me. I can handle half a beer!* His second reaction made more sense. *She wasn't just offering, she was testing.*

Still, only half a beer. He almost broke out in a sweat staring at the bottle, fighting the urge to grab it and chuck-a-lug it down. Rasmussen's words teased his thoughts. *Get thee behind me Satan.*

He sighed—hopefully she didn't see—and said, "No. Coffee is the strongest thing I drink these days." It was a lie, but he didn't want her to start doubting him.

They finished dinner. Much of the time the conversation dealt with cases they each were handling, not by patient's name, but by medical conditions. Boring to Jake, but he didn't let it show. Now and then, to keep him in the conversation, Warren asked what he was going to do regarding the estate; how long was it going to take to wrap it up; what problems, if any, did he anticipate.

Jake gave him general answers, the best he could do since he had no idea what, if anything, he might uncover. He hoped something might develop with the hit-and-run but he didn't hold out much hope and didn't say anything about it.

As they walked to their cars after dinner, Warren suddenly stopped and said, "You know what, Amy. Why don't you and Jake hit some tennis balls?" He turned to Jake and said, "Amy loves to play and with my kind of practice, I have to do a lot of pre-visit reading to get ready for patients and don't always have the time."

That hit Jake like a bucket of cold water but after a momentary hesitation, he said, "That would be fun but let me get into shape first." He thought Warren's suggestion was a friendly gesture. *Could be the man is genuinely easy to get along with. Nate may have had him pegged wrong.*

Amy said, "I can play early in the morning or at night. I see patients beginning at ten and close the office doors at five. Warren does not like to get up early." She laughed.

Warren smiled and playfully wagged a finger at her. "Especially if I've been up half the night reviewing patients' files for my next day's work."

Jake promised to call.

As they parted company, Amy said, "I dread tomorrow. I have to go home and write a eulogy I can't believe is necessary. Mom and Dad should be alive. *Damn it. They should be alive.*" She cried. "Christmas is coming up. We used to have such great times."

Warren put his arm around her shoulders and pulled her close. "It'll take time, sweetheart, but it'll get better. I promise."

"Sorry, it catches up with me sometimes."

Christmas. It had been a long time since Christmas meant anything to Jake. Depression began to crawl over him like a viny weed smothering everything it covered.

* * * *

Jake drove back to the McGuire's from the restaurant. Working was much more appealing than sitting on his cot fighting off depression and thinking about something to drink.

The McGuires' phone machine contained no messages. Likewise, there were no threats in the opened or unopened mail and no files that suggested there ever had been. He reminded himself that it was only his speculation that there was more to the hit-and-run than an accident. Nevertheless, it still bothered him that they were running with the traffic, not against it as was their habit. And why did the driver hit them with such force?

He did a quick scan of Nate's computer files and found nothing sinister; no letters responding to threats or claims, no claims or demands initiated by him. He shut it down.

Nate's in-box contained travel brochures; all sorts of exotic places he and Jen must have been considering. He noted a number of solicitations to contribute to various causes and one slick, black and white brochure on African art. Jake just glanced at them. Junk mail as far as he was concerned. He had no interest in traveling anyplace or giving anything to anybody. And he certainly couldn't afford art even if he wanted any, which, he didn't.

He made himself a note to ask Walter about negotiations with Nate's partners. *Were any of them angry enough to have them run down?*

As he turned off the lights and moved toward the front door, something caught his eye, a movement on the patio, made aglow by the outside security lights. *What the hell! A burglar? No. Hell, it's Phillip. What's he up to?*

Jake watched the McGuires' son try the back door. It was locked. Frustration showed on the young man's face. He retreated into the yard evidently in search of something. He dug a brick out of a flower bed on the lower patio, brushed his hands on his jeans and approached the house. He motioned left with his arm. Another man came from inside the open garage door to join him; thin but unlike Phillip, muscular and a head taller. In his hand, was what looked to Jake like a length of two by four. Phillip waved the brick to show what he'd found. The thin guy gave a nod in return.

Phillip said something during their hurried rush up the steps onto the upper patio. After they had cleared the top step, Jake threw open the door stepped outside. He pointed at them and said, "Stop right there! I've called security. They're on the way. You'll be arrested."

"It's my house. Half anyway. I can't be arrested for getting into my house. Come on, Billy," Phillip said to the other guy. He gestured for the guy to move a stride left, which he did.

Trying to flank me, Jake thought and surreptitiously searched the patio for anything he could use as a weapon. The only thing within reach was a bonzai plant in a pot.

The men resumed their walk toward the rear door. Phillip held up and said, "You'd better get out of our way. We don't want to hurt anybody. I just want to get my things. I'm entitled to my things!" He practically screamed the last.

Billy muttered, "Yeah."

"I think we're basically in agreement gentlemen. I don't want to hurt anybody either. And, I agree that you're entitled to your things. But, you're going to have to arrange that with your sister."

"I'm getting my damn things!" He waved his brick and Billy followed suit by shoving his two by four in front of his body like a spear. They walked forward, spread a bit more.

Jake wished he had called security. Without a second thought, he yanked the bonzai plant out of the pot and swung it. The men saw what he was doing and stepped back, well out of range. As Jake began his swing, Phillip heaved the brick at him. Jake saw it coming, but mid-swing, all he could do was lean away from it. It grazed his left shoulder with a numbing thud. Jake was relieved that his shoulder still worked.

The root ball missed the men by a good two feet, but the loose dirt and potting soil on the root ball didn't. It sprayed directly into their faces. And that sent them back another step, pawing at their eyes.

Billy lost his footing and fell down the steps onto the lower patio floor. His head bounced off the pavers with a loud pop. He rolled to his knees to get up, but his head wasn't sending the right messages.

Phillip glanced down at his friend. That gave Jake all the opening he needed. He shoved the root ball into Phillip's face and knocked him backward. He tried to dance down the steps backwards, but failed and landed with a loud bump on his backside.

Jake jumped down the steps to pick up the two by four before either of them recovered. He held it over the two men.

"If you try to get up, you'll be picking splinters out of your heads." He swung the board around like a baseball bat. Phillip looked like he was going to challenge him, but a "swish" of the board an inch or so from his face, forced him back.

He pulled at his friend's shoulder to sit him up. "You've half killed him!" He shouted at Jake.

"Only half? I'm slipping."

"*Billy! Billy!* Are you okay?'

His friend looked at him with glassy eyes, blinked then said, "Just knocked my head when I fell." Billy shifted his look to Jake and the two by four. He made no move to stand.

"If you go out the way you came," Jake said, "I won't have you arrested."

"It's my house!" Phillip repeated, with a wave at the house.

"It may be one day, but now it isn't. So, get out!" He poked the two by four at their faces.

"Let's go, Phillip," Billy said. There was no fight left in him. "There'll be another day."

Jake said, "There'd better not be. There'll be an armed guard here after today. He'll shoot you if you try to break in." He was bluffing, but they didn't know that.

"My personal stuff is in the house!"

"You'll have to take that up with your sister."

"Can we go out through the house?" Phillip asked.

"No."

"Stupid jerk!"

"Keep it up. I have the big stick." He waved the two by four at them.

"Come on, Phillip. Help me up." Billy reached up with his hand.

Phillip glared at Jake and said, "You'll pay for this!"

"I doubt it," Jake said.

Phillip helped him to his feet and they stumbled off behind the garage where they'd presumably climbed over the fence to gain access. Jake watched them disappear into the shadow behind the garage and listened for their car to drive away.

Jake rubbed his shoulder and walked back inside, suddenly tired. *I wonder if they would have killed me? Probably not.*

But, the boy had thrown a brick at him.

Even though tired, he had to let Amy know what had happened. His call went to her message center. He said what had happened and recommended having the security service install cameras to monitor the grounds for intruders and to increase the surveillance drive-bys.

After punching off, it suddenly hit him—the pressure of the last hour no doubt pushed by the depression that had been haunting him since Amy mentioned Christmas. And seeing how happy Amy and Warren were brought back memories he wasn't ready for him. It all crashed down on him without warning. Panic followed. He broke out in a sweat.

I need something to calm my nerves or I'll explode. Wait a minute! I promised everybody I was off the stuff. I am off. Get thee behind me Satan. Get thee behind me!

It didn't work. He couldn't shake the pressure. It seemed to smother him.

I may not be able to finish the job. I may be finished. Damn, I need a beer. Two beers at the most. I'll get calm and then I can plow right into it. Yeah, a couple of beers will help.

He drove to the nearest liquor store and bought a six pack. He drank three bottles in the parking lot outside the liquor store and reached for a fourth, but by that time, he could feel the relaxing glow wash over him. He hated himself, but he felt relief nonetheless.

He drove to Sunrise House. Minnie Sue heard him come in, but she had been alerted about his job and that he might be out late. She made a note but saw or heard nothing worthy of a report.

He climbed into bed and lay there for a while, staring at the ceiling. He rolled over and saw the Bible on his bedside table. He wanted to read, but that would require a light and a light would provoke a reaction from his roommate, so he decided to pray instead. He prayed that the Lord would let him die in his sleep.

But that did not happen. Instead, he woke the next morning before dawn, shaky and with a headache. To avoid facing himself, he pulled on his jogging togs and ran to the beach. The headache diminished to practically nothing. The ache he felt from his failure however hadn't diminished a bit.

At breakfast, he forced down two cups of coffee and a plate of scrambled eggs. He poured himself another cup of coffee and alternately drank and stared into the cup.

I'm worthless. I had a second chance and I'm blowing it. I can't control my need for a beer. I can't handle pressure anymore. I might as well tell Walter to get somebody else. I can't do it.

For some reason he recalled the conversation Rasmussen said he had with God. He wanted to quit but God wouldn't let him.

He made it. Damn it all! Why can't I? I have to make it. I'm fooling myself. I can't make it. Next time I feel pressure, I'll want another beer. Sooner than later, I'll be killing a six pack without stopping. Wait a minute. Sister Brigit! I wonder if she can help?

He checked the wall clock in the kitchen. Way too early for her to be up and about. Trying to stay busy, running from the devil, he drove to the Rec Center and rented the ball machine for an hour. It was exhausting, but for the most part, he hadn't had to shove a single thought out of his head. And, for sure, they were all hanging around like vultures just waiting to pounce.

After a shower, he dressed and drove to the Catholic Church.

He chided himself. *I don't know why I'm doing this. Sister Brigit can't help me. Nobody can.*

He went anyway.

Chapter

6

He found her in the church sanctuary checking the pews for what parishioners might have left. She wore her nun's habit, black flowing robes with white wimple.

"Sister Brigit," he said.

She turned, puzzled for a second then said, "Oh. You're one of the men Bessie looks after. Let me see, Jake, isn't it? Jake Carson."

Jake acknowledged her assumption. "I need to talk to someone. You're the only person I could think of."

She asked him to sit down in the pew she was in. "I am pleased that you sought me out." She sat down, hands in her lap, with a faint smile, facing him. "What is bothering you? I'll help if I can."

He told her about his drinking problem, his disgusting history and now his second chance. "I'm about to blow it." He reluctantly admitted to drinking three beers the night before. "I wanted to relieve the pressure. I felt terrible afterwards. Now, too. I feel like killing myself, frankly. I have a second chance at life. I need it but I don't think I can handle it. Every time I face a problem, I think about a beer. I'm *desperate*."

She reached out and put her hand on his shoulder. "I can see in your eyes that you're a good man, Jake Carson. From what you've told me, you've been a sinner, and you're trying to put your sinful ways behind you. But, Satan has a strong grip on your soul. He wants you to serve him. You need help. I'll pray for you." She lowered her hand.

"I need more than your prayers, Sister Brigit. I appreciate your prayers, but I prayed hard before I slugged down three beers last night."

She stared at him thoughtfully. "Perhaps you're right. The Holy Word says that the Lord works in mysterious ways, Jake Carson. I know that to be true. Last week, I received knowledge from someone about a drug called gabapentin. I hope I said it right."

Jake shook his head. He'd never heard of it and had no idea whether she was even close.

"Ordinarily, I wouldn't look to drugs as a way to solve a problem with another drug. Alcohol, in my mind, is a drug."

"It is. Alcohol dulls my senses so that all I care about is another beer. Alcohol makes my problems go away. Unfortunately, not for long."

"That is a tragedy. God, help this man." She touched the crucifix she wore around her neck and stared upward when she said that.

Jake shook his head in despair. *I'm ready to die. Will He help me do that?*

"You stay here. I'm going to do something that may be illegal in the eyes of the law. But, I don't think it is in the eyes of the Lord." She left him sitting in the pew, staring at her black robes as she walked away. Fifteen minutes passed. Jake was ready to walk away. There was no hope for him. Then, the door to the office she'd entered opened and she came out smiling. Her smile brought him to his feet.

"A friend of God is going to help you," she told him. "The friend is going to bring over samples of that medicine. There'll be instructions on the packages. I want you to take it. It will help you sleep and it will help you control your urge to drink alcohol. It will take some effort on your part as well."

Jake was speechless. Minutes before he was trying to figure out how to die and now he was being offered help.

"Thank you Sister Brigit."

"No, it is God you should thank. All I do comes from Him. He must be looking out for you Jake Carson. He sent someone to tell me about the drug and then you came in with a need for it. Go now and come back in two hours. If you have the determination, the drug will help you break your habit."

She asked him to get on his knees with her and pray for help. He did. It was the first time in his life he had ever done so. In fact, it was the first time in his life he'd ever asked anybody for help.

When they had finished, she said, "You have asked for God's help. He will give you the help you need. You must do your part as well."

"I will."

* * * *

He waited at Sunrise House for the two hours to pass. The thought that he might get help elevated his spirits and brought a smile to his face. It was the first time he had felt happy in years. Sure, he still felt the pressure of his failure, but knowing that relief was on the way gave him the strength to shove the pressure to one side.

Bessie walked by the table he'd taken to drink coffee while he waited. "Jake," she said. "I see you have a Bible. Have you turned to the Lord for help? I think you are doing better." She studied him a second or two. "In fact, you look like you've had some good news. Have you?"

"I guess I have."

"I pray for you, Brother Carson. I'd like to read the Bible with you sometimes. I'm a born-again Christian. I was a sinner until I let God into my life. I've never regretted it."

Her concern surprised him. She'd always seemed so insensitive, so hard. "Thank you, Bessie. I'd like that." He told her about the medicine Sister Brigit was trying to get for him and that was what he was waiting for.

"Bless her," she said and went on about her business.

And, when he felt enough time had passed, he jogged to the Church, letting his senses pick up sights, smells and sounds. He needed his mind to be thinking of things besides his failures.

At the Church, a young nun gave him a paper bag, explaining that Sister Brigit had been called away.

To the McGuire's burial service, he figured.

He asked for a glass of water so he could take one dose of the medicine then. The literature in the bag said that the drug had been developed to treat epilepsy but had seemed to help patents quit or abstain from drinking.

By the time he'd returned to Sunrise House, his mood had improved even more.

Bessie noticed. "You must have picked up the medicine."

"I did and I think it's already helping."

"Praise the Lord," she said touching the cross hanging around her neck.

He took a second shower and dressed for the day. He was ready to pick up where he'd left off the night before, inventorying the artwork and furnishings in the McGuire's home that might have extraordinary value. There was no urge to pop the cap off a beer and drink it down. In fact, he threw the remaining bottles into the first trash can he passed.

He laughed at the irony of his situation. He had started drinking to get his mind off the pressures of his work. Since he'd been kicked out of that life, he drank to get his mind off getting kicked out.

* * * *

His intent was to have a stroll about the McGuire house with a pad of paper and list anything that looked valuable. Armed with the list, he'd ask Amy what items had been assigned to the trust, either directly via documents of title or indirectly via the sweeping language of the trust. Anything else would have to go through probate.

First though, he made a pot of coffee. They had an espresso machine so all he had to do was wait for it to warm up. With a cup of espresso in hand, he decided to read the *La Jolla Light* he'd picked up in the driveway when he retrieved the mail from the box. That was a definite change in his usual approach to problems. In the past, he'd have jumped right into his marching orders of the day.

Except for being slightly relaxed, he didn't feel any repercussions from the drug. That was a relief. The printed information with its list of possible side effects had scared the heck out of him.

More details about Nate and Jeanette's deaths made the front page of the newspaper. From the story, he decided, a reader might very well conclude that both probably went straight to Heaven and walked on water to get there.

That could apply to Jen, but not to Nate. Notwithstanding what Sister Brigit believes, Nate was one tough son of a gun.

But Jen ... he remembered sitting where he was then, having coffee with her. She'd invited him on the spur of the moment to talk. Except for business associates, and they didn't count, she had few friends. Nate was in Dallas talking to some oil people about investing in California real estate. They just drank coffee and visited. It was a sweet moment and he could see her smiling face still, as though she were sitting across from him.

Such a precious person ... and captivating woman. There was always joy in her voice. She made me feel good, just to be with her. How could I have been so blind?

He shook his head as if that would rid it of her memory. It was like yesterday. He forced himself to read the next story.

It was the story about Rasmussen's new age Christian movement holding a special service at the Catholic Church Saturday afternoon. *The one he told us about the other night.* It quoted him as saying that he'd talk about their mission in Africa. The public was invited. Jake wondered how Rasmussen got the church to allow the service. He had heard that the Catholic Church rarely, if ever, opened its doors to a service by another religion. Sister Brigit had mentioned Father Posey. He assumed she must have prevailed on him to allow it.

Two guys in green coveralls and a ladder showed up from the security company. They were equipped with tools and boxes containing security cameras which they mounted at various locations around the outside of the house. If anybody came in, they'd be caught on camera and their presence would trigger a visit by an armed security squad.

Amy called to tell him to expect them. He told her they were already there.

"I'm sorry it happened," she said about the fracas of the night before. "I read Phillip the riot act after the funeral service. He said you started it."

"Right. He had a brick and his friend had a two by four headed for the back door. If that bonzai tree hadn't just been re-potted, I might have had the brick and the two by four as a midnight snack."

"He says he'll put together a list of his personal belongings. I'll have somebody from the security company there when he picks them up. I'd like for you to be present also. Phillip says his list won't be complete but the stuff that's his will be obvious. I'll let you know when."

He would be there. He expressed his sorrow for having to bother her on "such a sad day."

"You weren't the cause, Jake. And, you had no choice. I'm just glad you were there."

After he'd ended the call, he booted up Nate's computer and sent an email to Walter documenting what had happened the night before. The idea of a cold one floated through his thoughts before he could stop it. He looked toward the kitchen, specifically the refrigerator; the source of cold things with great tastes.

Wait a minute. With renewed resolve, he mumbled his usual mantra about Satan getting behind him and strangely it worked. *Sister Brigit's medicine with God's blessings.* He poured himself another cup of coffee and enjoyed it, a first for him in as long as he could remember.

He toured the house, inspecting for valuables. For the most part, he saw nothing he hadn't seen before when he'd been there as a guest. However, there were three bronze sculptures he hadn't seen before; impressive. All were a foot or so high and less that that wide. A miniature brochure under one identified them as the impressionistic works of a German artist, Herman Rosa. Jake had never heard of him but the brochure suggested the artist was of some renown in Germany in that his sculptures conveyed the impression of energy.

There were also two large sized oils, both signed, in the living room which he also figured were new. That's when it dawned on him that he was going at it all wrong. *The smart thing would be to ask Amy for a list of things which had been transferred into the trust. Anything not on the list has to be probated if it's anything of value.*

He called and left a message with the receptionist who promised that the "doctor" would return his call as soon as she could. She'd been out that morning and was trying to catch up.

Jake was faced with what to do next when he remembered something else he could do—call the accountant to see what he knew about Cynthia Berger, the girl Nate had dumped. Amy had given him the accountant's name, Chuck Samuels, and phone number and had called to authorize him to release information to him.

Samuels picked up his phone on the second ring. Jake introduced himself and said, "I'm calling to see if you can help me with my investigation." He explained.

"Sure, I know about Nate's little adventure with Cynthia Berger, his Administrative Assistant. Some of the high fliers, like Nate, hire pretty young women as window dressing and called them Administrative Assistants."

Evidently Nate couldn't resist his own window dressing.

"Nate told us to cut her a severance check for thirty thousand."

Severance for what? The relationship?

"Is that normal?"

"It probably wasn't, but who knows what normal is? She'd been with him for about five years. The problem was, she was making noises, Nate said, when he was trying to negotiate a settlement with his partners. So, to shut her up, he paid her off. Kind of normal, wouldn't you say?"

"With Nate, I suppose it was. Anything happen after that?"

Not that he had heard.

There was no address for her in the accounting firm's computers. It hardly mattered. Jake's old firm had access to a skip tracing service that could find practically anybody's address.

"Was anybody else making threats against the McGuires? Nate in particular."

"Odd you should ask. A guy from the police department, Demarco, I think was his name, asked the same thing. He said as far as they were concerned, the McGuires were killed in a hit-and-run accident, but they wanted to make sure nobody had been gunning for them."

"I guess you told him about Cynthia Berger."

"I did. He didn't think she was a problem. She'd been paid off and was apparently satisfied. However, there was one other wrinkle."

"Somebody else making threats?"

"Kind of. Aaron Bradley did a lot of Nate's ... well, dirty work. Nate would have called it field work."

"His name was the one anyone would see if they came looking instead of Nate's."

"Something like that, I imagine. Technically he was a real estate broker but he worked almost exclusively for Nate. Putting deals together, pulling strings to get approvals, if you know what I mean. Nate's bag man, I gathered, although Nate never said as much. Nate had us send him checks from time to time. Some pretty big. I also think he got paid from escrows he'd worked on. Nate told me that. Lots of double escrows Nate just as soon the partners didn't know about."

"So, Bradley made threats? Pay me or I'll talk to the partners."

"I'm not sure. Nate didn't tell me and he didn't talk much about his money arrangements. But, one day he called and told me to cut Bradley a check for $50,000 and put a special endorsement on it that said, 'in full settlement of any and all claims, past, present or future.' When I asked him what it was about, he said that 'the man claims I promised him a partnership. I didn't, but I don't want him mudding the waters while I'm trying to settle my accounts with my partners.'"

"In effect, Nate paid him off like he did the Berger woman."

"That's the strange thing. The check was never cashed. I told Demarco who gave it a 'hmm.'"

"It's worthy of a hmm. That one might be worth looking into."

"I got the impression Demarco thought so too."

"Didn't Nate ever wonder about it?"

"Yes. He said he'd tried to reach Bradley but he didn't answer his phone."

"I told him maybe Bradley was having second thoughts. He said, 'Yeah. It's like the bastard to try and sweat me.'"

"I doubt Nate could be sweated."

Samuels laughed. "Just before he was killed, the last time I talked to him, I asked if he'd gotten in touch with Bradley. He said no and doubted he would. There was no need."

"I guess he'd given up."

"I suppose."

Jake thanked him. *Doubted he would. What did that mean?*

He stopped by the firm's offices to use one of their computer services to check an address and phone number for Cynthia Berger. She had a downtown condo and two phone numbers, one presumably her work number, the other a cell phone. He'd call the cell number the next day.

He was relieved that he'd been able to slip in and out of the offices without being noticed by anybody.

* * * *

After dinner, he felt good enough to rent a ball machine at the Rec Center. Two times in one day! He hadn't had such enthusiasm for anything in a long time. After thirty minutes, he was certain he was going to die from exhaustion but he began to see a semblance of his game coming back. It was reassuring.

For the first time in months, he began to feel better about life. He was actually doing something besides sitting in the dark, drinking beer and feeling sorry for himself.

He silently thanked Sister Brigit for the help she'd given him, adding a silent prayer. He read from 1st Timothy about Jesus coming into the world to save sinners. He acknowledged that he was a sinner and needed saving. When he closed the Book, he felt better.

Following a sudden urge to do something good, he left his room to find Minnie Sue. She was sitting in the gloom of the kitchen by herself, staring at the newspaper, but not reading, just staring.

"Minnie Sue," Jake called out as cheerfully as he could. "I've been meaning to tell you how grateful we all are that you are here. We appreciate all you are doing to help us break the bad habits that got us here in the first place."

Her face brightened with a smile. It was the first time he'd seen her smile since he'd been there. She thanked him for telling her. "I try to do some good," she said. "It's not always easy. It's nice to know you notice."

He saw tears form in her eyes and turned away.

Amy called later that evening. "Sorry to be so late," she said. "I didn't get out of the office until after six. I didn't want to go in at all, after the services, but people get sick and they want to see a doctor no matter what."

"They somehow assume that you never have problems."

"Uh huh. So, what do you need?"

"I did a quick look through the house and spotted some bronze sculptures and a couple of signed oils. It occurred to me that you might have a list of art objects Nate had put into the trust. If I had that, I'd know better what to list for the probate."

She said she could make a list but she already knew about the sculptures. "Mom and Dad bought them during the last trip to Europe. Dad had intended transferring them to the trust along with the oils. They bought the oils at the last Laguna Art Festival, at an auction. He got involved in settling with his partners and just never got around to it. Together, Dad said they might be worth a couple of hundred thousand, maybe three." She didn't think there was anything else. Even their cars had been transferred into the trust.

She'd fax the list to the house—the office had a fax machine— in case there were artworks she'd overlooked.

That simplified matters for Jake. In fact, that meant his work was almost done. Of course, there was the "hit-and-run" but it seemed unlikely he'd ever find out who did that. So, as a practical matter, there would probably never be a claim for the estate to assert.

He again offered his condolences and thanked her for calling back.

Chapter

7

The next morning, with renewed enthusiasm, Jake showed up at the firm's offices to prepare a report of what he'd done so far including the altercation with Phillip and friend. He was deliberately early to avoid seeing the other lawyers.

On a roll after the report was finished, he prepared papers to have Amy appointed executrix of the estate. It was legal work, but his name wouldn't show up on anything. It just felt good to work again! For once in a long time, he was thinking about something other than when he could have his next drink.

He left the report and the probate documents with Walter's secretary and was walking out of the building when he ran into Walter.

Walter wanted more details about Phillip's attack. "I read your email, but have been too busy to call."

Jake had nothing to add to what he'd already reported but went over it again. Afterward he asked, "How was the funeral service? I assume you went."

"I did. I think Amy expected it," he said. "Not a big crowd, actually. Some perfunctory attendees, like me. Phillip was there with a friend."

"I think I met him." He described the young man with the two by four. "Billy."

"That's him. Amy gave a moving eulogy at the graveside. I don't think Phillip shed a tear."

"I'm not surprised. He's out of sorts because he wanted to get in the house to get some personal things," Jake said. "Amy doesn't trust him to limit himself to personal things. She's asked me to be there with a guy from the security firm as a backup."

"That ought to be fun."

"Yeah. I imagine his friend will be with him."

Jake told him about the report and documents he'd prepared for Amy's appointment.

Walter frowned. "I'll have a look. You're not supposed to do any legal work. What if somebody saw you?"

"Paralegals prepare documents all the time. They don't sign anything. My name doesn't appear on the documents and nobody saw me. And, if you don't like them, throw 'em in the shredder. I won't charge for the time."

He shrugged. "No, I'm sure they'll be okay. Just be careful about what you do. Follow me upstairs, if you don't mind. I'm expecting a phone call."

Jake hesitated, but said okay.

The secretary, in by that time, brought coffee. The phone did not ring.

"That's the way it always works out," Walter said. "I get here early for the call and he's late."

"I have a question while we wait," Jake said. "When Nate was wrapping up his partnership, how'd the negotiations go? From what I've heard, Nate seemed worried about them." *Nate had said he didn't want Cynthia Berger or Aaron Bradley making noises while he was winding things up.*

"I got that impression too. I never met the partners, only their attorneys. They were a tough bunch, arrogant, big firms from LA and New York. I got the idea their clients were just as tough. People with big money usually are. The negotiations were brutal. Nate insisted on being part of them. I got the impression that the partners didn't like the fact that Nate was wrapping things up in the first place. They felt like he had some kind of continuing obligation to make them money." He shrugged. "On the substantive side, they claimed their client's risk capital should have preference over Nate's expertise in developing the properties. Nate was squeezing them for everything he could. He didn't need the money. He just wanted to win."

"Sounds like him."

"One day, Nate laughed at them for refusing to compromise. He told them, 'If you think your money is more important that what I do, why don't we let the court decide? I'll win and you know it. This is my town. You're strangers here.' That pretty much ended the negotiations. I can't say they were happy, but they did okay in the settlement, I think."

"A gutsy bluff by Nate."

"I agree, but it worked. The attorneys knew the hometown boy would get special treatment, especially one as successful as Nate had been. Though nothing was said, there was an implicit suspicion that Nate had likely spread enough money around to make certain he would get special treatment."

"He did have a bag man."

Walter looked shocked.

"Guy by the name of Aaron Bradley. Nate had to pay him off. You ever hear about him?"

"Not that I can recall but if Nate had been doing anything under the table, he wouldn't have asked my permission."

"Did anybody threaten Nate?"

"Not that he ever said. Of course the partners weren't around for the negotiations. I doubt they intended exchanging Christmas cards afterwards, but it was always a money arrangement anyway. Why are you asking about threats?"

"The accident bothers me." Jake explained why.

"If anybody had been upset enough to kill him, they'd have been better off killing him before the agreements were signed. That way, they wouldn't have had to deal with Nate."

"Unless they didn't find out what he'd been doing until afterwards and wanted revenge."

"Could be, but I haven't heard anything. If those guys discovered any hanky-panky, I think I would have heard. They weren't bashful."

"Do you mind if I talk to the cops? I told the police unit at the scene that I was working as an investigator for you."

Walter looked shocked for a second. "I suppose you are, in a broad sense of the word. The accident is peripherally related to the estate ... and the probate. Any recovery would inure to the benefit of the estate. I didn't know you'd done that. Let me know, would you, when you branch out like that? In case somebody asks."

Jake promised but inside, he didn't like the notion of having to tell Walter what he was doing. It was insulting, but he wasn't in a position to do anything but accept it.

"Don't spend a lot of hours. The partners think you're doing clerical and leg work. Let the police do their work and you do ours."

Yeah.

"I ordered cards. I'll pay for them."

Walter wagged his head. "That's okay. I think we can cover cards."

Walter's phone rang, Jake cue to say goodbye.

He went to the vacant office Walter had said he could use and called Demarco, the police officer he'd met on Muirlands, the one who had called Samuels.

"James Demarco," the man said.

Jake identified himself.

"At the accident site, right?"

Jake agreed.

"I remember. What do you need?"

Jake said, "I had a thought I wanted to run past you."

"Shoot."

He told the officer that Amy McGuire, their daughter, said the McGuire's habit was to run against traffic, not with it. It struck him as odd that they'd have been hit in the back if they were running against traffic.

"I take your point, Jake, but where does that get us? Do you know of anybody with an axe to grind against them?" He was careful, Jake noted, not to mention Aaron Bradley or Cynthia Berger even though Jake knew he'd been told about them by Samuels.

Jake gave a general overview of Nate's conflict with Aaron Bradley and the check Nate had cut for him. Cynthia Berger's conflict with Nate had been successfully resolved using the "throw" method. *Throw money at the problem and see if it goes away.*

"I don't see that as a problem. Apparently they'd settled on $50,000."

"The check was never cashed. Bradley might have been thinking he was entitled to a million for all I know. Who knows how far anger will drive a man?"

"Hmm, well, you could be right. When people start thinking revenge, money doesn't matter. Could be we need to see if any stolen cars have been picked up with smashed front ends. I'll check it out. Actually, I already knew about the Bradley guy and his claim for more money. I've put a tag on him. I'll see what pops up when I locate him. It's still down as an accident on our books, but we want to dot our i's and cross out t's in case somebody complains down the road. The McGuires were important people."

"I believe they were. Would you call me if you come up with anything? I'd like to wrap up my investigation."

He would.

Jake next opened an Internet search for suits filed against the McGuires in the past year. Anything earlier than that would not likely have been the source of continuing animosity. Only one filing caught his attention. Cynthia Berger had filed a suit for sexual harassment but had dismissed it with prejudice before it was served. Nothing on Bradley.

Berger probably agreed not to talk about it but with Nate dead, the agreement might not have teeth.

He called her cell number.

"Cynthia Berger," she said.

"Cynthia, I'm Jake Carson. I'm doing some leg work for the Hoffman firm. We're handling the estate of Nate and Jeanette McGuire."

It galled him to say the "Hoffman" firm. It had been his. "I saw from the files that you were Mr. McGuire's Administrative Assistant. I thought you'd be a good person to ask about his financial affairs. The ones I can't find on the books, if there are any. Mostly I'm just cleaning up a few lose ends."

"Who'd you say you were?"

"Jake Carson."

"The name sounds familiar."

Nate might have complained about me to her.

"Everybody says that. Somebody told me there was an actor named Jack Carson. Maybe that's why."

"Uh huh."

"Are you available for lunch?"

"What'd you say you were doing?"

"Investigating the McGuire estate. My job is to make sure nothing and nobody gets left out. You were as close to him as anybody. I was hoping you could help."

He heard her laugh, a scoffing laugh. "Oh yeah! Well, I was as close as Nate wanted me to be. When he got ready to take his chips off the table that was the end of it. He said he never wanted to see me again."

"But, you were his administrative assistant. That's an important job, isn't it?"

She laughed again. "I was a lot more than that. He promised me all sorts of things, condo, car, money."

"Bonuses?" Jake played it dumb.

"You could call it that. In the end, he just paid me off. But not before I raised a stink."

"You want to tell me about it over lunch? And anything else you can remember about his affairs."

"I signed an agreement saying I wouldn't talk about it, but with him dead, I can't see the harm of it. Besides, I'm hungry. Where to you want to eat? I work downtown. He gave me a damn good letter of recommendation. Part of the deal."

I bet.

They'd meet at Mr. A's, the restaurant at the top of a building at eye level with incoming air traffic. So far none had hit the restaurant. Many of the cities prominent lawyers ate lunch there with their clients. Some around town figured a good air crash might do more good than harm.

* * * *

Jake waited for Cynthia Berger outside the elevator. He wore the suit he'd bought with money Walter had advanced him, without a tie.

He had no problem recognizing her. She was a tall, dark haired, dark eyed beauty dressed in an elegant black dress that showed her shoulders. A broad smile fixed in place showed lots of white teeth; silky hair casually draped over her shoulders captured sparkles of the overhead lights.

Great shape. Probably works out every day.

65

But, there was more to her than physical attributes, she had a sophisticated air about her, smart. Jake could see how Nate might have been challenged by her. Maybe challenged was not the word he was looking for, he joked to himself.

"Cynthia?" Jake said. "Jake." He pushed out his hand. *Mid-thirties,* he decided. *Nice perfume.*

"You look familiar," she said with a reflective frown. "Were you ever in Nate's office?"

To keep things at arm's length, Jake said no. Besides, he doubted ever seeing her. He was sure he'd have remembered. She accepted that.

As they were about to go into the restaurant, the elevator dinged again and a rough-looking guy in a worn jeans outfit, including a matching jacket, strode out, panning the area. Unruly hair in need of a trim and an angular face showing a couple of scars.

Been in some fights, Jake thought. *Tough guy.*

"My brother," Cynthia said. "I asked him to join us. Larson!" She called to him.

He made a sound that didn't fit anything understandable and hurried over.

"Larson, this is Jake Carson," she said.

Jake stuck out his hand. The brother ignored it. Jake shrugged. *So, it's adversarial.* Nothing new, but he did feel the pressure. In the old days he'd have laughed it off. Now, he wondered how he'd react.

"She said you wanted to ask questions." He jerked his head in Cynthia's directions. "I'm here to make sure you don't pull any crap. That's what the McGuire dude tried. I ain't havin' her end up holdin' the bag."

Cynthia looked at Jake and said, "Larson is protective. He talked to Nate on my behalf."

"Hell yeah. I talked to him. If he didn't pay up, I told him, I'd beat the crap out of him."

Limited vocabulary, "crap." I doubt Nate would have backed down, but on the other hand, he probably wanted to keep his dirty linen hidden.

"Okay with me," Jake said. "I'm just looking for anything related to the estate. I didn't know the man."

That seemed to satisfy the brother. They went inside and grabbed a table.

She ordered wine; her brother a beer, out of the bottle. Jake wished they hadn't. He was feeling the urge for something strong himself. He took a deep breath, recited his mantra about Satan and asked for coffee. Each time he looked at what they were drinking, he cursed himself for being weak. But, he was glad to be able to resist. *Sister Brigit's medicine must be helping.* He also gave silent credit to his Biblical readings which acted as shoring against the pressure he was feeling.

He looked across the table at the beautiful woman. At one time, he would have been tempted, like Nate obviously had been, but that was then and this was now. His self-esteem was so low just then that even flirting seemed beyond him.

She didn't hold back. "Nate was a ruthless, selfish bastard. He put on a good act to get me in bed. He promised me a condo. I moved in. Turned out he didn't own it. His partners did. Same with the car. I sued him—"

The brother interrupted. "I made her. He wouldn't 've paid her squat otherwise."

"Yeah. He paid me off. And got me the car."

Jake frowned. "You said he was ruthless? You mean in business?

"I mean in everything. He took what he wanted."

"Sounds like he might have made enemies."

"I'd say. He shafted everybody he ever dealt with including his sweet wife."

"For example?"

"Aaron Bradley for one. He stormed into the office and threatened to beat the hell out of Nate when Nate decided to settle up with his partners and retire. Bradley claimed Nate had promised him a partnership and wanted part of Nate's payoff. They almost fought. Bradley was a big man but Nate was in great shape and didn't back down. Nothing happened."

"When did that happen?"

"I'm not exactly sure. I'd say about four months ago."

"What came of it?"

She shook her head. "I don't know. Bradley never came back. I got the impression that Nate worked things out with him. They talked on the phone afterward. Arguments and threats were a way of life for Nate. He just laughed at them."

"Anything else?"

"He screwed his partners."

"How so?"

"He billed stuff to the partnership projects that should have been billed to his office building. I know that for a fact. Padded the construction budget. Double-escrowed the land deals. Had Bradley phony up land values with friendly appraisals."

Jake knew about that practice. Hire a MAI architect, give him an early Christmas present and request a "made as instructed" appraisal.

Probably other things too," she continued. "Bradley helped. He knew everything that went on."

Larson jumped in to say, "I told him I'd make sure his partners found out 'bout the crap he was pullin'. He told me not to threaten him. Big man, gonna beat me up. Like he could." He was ramping up to rage level. "I made the dude pay Cynthia! Not nearly what he owed her! I—"

Cynthia interrupted him. "It was enough, Larson. I didn't want you to get into any more trouble."

Any more trouble? That likely means he has a record.

"Scared you, did he?" For some reason, Jake took a dislike of the man, his bluster and angry arrogance.

He came out of his chair like he was going to fly across the table, fists first. "You don't know what you're talking about. I could 'a knocked him on his butt in a second."

"But you didn't. Did you ever consider why you didn't? What do you do for a living, Larson?"

Still standing, he said, "What is it to you, buster?"

"Just curious. You claimed to bluff Nate McGuire down. I doubt you did. From what I understand, he didn't bluff easy."

"Yeah. Well he did. And, I'm about ready to wipe the floor with you! You—"

"Larson! Cool it!" Cynthia said. "Stay calm. Just answer the question. It's no biggie."

He stared at her for a second, then at Jake with his jaw clinched. Finally, he let go a big breath of air and said, "I ... do odd jobs. Here and there." He sat down with a plop and stared over Jake's head with an angry scowl on his face.

Basically unemployed. Probably a dealer, trying to stay one drug deal ahead of the law.

The next thing just popped out. Jake knew he was pushing his luck, but he let it go anyway, "You sell drugs, don't you?" It gave him some degree of pleasure to say that. The guy's chip-on-the-shoulder attitude just rubbed him the wrong way. He'd dealt with people like that a lot in his past and he'd never gotten used to it. "It's okay. I'm not the law."

Larson practically leaped to his feet and with fists on the top of the table, he leaned over and said, "You shut your mouth now or you'll be needin' dental work! No, I'm gonna fix you right now." He made a move like he was about to do just that.

Jake stood, threw his napkin on the table and said, "Don't let your mouth overload your limited intelligence. One swing and you'll be tasting dirt. And, after that, your parole office will be hunting you down for violating parole. Have a go." Jake motioned at the man with his arms. It was all a bluff, but Jake had learned when he was practicing law, sometimes the only way to back a blusterer down is to bluff.

The restaurant patrons close enough to hear the commotion put down their forks and turned to watch.

Cynthia walked around and put her arms around her brother. "Leave him alone, Larson. You don't want to go back in."

He shrugged her off. "I'll remember you, dude." He pointed at Jake.

"I hope so," Jake said. "I can't say I'll remember you, but I will give you something to think about. I'm licensed to carry. I doubt you ever could be. Keep that in mind when you're remembering. By the way, you just threatened me. You know what I mean?" He lifted his eyebrows. Larson got the message, a parole violation itself.

Larson and his sister rushed off together. Jake paid the bill and left.

He passed a bar on the way back to La Jolla and wanted to stop so bad he could taste the beer. *Pavlov's dog,* he thought. He willed himself to keep driving. It wasn't easy.

His ringing phone might have saved him. It was Cynthia Berger. "Mr. Carson," she said. "I'm so sorry about what just happened. My brother loses his temper and acts stupid. Please don't turn him in. Please. I'll make sure he doesn't do anything even more stupid."

"Tell you what," Jake said. "I'll forget what just happened, if you'll answer my questions the next time we meet."

"What questions?"

"The ones I never got to today. Next time though, come alone. Less distraction."

She agreed.

"I remember you, you know. Your picture was in the paper. You're the guy Nate said was sleeping with his wife. He got so upset about it. I had to laugh. He was having an affair with me and complaining that his wife might be doing the same thing. He threatened to have somebody beat you up. He talked to somebody on the phone. I don't know what came of it."

"I beat myself up instead."

Chapter

Jake changed clothes at Sunrise House and went to the Rec center where he rented a ball machine for thirty minutes. Surprisingly, he was actually hitting the balls back and when he practiced his serve, he was up to 50%. An old guy had been eyeing him practice and seeing an easy touch, asked if he wanted to "rally a few."

Jake said sure after the requisite apologies for being out of shape and rusty. The guy didn't mind. In fact, that's why he asked. Of course he didn't say that in so many words, but Jake got that understanding.

They rallied for about thirty minutes. Jake's blood lust got up after the guy began to hit cross courts causing him to have to run balls down and put them back in the middle with nothing on them, easy put-aways for the old guy.

Jake remembered the counter to the old man's strategy, hit the balls back to the corners so the guy would have to retreat and move to get to them. After that, they played even tennis, including serves. Jake felt ready to play. He wondered if he should ask Amy and decided he would. Anything to keep his mind occupied with something other than feeling sorry for himself.

He got her answering machine instead.

Dinner with Warren, no doubt, Jake decided. It was Friday, after all, the evening most professionals go out to put the pressures of the week behind them. He once did that although the pressure got so bad before he burned out, that he began his decompression early in the week and never stopped.

All alone in the halfway house—inmates didn't count— instead of a sunrise, he felt a depression coming on. He reached for the Bible, but reminded himself it was time for another pill which he took and lay down for a nap. When he awoke, he felt better and it was time for dinner. He didn't have to resort to his mantra.

Sister Brigit came by the house after dinner to ask that as many as possible come to the church the next day for Brother Rasmussen's talk on their current mission. She had been told he was going to talk about the Central African Republic. That was of interest to her because of the strong Catholic presence in the country and because she had served with the Catholic mission there for three years before being assigned to La Jolla.

Jake wished she hadn't come by. He had intended missing it, but since she'd helped him with his problem, he felt obligated to go. Before she left, he caught her alone and thanked her for the medicine.

"I don't know if it's the medicine or the psychological impact of a placebo, but whatever it is has made a difference. I'm better able to control my urge to chuck-a-lug a beer every time I feel a panic attack or a wave of depression."

"Pray to the one who made it possible. I'm only a vessel from which God's mercy flows. I tell you this, Jake Carson. God is faithful and he will not let you be tempted beyond your ability, but with the temptation he will also provide the way of escape that you may be able to endure it. I think he has provided you the way of escape. I speak to you from Corinthians."

He promised to be at the church.

After dinner, he went back to the McGuires' home to meet with a realtor about a valuation. Since the house had been deeded to the trust, its value wasn't critical to the probate, but with Phillip panting to get inside, he thought a value might be useful to Amy in the future.

The broker was waiting outside the gate. Like most in La Jolla, his car wasn't cheap; it was a new BMW. Jake drove an old Chevy.

He showed a smile and stuck out his hand. He was about Jake's height, was in good shape and wore a dark gray silk suit. Exercise and good diet were a way of life for the rich and famous that lived in La Jolla and for those who depended on them for a living. That'd included real estate brokers.

Jake introduced himself, punched in the security code and asked the man to follow him inside.

"Actually, I know this house," the broker said as they strolled through. "Mr. McGuire had me come by last year to value it. I was sorry to hear he'd been killed. It's a damn shame."

Jake agreed.

"At the time," the man continued. "I think he was considering putting it on the market. I've updated my numbers from comparable sales since then. I'd value the house unfurnished at six million plus. Furnished, I don't know. They have some expensive things. I'd have to get some help to value the furnishings and the art works." He reached into his briefcase and handed Jake a valuation sheet and a recommended list price of seven million, to give some negotiating room.

Jake thanked him and showed him out.

"If you guys decide to list it, keep me in mind."

Jake told him they would.

He retrieved the list of art objects faxed to the house by Amy. It listed everything Nate had transferred into the trust. He walked through the house, checking to see if anything, other than the bronze sculptures and the two oils, else had to be listed for probate. At the door into the master bedroom, he hesitated. He had avoided going into the room, reluctant to wake the memories that lurked inside.

The first thing he saw after he entered was a large picture of Jen, framed and hanging on the wall facing the bed. He stared hypnotically at it; her smiling face; her eyes and her innocence. It was almost like she was in the room with him. He took a deep breath and let it out in a loud sigh.

"Jen," he said, choking back the tears. An overwhelming sense of loss flooded over him. That was followed by an equally overwhelming sense of guilt. He wanted a beer, two beers, to wash away his feelings. He turned to run down the hall to the kitchen, but hesitated.

"My life is on the line," he reminded himself and remembered Sister Brigit quoting from Corinthians. "I'm being tempted." He squeezed his eyes shut and muttered his mantra. "Satan get behind me." And, when he opened them, the urge to drink down as many beers as he could find had almost vanished.

"I'm getting better," he said. *Maybe I'm not being tempted beyond my ability to resist.*

He saw nothing in the room that wasn't on the list but while there he searched through her end table for a photo and found one, wallet sized. He took it.

* * * *

Amy called as he parked his car on the street across from his court-assigned home. Indeed, she and Warren had gone out for dinner. And, she'd love to play at the Beach and Tennis club the next morning around nine. They'd find him a partner.

"If you can get here at eight, you can have breakfast with us." He'd make it.

The Beach and Tennis Club. They travel in high circles. Jake was apprehensive about playing there. From what he remembered, having played there years before, the Beach and Tennis Club had a number of hot dogs playing, serve and volley; win at all costs.

He wished he hadn't asked.

He read his Bible before falling asleep.

* * * *

At breakfast with Amy and Warren, keeping the conversation off him, he talked about the artwork that would have to be included in the probate. They didn't know enough about it to do much more than acknowledge the revelation, but it did the trick. Nobody asked questions about him. Jake also mentioned the broker's opinion of value on the house and asked what Amy planned to do with it.

"I think Phillip wants it," she said. "He's hinting."

"That would be a disaster," Warren interjected. "I like the boy but ..."

Amy gave that an agreeing twist of her head. "I can dissolve the trust when he reaches thirty five, a year from now. If I give him the house, what he does with it wouldn't be my problem."

"The probate might take a year," Jake said. "You could get the court's approval on the distribution of the trust's assets at the same time. That'd avoid a later claim by him that he somehow got the short end of the stick."

"I'd say keep it," Warren said. "You would take care of it. You owe it to your mom and dad."

Jake told Amy that she, as the trustee, would have absolute discretion as to the distribution. That was how Nate and Jen asked him to set it up, before Nate terminated his involvement in their affairs.

The court would have no option but to accept her judgment even if Phillip contested it. They wouldn't be friends afterward, but from what he'd seen, they weren't friends anyway.

"Then, that's what you should do Amy," Warren said. "I don't want to see you having to deal with these issues twice. Phillip's a good lad at heart, but I'm afraid he doesn't have the maturity to take care of your home. I'd hate to see it ruined."

Lad? Where did that come from? Jake wondered.

"Thank you Warren. You're a sweetheart to care," Amy said touching his arm.

"I love you. I will always care." He put his hand on hers and leaned over to kiss her on the cheek.

Yep. He wants the house, Jake thought cynically then rebuked himself. *Give the man a break.*

"There are a couple of other houses in the trust. One in Rancho Santa Fe. Dad told me it was worth over five million a couple of years ago when he transferred it in. He picked it up in a real estate deal. Phillip might want that one or one in Del Mar. Both are leased right now."

They talked about that and some valuable commercial properties held by the trust. Both the McGuire children were going to be wealthy, Jake concluded. Phillip could open a string of storefront cooking salons. *He could go broke even faster that way,* Jake thought.

Before leaving for their court, Amy said, "I almost forgot. Jake, Phillip wants to meet at the house Sunday afternoon at one to pick up his personal things. The security service will have someone there to make sure that's all he picks up. I'd appreciate it if you'd be there as well."

No problem, Jake told her.

* * * *

An older guy joined them at the court. Not only was he steady, he hit like a mule and had a great serve. Jake found out later that he'd been the club champion a few years back. Amy and Warren were both good. Warren played like he was born with a racquet in his hand. He just floated over the court; had beautiful strokes and rarely missed anything. Amy was more a scrapper like Jake. She had to work for every shot.

Jake played defensively, concentrating on not making mistakes, avoiding hitting anything risky. Now and then, he had flashes of his old game, but flashes were about all they amounted to. In the end, he and his partner lost the first set but won a tie breaker in the second, thanks to his partner's sterling play. He couldn't be sure, but it was possible that Amy may have missed a couple of key shots she would have ordinarily put away for winners. Whether real or imagined, Jake nonetheless thanked her in his thoughts.

Jake didn't apologize for his play. It was his first outing in years. He was pleased to have played as well as he did. During beer time afterward, he did so want to join in, but was deathly afraid he'd fall back into the pit he'd climbed out of. Citing Rasmussen's service that he had to attend, he excused himself and avoided the temptation.

* * * *

Jake arrived at the end of Rasmussen's sermon, hoping Sister Brigit did not see him enter the church late. She was sitting up front, easily recognized by the traditional nun's black habit she wore. It always looked like it had just come from the cleaners. No priest was in sight. He wore his new suit, including a tie.

The church was filled to overflowing. And, from the looks of some, all of the "inmates" of the halfway houses were among them. Also present were the media people Jake had seen at the beach as well as others. A number of cameras were pointed at the pulpit where Rasmussen finished his sermon.

Stern, he thought, *does a good job getting Rasmussen coverage.*

Jake carved out a place to stand at the rear.

Rasmussen was paraphrasing Matthew when Jesus was talking about Judgment day. The guitar hung around his neck. In front of the pulpit were the four young people Jake had seen at the beach, dressed in green and white. Rasmussen was in all white as before; his beard just as white as his suit.

"All the good people he put on his right. All the bad people he put on his left. He's telling the good people why they were chosen to sit on his right —"

Someone near where Jake stood shouted, "Amen Brother Rasmussen." The man appeared to be one of the homeless souls Jake had seen begging for money along the La Jolla streets.

They must have sent out busses for them.

"Thank you, brother. Jesus told the good people, 'I was hungry and you gave me food. I was thirsty and you gave me drink. I was naked and you gave me clothes! I was sick and you ministered to me.'" Rasmussen smiled and looked about the crowded church. "Don't you just know that somebody must have asked, 'Lord, when did we do that?' He didn't know when! Of course he didn't know, but Jesus had an answer for him and this is the message I pray all of you will carry home with you. If you heard nothing else, hear the words of Jesus."

Rasmussen stood silent with head bowed before raising his head for a quick pan around the room as if to check whether all were listening, then began to speak in a slow, solemn voice. "Jesus told the man, 'It is not what you did for me. It is what you did for the least of my people. For, what you did for them, you did for me!' And, there it is, ladies and gentlemen. Words of wisdom from our Lord. Our mission has done and will do the Lord's will for the least of His people all over the world and we will continue to do so. It is the Lord's commandment to all of us!"

The four apostles began to sing and clap their hands. Of course, Rasmussen strummed his guitar and sang along. Jake couldn't pick out anything he understood. Half a dozen other apostles, also dressed in green and white, picked up offering plates and spread out to go up and down the aisles.

Brother Rasmussen recited Bible verses about giving as the plates were passed, "Deuteronomy. Give generously and the Lord will bless you and all you do. Proverbs. Do not hold back from those in need. Matthew. Give to the poor but don't brag about it. Luke. Invite the poor to your table. You will be repaid at the resurrection. Mark. A poor widow came and put in just a mite. Jesus said, 'this woman has put in more than all of you. She has given all she has.' Corinthians. God loves a cheerful giver. Luke. Give and it will be given back to you. Give so we may do for the least of his people."

The man knows his Bible.

More strumming of his guitar; more singing and clapping by the four apostles.

When the apostles with the offering plates had finished, Brother Rasmussen said, "When I began, I promised you news of our latest mission in the Central African Republic. We entered the country with no religious or ethnic banner other than God's and thought that would gain us safe passage. It did not. Let me introduce Aga Metefara, our missionary from the Central African Republic."

A slight black man wearing glasses, balding with a black beard showing gray patches, stood and turned with a slight bow. He wore a black tunic buttoned down the front, over matching pants and sandals. "Thank you so very much for invitation to me," he said, his tone sing-song and upbeat. "I tell you about our mission. We had planned for two years and prayed civil unrest would settle but alas, it was not."

It appeared that he paused to wipe tears from his eyes.

"Two brothers were killed. I am so sorry for them and their families. Our planes flew into airport near Warab in Sudan. From airport we use truck to get supplies into CRA. We want to fly into Zemio, closer but Zemio under siege from rebels. No so lucky in Sudan, our mission. There was a rebellion there as well. All roads are so bad we had an extra truck with men for road repair during our journey. There were many checkpoints. Each rebel group want something from us." He began counting on his fingers as he spoke. "We receive written assurances from Muslim leaders, Seleka, and Christian rebel leaders, the anti-balaka, that we be granted safe passage. —"

A media reporter raised his hand and asked, "Unclear! What's anti-balaka?"

"I am sorry. I try to explain, but I forget. Anti-balaka is ones against use of machete. Machete is weapon most used by rebels in past. Now, rebels use automatic weapons."

"Thank you. What percentage of the country is Catholic?"

"Less than thirty percent. Majority is Christian. Muslins now fifteen percent. Many religions work for peace. Archbishop of church in Bossanga now joins muslins and Christians in prayers for peace. Many organizations bring aid for people. I fear it is not enough." He wagged his head wearily.

Rasmussen said, "One problem was the LRA, the Lord's Resistance Army. We talked directly to their leader but he did not get the word to his soldiers. Or, they were ignored."

Metefara continued, "LRA soldiers are Tongo-Tongo in the local dialect, those who never sleep and march at night to catch anyone not aware. We are stop by them. Our brothers say no to give our supplies. Then they shoot. We also, but troops from Uganda's Army force come. These rebels very bad men. Many bad men there. Catechists suffer most in war. That is name given for Catholics. Catechists. Yes."

He described some of the accomplishment of the mission. "We install pump at village to bring drinking water back; help Red Cross give aid at refugee camp near Obo; help Doctors without Borders, you know, get generator running to have power."

Rasmussen interrupted to say, "What Brother Metefara hasn't told you is that he was beaten while trying to protect the mission's video cameras and pictures of the harsh living conditions facing the people there. And, the senseless bloodshed."

"If beating is necessary for God's work, Brother Rasmussen, I take two."

"The Lord loves you, brother."

"He is my master, Brother Rasmussen."

Metefara finished his report saying that though they did build a multipurpose building and hold a service with promises of instructions in at least one of the trades, they did not put a steeple on top for fear one of the rebel groups would burn it down as soon as they had gone. They left several missionaries in the small village west of Obo to instruct the villagers in ways to improve their coffee crops and to revitalize their timber industry. Invading troops from other countries had destroyed entire forests that needed to be replanted.

The congregation stood and applauded the slight black man who bowed with praying hands.

"You will be in our prayers every day, Brother Metefara," Rasmussen said as he addressed the congregation. "Brothers and sisters our mission is a just one but our needs are great. I will read you a letter from Prince Charles. He heads a large charitable organization in the United Kingdom,"

He read the letter praising the New Age Christian mission and its good works and "enclosed" a check for $100,000. He paused, raised his arms and said, "I want to thank two people of this church who heard the words of Jesus, Nate and Jeanette McGuire. God bless them both. We were hungry and they gave us food. I pray for their souls."

Nate made an impression on Brother Rasmussen. I wonder if Jen was responsible. It wasn't like Nate to give anything away. Must have been an earth-shaking sum to draw that kind of praise, Jake mused. *Right up there with Prince Charles.*

"And, a special thanks to Sister Brigit and Father Posey who made today's service possible." He asked her to stand but she shook off the request.

Jake knew enough about the Church to know that Sister Brigit must have had the approval of a priest—Father Posey?—to have allowed the service. Since no priest was in attendance, he wondered if perhaps the decision was somewhat controversial. It was nevertheless impressive to hold such a service in the Catholic Church. *Adds a touch of authenticity to Rasmussen's mission.*

A reporter for one of the television stations covering the service asked if Rasmussen and members of his staff would be available for interviews afterward.

"We most certainly will," he said.

When the question was asked, the dark haired man Jake had seen being interviewed on the beach the Sunday Rasmussen was giving what amounted to an impromptu sermon, turned to face the questioner. *Stern, the man who counts the money and most likely arranges for the media coverage,* Jake recalled an earlier thought. Sister Brigit was seated beside him.

"And, while we're doing that, the rest of you, should you be interested, are invited to share a small offering of food in the parking lot," Rasmussen said. "All donated and all served by cheerful volunteers. And, before I forget, we will be holding special services in all the La Jolla churches and synagogues this week and the next. You are all invited. "That information had been in the Light, along with a schedule of their special services in churches and synagogues all over San Diego County.

The homeless had begun stampeding out the doors after Rasmussen announced that food was being served. Others in the church, including Jake, closed in on Rasmussen, Stern and Metefara at the front where the cameras and news people had gathered for their interviews. They had split up so the interviews could be conducted simultaneously.

Many of the others had taken out their check books and were already filling in the amounts.

Jake listened to the Stern interview. "At the end of a tour, such as the one we're on now, we call a board meeting to consider the donations we collected. With our funds in mind, we evaluate proposals for help from missionaries all around the world although in recent years we've concentrated on Africa. We allocate money for expenses and divide the rest into missions."

He spoke with a no-nonsense confidence, Jake concluded as he moved near enough to hear the Metefara interview. He talked about the atrocities being committed by practically all those with weapons. "Even villagers with no weapons are killed for the little they have. Yes. Rebels take food, clothes, animals. I cry for their salvation."

Sister Brigit asked him, "Did you speak to the Archbishop? I served under him while I was in service in the country. He's a wonderful man."

"No, I did not. He is in Bossangoa. It is distance from our mission in northeast Prefecture. Brother Goporo of our mission visit with him. The Archbishop is well, but is stressed."

"I can imagine," the Sister said, "If you do see him, tell him I asked after his health. And, tell him that I pray for his safety and success. I will keep trying to contact him."

He promised to get her prayers to him.

Jake moved to where Rasmussen was talking, big smile, friendly and encouraging all questions. Enjoying the spotlight, Jake concluded.

Responding to a pointed question about how they spent the money they collected, which he interpreted broadly as being applicable to him, he rubbed his beard as if carefully considering the question before saying, "Jesus had only the clothes he wore. I wish for no more in carrying his message. I get nothing from the mission but the food I eat and the clothes I wear. I live in the old motor home Brother Stern procured for me. It does not belong to me."

Listening to the recitation of conflicts which appeared to have no end left Jake frustrated. His mindset had always been on solving problems, not listening. The conflict turned his thoughts to a cold beer. In fact, that was all he could think about. He walked outside to see men and women from halfway houses, street corners, and street medians all around La Jolla, gathered around buffet tables, shoving food onto their paper plates. Their frenzy temporarily took his mind off his urges and strengthened his resolve not to give in to his urge. The passage from Corinthians about being able to resist temptations came into his mind.

Chapter

9

Just how much had Nate and Jen given to the New Age Christians and why? That was the question that had dogged Jake during his drive back. Was it a token sum that Rasmussen embellished on to motivate the others to contribute or was it substantial? The answer had no relevance relative to his investigation, but he was curious.

Hmm. Their tax returns would show what they had given. He recalled Amy saying that the accountant kept Nate's files in his office. *Frustrating!* The accountant would not be in his office on Saturday and he hated to bother Amy. She probably would know, especially if they contributed a substantial amount.

It struck him that Sister Brigit might know. She seemed involved.

He turned around and drove back to the church to ask. The tables had been cleared away. No one remained. Not even the usual debris. Whoever was in charge had done a great job cleaning up.

He found the Sister in a small office down a walk way off the sanctuary, bent over a desk working away, intensity showed on her face.

"Sister Brigit," he said.

She straightened and turned to see who had addressed her. "Oh, it's … drats … let me see … Jake Carson. The man's who's fighting his demons. Right? My memory isn't what it was."

"That's right. I'm fighting and you're in my corner." Jake figured her for eighty if not more.

"God's in your corner, Jake." She stood. "I was just writing the Archbishop in Central Africa to see what I can do to help him in his hour of need. You may have heard. I served under the Archbishop when I was there."

"Yes," Jake said.

"I was so distressed by Mr. Metefara's report. Those poor people. But, why have you come? Do you need more medicine?" Her face softened.

"No. I still have some. It has helped more than I can say. I thank you." He couldn't recall if he'd already thanked her or not. He'd been distracted, but knew distraction was no excuse for thoughtless behavior. His mother taught him that. "No, I came by to ask a question that relates to something you and Brother Rasmussen have talked about a number of times; Nate and Jeanette's support of the church and Rasmussen's New Age Christian missions."

"They were most generous. But … why do you ask?"

He explained his role as an investigator for the McGuires' estate and said, "I was curious about the amount of their support. You could say if it comes up, I might be in a position to at least discuss their history with the executrix of the estate. Should she want to continue that support." While that was a possibility, he knew it was not likely that Amy would do that. However, he felt it might soften his request for information.

"That would be most helpful of you. Hmm, now, what can I tell you? I am not sure. You're asking about church business. I'm not sure I can divulge much." She touched the necklace around her neck and stared away in thought.

Jake waited.

"I'll tell you this. Nearly three years ago, Preacher Rasmussen introduced himself to the church and to me. He said that Nate and Jeanette McGuire of our Church had become supporters of their missions."

Jake opened mouth to ask a question, but she waved him off. "When I asked why he was telling me, he gave me a check for a few thousand dollars which he said Nate and Jeanette had suggested he give to the church. Without divulging anything specific, let me say the amount was under $20,000. Each year thereafter, Preacher Rasmussen has shared a like amount with the church, also taken from contributions given to his mission by the McGuires. Father Posey took the contributions into account in agreeing to allow Preacher Rasmussen to hold his service in the Church. He was not in favor of it, I must tell you. May God forgive me if I've said too much."

"As an ex-lawyer, I'd say you've covered yourself and the Church admirably. I don't suppose you know, in ballpark numbers, how much they gave to the missions? Also, as a matter of curiosity, was Jeanette the giving party or was it Nate?"

She shook her head. "That information was never imparted to me. Not the amount or if one or the other of them did the actual giving. Preacher Rasmussen gave both names. Have I been helpful to your investigation?"

"Yes. You have. I'll give your information to the executrix in a report." That much, he would do.

He thanked her and wished her well in her efforts to help the people of the Central African country.

She said, "I pray we will do some good. I'm so appreciative that people like Preacher Rasmussen have heeded God's call to help his people. The Church has a similar program, but the needs of the people are great and require help from all."

Jake took his leave, his curiosity still unsatisfied. It just didn't seem like anything Nate would do. Of course, the amount might have been peanuts by comparison to his net worth and income. Put a few bucks out and get a lot of ego satisfaction. Who knows? He'd ask Amy for more information Monday then forget it.

His phone beeped as he got into his car. Demarco had called but Jake had his phone turned off for the service and had forgotten to turn it back on. He called back. Demarco answered.

"Jake Carson returning your call," Jake said. "What's San Diego's finest doing working on Saturday?"

"Sometimes I need some time away from the wife and kids, you know. I come in to check if anything new'd showed up in my in-box. It had. Thought I'd call and tell you. We tracked down Aaron Bradley. Guess what, he's dead. Killed during an altercation with a witch. Halloween night. What do you make of that?"

"A witch?"

"That's what the report said. A witch," Demarco said.

"My suspicious side says it's too much of a coincidence to ignore. A man threating Nate McGuire getting killed under, to say the least, odd circumstances."

"I'm as suspicious as anybody. You get to be in my business, but it doesn't strike me quite that way. Sure it's a bit odd, but I don't see a real connection between his death and the McGuires'. Nate McGuire would have been the logical suspect to kill Bradley, but from the description of our eye witnesses, the witch wasn't as tall or as big as McGuire. And, for sure, Bradley didn't kill the McGuires. He were already dead."

"Odd though," Jake said.

"I suppose. I did a check for stolen cars and trucks. Found one in Pacific Beach, a car, with broken head lights. The fragments we picked up at the scene matched."

"What did the owner say?"

"Jeff Wagner. He'd reported it stolen the morning the McGuires were killed. Said he got up and it was missing. He always left the keys in it. Said it was common knowledge. An old car. He didn't figure anybody would be interested. We found it a few blocks away."

Jake laughed.

"Yeah. I laughed too, but he had an alibi. Because we found it near Wagner's apartment, we think someone who knew him, and knew he left the keys in it, took it for a joy ride."

"Find anything?"

"No. Of course, we wouldn't expect a confession from anybody. Prints matched Wagner's. None on the steering wheel. Probably wiped. Anyway, my boss says we keep the case for now. He told me I could spend a few more hours on it before we give it to homicide. PB is close to La Jolla. Could also be somebody came looking for an old car to steal—easier to hot wire than a new one—and found that one with a key already in it."

"Is it okay if I check back from time to time to see how you're doing?"

It was.

After punching off, Jake remembered he should have asked about Larson Berger and called back.

"Yeah," Demarco said.

"Have you ever run into a guy by the name of Larson Berger?"

"I haven't, but I've heard the name. He's a small time drug dealer. Got caught once, I think. Our drug squad keeps a watch out for him. They'll catch him one of these days. It won't solve the problem, but every dealer we take off the street helps the fight against drugs."

"Has he ever done anything violent?"

"No. Why? He threaten you?"

"Not really. I just ran into him and he wanted to bluster so I thought I'd ask in case I needed to watch my back."

"I don't think you need to. He's a blowhard, hothead."

Jake thanked him.

After he hung up, Jake felt the despair of loneliness creeping over him as he drove toward Sunrise House and parked nearby. *If I go inside, I'll get depressed and be tempted to go out for a six pack.*

He didn't have a friend to call and there wasn't anything he could do at the McGuires' home. In fact, there was very little else for him to do relative to the estate.

Cynthia Bergman! I could call her. She owes me one. Likely has a date. If she doesn't there has to be something wrong with the men in San Diego.

So, he was faced with drinking a six pack and feeling like a failure for good reason or facing rejection. He opted for rejection and punched in her number. Surprisingly, she answered.

Jake introduced himself and said, "You said I could call and ask the rest of my questions. I know its Saturday, but I'm free so I decided to call."

"Hmm. Me and a friend I work with are going to do the equivalent of a pub crawl in the Gas Lamp district. Listen to some music, meet some people, have a bite and have a beer that somebody else buys." She chuckled.

"Sure," Jake said. "I understand—"

"No. We can do it next week. The debt I owe you is more important than a night in the Gas Light district. Where would you like to meet?"

"There's a Japanese noodle place in Clairmont Mesa—"

"I know the place!" She rattled off the name. "My favorite little restaurant. And their hot sake is great."

They'd meet at six.

* * * *

They drove up about the same time. Jake had taken off his tie and exchanged his suit coat for an old suede thing he had in a closet at, what he hoped was, his temporary home.

She was in her canary yellow B'mer. No Larson, Jake was pleased to note.

She was stunning in black, tight fitting pants and white pullover with orange accents. Not a hair out of place.

I'm depriving a lot of guys in the Gas Lamp district their thrill of the day, Jake thought. He greeted her with a hello then let it dissolve into a quick hug initiated by her. In his past life, a full body hug was his norm, but circumstances had left him more restrained.

They made small talk while giving their noodle orders, whole wheat noodles with chicken, the spicy version with hot sake.

They enjoyed the sake while waiting for their noodles.

She worked for a commercial real estate firm downtown not far from where she lived. They developed condos as well but preferred commercial. Jake was impressed with her knowledge.

"I started the day after Nate let me go. The bastard."

"How long have you been with them?"

"About three months. Nate began to close the office after he notified everyone he was retiring. He kept me on for a while then out of the blue, said he didn't need me anymore. Just like that. I was out. I went everywhere with him the five years I worked there. You know what I mean."

He did.

"A second wife. From what he said, I think you were doing the same with Jeannette."

She hadn't actually accused him of sleeping with Jen so he let it pass with a nod of his head.

"Nate was furious. He called somebody, I think Aaron about having you beat up. Then he found out you were a lush and about to be disbarred so he took it back. He made up with Jennette." She looked at him hard. "You ... are you on the wagon? You don't look all that bad."

He laughed and gave her a summary of his skid into the halfway house. "I've been trying to make a comeback."

She laughed as well. "It looks good on you." She added a warm smile. "I'm not seeing anyone at the moment."

That brought an involuntary smile to Jake's face. He couldn't recall the last ... well he could—Jen brought the last one to his face. "Thank you. I'm not traveling in your neighborhood right now, but if I move closer, I'll give you a call."

She gave a smiling nod in reply.

Their noodle bowls arrived, steaming hot.

"Mind if I talk while we eat?" Jake asked.

She didn't.

"Okay. I'll be frank."

"Saves time."

"Let me set the stage," Jake said and explained what had bothered him about the hit-and-run "accident."

"You think?" she asked. "Somebody killed them?"

They sandwiched in scoops of hot noodles and spicy sauce between conversational lags. Pausing now and then for sips of sake.

Jake shook his head. "I'm not sure. That's what I'm investigating. For example, it occurred to me that Larson might have been so offended by Nate's putdown—I'm assuming—that he finally worked up enough courage to take revenge. Justifying it as on your behalf."

She gasped, putting her hand over her mouth. "I can't believe that. Well, maybe ... No. I don't think he'd ever ..." She looked away, as if assessing the possibility.

She turned her eyes toward Jake. "Is this a confidential conversation? It has nothing to do with Nate's death."

In that case, it was.

"Larson mostly deals drugs. Nothing big. He has a contact who supplies him his overflow. Larson has three guys who sell for him. It's not a regular thing. The guy doesn't always have overflow. He has one conviction for possession. I love my brother, but I don't approve of what he does."

"He'd headed down a rough road. The San Diego drug squad keeps a watch out for him. They'll catch him sooner or later and he'll end up in a maximum security prison with some pretty tough guys."

She signed. "He knows. I'm working with him, trying to get him to change. Taking him to church. That's why I asked you not to tell on him. I don't think he'd ever do anything like run somebody down! He may puff up like he would, but he'd find a way to back down at the last minute."

"Can you ask?"

She shrugged with a twist of her head as if considering his request.

"Would you tell me if he said he did it?"

Another twist of her head. "I don't know, Jake. Is it okay if I call you Jake?"

He hadn't been called Mr. Carson lately. Jake was a step up from "You" or "Carson."

"You'd report it if I did, wouldn't you?"

"I'd have to."

"That's your answer then. I'll ask but I'm not promising you I'll tell you anything."

"Being together like you were, I'd guess Nate would have told you if he had been having troubles with anybody else. Did he?"

"There was Aaron Bradley. I told you about him, didn't I? Yeah, I did. Nate was a tough guy. I've seen him knock people down, men of course, on the job, when I traveled with him. But I think he was wary of Aaron. Aaron was a big guy."

"He's dead."

"Aaron is dead! How?"

Jake explained then asked, "Did anybody else threaten Nate. How about his money partners? I understand you threatened to tell them what Nate had been doing. How he was skimming."

She grimaced with embarrassment. "Oh my. I'm so embarrassed. I would never have said anything. Nate just made me mad. You know, I loved him. I was hurt when he said it was over. I said things I shouldn't have. I knew a lot of what Nate had been doing, that's for sure, but I was just blowing off steam."

Jake emptied his sake cup and refilled it and hers. He tilted his noodle bowl to get the last noodle and a scoop of sauce.

"He paid you off."

She nodded without looking at Jake. "He took care of me. God, I think I might still be in love with him."

"Did you ever complain to Larson about it?"

"I did. And, sure he blustered. That's why you're asking, but he never said he was going to do anything."

"What about his money partners? Did you ever talk to them?"

"No. Nate talked about them. He was already in bed with them when he hired me. As far as I know, nobody ever threatened him. He was making money for them, even with the skimming and double-dealing. They weren't happy when he decided to retire. He told me that, but it was about money and dividing up property after that. They got their attorneys and Nate got his. Your firm. But, Nate did most of the negotiating, he told me. He said you would have been better. He said that under his breath. You stayed on his list for having an affair with Jeannette. You did sleep with her didn't you? Nate said you did, but I got the impression he was never quite sure."

He decided to stick with his story and hedge. "I enjoyed her company. She had a magic way about her."

She smiled with a knowing wag of her head. "Yeah."

"So, how'd he find the guys with the money? I understand they were not local."

"A guy used to come in to see Nate. I think he was a money broker or something. Maybe he managed a syndicate that lent money to developers. Could have been some under-the-table stuff. I got that impression. Nate didn't want to talk about it much."

"Money laundering?"

"Nate never said specifically, but I got the impression the money didn't come from banks."

Interesting. If they suspected Nate was cheating them, they might have retaliated. "Did the money broker have a name?"

"I'm sure he did, but I don't recall ever hearing it."

"Was he local?"

"I kind of think he was. He dropped by now and then. They had lunch. Nate took him on tours of the projects. Office buildings mostly. They were almost all leased up before the certificate of completions were filed. Nate was good. Jeannette too. She handled the leasing and she knew what she was doing. I was impressed."

I was too, Jake thought.

"Did Nate ever give any hints that the partners weren't happy? Let me make that stronger. Did he ever say anything that suggested the partners were unhappy enough to kill him and Jeanette?"

She stared into her bowl thoughtfully for a second or two before answering. "No, I can't say that he did. Of course, by then, he was trying to get rid of me toward the end so he wasn't confiding in me like he once did."

"And you never got a name ... for the money broker?"

She shook her head, no, before tilting the bowl up to finish the noodles Japanese style.

"What'd he look like?"

"He was well-dressed. Never said much to me. I didn't pay much attention to him. He'd stalk in, say, 'Nate in?' and without waiting for much of an answer, barge into his office. Nate never objected. You know what he used to say?"

Jake did. "Money talks. Bullshit walks."

She laughed. "Money could also walk into his office. Nate never complained."

"Was Nate into anything else controversial? He sometimes went high risk."

She hesitated as she thought back. "I don't think so. Mostly, he seemed focused on winding up the joint ventures and traveling. Somebody sent him a brochure about African art. I got the impression it was some kind of investment. I don't what became of it. He never said."

Jake recalled seeing an African art brochure at the McGuire's home.

"If you remember anything else, call me," Jake told her in the parking lot.

She would. She reached out for him, gave him a close parting embrace with a long—Jake thought—kiss on the cheek. She followed that with a mischievous smile and look into his eyes.

"Call me sometime," she said as she slid into her expensive sports car to drive away.

He mumbled a promise.

He had enjoyed the dinner with Cynthia, even if it was a working dinner. It had been his first real social outing with a woman in a long time. *I can see why Nate would want to have an affair with her. Nate wasn't the best looking guy around, big and tough, and rugged to be fair, but not movie star handsome.*

Chapter

10

On his cot that night, Jake read his Bible. He just read whatever it opened to. It had opened to Ecclesiastes. The book talked about a time for everything, in particular, a time to laugh and a time to heal. He closed the book hopeful that it was his time to do both.

Afterward, he took stock of what his investigation had turned up. Nate was skimming his partners, but there was nothing to indicate they knew about it. Even if they did, how would anyone they hired to do something about it know about the old car with the key in it?

Could they have stumbled onto it? Hard to believe, but possible.

Larson didn't seem to figure in their deaths although hit-and-run was a sneaky act. Something he could do with the few guts he had. Certainly not Cynthia. Nate broke her heart, but she should have expected it. Besides, she did all right in the settlement.

Aaron Bradley seemed to have an axe to grind but Nate paid him off, or was trying to. Nate didn't kill him. The description of the witch, given by the witnesses, didn't match Nate's description. He might have had it done.

He was about to fall asleep when he remembered drinking sake with Cynthia. He laughed out loud. *I must be recovering ... healing. I didn't chug-a-lug it down and lust for more.*

* * * *

The next day, he drove to the McGuires' home early to have a look around before Phillip showed up at one. Jake wanted to have the contents firmly in mind before Phillip stalked in demanding this and that.

Phillip showed up thirty minutes early with his friend, Billy. His early arrival was no big surprise to Jake but since the security guy hadn't showed, he made Phillip and his friend, Billy, sit on a bench and wait in the foyer. He leaned against the wall and waited with them.

Phillip immediately began to complain. "Why can't we just go into my bedroom and look around?"

Jake was amused that he hadn't tried to storm past. *Perhaps my bonzai attack made an impression.*

"Because Amy told me you were to wait until the security guy shows. That way, there will be no dispute about what you took and what you left."

"What a hard-ass you are."

Billy agreed with a grunt.

Thankfully the security representative showed up as Phillip and Billy began to get restless.

"Larry Weaver," the man said by way of introduction.

Jake introduced him to Phillip and Billy and suggested that they head to Phillip's old bedroom. It was the one with posters of musical groups decorating the walls.

They strolled around, picking up this and that, and looking. Now and then, they'd put something on the bed that they intended taking. Mostly CDs, a player and a few clothes. It looked to Jake that they mostly just wanted to look around to prove they could, to satisfy an urge.

"I may want to come back," he announced as they took the last load to the pickup truck they come in.

"Call Amy," Jake told him.

"You think you're hot stuff, don't you?" Phillip said. "If Dad had put me in charge like he *was going to* you wouldn't be allowed to set foot in this house!"

"He didn't though, did he? So, we'll do it like Amy says."

They stalked off.

After they were gone, Jake sent an email to Amy with a copy to Walter detailing the visit and what was taken.

He sent a second email to Amy asking if she could meet with him at her convenience regarding charitable contributions made by her Dad to the New Age Christian mission. *I'm just curious,* he told her. It wasn't billable time so he didn't feel guilty.

Jake set the alarm, locked up, and left figuring it was likely the last time he'd be in the house. He'd make a final report to Walter the next week. He wasn't sure he'd done what he started out to do, that is, somehow make amends to Jen, but in a vague sort of way, he was satisfied. His work on the estate was like a visit with someone dear after being separated for a long time.

Sunrise House had chicken and mashed potatoes for dinner. He ate without a thought about a beer. He didn't dare think he'd broken the habit, but he felt good about himself. He'd gotten interested in life again.

Later that evening his phone beeped with a text message from Amy. She could meet him for breakfast at the place across from the old post office in La Jolla at seven thirty. Warren couldn't make it. He had an early assignment.

Though a challenge, he texted her back and said he'd be there.

Bessie was taking a rare night shift and came by to speak to Jake. He was alone. His roommate had overnight privileges at his parent's home. "Mr. Jake," she said. "We've noticed that you've quit sneaking in your bottles of beer. Are you drinking 'em outside or have you quit?"

"Well, Bessie, I can tell you that I've quit. I was given a job and a chance to kind of start over. It hasn't been a long job and I don't know where I'm going from here, but for some reason, I've turned the corner."

"I've prayed for you. You didn't truly belong here. I hope they'll let you leave soon. I've been giving you good reports."

"When I first got here, I didn't think you liked me, Bessie."

"I didn't know you when you first got here. Frankly most men I've met are scum and think no higher than their underwear, but I've come to believe that you are different, lately anyway. You seem more in control of your life instead of the other way around. As I said, lately anyway."

"It means a lot to me to hear you say that. I've been a long time in the dark. And, it was controlling me. You've brought light into my life. You and Sister Brigit."

"Maybe it's time you had a little light. I'm blessed if I can help you."

He thanked her, a rare friend.

* * * *

Amy had already secured a table for them for breakfast. "I saw you park and ordered coffee. I assume you wanted a cup. That's all you seem to be drinking." She smiled.

"Rub it in. Deserved. I'm getting better, however." He told her about the sake he'd had Saturday night.

"I'm glad you wanted to meet," she said. "Can you take a compliment without thinking I'm inviting you to bed?"

He laughed. "It has been a long time since I've had one of any kind. Please."

"I can see why Mom liked you. I suppose why you were a good lawyer. You have a presence about you. A commanding presence. I enjoy being with you. You make me feel secure; good somehow. There."

"I'm blushing. I thank you. It has been a long time since anybody said anything that nice to me. May I reciprocate?"

"Recip away," she said. "Doctors need a little medicine too. A pat on the back is always welcome."

"I … well, you remind me of your mother so much, I can't look at you without thinking I'm with Jen. You have the same captivating smile, the innocent look in your eyes. There was a magic aura about Jen and you have the same magic. I'm almost afraid to look into your eyes for too long. It melts my heart."

"That is a compliment. Not deserved, but appreciated. I'll tell Warren he'd better shape up. Thank you." She looked away. There was no expression on her face.

Jake noticing, forced a nervous chuckle. "You're welcome. I'm sure Warren does okay."

Damnit. That just slipped out. A mistake. I may have stepped over the line. Damn it to hell. This is not the old days. I'm trying to claw my way out of a hole. Piss her off and I'm back in the bottom. Stupid.

He looked at her face for a sign but saw none. *Okay. Pull back and act like it never happened. It was a compliment. That's all. Hell, it was more, I know it. She probably knows it too. Maybe I should apologize.*

The waiter refilled their cups and took their orders.

"Ask your questions," she said, staring at her cup.

Jake looked at her face again. *Nothing.* She was sipping coffee. *Okay, get on with business. Change the subject.*

"Right." He sighed. "I've run into a Brother Rasmussen who heads up a religious mission called New Age Christians. He's made a couple of references to donations from Nate and Jen. Sister Brigit of the Catholic Church corroborated that. From what I knew about Nate, he never gave away money unless he expected a return. Jen would have, but not Nate. I was wondering if you know anything about it. It has nothing to do with the probate. It just struck me as odd. Like Nate and Jen, if you don't mind me bringing it up again, jogging on the wrong side of the street."

She frowned, took a second of two for another sip of coffee. Then, after clearing her throat, she looked at him and said, "I know about the donations. The first was three years ago. The trust was revocable then but the money came from the trust account so I knew about it. I was the trustee. Dad told me about them. He made them over a three year period, each $150,000. The last one came this year after Dad had made the trust irrevocable. All tax deductible, he told me since it went to a non-profit, charitable company."

$450,000! "Did he say why he donated so much? Even if he had been in the 50% tax bracket, that's still a lot of money to put on a schedule A."

"I asked him. He gave me that little grin he had, like he knew something I didn't or was putting something over on somebody and said, 'You know I never do anything without expecting a profit.'"

"Did he say what profit?"

"No and I knew not to ask. Now and then Dad broke the rules if it suited him. You may know that."

He did. That was why Nate always needed good lawyers. That more or less confirmed Jake's suspicion that there was more to it than merely a donation. It was a sizable donation, so the expected profit must have been equally sizable.

"Any ideas about the profit?" he asked.

"Not a one. It was Dad's money."

Maybe his expectations died with him.

Breakfast came and they ate without talking for a few minutes. Jake had to force himself not to apologize. *Maybe she'll just forget I made a fool out of myself. I'm little more than a bum living at a halfway house. Good God, Warren could eat my lunch. What the hell was I doing?*

During a break for a coffee refill, Jake asked, "Did your dad ever talk about Aaron Bradley? He was Nate's ... for lack of a better description, bag man. I gather he did odd jobs for Nate, investigations and under the table things. He knew who had their hands out. When Nate decided to retire, Bradley became upset. He claimed he'd been promised a partnership. Your dad paid him off, well tried to, the check was never cashed."

Amy looked surprised. "Gosh! I never heard anything about any of that. It was like Dad not to get me involved, just like the charitable donations you mentioned. Sorry I can't help. Even after he made the trust irrevocable, he stayed on the trust checking account. In fact, I never wrote a check out of it until he ... was gone."

"He also paid off Cynthia Berger. Did you know that?"

"No. Frankly, I never looked at the bank statements. As far as I was concerned, he was in control. After he made the trust irrevocable, he had the statements sent to my office. Even before, as I recall. 'Give the trust more legitimacy,' he told me. I haven't been opening them. I suppose I should start."

"Probably a good idea. You need to know what your dad was doing."

"I'll take a look. The old ones might be in the house. In the file cabinet, unless he threw them away."

"He must have. I didn't see any."

"How did you get into that? The donations?"

"I was searching for something to tie somebody to the hit-and-run. Bradley is dead, but his death was kind of odd, like Nate's and Jen's so it sticks in my mind. Samuels told me about the checks to Bradley and Berger. And, when I heard Rasmussen talking about a donation by Nate and Jen, I was curious. I would have asked Samuels, but figured you'd know more than he would."

"I can see how you would have been curious. I would have been as well, except for what Dad told me. Sorry I don't know more."

He debated whether he should call Samuels, but decided he'd chased it as much as it needed to be chased. Amy told him Nate was looking for some kind of profit from the donation. Looking at the donations in that light, it made sense. *Now, all I need to do is find the profit he expected.*

He asked her about Nate's money partners. Did she know how they reacted when he announced his retirement? Cynthia's comment about Nate's skimming was in the back of his mind, but he doubted Amy would know about it, so he didn't bring it up.

"I know a little about Dad's money problems. I had just met Warren. Years ago now. We hadn't moved in together yet, but I invited him to dinner. I think Dad liked him at first. Mom did. He was doing his best to charm them. The banks were apparently balking at lending Dad any more money so he was looking for private investors. A few weeks later, Dad said he'd found private money. They wanted joint ventures instead of lending which was okay with him. Dad always figured he was going to get the better of any deal he went into."

"I heard that Nate dealt through a money broker. Did he ever mention him?"

She shook her head, no. "A couple of months ago when Dad was winding up the negotiations, he was laughing about how the partners were trying to jack him around but he wasn't having any of it. Do you think they might have had something to do with the hit-and-run?"

He could see that it still pained her to mention their deaths. "I haven't found anything that points in their direction."

"Too bad."

"Yeah."

Now, I'll test to see how much damage I caused with my stupid compliments.

"Well, Amy, I've finished my assignment as far as the probate. There won't be much to probate. I'll make my final report to Walter today."

"Hmm," she said.

I guess that says it all. I screwed up. I think I'll get roaring drunk tonight.

He opened his mouth to apologize, but let it go. *It's too damn late.*

They finished breakfast in silence. Toward the end, she looked up and said, "What if I retain you to continue your investigation into Mom's and Dad's hit-and-run? I'd pay you fifty dollars an hour for ten hours a week, for one month. Would you be interested in anything like that?"

Damn. Maybe I'm still alive.

With a smile on his face and a sigh on the inside, he said, "Thank you. I, uh, I am pleased you'd want me too. Frankly, I'd work for you for nothing, but I'll need gas and some expense money so I'll accept your offer."

With a hug, they said goodbye. He kept the keys to the house.

He drove to the firm's offices and typed his final report including his suspicions that Nate's and Jen's deaths were likely deliberate and probably related to Nate's business activities. He did not say anything about Amy's offer that he continue the investigation. He didn't see a conflict.

Chapter

11

Walter looked over his final report, nodding at appropriate passages. He looked up with a half-smile and said, "Well, I think that does it. It's not up to us to investigate the deaths of Nate and Jeannette, of course. I appreciate your observations. I'll pass them on the appropriate police department. I assume that might be homicide although, I'm sure you agree, that you are speculating about the cause."

"Yes."

"I appreciate that you stayed sober, if I may be direct. If you stay that way, I'm sure that eventually you'll be reinstated. Frankly, I don't know if you'll be offered a position here. By the same token, I can't say you won't. I'll recommend you. I know it won't be as a partner."

"I'll be starting over."

He nodded.

"I brought in most of your big clients."

"I know you did, but the other partners have satisfied their needs. Certainly they are not ready or willing to let you take them back. That's the reality. You know how it is. You lose your place in line, you have to go to the rear."

"I understand. I'll continue as I have for now. If and when I get reinstated, I'll make a decision about what I might do then. Thanks for letting me work on the McGuire estate."

They shook hands. Jake left. A certain bitterness stayed with him. He was confident his old clients would return to him once they were certain he was completely recovered though he was equally certain they'd wait until he'd had a few successful trials under his belt before they did. For now, he'd stay at Sunrise House, and take such menial tasks as Walter and his of firm shoved his way. Mostly though, his interest was in investigating the McGuire's hit-and-run … for Amy.

How am I going to do that?

He drove to the McGuire's estate and called Cynthia Berger to ask if Nate had anybody else he used for dirty jobs, like killing Bradley. She picked up right away. He identified himself and asked how she was doing to ease into the conversation.

She said she was okay then, "I was going to call you, but I keep finding reasons to put it off. I talked to Larson about … well, doing anything to the McGuires. You'd asked me if he had. He hemmed and hawed, I don't know, acting like he did, but in the end, when I pinned him down, he says he was just thinking about it. I guess I believe him."

"Did he have an alibi?"

Silence then, "Not one he would share with me."

Hardly a ringing endorsement, Jake thought, but it was the best he figured to get. She'd be protective of her brother and give him the benefit of a doubt.

He told her the reason for his call. "Did Nate use anybody, other than Bradley, to do his dirty work?"

"Not that I ever heard about. Bradley did it all. Nate trusted him."

Jake thanked her.

"Oh, by the way," Jake remembered something else he wanted to ask. "A little background first. Amy, Nate's daughter—"

"I know Amy from the office. I like her."

"Good. She's the executrix of the McGuire's wills. She's also in charge of their trust. Phillip keeps claiming Nate was going to change everything and put him in charge. Did you ever hear them discuss anything like that?"

"I remember the last time Phillip came in, a week or so before Nate fired me. He was all red-faced and bristling like he was ready to fight somebody. I assumed Nate. Anyway, he slammed the door behind him. I heard talking but I couldn't hear what was being said. Phillip did most of it. Finally I heard Nate shouting curse words. Phillip said something and stalked out. He didn't speak to me going in or going out."

"Is that it?"

"Not quite. When Nate came out, after Phillip had gone, he said, 'That boy can come up with some wild-assed ideas to convince me he has a set of balls.' He laughed."

"Did he say what he meant?"

"No."

He thanked her. "If you remember anything else give me a call. Especially if Larson starts taking my name in vain."

She would.

He was none the wiser about Phillip, but if he had to draw a conclusion, he'd conclude that the boy had read something into what Nate hadn't said, rather into something that he had said. Notwithstanding that, Nate had not changed anything.

Jake was convinced that Bradley was murdered and that it was too odd a coincidence to think it stemmed from a spontaneous squabble with a Halloween witch. If Nate didn't do it, as was apparently the case, then who did. And why?

I wonder if Bradley's $50,000 check was found. He'd call Demarco.

And, it still nagged him about Nate saying he intended to make a profit from his four hundred and fifty thousand dollar donation to the New Age Christians. It had been three years since he made the first donation, so where was the profit? What kind of profit was he expecting? Money or what? A money profit should have gone into the trust account unless he had a separate account he hadn't told Amy about.

If Nate expected a profit and hadn't gotten one, he would likely have been asking why. I need to know more about the profit before I start barking up the wrong tree.

He half wished he'd gone to the special service at the Baptist Church and talked to Alan Stern. He'd check the *La Jolla Light* for Rasmussen's next service.

There should be a copy around here.

He found it in the family room. A special service was scheduled that evening in a non-denominational church near Del Mar. He'd go.

* * * *

He arrived early. The four green and white clad apostles had found a place to stand so they wouldn't block the congregation's view of the Brother delivering the Word from the lectern. Jake didn't see Rasmussen or Stern. He figured they were off someplace making peace with the resident preacher, as in tendering a healthy contribution.

I assume the guy from the Central African Republic will be here as well. Something for everybody. Rasmussen with his rosy feel-good sermon and Metefara with his reality. He had witnessed the needs of the people there firsthand and his words opened checkbooks.

It sure opened Nate's.

Ah. Metefara was walking into the church with Stern. Jake hurried over to intercept them before someone else could. Media people stood in a group at the rear of the church, but they appeared to be waiting for Rasmussen to show.

Stern does his job well.

"Mr. Stern," Jake called as he neared the two men.

Stern looked up. His face was without expression. With a gesture, he waved Metefara on. He headed toward a door on the opposite side of the church.

"Yes?" Stern replied.

Jake introduced himself and handed him one of the cards he had printed. It identified him as a "Contract Investigator" for the Hoffman firm.

"Carson?" He frowned slightly. "I don't think we've met."

"No. I'm working for Amy McGuire, the executrix of the Nate and Jeanette McGuire estate. They were killed in an accident."

Stern shook his head slightly as if to say, *"What does that have to do with us?"*

Jake answered. "Going over their affairs, the McGuires donated $450,000 to your mission over the past three years. Can you tell me anything about that?"

"The McGuires. Of course, I recognize the names, Mr. Carson, but all donations and all communications between donors and our mission are strictly confidential. Surely you must understand that, working for a law firm." He glanced at the card with a puzzled look. "I know your name. Weren't you ... a lawyer ... at one time? I read something in the paper."

Jake recognized the ploy as one he'd often used when he wanted to shift the focus away from whatever was being discussed to something that would require a response. Jake's counter was to ignore the ploy which he did.

"Since both are deceased, it would not violate any rights of privacy for you to explain why the McGuires, who previously had had nothing to do with your mission, suddenly begin giving you substantial amounts of money."

For an instant, Stern appeared to glare at him. Then, he smiled and said, "What part of what I said didn't you understand, Mr. Carson? I said all transactions with our donors are confidential, dead or alive. I understand your quest for information, but I don't see its relevance to anything. Donations are used for our missions. If you like, I can send you one of our annual statements showing how much money is collected and how it is spent."

"Thank you Mr. Stern. I would not be interested in a statement your accountants have put together using information you supplied. I am interested in why the McGuires gave you such a large sum of money. From what I've been able to determine to date, no one in the San Diego area has donated such a sum." He deliberately made that assumption. He'd often done that with hostile witnesses to get them to make admissions against their interest.

It did not work with Stern. "I can't comment on what you *claim* you have determined, Mr. Carson, but let me say again, I will not disclose anything about any transactions between our donors and our mission. Am I making myself clear? I don't mean to sound rude, but our attorneys have made that clear to us. Since you were *once* an attorney, you should understand that! We never discuss donations. Your questions border on being offensive so I'll speak bluntly. I am an attorney. Not disbarred." He nodded at Jake.

That stung Jake but he didn't let it show.

"You questions are not relevant to the probate of their estate. I know that and if you went to a reputable law school you should know that as well. So, if you will excuse me, I have promised the media a short meeting before Brother Rasmussen's service."

He turned to leave without giving Jake a chance to ask another question but Jake called out. "You are wrong Mr. Stern. Mr. McGuire left instructions that he expected a profit from the donations. I'd say that made my questions relevant. Wouldn't you? That gives the estate a claim against your mission which it will most definitely press in court … of course using an attorney with reputable credentials." Jake abruptly turned away.

He heard Stern say, "That is ridiculous. The only profit one realizes from a donation is a Biblical one. Check Proverbs. You will waste your client's money."

Over his shoulder, Jake said, "We'll see." He felt a certain satisfaction in leaving it like that. The exchange had left him thirsty for a beer. He thought of Sister Brigit and recited his mantra until the thirst diminished.

As he walked away, he spotted Sister Brigit at the entrance to the church, evidently there to hear more news from Metefara.

Jake read the newspaper accounts of the service in the morning newspaper. The congregation was generous with its support for the mission. Reference was again made to the contribution from Prince Charles. That put the stamp of validation of their mission. *If the future King says they're okay, they're okay.* No mention was made of the McGuires, but they were Catholic and not likely to be much of an influence on a non-denominational congregation.

* * * *

Walter called the next morning. "What are you up to Jake? I just got a call from an attorney in LA, a heavy-hitter with a good reputation. I ran into him when Nate was wrapping up his partnerships. He says you were slandering the New Age Christian mission within earshot of a number of people. He says he has affidavits. He also says his client will file suit if you do it again. What's more, the suit will include us. You could not have been working for us at the time. You've finished your assignment. Isn't that right?" He added a name at the end.

"I'm working for Amy. Freelance. I gave him a card showing the Sunrise House address. There was no one within fifty feet of us. Any affidavit is a fabrication. I assume you told him I was not working for the firm."

"Of course. What were you doing?"

"Amy asked me to follow up on something Nate had said to her." He recited the gist of his conversation with Amy about Nate's announced "profit" motivation. "Stern—he more or less calls himself the financial director of the Mission as well as a lawyer—said that Nate's profit expectation was Biblical and directed me to Proverbs. I don't see any slander in anything I said and seriously doubt a jury would either. The so-called heavy-hitter was just rattling your cage to rein me in."

Jake recalled that the attorney had been a party to the negotiations between Nate and his joint venture partners. Big reputations never bothered him. When he took on a case, he prepared as if the other side would have an attorney with a big reputation. Through preparation usually trumped big reputations.

"The firm does not want bad publicity regardless of the merits. I think you can understand that."

"Likewise, I don't think the New Age Christian mission wants publicity. Bad publicity dries up donations."

"I couldn't care less about that mission, whatever it is. I care about the firm and my position in the firm. I hired you to investigate the McGuire estate, remember?"

"I do and I thank you. I'll throw away my cards." He wouldn't, of course.

"Do that."

Walter asked that he come by the office to settle up. He could leave the cell phone he'd been using.

* * * *

Jake picked up a check for his services. It was generous. He used some of it to buy a pay-as-you-speak cell phone from Wal-Mart. He called the people who needed his new number including Walter. He still wanted the odd jobs that the firm dished out. He left messages for most, but Demarco answered.

"What's up?" he asked.

Jake told him he was looking for a way to link Bradley's murder to the McGuire's deaths. "I thought I'd start with Bradley's computer files. Did he have one?"

"I'm pulling up his file as we speak. Yep. He owned a computer. Mostly the files showed that he belonged to five dating services and had memberships in a bunch of porn sites. Other than that, not much on it."

"Did they find an uncashed check for $50,000?"

"As a matter of fact, they did. It had been endorsed and a deposit slip filled out. So far we haven't found any next of kin to give any of it to."

"How about correspondence? Letters?"

"Other than dating services?"

"Right."

"I'm looking. No. I don't see anything."

"What about the witness reports?"

"You want me to read them?"

"If you don't mind?"

"Tell you what. Why don't you come down here and read them. I've got other things to do."

"Thirty minutes."

* * * *

Demarco put a pile of papers on a table in a small conference room ordinarily used by lawyers and told him the computer was available if he wanted to have a look. Jake said he'd wait.

"We have a bag of junk mail if you want to search that. Brochures, things like that. We didn't see anything relevant," Demarco said with a shrug.

"I throw away most of mine."

"We will eventually I imagine. Right now it's still an open case. We also have his phone records."

"Maybe later."

Demarco left.

Jake looked at the endorsed check on top of the pile of papers. It was dated a couple of weeks before he died. *So, Bradley had accepted Nate's offer.*

Nothing else in the papers told him anything. The witness reports pretty much contained the same information Demarco had already told him except for the auto engine the witnesses heard start up immediately after the witch rounded the corner. The tires had squealed.

The witch must have had somebody waiting. 'Means it was a planned provocation and killing, not a spontaneous argument. Unfortunately, there's nothing on the table to tell me why.

He felt the pressure that comes from frustration and wrapped up his review.

He found Demarco and told him he'd finished.

"If you come up with anything, let me know," Demarco told him. "By the way, aren't you Jake Carson? Used to be a pretty good lawyer. Nobody around here liked you until you got disbarred." He laughed. "I think they considered giving everybody half a day off to celebrate."

"Yeah, I don't blame them. I messed up pretty good."

"You off the booze?"

"Been off for a while. I'm enjoying doing something besides passing out."

"I guess I'd better not offer to buy you a beer."

Jake laughed. "Only one thing better than a beer."

"What's that, three?"

"Yep. If I come up with anything, I'll give you a call."

"Good luck to you. I've known people, good friends, who weren't able to give it up. It ultimately killed 'em. I'm always glad when somebody can. How'd you do it?"

Jake embellished a bit and told him about the Bible Rasmussen had given him and the Satan mantra he recited to himself when he really got stressed, omitting Sister Brigit's bootlegged medicine. No need to risk getting her into trouble. "Got a little Christian help, I guess you could say."

"God bless you, Jake. I'm a Christian myself." He shoved out his hand. "You're the first Christian Detective I've ever met." He chuckled.

"I've been called a number of things, but never a Christian Detective."

Chapter

Jake had been considering drinking a beer from the McGuire's refrigerator, but Demarco's encouraging words took the edge off his intentions. Instead, he made himself a cup of coffee and stared into the back yard.

His new phone rang. It was Amy. "Sorry to bother you Jake, but I wonder if you'd mind meeting Phillip at the house this afternoon. He says he wants to pick up some shoes and things."

"Well, as it just happens, I'm at the house now. I hope you don't mind. I was having a cup of coffee and thinking. What time will he be here?"

"Actually, I'm glad you using the place. Phillip says he'll be there at one thirty? Will that be okay with you? I didn't call the security service."

"It should be okay. If he causes trouble, I'll call them from here." Before punching off, he briefly related to her his confrontation with Alan Stern, the financial manager of the New Age Christian mission and promised details in an email.

He hung up and opened the gate.

* * * *

At one thirty, the doorbell rang. Phillip and his friend Billy were outside. A glance told Jake they'd brought the pickup truck.

He invited them in.

"Mind if we get something to drink?" Phillip said.

Jake shook his head. Already Phillip was pushing his limits. "Okay. Both of you stay together."

"That's insulting!" Phillip said. "D'you think we're going to steal a glass of water? What garbage!'

"I don't think anything. I'm responsible and if you don't want to follow my rules, I'll call the security patrol. You decide."

"Come on Billy. We'll have to do as the jerk says."

Jake let the insult go.

They brushed past him en route to the kitchen and the refrigerator, got drinks and headed to his bedroom where they proceeded to pick up shoes from the closet. While at it, they took a couple of coats.

"I want one of Dad's paintings for my apartment," Phillip said. He gestured toward the living room.

"You can take your personal belongings. That's all," Jake said. "If you try to take anything else, we'll have trouble."

"There are two of us and one of you," Phillip said.

"True," Jake said. "But, I have this." He pulled the hammer from under his coat and waved it at them. He'd found it in the garage after Amy's call.

"Hoodlum!" Phillip said. "That's a threat. I think I'll file a complaint."

"File away. You attacked me before. I've reported it. If you attack me again, I'll report that as well. Also, I'll report that you threatened to take property that belongs to the estate. I think that qualifies as a criminal offense."

"Our word against yours. You''re a burned-out drunk and disbarred lawyer, living in a house for criminals."

"Partly true, but you'll still be arrested on my complaint and have to spend a night in jail."

"I hate talking to thugs," he said. "Let's go, Billy."

They marched out, slamming the front door behind them.

Jake breathed a sigh of relief. He wouldn't have used the hammer, but was glad it stopped Phillip and his friend from testing him.

He sent Amy an email detailing what they had taken and Phillip's attempt to take a painting from the living room.

Walter called next. "I just got a fax from the firm in LA. I told you about the attorney who'd called me. The fax documents what he told me. We're on notice."

"I still think it's a bluff to warn me off."

"Bluff or not, if you try to approach any member of the New Age Christian mission, with questions about private transactions between the mission and its donors, they will file a complaint and request a restraining order against you. I told them you were no longer working for the firm and gave them your half-way house address. I expect you'll get a letter putting you on notice."

"I appreciate your call. Does that mean I should look for dog work from other law firms?"

Silence, then, "What I told them was true. When I got the fax, you were not working for the firm. If we give you work in the future, it will have nothing to do with the mission so I think we'll be safe. Unless you'd rather not work for us."

He was quick to throw that last line in, Jake thought.

"Call me when you have work."

I think I touched a nerve. Those missionary people are sensitive folks. They could be bluffing about the restraining order. However, when I approach them again, I'll be careful not to ask questions about transactions.

He hadn't figured on approaching them again, but that was out. He'd approach Rasmussen for sure after they'd threatened him and tiptoe around the issue. His theory, when practicing, was to pursue any issue someone didn't want pursued. While Stern's objections might have been valid, he seemed unnecessarily belligerent about making them. At any rate, it rubbed Jake's nose the wrong way and he wanted to return the favor.

He locked up and drove to Sunrise House. Chores had to be done.

Around twelve that night, a knock on the door got the night matron up. A policeman was at the door. "Do you have a Jake Carson living here?" he asked.

"Yes. Is anything the matter. He's in his room."

He explained that somebody had knocked in the windshield of Jake's car. By that time, Jake had heard and was up.

"Give me a minute," he called out, got dressed and followed the officer to where he'd left his car.

Sure enough, both sides of his windshield had been caved in by something.

He wondered if his insurance would cover a new one. The officer was apologetic.

"Now and then, kids in the neighborhood do this sort of thing. Sometimes it's part of some kind of ritual. Doesn't look like the door was opened so nothing was likely taken. The lady across the street heard the commotion and called it in."

Jake was fairly certain it wasn't neighborhood kids. Phillip was his choice. He got back in bed and agonized about it the rest of the night. He'd been taken advantage of and couldn't do anything about it. He wished the kitchen had a refrigerator with a six pack but was thankful it did not. He would have finished every one. As it was, he woke with the urge still in his mind. Breakfast chores did little to sweep the urge away.

He called his insurance company and after the usual haggling, the guy sent him to a windshield place to get it replaced. Thankfully, it wasn't far. He had to drive with his head out the window and was glad a traffic cop didn't stop him. *That'd be insult to injury.*

It took until noon and he had no choice but to wait. He sat there and stewed and read old waiting room magazines and drank old coffee until they were finished. He tried to come up with some way to retaliate against Phillip but couldn't. Besides, he grudgingly told himself, it might not have been Phillip. *How about somebody working with the mission ... at Stern's request? Am I getting paranoid or what?*

* * * *

Bessie had sandwiches for lunch. He was glad to get one. He was one of the few inmates in residence for lunch that day so he and Bessie sat together.

"Will you ever get ... what, reinstated so you can be a lawyer again?" she asked.

"Frankly, until now, I hadn't given it much thought. However, now that you ask, I think I will petition the court to reinstate me."

"I'll tell them you are okay. I think you're a fine Christian man. Any man who reads the Bible like you do has to be good. I believe that, Jake."

"It means a lot for you to say that, Bessie. Thank you." He knew it would be a bit harder than having her say he had recovered and should be reinstated. Not all judges followed the Teachings. He'd need somebody, medical, to give an affidavit that his blood had been tested regularly and hadn't shown any sign of alcohol consumption. And, who could say what the judge would require? He drifted back to his room to think. *How can I approach Brother Rasmussen? Do I even want to? They have a right to protect their donors. If I were their lawyer, I'd tell them to keep the details confidential. So, why would I risk getting sued for invading someone's right of privacy? Does a dead person have a right of privacy? The last time he looked, the dead did not, but the courts often only gave lip service to the rule, especially if other interests were involved.*

It could be that Stern was asserting the mission's right of privacy. *Where would that lead me? I may be in a gray area of the law.*

At the end of his mental wanderings, he decided to see if he could somehow isolate Rasmussen from Stern and ask him the questions. *How can I do that? Catch him after a special service!*

* * * *

Jake waited patiently in his car for the New Age Christian's special service to end. It was held at a community service center in the county near Poway. Jake had consulted a newspaper for the time and place. By holding it in a community center, the newspaper story had said, all denominations could attend.

If the number of cars were an indicator, it was fairly well attended. Jake parked half a block from Rasmussen's old RV to wait. Stern came in a separate car with a man and a woman, all casually dressed. The apostles and Metefara came by van. The apostles poured out smiling, already singing and clapping, when Rasmussen came out of his RV, dressed in white, also smiling and waving, his guitar strung around his neck. Metefara, with what appeared to be a look of worried intensity on his face, followed unobtrusively holding a brochure. *His talking paper,* Jake assumed.

They went inside, passing well-wishers along the walk way. There was a sense of celebrity about them. Of course, the media had shown up to tape and interview. Stern and his entourage slipped in after the rest had gone in.

About an hour later, people began to pour out. *Presumably the ones who hadn't brought check books and who didn't have an interest in standing next to Brother Rasmussen or Metefara for a photo.*

Finally, when the outflow reached the straggler stage, Stern with the man and woman he'd come with, popped out the door and drove away. Soon thereafter, Metefara and the apostles got into their van and followed. Rasmussen was close on their heels, waving and smiling, shaking hands and hugging any woman with outstretched arms. His driver, who'd waited in the RV, took his guitar and urged him inside.

The RV pulled away. Some attendees crowded along the sidewalk to wave goodbye. Jake followed. He figured it'd head to a decent RV park, one that would accommodate a 30 foot motor home, Jake's estimate of the RV's length.

The RV exited Interstate 8 and headed north on I-5 in the direction of Escondido. Jake couldn't recall an RV park along 15, but he assumed there would be. Thirty minutes later, the RV was rolling past the exits to Escondido. Jake was grumbling. *Has to be an RV park nearer San Diego.*

Finally, a few miles north of Escondido, the RV took an off ramp and headed east into the foothills where it turned onto a small, winding paved road. Jake stayed sufficiently far behind to avoid being seen. A few minutes later, Jake rounded a bend in time to see the RV entering a gated lane. Jake continued on, searching for some place to turn into to get an angle on where the lane led.

Seconds later, he found a place to pull off the road and look back at a sprawling ranch-style home sat on top of a hill. It was white with dark trim, all one level. A small porch protected the front door from the weather.

On a bricked apron in front was the car driven by Stern and the apostles' van! There was no RV, but Jake did glimpse what appeared to be a man in white entering the front door. *That has to be Rasmussen.*

Shrubbery and trees around the house blocked a clear view, but by getting out of the car, he was able to spot the rear of the RV in a clump of trees below the house.

Lights came on in the house at dark, but no one left. Finally when it was completely dark, Jake drove away.

I'll come back in the morning to see what has happened.

* * * *

At Sunrise House, he asked Bessie if she had a pair of binoculars. She didn't. He drove to the McGuire home and searched around but was likewise unsuccessful. Frustrated, he called Amy and told her where he was. He inquired about a pair of binoculars and why.

"The guy who counts the money for the New Age mission rubbed me the wrong way when he refused to talk about it Nate and Jen's donations. So, my plan is to get Rasmussen—the preacher—alone and ask him. I don't see how it has anything to do with the hit-and-run, but the amount of the donations, knowing Nate, made me curious and I don't have anything better to do. That's why I'm not putting it on your tab."

"Actually, I am curious too. It wasn't like Dad to do that."

"Nate's cryptic comment about making a profit added to my curiosity."

"Log in your hours. I'll go with your instinct. If your bill gets high, I'll just tell you to quit. About the binoculars. Dad kept a pair in the garage, in a cabinet at the back. He kept camping gear in it."

He would find them.

* * * *

After breakfast the next morning, Jake drove to his vantage point. The RV was still where it had been parked in the clump of trees. Stern's car and the van were gone.

Using the binoculars, Jake could see Rasmussen wearing a white robe, wandering onto the back patio holding a cup of coffee. He sat down, apparently, to enjoy the morning view. Soon, a woman joined him. Not one of the apostles, as best that Jake could see, but relatively young. She bent over, kissed him on the cheek and sat in the adjacent chair to enjoy a cup of coffee with him.

He said he lived in the RV. Not last night. Who owns the home? I'll ask Demarco to track it down.

* * * *

Jake called him as soon as he had returned to La Jolla. "James, I was wondering if you wanted to have lunch. I'll be in your neighborhood."

"Oh yeah. You want a favor, is that it?"

Jake laughed. "You're too quick for me."

"Pick me up at twelve. I'll take the lunch and then decide on the favor."

"Fair enough."

He drove to the McGuires, took a coffee break and sent Amy an email telling her what had happened. He was beginning to accept a coffee break as a good substitute for a beer break. The urge for a cold one hadn't disappeared altogether. He just had to keep running from it. Keeping busy and staying free of frustration was a good antidote. Sister Brigit's medicine and his mantra were the bulwarks.

* * * *

Demarco was waiting at the curb in front of the building where he worked. "Where you been? I've been waiting, Jake." He smiled.

"Yeah? I was parked down the street waiting for you to show." Jake said with a grin.

"I should have known. Lawyers have an answer for everything. Where are we going?"

"Hamburger place down the street. Best in town."

"I was hoping for someplace with a beer."

"They tell me beer can get you into trouble. I should say, can get me into trouble."

"Tell me your favor. I won't be able to enjoy my burger wondering what it is."

Jake gave him the donation story, what Rasmussen had said about the generosity of the McGuires; Nate's "profit" quip to Amy; Stern's attitude when asked about the donations and the hilltop ranch home where Rasmussen spent the night with a friend.

"So, you want the public to spend its money to see who owns the place. Is that the favor?"

That was it.

"I go into my boss and tell him a Christian detective wants the police department to do his work for him. You know what would happen if that ever got out?"

"I was counting on your skills to make certain it never did. And, in exchange, if I come up with anything actionable, you'll get it on a platter."

"Best offer I've had today. I've had two hang-ups telling me what I can do with myself and one telling me about my mother."

They got their burgers and fries; Demarco's with a chocolate shake and Jake's with coffee.

"You know you don't have much to back up your suspicions that something may be funny about the donations. However, I think I agree with you. Who gives away that kind of money without expecting something in return?"

"Plus, Rasmussen said he lived in that old RV. At least last night, he didn't and—"

Demarco interrupted saying, "And if he lied about that, ladies and gentlemen of the jury, how do we know he hasn't lied about other things? Isn't that what you lawyers say?"

"When I was a dues paying member of that much maligned association, I might have said things like that. And, there's that thing the proud members in blue say when they're on donut break, 'where there's smoke, there's fire.'"

"We don't actually say that, you know. Well, while we're donut breaks."

"Uh huh. Hamburger's good," Jake said.

Demarco agreed. "Best fries in town."

"Well, are you going to bootleg the favor?"

"I thought that was settled before you picked me up. I have a gut feeling you're onto something. If you get into trouble we can arrest you. If you get lucky, we can take the credit. Sure I'll do it."

Chapter

13

Jake drove to Sunrise House to change into the shabby clothes he wore when living from drink to drink, the same things he'd had on the first time he'd run into Rasmussen and his New Age Christians.

Bessie saw and suspected he was up to something. "What are you doing now, Jake?"

"I'm on the scent of someone who may not be what he says he is. I read someplace, the Book of James, I think, where it says if we know the right thing and fail to do it, that's bad." He smiled.

"Well, don't let me stand in the way of a man who's trying to do the right thing." She gave him a goodbye pat on the back.

He took I-15 back to the exit north of Escondido and drove to his observation place on the winding road overlooking the home where he seen Rasmussen and his friend that morning. The RV was still where it was parked that morning and there were no other cars in front of the house.

He drove back to the gated lane and parked a hundred yards away where the road widened. The gate was intended to keep out vehicular traffic, so was barely a challenge to Jake. He slid through a gap between an anchor post and the fence that wrapped around the property. The walk up the steep asphalt covered lane was harder than getting past the gate. He felt pressure to hit Rasmussen with all his questions before Stern showed up.

He paused when he neared the RV. It rested under the shade of mature eucalyptus trees on a dirt pad. Protected by the RV, Jake looked carefully at the house, searching for any signs of anything with sharp teeth. He figured there were none because they'd have been barking by then. And, he'd seen none when spying on the house.

He took a deep breath, told himself to be effervescent and strode forward, onto the porch to the door. He pushed the doorbell. It rang loudly, but no one showed up. He pushed it again. That time, he heard voices. Seconds later, a woman still in her robe from the morning opened the door. Jake couldn't help but notice that she wasn't a bad looking woman, glamorous in fact, round face with olive skin, blond, nice figure, and probably not much over forty—Rasmussen had to be pushing fifty. She wasn't smiling however.

She'd opened the door wide enough for Jake to see Rasmussen a few feet behind her in the house's central hall. He had dressed, but wore slippers. *Not nearly as impressive as he is dressed in his all white suit.* His beard poked out here and there as if in need of trimming and combing.

Jake waved to Rasmussen and barged in., "Brother Rasmussen! I can't tell you how glad I am to see you. I just had to thank you in person! Praise the Lord!" He patted the big man's shoulders. "I can't tell you how much I'm in your debt. Yours and the Lord's!"

The woman turned sideways to stare back at Jake and Rasmussen, a puzzled look prominent on her face.

"Wait a minute," Rasmussen said, pushing back with his hands. "How did you ... the gate ..."

"Yeah," Jake said. "A limb got caught up under it so I pulled it out. It closed okay. No worries there, Brother."

"But, I mean, ... the no trespassing sign." Conscious of how he must look, he rubbed at his beard with the back of his hand, trying to smooth it out some.

"Wasn't no sign. If there was, I would'a stopped. I obey man's laws and God's." Well, there was a sign on the gate, but Jake ripped it off and threw it across the road.

Rasmussen blustered on, "How ... I mean, how'd you ... who are you?

The woman closed the door behind Jake and watched.

"Don't you remember? I'm the guy with the beer in the bag. By the beach. You told me God said alcohol bites like a serpent and stings like an adder. You prayed for me and it worked. I ain't had a drink since that day." Jake stepped forward and hugged the man.

Rasmussen forced a smile but stepped back, almost brushed his shirt as if to rid himself of Jake's intrusion. "I thank you ...

Brother. I ... I'm ... well, how did you find m... where I'm staying while in San Diego? A friend invited me."

"Is that so? It's nice. I was at your Poway service ... at the community center. Man, that was uh impressive sermon you gave. All those people loved you, Brother. I couldn't get close to thank you ... and I can tell you I tried."

"Yes, but how—"

"Well, I was going to ask one of your apostles where you stayed. Dressed in green and white! They're lovely, Brother. Just lovely. And they sing pretty. I mean to tell you, real pretty. I got close and heard one of 'em tell another where they were going and danged if I just didn't put two and two together and here I am. I parked on the road. Wasn't sure what I'd run into if I tried to climb that hill in my old car. My transmission ain't what it was."

"I'm pleased I was able to help you ... I didn't get your name."

"Brother is good enough for me. To the Lord, we're all brothers. I've been reading that Bible you gave me." Jake turned toward the woman. "Hello, ma'am. Nice wife you have, Brother Rasmussen. I wish mine was still alive. I lost her to the Lord. That's what it says in the Bible and I believe the Bible."

Jake glanced at the woman who, he thought, smiled at the last thing he said. He also thought he detected a slight frown and head shake by Rasmussen. *I think she's enjoying this.*

"I don't guess I could bum a glass of water from you before I go? Whooeee! It was hot coming up that hill. I got me some exercise. Whooeee! I can tell you that." He added a grimace to reinforce his discomfort.

Rasmussen opened his mouth like he was going to object but Jake brushed past. "Don't you worry, Brother, I can find the kitchen."

"Hold on ...Brother. I'll get the water." It was too late by then, Jake was well past. He strolled past framed photos. He recognized Rasmussen and his wife in them along with other people, well dressed people as if all were taken at functions. *I'm assuming she's his wife.*

The kitchen, dining room and living room were one large open area at the end of the hall, vaulted ceiling, painted, with a canyon view out the back. The kitchen was on the right side.

Jake hurried over, opened a cabinet, pulled out a glass and filled it with water which he drank down as if famished. All the time, he was taking in the living room and its contents.

In the living room, a Christmas tree stood, fully decorated. A few wrapped boxes lay on a colored blanket underneath. It reminded Jake that Bessie wanted one of the inmates to help her get a tree for the halfway house. He supposed it would be him.

The only relevant things he saw were a couple of brochures. *Looks like one Metefara was holding at the last service I attended.* He couldn't tell about the other one. It looked different, familiar somehow.

Jake put the glass down and said, "Well, I reckon I'd better be gittin' on. Things I gotta do."

"Uh, just what is it that you do, Brother?"

"I'm a handyman. I do what anybody'll pay me for. Just enough to keep body and soul together. I'm back in church now, thanks to you. I'm Catholic." He touched the cross he'd borrowed from Bessie. "I was there when you gived your sermon. It was beautiful, Brother. It pushed the sin right out of my mind. And, I can tell you I had lots of it to push."

"I'm always pleased to serve the Lord and to help people," Rasmussen said. "I appreciate your coming. Now, I have to sit down and think about our next service. There's no rest for a servant of the Lord."

"Amen, Brother. You know, now that I think on it, I have something on my mind I'd like to ask you about. Do you mind me asking a question? It's about something I heard at your service. At the Catholic Church."

Rasmussen seemed a bit flustered. He glanced at the woman. She gave him a sly smile with a twist of her head as if to say, it's your shot, you take it.

"If you make it quick. I do have much work to do. You can understand. I'm a handyman myself, doing odd jobs for the Lord."

"Yes, Brother. I do understand. You see, I was sitting close to a young woman who was talking to some people next to her about her daddy and mama, Nate and Jeannette McGuire. She said they'd died. I guess you know that 'cause you talked about them in your sermon."

"Brother Nate and Sister Jeannette. Yes. Wonderful people."

"Well, this young woman was saying how her mama and daddy had gived the mission $450,000! Wow! $450,000! I ain't never seen that much money in my whole life and ain't likely to ever see it. Is that what you were talking about in your sermon? That money they gived you?"

"Well, I, uh, I ... Brother Nate and Sister Jeannette have been very supportive of our mission. That's true. I wish we had more like them."

"I wish I had some like them supporting me, Brother Rasmussen," Jake said with a smiling nod at the woman who'd sat down in the living room to watch, still looking amused.

"Three years, she said. There's was one other thing she said that I just couldn't understand. Now, this one is hard Brother Rasmussen. She said ... if I understood it right ... the mission was going to give Brother Nate and Sister Jeannette a profit on that donation. How in the world could that be, I asked myself. I've gived money to the church. Not that much, more like the widow's mite the Bible talks about, but some. I ain't never been promised no profit. That worried me some and I'm sure enough glad I remembered to ask you about it. Can you tell me how they were going to make a profit?"

Rasmussen almost turned away. He did look out the floor to ceiling window at the rear of the living room as if collecting his thoughts. The woman leaned forward; a definite smile showed.

She is absolutely enjoying watching Rasmussen squirm.

"Well, now, Brother, I don't think I can answer that question. They didn't actually donate the money directly to me. Few folks do. So, I don't know about a profit. I call your attention to Luke wherein he quoted Jesus as saying, 'Give and it will be given to you. For by your standard of measure it will be measured to you in return.' I assume that was the profit he was talking about."

"It may be. It may just be. I've heard stories about Brother Nate. And, I can tell you, I'd be hard pressed to think that's the profit he was talking about. Some say Brother Nate never put a nickel on the table without keeping one finger on top of it."

By that time, Rasmussen was shaking his head.

"I just wanted to ask you," Jake said. He knew he would get no more from the man and he also knew he'd better get out of there before Stern showed up.

He thanked both for their hospitality, thanked Brother Rasmussen again for "delivering me from the evils of drink."

"It's my job, Brother, to minister to those in need," Rasmussen said as he urged Jake to the door. The woman gave Jake a slight wave before he turned away.

"Ma'am," Jake said with a nod.

The door slammed shut behind him. He hurried down the steps, but hesitated and went back to the door to listen. From inside, he heard the woman laughing. Rasmussen's reply was muffled.

There may be more to Brother Rasmussen than I imagined ... or less.

He stopped for a look in the windows of the RV as he passed. It didn't look as if it had been outfitted for full-time living.

Jake went down the hill faster than he came up and breathed a sigh of relief when he squeezed past the gate.

He drove to the McGuire's and emailed a report to Amy. He said that he didn't see any relevance in what he'd just done to deaths of Nate and Jen, so he wouldn't charge for the hours he'd spent. Besides, it was too much fun to charge for.

Bessie got her cross back and Jake went about his chores for the evening dinner.

All in all, it had been a good day and he never once thought of a beer.

Bessie visited with him before she left for the day. "I prayed that you'd be successful, Brother Jake. Were you?"

"I think it was but I have to wait to see what might hatch from the seeds I planted."

"I trust that you sowed your seeds bountifully so that your harvest will be plentiful," she said giving him a hug goodbye.

"We will see," Jake told her.

* * * *

Rasmussen called Stern as soon as he regained his composure. "Some goofy guy was just here! I couldn't believe it. Right here in my damned house! Said he overheard the singers talking about the address. By God, you'd better tell them to keep their mouths shut in the future."

"Didn't the son of a bitch see the No Trespassing sign? You should have had him arrested."

"I sent Tammy down there to look. There was no sign. I don't know what happened to it. Some kids must have torn it off."

"What'd he want?"

"Ah, hell, he went on about how I'd saved him from drinking. Turned his life around, that sort of thing."

"Yeah. Sounds like a goof ball. Drank so much his brains have turned to ashes. The only time he thinks is when he shakes his head and the ashes stir."

"I'm not so sure, Alan. He asked about Nate and Jeannette McGuire. Wanted to know about their donations. The profit they expected."

"Profit? What'd the guy look like?"

Rasmussen described Jake, rumpled clothes, old shoes, hair not combed, talked rough. Of course, the Jake he saw and talked to wasn't the Jake who had confronted Stern.

"Hmm. That could be the same guy who button holed me after the service in the community center. He was asking about profits also." He described Jake Carson.

"They don't sound the same. This guy wasn't all that polished and not well dressed," Rasmussen said. "He said we gave him a Bible during my impromptu sermon in Bird Rock. I barely recognized him. I think he was the guy with the bottle in a bag. I was doing a little theater to spice things up. He lives in a halfway house."

"Probably nothing to worry about, Eric. It profited a man nothing if he gains a fortune and loses his soul. Is that close to what you preach about?"

"It's in the neighborhood."

"That's the profit Brother Nate was talking about. Saving his soul. You just keep preaching your inspiring sermons."

"He saw Tammy."

"So what. Even a man of God is entitled to a woman."

Rasmussen was satisfied. "I like to keep my private life private. And, I don't like what I do getting mixed up in what you do."

"All I do is count the money we collect and decide how to spend it to do good for everybody, including you."

Chapter

14

After dinner, Amy called. "I'm impressed. You do stick your nose in, don't you? I read your email. What were your impressions? I want to hear about the things you didn't put in your email."

"I don't think Rasmussen is the monkish guy he makes out. In his sermons he says he lives in that old RV. It didn't look lived in to me. He lives in an expensive view home. Says a friend's letting him use it, but his pictures are on the wall. Also, he lives with a beautiful woman. So, he's not celibate or poor. Not that he's said he was, it just the impression he tries to give."

"You think it's a scam?"

"I can't go that far. Certainly they seem to be putting out the money for the missions. Central Africa is the current one. They even brought over a guy, Metefara, for a report. But, he's conning the public a bit. I don't know if he owns the home or not, but I'm trying to find out." He told her about the favor he'd asked of Demarco.

"What will you do with the information?"

"I don't know. I asked the preacher, Rasmussen, about Nate's 'profit.' He was flustered, but he didn't give anything away, if there is anything to give away. Basically, he gave me the same Biblical response that Stern did. I may have told you, Stern is their financial manager. Yeah, I remember now. I did tell you."

"The arrogant guy."

"That's the guy."

"What else can you do about them?"

"Nothing actually. I enjoyed getting into it, though. Reminded me of the old days when I practiced law."

"Do you think you ever will practice again?"

"If I can get reinstated I will. I'll have to prove to the judge assigned to my case that I've stayed sober for a period of time that will satisfy him. He has to be convinced that I've recovered and am mentally fit enough to take the pressure of a legal practice without falling back into the same black hole."

"Can I help?"

"I'll need a doctor's certificate that my blood tests are negative for alcohol. So, yes, you can help."

"Why don't we talk about it between games? Are you up to hitting a few? I need to work off some frustration. It's getting harder and harder to deal with the drug companies. They take forever to authorize medicines for my patients."

He'd meet her at the Beach and Tennis club in twenty minutes.

* * * *

Jake thought she looked great in her white warm-ups. She greeted him with a tight hug and a smile.

No sign that I offended her at breakfast. He was encouraged.

He got a whiff of her perfume. Faubourg, he thought. It had been a long time since he'd been close enough to a woman to enjoy her perfume. Jen was the last. So lost in thought was he that he almost forgot to turn loose. It was like being with Jen all over, but it was different too.

"I love your perfume," he managed to say. *Be careful,* he reminded himself. *You got away with it before. Don't press your luck.*

"Thanks. Mom gave it to me for Christmas one year. I've used it ever since."

"She had good taste." She was so much like her mother, he thought. He became so caught up in looking at her, he almost stared.

"Let's play," she said with a knowing smile.

They rallied a few minutes then played a set. She played better but he was in almost every game and only lost 6-3, one service break.

"How about a beer?" she asked. "No. I'll have the beer. You get the coffee. I need to swear that your blood is free of any alcohol."

They sat at a table away from the dinner crowd. Her face still was rosy from the match; her hair pulled back and tied behind her head.

Indeed, she ordered a beer. Coffee for him. He felt strong enough to drink a beer, but he was deathly afraid he couldn't handle it and the last thing he wanted to do was make a fool of himself in front of her.

"You played well," she said.

"Thank you. I felt good. You played great."

"I enjoyed playing with you. We have the same kind of game. Get it back and make the other guy win the point."

Jake laughed. She was right.

"How's Warren?" he asked. He recalled the ease with which Warren floated around the court, hitting perfectly placed balls back practically every time. Jake had never seen anybody play with such natural talent.

"He's away in a meeting."

"Medical thing, I suppose. Lawyers have to put in so many hours of continuing education. I suppose doctors to also."

"We do, but no, it's something to do with money. He dabbles in other things. I suspect that's why he doesn't want to have an office, he'd rather dabble. Never wants to tell me, but I hear bits and pieces when he talks on the phone. We've kind of reached the old-marrieds stage. He does his thing and expects me to do mine." When she talked, she smiled and her blue eyes looked directly into his. It felt hypnotic to Jake.

Damn. That has to mean something!

Involuntarily, when he put his cup down, his hand stayed on the table and slid an inch or so toward hers. His eyes never left hers. She broadened her smile a bit and moved her hand so that the tips of her fingers touched his. It sent a jolt through him he didn't think he'd ever feel again.

He sighed ever so slightly and whispered, "When I look at you like this, I think I can see your beautiful and tender soul. I know I shouldn't be saying that. I apologize to you ... and to Warren."

She looked down at the table; her smile faded. "You've no need to apologize. I always feel so comfortable with you. Somehow it's like we've known each other forever. Maybe I should apologize to you."

"I know you and Warren are engaged. He's everything I'm not, successful, a handsome guy and frankly, as you know, I'm nothing and have nothing. But, I do thank you for this magic moment. I will cherish it."

"Don't sell yourself short, Jake. You have something Warren does not have. There's something about you ..."

He almost believed it. It seemed impossible.

Her hand squeezed his. She rose from her chair, leaned over and kissed him on the lips. "If we never have this moment again, Jake, I want to remember it."

"It will be etched in my thoughts forever, Amy."

Then, as if both were embarrassed by what had happened between them, they spoke no more of it, just spent the remaining few minutes talking about the match. She hugged him when they parted. The scent of her perfume lingered after she'd turned away. At her car, she paused for a look back. Seeing him still standing there, she smiled and waved before driving away.

The moment between them lingered in Jake's thoughts like something delicious as he drove home. It had been so long since he'd felt anything for anybody and even longer since anybody had cared for him. And, he remembered the last time. *Ironic. Jen was the last.*

However, he reminded himself, she was still engaged and he was still one mistake from becoming homeless.

Tonight was probably a fluke, but I'm going to enjoy it. It'll keep me going awhile longer.

* * * *

It was still early, eight thirty, so he'd beat the house's curfew even though the night matron had been alerted to expect him late since he was working. Nevertheless, he did not want to draw attention to himself.

He drove past the Catholic Church and turned on a dimly-lit side street that led to his destination. His eyes loosely fixed on the street, his thoughts still back at the restaurant; Amy's face glowing as if she were still in front of him.

"What!" He saw something that snapped him out of his reverie. It looked like … it was! Sister Brigit being attacked by two men in black. He pulled to the curb and jumped out. One man saw him and said something to the other. Their faces were covered so only their eyes showed. One man had just hit Sister on the head with a small sack of something, knocking her to her knees. Jake recognized it. A blackjack!

"You bastard!" he shouted.

The other pulled the small fanny pack from around her waist. Both men turned when he shouted. As they did, Jake crashed into the back of the man wielding the deadly weapon. He swung, but it passed over his back. Jake drove him into the small picket fence along the sidewalk knocking him to the ground. Jake rolled over in time to kick out at the other man who'd rushed over to give his accomplice a hand. The kick sent him staggering back with a grunt. The guy with the black leather weapon rolled to his feet as did Jake, but instead of hanging around, turned and ran away.

Jake's first instinct was to chase after them, but the sight of Sister Brigit lying on the sidewalk, unconscious, stopped him.

He reached into his pocket for his phone and called 911 with a request for an ambulance.

Telling the ambulance drivers he was her brother, they let him ride to the emergency room at Scripps Memorial Hospital. One of the police cars followed. A second stayed at the scene to tape it off to secure any evidence that might have been left.

At the hospital, Sister Brigit was rushed into an emergency room. She was conscious, but only barely.

Jake gave the police officer a report of what he witnessed. "They grabbed her fanny pack," he said, shaking his head. "Makes no sense unless they were desperate. I bet she didn't have more than a few dollars in it."

"Probably not the money they were after, Mr. Carson. Probably after the keys to the church. They'd let themselves in and steal anything of value they could sell at a swap meet. Nobody asks for a bill of sale at those things. I called for a car to patrol the church tonight."

"I guess she was taking her evening walk. You might want to advise her to walk on streets with better lighting."

The officer agreed.

Jake waited until the emergency room doctor came out and said Brigit was okay. "Slight concussion. We'll keep her for a few days, but she should be okay."

Jake thanked him and went to his temporary home. He heard the night matron stir, likely checking the clock and making a note. He'd explain in the morning why he was so late. It was after midnight. He'd also announce to the others why Sister Brigit would not be dropping by for her early morning devotional.

The next morning, he got up to do his chores even though his body wanted a couple more hours sleep. At breakfast, he announced what had happened to Sister Brigit. A couple of men asked when they could visit and how they could get there. Jake didn't know, but Bessie promised them she'd call since she also wanted to visit. She offered to let those interested ride with her.

Jake knew Amy was not a practicing Catholic but probably knew Sister Brigit. So, he drove to the McGuire's home and emailed her a report about what had happened. He wanted to say something about what had happened between them, the magic moment, but thought it best to let it go.

He called the hospital to check on Sister Brigit and was told that she was resting comfortably. "She can have visitors between two and three this afternoon," the nurse told him.

* * * *

Hospital rooms always had funny smells as far as Jake was concerned, like Lysol or medicine or something metallic. And, the colors were always bland like somebody was afraid to show color for fear of upsetting a sedated patient. The television was off in Sister Brigit's room. Her bed was raised. She was sitting up; a half conscious look marked her face.

"Come in Jake Carson. I remember your name," she said with an effort, barely above a whisper. "They tell me you saved me."

"Not really," he said. "They'd grabbed your fanny pack and hit you over the head by the time I got there."

"I mean afterward. Calling the ambulance. Who knows how long I would have been on the walk if you hadn't come along."

He agreed. "Maybe you shouldn't walk that late at night, especially on dark streets."

She sighed. "Goodness yes. I know. I've been so worried about the Archbishop and his work in CAR—that's what I call the Central African Republic—, all those poor refugees. We are all trying so hard to help but there just aren't enough resources to go around. I just had to get out and walk it off. Metefara's report was most upsetting.

"I know how that must feel," Jake said.

"I've been to two of Brother Rasmussen's services ... to get as much news as possible. I gave Metefara two letters for the Archbishop. I've tried to mail, but I'm afraid regular mail isn't getting through. I'm desperate for news. Metefara promises me he'll get my letters to the Archibishop, but I could tell he wasn't at all confident about it."

"I understand. I wish there was something I could do."

She closed her eyes for a second or two. "Sorry," she said when she opened them again. "This medicine. Makes me sleepy."

"I'll leave you. If you think of anything I can do, call me." He wrote down his number and gave it to her. "We miss you at the half-way house."

She smiled.

He wasn't sure that was true, but said it to cheer her up. Some of the inmates would miss her, but some didn't care one way or the other.

* * * *

Bessie gave him a message from Walter Hoffman about a job. He called back and accepted.

After dinner, he drove to the McGuire's home to pick up the mail, a task he'd told Amy he'd do. And, he needed something to do to take his mind off his loneliness. It didn't work. When he walked in, the first thing he did was eye the refrigerator. He opened it for a look. It contained half a dozen bottles of Stella Artois, great tasting beer. He picked up a bottle and held it up for a look.

One beer. I'm sure I can handle one beer. No you can't. YOU CAN'T. YOU CAN'T. Get to work. God's mercy! Remember? God's mercy! Get thee behind me!

With considerable effort, he turned away. The effort brought a sweat to his forehead.

There was a pile in the mailbox, mostly junk, including solicitations for contributions. He brought it inside and forced himself to concentrate on it. He was glad to have it to do. *Otherwise, I'll go mad.*

The junk mail reminded him of something else he wanted to do, but the reminder didn't quite make it into his consciousness.

He put the "real mail" in a sack for Amy and sent her an email saying that he'd drop it off at her office the next morning. That was their arrangement.

The mail included what looked like household bills and junk mail. The junk mail contained a number of colored travel brochures. He put the brochures in Nate's in-box with the others and wondered why he was doing it since Nate and Jen weren't going anyplace. *Maybe Amy and Warren can use them.*

The rest of the mail, he put in a sack for Amy to throw away later. Then he remembered what he wanted to do—look through Bradley's junk mail for anything that might point to what he might have been doing.

Feeling better for having done something positive, if looking through mail qualified, he drove to the Rec Center and rented a ball machine. He set it on high speed and slugged it out for 30 minutes. Satisfied and no longer so depressed he needed a beer, he drove back to Sunrise House and parked in on the drive way apron for the house in case anybody was running around with a brick. The night matron's car, much newer than his, was also parked there.

As he entered the front door, he felt like he'd been running from the devil holding a beer and the faster he ran, the more distance he put between him and the beer. And, finally as he closed the door behind him, he felt like he'd outrun the beast one more time. He thought Sister Brigit had told him something about temptation, but he was too tired to remember.

He slept well that night.

＊ ＊ ＊ ＊

He left the McGuires' mail with Amy's receptionist and drove to the offices of his old firm for his "work" assignment. The office manager handed him the documents someone had approved for him to serve. "You don't look so red faced today. Eyes aren't red rimmed either. Have you come up with some way to disguise your hangovers?"

Jake looked left and right as if checking to make certain no could hear then leaned in close and said in a whisper, "Don't you know it. I met this doctor who gives me some pills that knock my hangovers in the head. Hell, I drank a six pack last night and slept like a log. Do you want me to see if she has anything that'll fix your stupidity? Maybe you could pass the bar. Those mail order law schools leave something to be desired don't they?"

The man had actually gone to a reputable law school, but lawyers who wanted to barb another lawyer often accused them of studying law via correspondence. The word around the firm, Jake had been told, was that the guy couldn't think under pressure. Jake's reply was that law wasn't the job for him since pressure was always present in a lawyer's life. He'd come to realize that the hard way.

Before the man could reply, Jake turned and walked away. If he ever needed a reason never to drink again, it was the office manager.

Walter was coming down the hall for his morning coffee and met Jake. "Got time for coffee?" he asked. Jake wished he had been quicker but agreed.

In his office, Walter said, "That hot shot attorney from LA called again. He said some guy in ragged looking clothes broke through a gate and tried to question the New Age Christian preacher at his home about Nate and Jeannette McGuire. He wasn't as belligerent and he didn't threaten a law suit so I assume he wasn't sure you were the one or not. Were you?"

Jake kind of figured Walter wanted a denial so he feigned surprise and said, "Goodness no!" He patted his clothes. "I've upgraded my attire and for sure I don't want to be the subject of a lawsuit. I want to be reinstated."

"I told him I seriously doubted you were the one. By the way, I had a chat with Amy McGuire. You have impressed her. She says she's ready to sign an affidavit that says you've have kicked the habit. You must have charmed her? You haven't lost that asset, old buddy."

"I don't charm anybody these days, Walter. I just do my job. I'm pleased that she called. I'll thank her if I ever see her again."

"She said she'd given you a couple of jobs."

"Yeah. I finished them. I don't know if she has anything else or not." He figured the less Walter knew, the less he could worry about.

"In a couple of months, maybe sooner, maybe we can petition the court to have you reinstated."

That sounded good to Jake. Serving papers, especially with his new frame of mind, was boring.

Chapter

15

Jake went about the menial task of serving the papers he'd been given. It came with a bitterness he could only barely shake. He shoved an Enya CD in the radio slot to take the edge off. Her music was relaxing and as best he could understand the lyrics over his car noise—and the fact that some lyrics, he was sure, were in Gaelic—almost all songs had to do with man-woman relationships. He remembered Amy; her tender kiss. How she wanted to remember that moment.

It seemed real, but it made no sense. No way in hell can I compete with Warren?

That realization renewed his urge to have a drink, but he was so mad at himself for being in the position he was in, he didn't need the mantra to resist it.

He'd served about half the papers when his phone rang.

"Jake, this is Demarco. How 'bout I buy the burgers and fries and tell you about Rasmussen's digs?"

* * * *

"Best burgers in town," Jake said when they'd sat down.

"Fries aren't bad either," Demarco said.

"So, what did you find out?" Jake asked.

He pulled a sheet of paper from his jacket pocket and read from it. "The house is owned by Eli and Tammy Reid with a mortgage for three quarters of a million in favor of an outfit called New Age Christians. Recorded five years ago. That should be right up your alley. The Christian thing," he joked.

"Rasmussen said a friend was letting him use it. Rasmussen's pictures were hanging on the walls, but I suppose it's possible. Some people take their pillows with them on trips. Maybe Rasmussen takes his photos with him."

"You thought Rasmussen owned it."

"Yeah. I would have put money on it. Reid must have some connection with the New Age Christians. That stands to reason. If he's letting the Rasmussens use the place. The pictures hanging on the wall bother me. And, I think he almost said, 'my home' when I was talking to him."

"You know them?"

Jake shook his head yes. "They do missionary work with—what I call—a purpose. They combine religious missions with the teaching of job skills. Right now they're busy in Africa. The McGuires contributed four hundred and fifty thousand to the cause. That's what got me interested. Nate wasn't known around town for his benevolent spirit."

"So I've heard. Man, four hundred and fifty thousand! That's a chunk of money. More than I'll make in a lifetime."

"Me too. I was trying to find out why. I know he got a good tax write off, but Nate McGuire said he expected a profit. That's why I was snooping around."

"How can you make a profit on a donation? Anyway, I ran a check on the outfit. A guy by the name of Alan Stern is the head man. He's the money guy anyway. Chief Financial Officer. A law firm in LA is shown as their address. The other officers are lawyers in the firm."

"I've met Stern. He's a hard-nose. Wouldn't give me the time of day. Claimed I was trying to invade the privacy of his donors when I asked about Nate's donation."

"I suppose you were."

Jake nodded.

"What do you make of the house thing?"

"I'd say the New Age Christian mission bought the place and sold it to the Reids who let the mission people use it when they're in town. Rasmussen lied when he claimed to live in an old RV."

"Not a crime to lie is it? If it were, half the corporate officers of every listed company in the country would be in jail."

"Yeah." Jake shook his head. "No, but it puts a taint on the man's credibility."

Jake thanked him for bootlegging the information. He had a few more legal papers to serve.

"No problem. Let's go for street tacos next time ... on you," Demarco said.

"For sure."

As they left for their cars, Jake remembered to say, "I'd like to come by and look through that bag of Bradley's junk mail you told me about."

"Why? Don't you have anything better to do? You see one piece of junk mail, you've seen them all."

"You're right but I'm looking for a ravel I can pull."

"Your time to waste. Call me first so I can get it from storage."

* * * *

He cogitated about Demarco's information. It didn't shed any light on what Nate had said about making a profit.

Nate must have been promised something for his donations. But what? The man had everything so what could the New Age Christians promise him that he didn't already have? Nate might have been trying to preserve his take-no-prisoners' image for Amy when he told her he expected a profit. It'd be like him.

His phone rang. It was Amy.

"How about a veggie pizza with me and Warren later?"

He accepted but asked if they could meet him at her parent's estate to take a look at the sack of junk mail she might want to throw away.

They'd be there in about an hour.

That gave Jake time to check in with Bessie to see if she had any chores for him. He knew the other inmates used every excuse they could to avoid helping no matter how much she pressed them. *Probably why they were there in the first place—lazy.*

He helped with the food preparation for that night's dinner and left. Bessie was appreciative.

* * * *

With a few minutes to spare, he sorted the junk mail into piles on the dining room table. It was a huge round thing with padded chairs for ten. A Georgian crystal chandelier hung over it. To save time, he also put the brochures from Nate's in-box in stacks. He segregated them into categories, travel, investments and one from the New Age Christian mission, showing what they were doing with the donations they collected.

He thumbed through the investment brochures. Most had to do with 401K plans. One was information about a syndicate formed to exhibit African Art. Almost like a solicitation, Jake decided, but it never quite made that jump. The back page showed a web-site address and a phone number.

Amy and Warren arrived. Warren in something trendy with a North Face label and Amy in what she was wearing when she closed her office for the day, absent her white lab coat, beige blouse and light brown slacks and tennis shoes, which she said helped because she was on her feet most of the day.

Warren stuck out his hand, big smile and his familiar "good to see you, my friend" greeting. Amy gave Jake a quick hug and peck on the cheek.

"I'm starving," she said. "Where is the junk mail?"

"I'm with you, darling," Warren said.

Jake led them to the dining room where he'd laid everything out. Anticipating the need, he'd brought in a trash can from the kitchen.

Amy made short work of the junk mail, throwing most away. A few things she stuck in a folder to look at later. She also threw away the travel brochures. "One of these days," she told Warren.

He agreed.

The investment brochures also made the trash can. She paused at the Art for the Ages brochure. "Better hang onto this one," she said. "Dad said rich people would go to art exhibits no matter the state of the economy. He put $350,000 in it a few years ago for the trust. I have a file on it."

"Great hedge against inflation," Warren chimed in.

"Don't you have some money in it?" Amy asked.

"Peanuts compared to what your dad invested. All the doctors were told about it. We were invited to a conference. One of the speakers talked about it. An information presentation. No solicitation to buy but it sounded good. You needed someone to recommend you before you could put money in. I think they're non-profit. I'm not sure."

They left for the restaurant, Jake following in his Chevy.

Nate's investment in the art syndicate was the early topic of conversation during their pizza dinner, the quality of the art and the range of exhibitions scheduled.

They ordered beer with theirs. Jake stayed with coffee.

"Has it made money?" Jake asked Warren about the art syndicate.

"The ones which have acquired a full portfolio are doing well. Some are still in the acquisition phase. They either purchase outright or lease. We were told to expect a number of years to put one together. On occasion, they run into problems getting the art exported from a country. That results in delays. Personally, I think some of the local officials have their hands out."

"In other words, if you are going to need returns in a hurry, don't invest," Jake said.

"Right you are. Once a syndicate has acquired a full portfolio, it goes on exhibition and another syndicate is formed. They project pretty good returns."

He has a bit of an upper crust English accent, Jake noted, recalling his use of the word, lad, previously.

"How much money is involved in one … syndicate?" Jake asked.

"You may very well ask, Jake. Quite a bit, it seems. Thirty to forty million depending on each syndicate's acquisition plan."

"Investors get paid from exhibition proceeds," Jake said, more as a question.

"That's what I understand. We get progress reports. My syndicate has thirty million in it now and the art pieces are all under contract as are the artists the syndicate feels it needs to open an exhibition. The syndicate managers try to get the more prominent artists to attend the opening of an exhibition. Give interviews to the media. It's very well done."

Jake agreed.

"Didn't you tell Dad about it?" Amy asked Warren.

"Not really. We discussed it at dinner one night. He seemed interested."

"He must have been. $350,000 worth!" Jake said.

"You know Dad. Knew him," Amy said.

"Yeah. Well, changing the subject," Jake said, "I've pretty much reached a dead end on Nate's donations to that new Christian mission. I haven't found out anything that sheds any light on it. And, they threatened me with a lawsuit if I bothered them again."

Warren looked at Jake and said, "Personally, I have an aversion to lawsuits." He smiled. "Court time is an anathema to billing time and those big LA firms can keep you in court until you starve."

"I agree," Jake said. He handed Amy the one sheet report given to him by Demarco. Demarco's name wasn't on it. "This is all I found out when I investigated. Nothing of any significance. The preacher, a guy by the name of Rasmussen and his wife, I assume, live in a luxury estate owned by Eli Reid and his wife, Tammy. The property is encumbered by a three quarters of a million deed of trust in favor of the Christian mission. Nothing that tells me why Nate thought he was going to profit from his donation."

"Impressive investigating," Warren said, "How'd you unravel that?"

"I followed the preacher after one of his sermons."

"Good sleuthing," Warren said.

"I suppose. It got me a glass of water."

Amy said, "Changing the subject again, are you two up to tennis tomorrow afternoon. I have a short day and I'd like to work out my frustrations on the court. Warren, can we find a fourth someplace?"

"Ah, tomorrow is not good for me. I have two pre-op reports. That'll tie me up for at least two hours. Why don't you and Jake have a go?"

Amy looked at Jake. For a second he thought she was going to touch his hand with hers but she didn't. "How about it Jake? Are you free?"

He was. She gave him a time.

"By the way, Amy, there's very little else for me to stick my nose into. I have one little thing to check and after that, I'm finished." He had in mind looking at Bradley's junk mail, too minor for discussion.

"I was hoping somehow you'd get a lead on who killed Mom and Dad." She choked up at the end.

"I was hoping the same thing." He had another idea. "Remember the hit-and-run car? Somebody knew the owner left his keys in it."

"One of his friends?" Warren suggested.

"Probably. So, did one of them do it?"

"Or let it slip accidentally? So some unknown person knew about the keys and took the car out for a ride." Warren supposed.

"Yeah," Jake said. "That might mean it was indeed an accident. Joyriding."

"Could be," Warren said.

"I think I'll check around to see who knew about the key."

* * * *

Dinner was something of a bore. Amy and Warren talked medicine, a subject he knew very little about and wasn't interested in learning more. He liked medicine when he was sick with something and just then, he wasn't.

Once, when it appeared they were between subjects, he asked, "How wide a range do you cover substituting for other doctors, Warren?"

"Good question. I try to limit myself to no more than a twenty minute commute. So far that has worked. I've been looking for office space around here that'll accommodate offices for me and Amy."

Amy looked at him with surprise. "I didn't know you were doing that."

He smiled. "That's because I haven't told you. Unfortunately, I'm a victim of success. I'm doing so well substituting, I haven't had the time to do much looking."

"You're making more money than I am, Warren. Why change?"

He patted her hand with a smile. "Some of that is my business income," he said, adding, "I'm trying to change … follow through on what I told your dad. He thought I should have an office and I took that to heart. I love you, Amy. If Nate wanted me to be more like the ant to get his approval to marry you, I'll be more like the ant, even though … well, just even though."

Amy's face lost its smile for a second. The reminder that her dad was dead brought back memories she's as soon forget.

"I'm sorry, sweetheart. I'm sorry to remind you." He reached out with his arm and squeezed her.

"It's okay," she said and took a sip of her beer.

After a sideways glance at Amy, he looked at Jake, sighed and said, "As you can appreciate, there are problems with that plan. In the first place, Amy'd have to sell her office space. And, I'd be opening an office without a single patient. She'd be supporting me until my practice built up. I would, most likely, continue substituting until it did, but the plan does have its uncertainties."

"It does," Jake agreed. *I'm impressed that the guy is willing to change his lifestyle to that extent. Ah, unless he has his sights set on Amy's inheritance. Don't be so damned cynical,* he thought, rebuking himself. It was a hard habit to break after years of practicing law.

He thanked them for dinner.

Healthy eating or not, if I ever pick up the tab, I'm ordering pepperoni pizza.

Chapter

16

The next morning, Jake called Demarco about looking through Bradley's junk mail. Also, he wanted a list of the people who knew Wagner left his key in his car. Demarco told him the mail would be in a bag on the conference room table. He would show Jake the Wagner list after he'd finished with the junk mail.

* * * *

Jake found the bag on Demarco's table, as promised. The room was warm, he was pleased to note. Though not by eastern standards where freezing and below freezing were the orders of the day, the Southern California weather was chilly. Jake wore the old blue coat he'd found on the beach. It advertised a surf shop in La Jolla. Jake figured a pumped up surfer left it after running a barrel, surfing under a high, curling wave. He expected somebody to tap him on the shoulder one day, demanding its return and hoped it was a little guy.

Soft jazz music played in the background. The room still had a musty smell to it, like it needed airing out for a week. Nothing mattered however, once Jake poured the mail on the table and began sorting through it. Mostly it was throw away stuff, supermarket circulars, restaurant offers, dozens of letters and flyers from people with real estate. *A holdover from when he sniffed out deals for Nate,* Jake thought.

Hearing aid deals, likewise for dental and eye exams. Banks offering credit cards with low interest, cell phones, outfits with great deals on car repairs; all about the same. He came to a brochure like the one in Nate's in-basket, a brochure about Art for the New Ages! It had been taken out of the envelope but the envelope was under it.

He glanced through it, something he hadn't really done with Nate's. It featured carved African objects, including real and fantasy creations, some large, three feet high, one even larger, many smaller. Photos of men and women working in makeshift studios. Jake assumed the photos were of artists whose works were shown in the brochure. The brochure also featured metal castings, smaller than the sculptures and an equal number of paintings, different sizes, mostly primitives but pleasing to look at.

"Very impressive," Jake said.

The last page of the brochure gave a list of galleries which had expressed strong interest in hosting exhibitions when the portfolio had been filled which was projected to occur within the next twelve months. An address, Las Vegas, with a phone number and email were given for parties interested in learning more about the art program; also a web site.

It was a non-profit organization and donations were solicited.

Nothing about investing, Jake noted. *Must mean they're operating without a permit to solicit investors. Or maybe if anyone expresses an interest, they'll produce a permit. Or, maybe if someone wants to put money in, they'll consider taking it. Like they did Nate's $350,000.*

He checked the date on the mailing envelope. *Middle of October. A couple of weeks before he died. Coincidence? Probably, but …*

Had Nate asked Bradley to run a check on it? No way I'll ever know, he thought.

There was nothing else of interest in the pile so he put it back in the bag, holding out the brochure.

Next, he went in search of Demarco and found him in a cubical in a room full of cubicles. Most were empty. Phones rang around the room, some were answered, some not. The room shared the same music he'd had in the conference room but lacked the musty smell.

Demarco looked up when Jake approached. "Did you find your needle in a haystack?"

Jake smiled. "I don't know." He told him about Bradley's Art for the Ages brochure; the fact that Nate had invested $350K in one of the syndicates.

"So, maybe McGuire told him it was a good deal and he was looking into it. He was getting a $50,000 check. He might have been looking for a place to put it. Not every coincidence is linked to a crime, Jake. However, I give you credit of finding something to sniff. I've learned not to get excited every time a coincidence pops up. I sleep better."

"I was thinking Nate asked him to check it out. You know, maybe he was wondering when he was going to get a return on his money."

"If you're thinking Bradley was killed because he was sticking his nose into some big time scam, think again. If that were the case, big time scammers wouldn't send a witch out to take care of a problem. They'd drive up and put a couple of slugs in the guy and be on the next plane out."

"I hadn't thought of it like that, but you must be right."

"That's why I get a lousy pension after living hand to mouth on slave wages for twenty years."

"Do you have Bradley's phone records?"

"Yes, we do and before you ask, as I'm sure you will, we did call that Art outfit, officially. Bradley had called them three times. They didn't recall if Bradley called or not but they did have him in their computers as having requested a brochure. And, that they sent him one. What does that get you?"

"Not much. Okay. On to the next subject. How about that list of friends who knew Wagner left his keys in his car? And, do you mind if I call them?"

Demarco looked at him, slightly frowning, and said, "If you mean what I think you mean, I don't want to know about it and if the stuff hits the fan, I don't know you."

Jake knew exactly what he meant. Jake had indeed planned on hinting that he was an investigator with the police department to get the people on the list to open up.

"I don't know what you're talking about."

"Good. Keep it that way." He reached into his drawer and drew out a sheet of paper. On it were the names, phone numbers and addresses of the people Wagner had identified as knowing he left the keys in his car. Wagner's name, phone number and address were also on the list.

"I'll save you some time, Jake. The department sent out three people to interview everybody on the list. We do our jobs around here and we do them well. Just to give you the bottom line, we were convinced that none of them had the motive or opportunity to take Wagner's car—he's called Wags, by the way—out for a joyride. You can waste your time or not, but you won't find out any more than we did."

"I won't. What about Wagner? What'd he have to say?"

"Wagner's your typical computer nerd, skinny, cuts his hair only when necessary. He works on-call for a storefront computer business, repairing computers and making house calls for the elderly whose computers have picked up a virus. That sort of thing. His living room looks like something out of a sci-fi movie, computers and monitors spread out all over. Get the picture?

"Yep."

"He's not like anybody who'd take his old car out and run anybody down."

"I agree. So, what's the story about leaving the keys in the car?"

"First of all, it's an old car. Secondly, the people we talked to say that Wags is not a conversationalist. You know the type, stuck for an answer if you ask how he's doing."

"I've met a few."

"He uses the old car as his conversational stick. It's old. It rattles. It's a junker. The seats have no cushion left. Floorboards are practically rusted through. If somebody steals it, he collects insurance. So, he leaves the keys in it hoping somebody will do just that. Get the picture."

"Yeah."

"Hell, he makes okay money, not rich, but okay. He could afford a decent car."

"I suppose he has a new one now."

"I suppose. I haven't checked." He looked at Jake and asked, "So, do you still want the list?"

"I think I'll only need Wagner's vitals, phone number and address in case I come up with a question. I still think somebody he told about his keys or somebody who knew about the keys, took it out and ran down the McGuires. I might come up with a question."

Demarco shrugged, reached into his in-box and handed Jake a list containing Wagner's information and like information of all the witnesses Wagner remembered telling about his car.

"Wagner's on there with the rest. Knock yourself out," he said. "We also canvassed the neighborhood for two blocks in each direction where we found Wagner's car. The reports are in the file if you want to have a look."

"If you didn't find anything, I doubt I will."

"We didn't find anything we thought significant. Nobody running away. Nobody looking suspicious. No kids who looked like they didn't belong there."

Jake thanked him and was on his way.

* * * *

Jake drove to the McGuires, booted up the computer Amy had left and typed in the web site address for the Art for the Ages syndicate. It was impressive, with all sorts of dignitaries endorsing it, art galleries all over the world welcoming exhibitions. The site was a virtual viewing gallery for many African art pieces, sometimes with photos of the artists, sometimes with a reference to their deaths. It talked about the efforts of the managers to raise money to acquire art for the world to view before it was destroyed by civil unrest.

Jake called the number and said he was interested in investing. "How do I go about that? I want to put in, say, a hundred thousand dollars."

The lady who'd answered the phone said, "I thank you for your interest sir. It is most commendable. We welcome interested parties, in particular donors. However, we do not solicit investors. All of our supporters come to us by of referrals. We are non-profit. How did you find out about our program?"

"A friend, Nate McGuire told me. In fact, he suggested that I give you a call." If they wanted a referral, they had a referral. How could they check?

"Mr. McGuire. Let me check my computer." Jake's hopes sank. Seconds later, she said, "Mr. McGuire has passed away,

I'm sorry to see. He was one of our supporters. I'm afraid you'll have to have someone else to recommend you. I'm sorry."

"Can't you bend the rules a bit? Nate recommended you highly and I have money I want to invest. I believe in your program. I think you're doing a wonderful thing, preserving art so that future generations will be able to see the treasured works of some very great artists."

"Thank you, sir. I do so enjoy hearing from people like you. It makes me feel like I'm doing something meaningful. And, I do wish I could be more accommodating, I really do, but we are strictly regulated by our Board. No exceptions, I'm told."

That was the end of that phone call.

So, they don't solicit investors and might not need a permit to sell investments. I imagine if a regulatory outfit tore into it, they'd find enough to shut them down, but that's not what I care about. I just want to find out what the heck they're doing. And, it doesn't look like I am going to.

He brewed himself a cup of coffee and sat down to drink it. He thought of a beer, but the urge wasn't strong. The second the thought popped into his thoughts, he recited his mantra and whether that helped or not, he was able to push away the urge. He looked into the refrigerator, found bread and cheese and made himself a sandwich.

As he enjoyed the sandwich and a second cup of the McGuire's coffee, he decided to interview Wagner in person. He'd always found that face to face conversations were more revealing than telephone exchanges.

He called the man's cell phone number.

"Hello. Wags here."

Jake said, "My name is Jake Carson, Mr. Wagner. I know you've talked to police office Demarco about the unfortunate hit-and-run involving your car, but I wanted to ask a few additional questions. I'm doing some compliance follow up. Could I come over? Say now?"

"I told you guys everything I know already."

"I understand, but I have to sign off as having heard it myself. It's just part of the red tape I have to put up with."

"Well, I have an appointment in La Jolla in an hour. A computer won't boot up. Maybe I can spare a few minutes. How long will it take for you to get here?"

Jake said he'd be there within twenty minutes. Wagner lived in an apartment complex in Pacific Beach.

* * * *

Jake rang the doorbell of the second floor apartment. A thin man with plastic-rimmed glasses showing unruly hair and a touch of acne opened the door, shy and looking every bit the nerd Demarco described. He wore clothes with mismatched colors that looked as if he'd slept in them.

Jake identified himself.

"Come in," the man said.

Jake walked inside, a note pad in his hand.

Wagner pointed to an old chair that Jake was almost afraid to sit in it looked so dirty. As if sensing that, Wagner hurried over and brushed the seat. Hair floated out and settled to the floor with visible traces of other hair.

"I bet you like pets?" Jake asked, sitting down in the chair, reluctantly. Hoping he would not get devoured by fleas.

"Dog and cat. I put them in a pen in back after you called."

"I won't take much of your time," Jake said, questioning his judgment in coming there. He asked for a repeat of the "keys in the car" story.

Wagner obliged him.

"Everybody says it's all I talk about. My old car. I take my dog and cat for rides in it. Well, I did do that. The insurance company paid me blue book for it rather than pay to get it repaired. I have a new car now. Well, it's different, not new."

"I see."

"Oh, do you have a card. The other officers had cards. I keep cards."

Whoops. Jake's thoughts raced about searching for a way to answer the man. He tried the easy way. He pulled out his wallet as if to retrieve a card. "Blast it," he said. "I told the girl to give me some cards. She must have forgotten. I'll send you one if you want me to, when I get back."

"I guess you have Id." He shoved his hands into his pockets and looked at Jake.

Jake was ready for that. He quickly flashed his wallet open to his bar card.

"California?" Wagner said. That was the most prominent thing on the card. Jake hoped he wouldn't see anything about being a member of the bar. Even that wasn't true anymore. "Are you a … plain clothes detective? Like the ones on television?" A suspicious look showed on his face. "Maybe I could call—"

Jake laughed to interrupt Wagner he could ask who to call. "You know what they call me?"

"No, sir."

"They call me the Christian Detective."

"Why do they call you that?"

"I don't put up with any nonsense. I don't drink. I don't smoke and on Sundays I take my family to church."

"Man. You are a Christian. My nick name is Wags. I don't know why though."

"I don't want to keep you so let me get back to this open file, the McGuire hit-and-run case. You gave officer Demarco a list of everyone you'd told your funny story to. Don't you tell your co-workers?"

He'd forgotten to add those names.

"How about people at the supermarket? Liquor store, places you buy stuff from regularly. Your dentist, for example." He almost added drycleaners, but decided that would be a waste of time, after looking at the guy's rumpled clothes.

"Yeah. Well sometimes."

"Those people aren't on the list."

"No. I don't think they know my name. Not really. I pay in cash. My first car was repossessed. I'm doing better now."

"How about rethinking your list? You need to add people who *do* know your name."

"I can do that if you think it's important."

"I do."

The man's phone rang. It was his appointment. He had to go. The lady was upset and needed her computer looked at right away.

He walked Jake to the door, locked it and ran on ahead to his car. It looked like a junker too. Jake wondered if he left his keys in it like he did the last. *I doubt it.*

* * * *

At Sunrise House, Bessie wanted him to replace a light bulb. He got the ladder out and put in a new one.

She asked if he'd petitioned the court to be reinstated. He told her he was seriously thinking about it. One thing holding him up was getting a doctor's certificate but he thought he had someone he could ask. That pleased her.

Amy called to say that Phillip had come by her condo that morning with a request for a million dollars.

"That's a lot of money."

"I'll say. And, I did say. He wants to buy one of those storefront cooking club businesses, in Hillcrest. He brought me the lady's financial statements including her income statements for the past three years. He's using a ten times earnings rule. According to that, the store is worth a million five but the lady's husband is pressuring her to sell out and retire so they can spend more time together."

"What'd you tell him?"

"I told him I'd think about it. I don't know much about business. Warren says the numbers look good. He thinks I should trade him the million for the house. Of course, the house is worth a lot more, but he—Warren—says Phillip is so desperate for the money, he'd probably agree. What do you think?"

Talk about being put on the spot, Jake's thoughts went into overdrive. It had been a long time since he'd looked at anything having to do with business. He tried to sound lawyer-like. "Well, numbers aren't always what they seem." He dredged up knowledge he'd almost forgotten. "Businessmen have a tendency to put happy faces on things. They resolve all differences in their favor. I'd recommend an audit of the woman's records. Certainly I'd want to see three years tax returns."

"Phillip says she has a backup offer. A doctor who wants to buy the business for his wife but she'll hold it open for Phillip because she feels he has a passion for cooking and will make the business flourish. She's not so sure about the doctor's wife who may be bored and looking for a diversion."

"Yeah. Sounds pat. Are we still playing tonight?"

They were.

"Well bring me the package and I'll study it. Tell Phillip you are not going to give him a million dollars until you've done some due diligence. If he loses the deal, there'll be other deals. Besides, you can tell him he may thank you if it turns out she has cooked the books to make the business look better than it is."

He asked for an address. "I'll drive by the place."

* * * *

The store was on a busy street, good traffic and good visibility. The store's sign said, "Save a Marriage, Cook Sexy Tonight."

It didn't do anything for Jake, but he didn't have a marriage to save and if he did and it depended on cooking anything sexy, he knew he would be lost.

Parking was a problem for the store, a big problem. He finally found a place. When he strolled in, two women were in the store having a look around. They left without buying anything. Jake pretended to shop. He visited the kitchen area to check their scheduled events. One was listed for the coming week. No visiting chef was named though a couple of posters did show named chefs for the future.

On the way out, he stopped at the checkout counter at the front. A middle-aged woman, Sue Tucker, busied herself sorting brochures. Jake introduced himself—Jim Taylor—and engaged her in small talk. She'd moved to CA from Texas; drove out after her husband died. Her children were married and still living in east Texas.

Jake had a similar story. Wife divorced him, took the children and moved to Colorado. He worked in a warehouse. "I make sure the orders get out the door the day after they come in. I work the morning shift."

He said he enjoyed talking to her. "You … free for lunch sometimes?"

She was. He took her cell phone number and promised to call. "Real soon."

It would be sooner than she thought.

He went back to Sunrise House and changed for tennis. He had to leave before dinner, but figured he could always get a bowl of chili at a fast food place if Amy didn't want to have a bite out.

Chapter

Amy had told him they would be on the last court in the complex, bordering on the street and the pitch and putt golf course. He headed in that direction and saw her walking ahead. She looked great in her white tennis togs, long jogging pants and jacket which she'd remove after the warm-up. It was still chilly, and even more so near the beach.

He caught up with her at their court. She greeted him with a hug. Her perfume almost stopped him cold again. He had to remind himself to turn her lose. She smiled as if she knew.

She handed him the folder on the store Phillip wanted. "I'll look at it tomorrow," he said. "However, I certainly recommend that Samuels look at it. And if he finds anything out of the ordinary, he should have a quick look at her books. She might keep two sets, probably does, well, maybe, but a good accountant, as I think Samuels is, should be able to spot anything suspicious."

"Phillip won't like that. He called me again, a few minutes ago, wanting to know if I'd approved his loan yet. Of course, he considers it a gift. Part of his inheritance."

"Did you put Warren's offer to him?"

"Not yet. Warren said I should wait until he's desperate. I think he wants to stall until Phillip will agree to anything."

They warmed up. She played relaxed, smiled at her misses and applauded Jake's winners. Jake was ready or thought he was. He tried to recall every mistake she'd made when they'd played before and planned his game around those. Unfortunately, she remembered those mistakes as well and anticipated Jake's plan. However, Jake was on his game. He played patiently, waiting for clear shots before taking chances. And, she matched him shot for shot. There were no service breaks and at 6-6, at the switch, she looked at him and smiled. "What do you say we call it a draw?"

He welcomed it. "I couldn't have played much longer anyway. You wore me out."

"You played well."

Instead of the usual handshake, she gave him a hug and kiss on the cheek.

Holding her close, he whispered, "Fifteen degrees separates me from a taste of Heaven." He enjoyed the warmth of her embrace and the wafting scent of her perfume.

For a second that stopped her. She pulled her face back ever so slightly. Then what he was saying hit her. She turned her face the fifteen degrees so that her lips touched his. He kissed her softly, letting his lips linger on hers, then passionately, holding her eyes as he did, watching the fire he was certain he saw in them.

Finally, she pulled back. "I think in anybody's book that would qualify as a decent congratulation, don't you?"

He laughed. "Yes. I've wanted to since the first time I saw you. There's a magic about you that grabs me and won't let go. But, I'll apologize for doing something I have no right to do." He was thinking of her engagement to Warren. "That's your cue to say, you'll let Warren know how much I enjoyed playing tonight."

It was her turn to laugh, though hers was more a chuckle. "No apologizes needed, Jake. Some things happen. We're human. Let's leave it at that."

She picked up her warm-up jacket and put it on, grabbed her racquet and began a brisk walk toward the gate.

Behind them, a car motor came on. The car raced away, but neither noticed.

At her car, she stopped and said, "Let me know what you decide about Phillip's offer to buy the store. I'll call Samuels in the morning and alert him that you'll contact him."

"I'll look at the statements as soon as I can. I enjoyed the game." He took a step toward her, but stopped.

"I don't know when I'll be able to play again. I'll call." She didn't smile when she said it and turned away before he could respond, a body language rejection, he figured.

What happened to 'We're human?'

He watched her walk away. She never turned. He felt like his life was draining away with each step she took.

I just kissed her with more passion than I've kissed anyone ... well since Jen. It felt so right. I guess it wasn't. Why did I let myself go? She's practically married.

A beer looked good right then. He didn't even bother with his mantra. He didn't care. He wanted that floating feeling; that don't-care-about-anything feeling he got after four beers.

He drove to the liquor store and bought a six pack. Next, like a robot, he turned his car toward Sunrise House, parking his usual half a block away. His plan was to sit on the curb and drink the entire six cans.

He got out of the car, holding the pack of beer. As he did, he heard a rustling sound, no, it was more. It was the sound of running shoes. He turned, his hand still on the door handle.

Two men were rushing him, one slightly ahead of the other. Both held knives. Nothing showed on their faces, but their intent was obvious. They meant to kill him.

The faster of the two raised his knife when he was a step away. The other man circled to the left to cut off Jake's escape. As the first man's knife began its downward plunge, Jake's mind was racing. In a blur, he yanked the door handle and pulled the door open. The man's wrist cracked down on the top of the door. "Ahhhh!" he cried out and staggered back holding his wrist. The knife dropped at Jake's feet, but he had no time to pick it up even if it would have helped. He'd never faced a knife in a fight.

Jake rolled away from the slash of the second man's knife. As he did, the six pack broke and Jake was left holding a single can. When the man drew back for a second try, Jake shook the can and pulled the tap, losing a stream of cold beer in the man's face. It slowed him long enough to wipe his eyes. "Jer," he yelled. "Damn it! Get in here!"

It did no good. "Jer," as the faster man had been called, was staggering backward, grimacing and holding his wrist.

"Broke it, m' wrist," he grunted. He turned to go back the way they'd come.

Using the time created by that exchange, Jake grabbed a second can and popped its lid and sprayed another flood of beer into the man's face and eyes. While he pawed it away, Jake picked up a third can and threw it as hard as he could at the man's head. It hit with a loud "clunk."

The man cursed and rubbed his forehead. His hand came away red. Jake hit him with the fourth can from his six pack. Square in the face. He cursed again and turned to run.

Jake caught him in two strides and kicked out with his left foot to trip the guy, who hit the street with a loud "thump" that left him dazed. Jake began pounding him with both fists as he tried to get to his feet.

"Jer! Need help back here!"

Jer stopped and turned. Seeing what was happening, he reached behind him with his left hand and pulled out an automatic. Jake saw the gun in the man's hand. He thought he had no chance but the man was trying to shoot with his left hand. Not only that, he had to aim high to avoid hitting his partner.

As Jake leaped left to roll behind a car, the bullet passed well over his head. The sound the shot made had the impact of a bomb blast on the quiet night. The second shot was even wider of the mark but it gave the man on the pavement time to get to his feet and run.

When the running sounds seemed far enough away, Jake rolled to his feet and followed. He rounded the corner as a dark car squealed away, too far away to tell the make much less get a license plate number.

Lights came on along the street. San Diego's finest would be there soon, Jake knew. He trotted toward the half-way house, but paused long enough to pick up the cans of beer and the carton. It'd be too easy for the police to get his fingerprints. That might have been okay but for the fact that he was trying to prove he no longer drank. Being caught with a six pack would knock that plan in the head.

He eased the cans and carton into the garbage can on the front porch and was in bed before the pulsating red lights of a police car sped down the street in front of the house. Since the lights of the half-way house were off, no one knocked. There were plenty of lights on in the other houses to keep them busy for a while.

Sleep didn't come easily that night as Jake's thoughts kept churning over the attack. He finally decided that the two men looked, in build and size, like the two who had attacked Sister Brigit. *They didn't wear masks as had Sister Brigit's attackers, but they hadn't expected me to be around to identify them. Not that I could have. It was too dark and everything was happening too fast.*

The next morning when the police got around to interviewing residents of the halfway house, no one recalled hearing anything, including Jake.

At breakfast, Jake pondered, as he had most of the night, what had happened. They were clearly trying to kill him. Only by luck had he escaped. He laughed to himself. Instead of the beer destroying the progress he'd made, it saved him.

Who tried to kill me? He asked himself. *And, why?* He had no answer.

He took the time to give a prayer of thanks. It was a first for him.

Later he visited Sister Brigit. She had been moved out of intensive care and was pushing to be released.

"They said I could go home this afternoon," she told Jake.

They visited for an hour. Jake didn't mention that he'd been attacked. What good would it do? She asked how the medicine was doing? He told her it was more help than he could have imagined. If fact, could he get a few more samples.

"If I ever get out of here," she said.

"Will you need a ride home?"

"Thank you. No, Father Posey is picking me up. I think he feels guilty for giving me a rough time about letting the New Age Christians use the church for a service."

He wrote his phone number on a piece of paper and gave it to her. "If you need anything let me know. I owe you, Sister."

"Your recovery is my reward, Jake Carson. Seeing you free of alcohol dependence had given my life new meaning. I'm in your debt."

She'd let him know when she got more samples of the medicine.

His indiscretion of the prior night caught up with him. Amy hadn't called, not that he expected her to. Maybe it was a good sign. She could have called and told him to bring the key by her office.

It was while he was mulling all that over he remembered a car starting and driving away while he was holding Amy. Was that related to what happened later. *Had somebody been following me?*

Who had a grudge against me? A big grudge. Phillip? Sure, but I only knew about his plan to buy a cooking club that day. And, would he kill me at this stage? Well, a million dollars was on the table but I haven't even decided what I'll say.

Bradley? He had an interest in the Art for the Ages syndicate. Probably at Nate's request, but I had only made the one call about it. And, I hadn't even given my name. $350,000 was on that table. Would somebody kill over that? Hmm. Somebody had killed Bradley.

What was left? Brother Rasmussen? I don't think anybody knows for certain I was the one who trespassed. Maybe they guessed. If so, why didn't the LA firm file suit like they threatened?

What about Wagner? I had asked him questions about the hit-and-run. I can't see anything threatening in what I asked. Nothing in what he'd told me should scare anybody into trying to kill me. Besides as far as he was concerned, I'm part of the police department. He wouldn't send anybody to attack me.

Larson? He'd know thugs. Was my putdown enough to push him over the edge? He'd probably want to give me a good beating. But murder? I doubt it.

He had no answers.

Maybe the guy whose jacket I found on the beach sicced them on me. He laughed.

He finally gave up stewing and got on with his next job. Amy hadn't called so he assumed she still wanted feedback on Phillip's request for a million dollars.

Since he would need for the accountant to look over the financial information Amy had given to him, he made an appointment with Samuels and drove to his office. Amy had alerted Samuels that Jake might be doing that.

* * * *

They talked in Samuels' conference room, a big change from Demarco's. Plush seats, carpeted floor, plants in the corners, accents here and there on small french-looking tables, all told, a pleasing ambience with a view and no musty smell.

Jake watched as the man, heavy-set with dark hair and bushy eyebrows sat hunched over the table and read the financial data through thick glasses. He finished and looked at Jake. "As far as I can tell from this, it looks like a fair deal. What I'll need are their tax returns to make a comparison."

Jake suggested that he call the owner and request the returns. "She wants to make a sale. Tell her you're reviewing her financial data on Phillips' behalf and that you need the returns."

Jake waited while he made the call. He expected her to refuse, but she didn't. She'd have the returns messengered over within the hour.

"Doesn't sound like she has anything to hide," Samuels said. "Half the time when I ask for returns, I get all sorts of excuses."

Jake said he'd call back after lunch. When he was back in his car, he called Sue Tucker at the "Save a Marriage" cooking club store. His theory had been and still was, nothing ventured, nothing gained. He'd rather get rejected trying to win instead of losing sitting on the sidelines.

"Sue," he said after an introduction. "Remember me?"

She did and seemed delighted to hear from him.

"My boss gave me the day off. Work's slack. He didn't want to pay me. Can you take off for a bite?"

She could. Give her thirty minutes.

En route, he called Walter. "Heard any more from that law firm in La wanting to put me in chains for asking a pertinent question?"

"No. Have you been asking again?"

"No. I stood corrected at the first threat."

"Good. Glad you called. I was going to call you. I may have a little job for you. Drafting a non-competition clause for a contract I'm negotiating. You were good at that sort of thing."

"I'd be glad to."

"I'll give you a call when it's ready."

Jake thanked him. That would be the first non-dog work he'd been given, except for the McGuire estate but he'd asked for that.

He also called Demarco. "I heard there was some kind of fracas last night on the street where I live."

"I heard. My first thought was that you'd finally stuck you nose too far into somebody's business. I guess not. Or, have you?"

"I guess that falls into the category of what you don't know, won't hurt you."

"Are you okay? I heard that shots were fired? Knives were found at the scene. You must have really made somebody mad."

"I'm okay. I can't figure out why anybody would attack me. I've been trying to stay out of everybody's way."

"For some reason, I find that hard to believe. I envy that kind of reckless disregard for one's safety."

"Would you mind asking around about Larson? He's the only one who clearly might have an axe to grind. I kind of rubbed his nose in it the only time we met."

He promised.

* * * *

Sue was on the curb waiting when Jake drove up. She got into his car.

"What tickles your fancy, Sue?" Jake asked.

She directed him to a small café around the block.

"I have to be back. She only lets me close the store for thirty minutes. You know, give or take."

Jake had a grilled cheese sandwich. She had the soup and salad special. Both had coffee to drink. Jake was beginning to consider himself a connoisseur of coffee.

"How's your day?" he asked after they'd ordered.

"It's been good. Slow in the store, but my daughter called me early. They're going to assume the lease of a Cajun place in Sulphur, Louisiana. You know what they're going to name it?"

Jake shook his head.

"The *Laissez les Bons Temps Rouler* Cajun Joint. Ain't that a hoot?" She explained what that meant; Let the good times roll.

"Be danged. I like that Cajun cookin'. I love a good crawfish boil."

"Me too. I miss 'em. She wants me to come back and help out. I used to cook some. I might do it. I want to be close to my grandchildren."

"But, you have a job." Jake couldn't have asked for a better opening.

"Not for long. She's selling out. Some young guy wants to buy it. She told him she has another offer. Push him a little." She laughed.

"Yeah. I know that game. Why's she selling? Business bad?"

"She says it's good! She runs a lot of specials in the back, the cooking part. We don't sell much at the front. I think her prices are too high. People can buy the same things at Wal-Mart for half. Maybe not the same brand, but it works the same as far as I'm concerned."

"I practically live at Wal-Mart."

"Me too."

Their food arrived.

"Smells good," Jake said and took a big bite.

She agreed and followed suit.

A few bites later, he asked, "How does she work her specials? I reckon she brings in … what do they call themselves … celebrity chefs? My wife like watching them cookin' shows."

"Since I've been there, she sends out flyers and puts ads in the throw away papers about her specials. If they buy one, they get two free."

"What does she charge for one special?"

"Right now, it's twenty five dollars a head."

"I don't see how she can make much money doing that? She have a lot of people coming in?"

"Some. I wouldn't say a lot. Lots of times the place is almost filled. Sometimes about half. I don't think the celebrity chefs are anymore celebrity than I am, frankly. The folders say they're all from France or someplace exotic. I've heard her talkin' to them. I think they're from around here. They try to talk funny when they're cooking. I try not to laugh."

"That is funny. How's the food they cook?"

"Come to that, she cooks most of it. The so-called celebrity stands up there and goes through the motions, but the stuff in the oven and on the stove, she's already cooked. It's okay, I guess. Lots of spices. Too many for my taste. I like spices, but if you put in too many, the food gets to tastin' funny. You know what I mean?"

"I don't know beans about food, Sue. I used to eat what my wife put on the table. If it had spices, it had spices. She used lots of garlic, I think. My breath would stink for two days."

"Lots of people love garlic. I think a little goes a long way."

"Me too. What's she selling the place for?"

Her eyebrows raised. "Including the merchandise, a million dollars."

"Wow. That would eat up my petty cash." Jake laughed. "You think it's worth it?"

She leaned over and said in a whisper, "I wouldn't give her a dime for it. Hardly anybody ever comes in. No parking 'round there. Except for the specials, she never advertises. And, for sure she doesn't make anything on the specials. Not at her prices and the giveaways."

So, she's cooking the books and Phillip is buying into a losing proposition. He's not going to want to hear that.

Jake took her back to the store and wished her well in Sulphur.

"It'll be awhile. Call me again. I love talking to you."

He promised.

His next stop was at the accountant's.

Chapter

18

Jake told him what he'd discovered.

"I'd have to audit their books to get a better handle on it, but the tax returns look good. I got them."

"Could be phony."

"No doubt. And, if what you're saying is true, my guess is that she keeps two sets of books as well. So, there may be no way to actually pin her down. What're you going to do?"

"I'll tell Amy. It sounds like a pure scam. Phony from the git go. Phillip will think she's conning him. And, if she says the woman's a crook, he'll run tell her and she'll get a lawyer and file a suit. I don't know what I'll do."

In fact, he wasn't even sure how to approach Amy, let alone give her any suggestions about how to proceed. He had to admit that a cold beer would taste great about that time. Almost involuntarily, he stopped along the curb of a liquor store and looked at the neon lights advertising various beers.

To heck with all this, I think I'm going to buy two six packs and drive to the beach. I'll sit there and drink until I'm in a stupor. Who needs this kind of pressure? I've offended everybody I've talked to lately. Well, maybe not Bessie or Sister Brigit, but everybody else. And, somebody's trying to kill me. What do I need this for?

He opened the car door to get out but hesitated for the traffic. His phone rang. *Blast it!* He punched the button. It was Demarco.

"Larson's been bragging about how he bluffed you down at Mr. A's. How he was about to wipe the floor with you but you turned tail and ran."

"He's full of it. Nothing about last night, I guess."

"Nothing our informant has heard."

Jake thanked him. Larson didn't seem like he was responsible for the attack. *I need to rethink what's been happening. Was it somebody at Sunrise House? Couldn't be.*

He closed the car door. His urge to drink himself out of his responsibilities had passed. For drill, he recited his mantra, but wasn't sure he even needed it.

I think it has something to do with Rasmussen, but what? Sister Brigit was attacked by two goons. Then me. The only thing we have been doing in common is attending Brother Rasmussen's services.

That made more sense than anything else he'd come up with. But, it was far from clear. He'd asked some pointed questions of Rasmussen and Stern, but what had Sister Brigit done? What could she possibly have to do with anything that would upset the Rasmussen mission? It didn't make sense.

He sighed in resignation and drove to Amy's office.

Might as well face her. It ain't gonna be easy, he thought, trying to make light of his dilemma.

* * * *

When he had stopped in front of the building where her suite was located, he hesitated. "I'll call instead. That'll give her a way to get rid of me without the embarrassment of having to face me."

He got her message center. It was a relief. He told her what he'd discovered and asked what, if anything, she wanted him to do next.

While he waited for her to return his call, if she was going to, he drove to Walter's offices. He needed something done. He figured Demarco's willingness to help was growing thin.

"Walter," he asked after his secretary announced him. "How're you doing? I thought I'd take a look at that job you mentioned."

"That's prompt. I appreciate it. Here." He slid a folder with his notes and the pertinent information across his desk to Jake. Jake opened it and had a quick look. It looked like no more than a thirty minute job. He'd done so many non-competition clauses, he felt he could do them in his sleep.

"Is an office available? One with a computer?"

Walter directed him to an empty office. Jake stood to leave. "By the way, Walter. Could you do something for me?"

Walter gave him his "ask it" look.

"We used to have a service that would check the criminal backgrounds of witnesses and sometimes clients we thought might be lying to us. Do you still have it?"

"Sure. You have a problem?"

"Not me. But, a woman has been bothering a Catholic nun I've been visiting with since I've been on the wagon. Not bothering so much as hinting. I just get the feeling she's up to something and I wanted to run a check on her."

"Sure." He gave Jake the code to login.

That was the first thing he did after he'd booted up the computer in the office Walter told him to use. He typed the name of the woman selling the store in the slot provided and hit the continue button. While he waited for a return, he began drafting the clause Walter had requested. He had the first draft done when the computer dinged that the information was ready.

The report showed the woman's present home and business addresses and phone numbers. Also that she was married to a bookkeeper, also with an office and gave his name. His office did a little bit of everything for small businesses, including financial statements, tax returns and business plans. Neither had criminal records but she had been charged with fraud in Tucson five years before. The charge was dropped when the complainant withdrew the charge.

Paid off, Jake thought. He read further. The fraud stemmed from falsifying the books and records of a business she partly owned.

Most likely her husband did the falsifying.

Since that was public information, he didn't think the woman could sue Amy if Phillip told her. The knowledge brought him instant relief. He printed out a copy and faxed copies to Amy and Samuels. On Samuels' copy, he asked him to check something out.

Afterwards, he revised his draft a couple of times and left it with Walter's secretary. His door was closed.

"Tell Walter I appreciate the business. Thank him, will you?"

She would.

Now, I wait.

And, while he waited, he drove to the Catholic Church to check on Sister Brigit.

* * * *

Not so surprisingly, she was up and around, though moving somewhat slowly. She was in the Church's rose garden, deadheading roses.

"I'm pleased to see that you have almost recovered," Jake said.

She sighed and sat down on a bench. "Well, as you can tell, I have some distance to go. I get tired. But, I am glad I'm not in the hospital."

They digressed about hospital stays in general, each complaining, though Jake's one stay in a hospital was decades before.

"I don't guess you've been to any more of Brother Rasmussen's services?" Jake asked, the main reason for his visit. Rasmussen was the only link they had in common.

"No. I don't feel up to getting out much just now. The last I went to was at the Community Center out from Poway. I wanted to get the latest on the Central African civil war."

"From Metefara?"

"Yes. He said about the same thing he'd said during the service here. The people are suffering terribly."

"So I understand. Did you ever hear from the Archbishop? I think you were trying to contact him."

"I had asked Metefara if he could get a letter to him. I haven't been able to contact the Archbishop by phone. And, I'm so worried. Metefara promised to do what he could."

"That should give you some relief."

She shook her head wearily. "Some. He said he managed to get a phone message to their Mission Manager however. The Mission uses global telephones. He says the Archbishop is doing well and sends his best to me. He appreciates my prayers. I'm not to worry he said. 'The Lord will provide for us.' That's just like the Archbishop. I've known him a long time."

"Metefara was lucky to get through."

"He was! I've tried and tried. Even called our embassy. Their phones are out as well. They only have local service."

"At least you know the Archbishop is safe."

"I sleep better knowing that. Metefara promises to deliver my letters even if he has to do it himself. Oh, by the way, I have another bag of gabapentin samples for you." She hopped up spryly and disappeared into an office a few steps away. Minutes later, she reappeared with a bag which she handed to Jake.

He thanked her, wished her well and promised to check in from time to time.

"Let me know if you hear from the Archbishop," he said as he was leaving.

He sat in his car and tried to make sense out of what she'd told him. Metefara's story seemed legitimate enough. *In fact, the man sounded sincere when I heard him speak. Would their Mission Manager have dropped everything to drive along perilous roads past rebel road blocks to get a message to the Archbishop? I wouldn't have. It could be that Metefara, seeing how upset the Sister was, deliberately told her a white lie. Currying the favor of the Catholic Church certainly wouldn't hurt their mission.*

He had nothing to do but stew. The only question was where to go to do it. At the halfway house, he'd have to visit with Bessie and just then, he didn't feel like visiting with anybody. He was depressed and didn't mind admitting it. A beer would taste good, but he was determined not to give in to the temptation.

Well, I'd rather wallow in self-pity and depression at the McGuire's estate than on my thrift store cot staring at bare walls.

No sooner had he parked and picked up the mail, his phone rang. It was Amy's office manager calling. "Dr. McGuire asks if you could meet her and Mr. Samuels at the family home in La Jolla at six. Phillip will join the meeting. Dr. Meyer will also be present. It's to discuss Phillip's interest in a business."

He told her he would. *No problem since I already am.*

Phillip and his friend were early. So, he had to babysit with them in the family room.

"You queered this deal for me, didn't you?" Phillip said.

"The deal was queered before I got there. All I did, if I did anything, was save you from losing your shirt. Better put, losing your dad's shirt since it would have been his money you would put into the thing."

His friend sat without speaking.

"You'd better shut up when my sister gets here. If you know what's good for you."

That brought Jake out of his chair. Only the ringing of the doorbell stopped him from taking out his frustrations on Phillip.

It was Samuels. Jake welcomed him. Driving up behind Samuels were Amy and Warren in her car.

Jake walked into the family room with Samuels, allowing Amy and Warren to come in alone. Jake wanted to avoid a confrontation with Amy.

"Phillip," she said when she and Warren strolled into the family room. They pulled out chairs as casually as though they'd come to a party and were waiting for the hos d'oeuvres. She held the papers I'd faxed in her hand.

Samuels and Jake followed suit.

Amy looked at Phillip and said, "I am turning down your request for a loan—"

Phillip immediately jumped up to protest, but Amy waved him to sit down.

"I'm turning it down because the seller looks like she is phonying up the numbers. Mr. Carson ... Jake would you tell Phillip what you discovered."

Jake handed Phillip the report he'd had printed, giving the woman's history, the charge of fraud.

"It appears that she might have attempted to do the same thing in Tucson several years ago," Jake said. "I also learned that to get the attendance she shows for her cooking classes, she's been running discounted specials. In addition, her French chefs may be imposters. If that is true, the business is probably not worth nearly a million dollars. In fact, it may not be worth anything." He looked at Samuels and asked, "Did you find out anything?"

"Yes. Their tax returns show some income the first year the business was opened, more the second year and $100,000 the third year. That looks pretty good. I'm assuming the tax returns are valid. Nothing stops people from preparing false returns. Very few people request copies directly from the IRS. However, even with the income she shows, she paid very little taxes. That's because of depreciation on three buildings in Tucson. I ran a check the buildings using our real estate service. They don't exist."

Jake picked up the conversation. "You see Phillip. She had no problem showing income from the business on her tax returns because she knew she wouldn't have to pay taxes anyway. She had nothing to lose. So, you come along and think everything is valid. Whereas in fact, she may be cooking the books."

Phillip said, "I don't believe any of this crap. All of you are dancing to my sister's tune to stop me from buying the business." He pointed at Jake. "And you are propping her up. This is all your doing and you're going to pay before I'm finished. Dad would have loaned me the money."

"Why didn't he?" Amy asked.

"He was going to. He had confidence in me. He knew I was capable. And you will wish you had listened to me!" He wagged his middle finger in Jake's direction.

His friend gave a nodding, "Yeah!"

Jake practically leaped across the room, snatched him out of his chair and walked him to the wall where he grabbed the front of his shirt and shouted in his face, "We're trying to do you a favor and you're acting like a dumb little kid." Jake felt Phillip's friend grab at his arm. Jake twirled around, snatched the front of his shirt and stood him against the wall beside Phillip. His hands pushed them so hard that both stood on their tiptoes. Their faces went white with shock at his sudden outburst.

"I'm going to tell you what you're not going to do. Okay! For starters, you're not going to smash my car windows again. Understand?"

Both men nodded.

"And you're not going to threaten me again. Understand?"

Both nodded again.

"Because if I catch sight of either of you hanging around where I live or around my car, I'm going to track you down and beat the hell out of you. Do I make myself clear?"

They nodded.

"Speak up!"

"Yes sir."

"Okay. Get out of my sight." Jake released his hold and let them sag to the floor. They immediately hurried out of the house.

Warren was the first to speak. "Well, I think you made an impression on the lads."

Lads again. Where does he think we are, merry old England?

Jake said, "I certainly hope so. I can only stand so much bluster." He was thinking how they involuntarily admitted to having broken his windshield.

Samuels said, "I was afraid things would get out of hand. You handled it well." He said to Jake.

"Thanks. Who would have thought those people would put on a scam that risky."

"It's scary," Amy said. "We were that close to being fleeced."

"Yeah. The numbers looked good until we started turning over the rocks," Samuels said.

Jake nodded.

"Well, if you don't need me for anything else, I'll be on my way," Samuels said to Amy.

She didn't.

Almost before the front door had closed behind him, Amy turned to Jake and said, "Sorry you had to endure that outburst from Phillip. I'm sure he'll go home and feel embarrassed."

Jake wasn't so sure. *Most likely he'll go home and begin plotting how he can get rid of me.*

Jake looked at them and said, "I guess this pretty much wraps it up for me. I've done about all I can do in connection with the estate and the … hit-and-run." He reached into his pocket and handed her the key. Inside, he felt regret because he'd come to enjoy the place as a quiet refuge, a place he could drink a cup of coffee and relax. *But, when it's over, it's over.*

Amy took the key. Her face showed a frown. "I thought you were investigating the mission, the New Age Christian mission and that art thing Dad put money into."

"There are a couple of ravels I might pull in my spare time, but I've pretty much reached a dead end on everything. I wish I had been more successful."

"Why not keep the key for now? Use the house to pull the other ravels. How much time would you need? I'd like to see you pull every ravel, as you say, that you can. Nobody else is doing anything."

"Amy, sweetheart, Jake knows what he's doing. If he says he finished, let the poor man go. He's already being threatened by some LA law firm for invading privacy rights. I'd recommend that we wrap it up." Warren put his arm around her shoulders and squeezed, then bent over and kissed her cheek. "We can't bring them back. I wish we could." He shook his head wearily and let his arm drop.

Amy looked at him, almost a stare, then at Jake.

"Are you willing to hang in a bit longer, Jake? I don't want to get you into trouble."

"Trouble is what I've dealt with most of my professional life. That doesn't bother me. I just didn't want to waste your money."

She glanced first at Warren whose face showed nothing then back at Jake. "Why don't we do this? Spend another 20, no, 40 hours pulling your ravels. Okay?"

Warren was shaking his head ever so slightly but said nothing. He gave Jake a plaintive look and shrug as if to say, *I tried.*

"I'd love the opportunity," Jake said and reached out for her hand.

She ignored it and put her arms around him for a big squeeze and kiss on the cheek.

Jake's insides lit up like a Christmas tree. She wasn't mad at him or least wasn't going to make an issue out of it. He did note that she said nothing about playing anymore tennis.

Chapter

19

He parked his car near the half-way house and looked back several times before shutting off the engine. Seeing no one, he switched off and walked inside, careful to keep an eye out for men running at him with knives.

The next morning, he drove to the McGuire's home and called Cynthia. "Quick question," he said.

"Okay."

"Do you recall Nate's cell phone number?"

Easily. She gave it to him.

"Second question. Let me preface it first by saying that two guys with knives tried to kill me the other night. Has Larson said anything about that? I assume he would know guys he could call on for a job like that."

"I'm flabbergasted. Wow! Were you hurt?"

"No. I escaped. Barely."

"Well, to answer your question. He still mentions your name braced with epithets. You bluffed him down. He won't forget that for a while. And you won't ever make his Christmas list, not that he has one, but he hasn't said anything about sending guys out with knives to balance his books. That doesn't mean he didn't. He just didn't tell me."

"You're his sister so I can't expect you to tell me, but I'd appreciate it if you would give me a warning if he does tell you anything like that."

"I don't want him to get into trouble. The cops have a way of knowing what's going on but if I hear anything like that, I'll let you know. Maybe I'd be doing him a favor. If pushed, I'd say he didn't do it and I know him pretty well. I believe he's trying to get his act together, finally. Okay?"

He thanked her.

Next, he turned on the coffee pot and called Demarco. "You said you had Bradley's phone records."

He did.

"I wonder if you'd fax them to me?" He rattled off Nate's home fax number.

"Damn, Jake. You're becoming a nuisance. I have to pull his records from storage and sort through them to find the phone records. Can't you come down here and do it?"

"I could, but you're closer. Street tacos?"

"Only for a Christian detective would I do it. Plus the street tacos … and chips." He laughed.

Half an hour later, Jake heard Nate's fax machine cranking out a fax. It was Bradley's phone records for the last two months of his life. He scanned it for the two he was curious about, Nate's cell number and the number of the Art for the Ages. He circled one in black and one in red. When he'd finished, he flipped open Nate's calendar and placed the phone records beside it.

He found that each time Bradley phoned The art outfit, he had called Nate. So, *he was doing some checking for Nate. He couldn't have gotten much however. They wouldn't tell me anything. Of course, he probably gave Nate's name and Nate was still alive to corroborate it.*

He pondered the implications.

My guess is that Nate was wondering when he'd start getting money. If so, he probably had been calling himself and sicced Bradley on them to see if he could find more. If Nate called them, it'd show up on his phone records.

He opened Nate's file drawer and there it was, a file with the title, "Phone Bills." He pulled out the bill for the month before he'd been killed and scanned down the list of numbers he'd called. There it was, the Las Vegas number of the Arts for the Ages headquarters. He talked ten minutes. *I wonder what they told him. Whatever it was, didn't satisfy him because he called Bradley soon after.*

His second call to them came after Bradley had made his first call. *He was most likely giving Bradley a recommendation. That's why they sent him the brochure.*

Nate also made three calls to Los Angeles. When Jake dialed the number, someone announcing a law firm answered. He excused himself for having dialed a wrong number and hung up.

He called Walter for the name of the LA law firm Nate's partners had used during the wrap up negotiations.

"I don't know it off hand," he said. "Why do you want it?"

"Amy has me checking Nate's contacts during his last days to see if maybe he'd called anybody who might have had an axe to grind. An LA law firm came up on his phone records and I wondered if it might be the same one Nate's partners had used."

Walter did not respond right away, obviously considering what Jake had said and the legal consequences of giving him an answer. Finally, he said, "I'm not sure I should disclose the name to you Jake. By the same token, I'm not sure I can't. If you use it, just to cover me and the firm, I'll ask that you not disclose how you came to have the name or the knowledge that it had represented Nate's partners. I have to have your agreement on that, Jake."

"No problem, Walter. I swear that I will not mention your name or the firm's. If I'm asked the question, I'll say one of Nate's employees told me, a name I will have conveniently forgotten."

Walter gave him the name and number. "Hmm," he said. "I didn't connect it until now, but the guy who threatened the restraining order against you is from the same firm."

"I'd have to say that is an interesting bit of information."

"I thought it might be. Of course, it's a big firm and undoubtedly has many clients, but it is an odd coincidence."

"The New Age Christian mission was incorporated by an LA firm. I don't remember the name, if I ever knew it, but I'll look it up. Maybe there's a link."

"Don't involve the firm. I don't want to lock horns with that bunch. They were tough during the negotiations and they have lots of bodies they can throw into a legal fight."

"I'll keep the firm out of it. And, if they sue me, they won't get a dime."

"With all due respects, Jake, good."

Jake laughed. For once his impoverished state might inure to his benefit.

After hanging up, he called Demarco for the name of the law firm he'd run across when checking the status of the New Age Christian mission. It was the same firm which had represented the partners and the same one which had threatened Jake. He thanked him.

Too many coincidences to ignore, Jake thought. *But, what can I do with it? Stern obviously has some connection with the firm since they incorporated the Mission. It's logical that he would have called to complain about me. It's not too farfetched to conclude that they might be called on by a New York firm to provide local representation for clients based out of state. If so, they'd retain a firm with a good reputation, the LA firm. So, that gets me nowhere.*

He went online to check the firm's roster of attorneys to see if perhaps Stern's name appeared. It did not. He also accessed Martindell Hubbell for Stern's name and found no listing. He tried a general Internet search for Stern and found only reports he'd made concerning the Mission's activities. He accessed the California Bar Association's roster of attorneys to see if his name came up there. It did not.

Dead ends, all.

He sighed. "Frustrating." A few weeks ago, he might have resorted to drink to relieve the frustration, but now just then. Sister Brigit's medicine and the support he'd gotten from reading the Bible seemed to be doing their job. It didn't hurt that he felt worthwhile again, doing something productive. Something he hadn't felt in a long time. And, he wasn't overloaded. He had learned that lesson. Don't let his ego overload his capacity.

What about Rasmussen? He must have complained to Stern after my intrusion but where does that get me? He doesn't live in the RV as he claims. And, for sure the pictures I saw on the wall where he's staying with his wife, presumably, weren't taken at religious events. But, none of that is a crime.

One thing he did know, he had to help Bessie with preparations for Christmas dinner. It was coming up and she'd asked if he'd help. That took priority over everything else.

Christmas morning, Jake got up and made a move toward the coffee pot. As he did, he heard Bessie and the two volunteer ladies who came in to help cook Christmas dinner, talking in earnest in the kitchen. From the looks on their faces, it was a serious discussion.

He sat down with a cup of coffee and waited to see if Bessie would share what it was. Indeed, she walked over with tears in her eyes, pulled out a chair and sat down.

"Jake," she said, touching his hand gently, "I am devastated. I have to tell you. I just can't believe what happened last night. Sister Brigit was killed. Burglars, they tell me. They came into the church. She must have been praying. They hit her over the head and stole everything they could cart off." She bowed her head and sobbed.

"What! I can't believe it!" Jake said. "Why would anybody kill that sweet person?"

Bessie shook her head. Tears ran down her face.

Jake reached out and put his arms around her shoulders. "I'm so sorry Bessie. Sister Brigit was one of the finest women I've ever known. Not a bad bone in her body. I guess it was the same people who attacked her a while back. Stole her fanny pack with her key. It's impossible to accept. The poor woman. She was absolutely dedicated to doing good. It's not fair. People like me are the ones who should be killed not Sister Brigit."

For a second time in his life, he lowered his head and whispered a prayer. He hadn't felt that much anguish since the Judge ordered him disbarred. He'd gone on a two day drunk that day. Not so this time. This time, he only felt despair.

"She would have given them all that she had. There was no need to hurt her," he said. "Have they arrested anybody?"

Bessie shook her head and half whispered. "They don't know who did it."

He drove to the church. Of course, it was sealed with "Crime Scene" ribbons. He asked one of the police officers for information and was told, "We're just beginning our investigation. As soon as we know anything, we'll hold a public conference and make an announcement. If you please sir, we are asking that all people stay away from the church while we're conducting our investigation."

Jake called Demarco from the parking lot. He knew it was not Demarco's department, but he figured he would know something.

"I don't know much more than you, Jake," he said. "I heard the guys talking about it this morning. It happened late last night. The church was supposed to be locked so they're thinking whoever stole her key used it to gain access. Her body was found in a hallway. They figure she heard something and went to investigate. They burglars must have heard or saw her coming and hit over the head. Apparently they took about $15,000 worth of stuff from the church including some stuff from her office. Her computer and a few art objects she'd collected over time."

"The price of a good woman's life. She was worth a lot more. What a tragic waste. She had been so concerned about the trouble in the Central African Republic, the abuse the people were suffering. She knew the Archbishop from when she was in service there."

"Yeah?"

"If they turn up anything, would you call me? I got to know Sister Brigit quite well. She helped me with my drinking problem."

"From what I've seen of you, she did a good job."

"Thanks."

He drove back to Sunrise House to help with the Christmas dinner. There would be no joy in the kitchen that day. Even some of the inmates, once they were told, went into a depressed funk. Sister Brigit would not be coming for dinner. The joy she always brought with her would be sorely missed.

* * * *

Mid-morning, he received calls from Walter and from Amy inviting him to dinner at their homes. Walter's was a courtesy and easily turned down. To his instant relief, Jake figured but thanked him nevertheless. He explained about Sister Brigit's death even though Walter did not know her.

Amy was cooking dinner at the McGuire's home when she called. Phillip and his friend had been invited and had promised to come. He explained what had happened to Sister Brigit and also about the house's duty roster that had him helping with dinner preparations.

She expressed disappointment that Jake could not make it and was as shocked as he was about Brigit's death. While she didn't know the Sister personally, she knew of her and held her in high regard. "Everyone did. Her death puts a pall over everything," she said. After a pause, she came back on the phone and added with tears in her voice, "It has been … everybody's dying. I … it's difficult for me to accept."

He asked, "What time will it be? Your dinner?"

"I'm not much of a cook so I don't know," she said. "Phillip and his friend say they'll help. They want to bring a couple of friends as well. I don't expect we'll sit down to eat until around two."

Since dinner at Sunrise House would begin closer to noon, Jake was certain he'd finish in time to drive over. In any case, he'd be there for dessert and coffee.

"Thank you," she said. "Although Christmas is a time for peace, I have to say that being in the house with Phillip and three of his friends, makes me uneasy, even with Warren around. I don't dare ask the security service to send someone so if you come, it'll be a big help."

"I'll get there as soon as I can."

Jake helped set the tables for the ladies; did the lifting of the turkey from its pan. It was a big turkey. It had to be to feed everyone assigned to the house. The whispered conversation had to do with Sister Brigit's death. He heard bits and pieces. "Sad that it happened this day … Jesus' birthday … Christmas."

When the pots and pans began to pile up, he jumped in and scrubbed them clean. By noon, the kitchen was clean and the food set out for the ten hungry men gathered outside the door. The smells had brought them close to the dining room.

Jake and the two volunteers served with Christmas music playing in the background. A prayer was said by Bessie for Sister Brigit before the first bite was taken.

The inmates ate with gusto. And, three jumped up afterward and offered to help clean up. Jake accepted their offer and left for the McGuire's. And, he was hungry.

* * * *

He walked into the McGuire's home to see Phillip in white chef's attire working in the kitchen. Amy stood nearby evidently between assignments as Phillip had taken charge. Warren was at the bar refilling his glass. He turned when he saw Jake, waved and shouted, "Welcome, Jake. Won't you join me?"

Amy looked and smiled. She reached into the refrigerator and handed Jake a glass filled with something red. "Here. I figured you'd like yours chilled. I won't tell a soul."

From her smile, he knew it was not wine. Indeed, a sip confirmed it. It was grape juice. Well, that was a change from coffee and it would look like he was participating in the Birthday celebration.

"Thanks," he said.

"Enjoy," she said over her shoulder. Phillip had demanded her assistance.

From where Jake stood, it appeared dinner would be turkey with dressing, vegetables, sliced ham and pecan pie for dessert. No one would go hungry. And, it looked ready. As Amy took a dish from the oven, Phillip called Billy to carve the turkey. He had been sitting in the family room with Phillip's other two friends.

Jake strolled over to where Warren stood and extended his hand. Warren smiled and shook Jake's hand like he was a long lost friend, big smile and all.

The guy looks younger every time I see him.

Behind him, from the family room, he caught a few words of a conversation the two friends were having. "… queered his deal … get the bastard …"

Jake sighed and laughed to himself. *I sure made an impact on Phillip and Billy. Scared the heck out of them.*

Ordinarily he might have taken issue, but it was Christmas and it'd be too easy for them to claim he was being paranoid. And, too, Sister Bridget's death still lay over his thoughts like a dark shadow that refused to lift. So, he made small talk with Warren while Phillip, Billy and Amy finished the dinner preparations.

Perhaps sensing how Jake felt, Warren wanted to know about Sister Brigit. "I didn't know her, but Amy says she was well respected and was always there for anybody who needed a helping hand. She will be missed."

Jake agreed.

Dinner was served, buffet style. It was delicious. More than delicious, Jake thought. He tried to give Phillip a compliment, but the boy wasn't interested in anything Jake said. He more or less shrugged as if a compliment was his due.

They ate in the magnificent dining room under the lighted chandelier. All had seconds and Phillip's friends went back for thirds. Two bottles of wine disappeared. Jake stuck with what Amy had given him.

The desert, pie with coffee, didn't last long either.

Phillip managed only one remark. When Jake got up to refill his glass, he said, "Don't overdo."

Jake took it as a joke and replied, "I haven't had a better claret than this in years." In fact, he had never had a claret.

Trying to end the dinner on a high note, Jake again complimented Phillip and Amy for a job well done. Everyone agreed. Amy passed the compliments to Phillip saying, "Phillip is the cook as Warren knows. That's why we eat out so often."

And, when it was over, Phillip and his friends left without incident though Phillip did turn at the door and give Jake a look. Jake wagged a finger at him.

Jake began the cleanup. It was twice in one day for him. Warren helped as did Amy.

Jake told them goodbye.

Apparently they were going to spend the night there.

* * * *

He visited with Bessie some. She was still depressed. Sister Brigit was like a real sister to her.

"I don't often wish ill on anyone, Jake, but I hope the people who did that to Sister Brigit, rot in hell."

Jake agreed.

"How could something like that happen? Don't people have any respect anymore? She was a nun. She wasn't going to hurt anybody. She would have given them everything they took."

"It makes no sense," Jake said.

"The funeral will be day after tomorrow. Will you go? I know you're not Catholic," Bessie said.

"I will be there."

"They will probably ask if anybody wants to say anything. I'd like to, but I always get my words tangled up."

"Sister Brigit will know your thoughts, Bessie. I'll say a few words." He climbed into his cot and tried to sleep. But, his thoughts wandered.

They found her body along a corridor outside her office. She was probably working in her office and heard the burglars, like the investigating officers said.

The earlier attack by two thugs came into his mind. They might have killed her then if I hadn't come along and stopped it. *The two thugs who attacked me with knives certainly intended killing me and, appearance wise, they resembled the two who had attacked her.*

What did we have in common? Rasmussen's mission! She was concerned about the civil strife in the Central African country and the Archbishop. I was concerned about Nate's expected "profit" from his donation to the mission.

Were we a threat? If so, I still am. I'd better be on my guard. I doubt knives will be used next time.

When he awoke, he was convinced that Sister Brigit had been killed because of her questions about the Archbishop.

As he drank his first cup of coffee, he pondered the *why* of his conclusion.

He let his thoughts spread out in all directions and run a "what if" analysis as they picked up steam.

What if Rasmussen's running a scam? What if Rasmussen's pocketing the money? *Okay, what if I'm right. How am I going to prove any of it?*

He cautioned himself. *Are you overreacting because your mind is biased from the scam Phillip almost fell into? But, if Rasmussen didn't have something to hide, why would he threaten a restraining order to shut me up?*

Was Nate part of the scam?

Chapter

20

At the McGuire's home, he combed carefully through all the files searching for anything that might resemble an investment somehow related to the New Age Christian mission. He found nothing.

He made a cup of coffee and sat at the family room table and thought. Two cups later, he had a glimmer of an idea. Nate had made a $350,000 investment in the Art for the Ages, the "invitation only" syndicate. Warren also put some money into it though not as much with the anticipation of a good return. A good return would mean a "profit." Was that what Nate was talking about?

He called Amy at her office. She was with a patient who called with an emergency, but seeing his name on her screen, took his call.

"I hate to bother you, but could you check the date of Nate's investment in the Art for the Ages syndicate?"

She'd have to call back. "Ordinarily I wouldn't be in today, but I have an emergency and another patient who needs to see me before leaving on a trip. I do travel medicine as well."

"I'll make it short. Check when you can. And, while you're looking, check the date Nate made the first donation to Rasmussen's the New Age Christians, the $150,000 donation. I'm looking for a correlation between his donation and his investment. I'm searching for the 'profit' Nate told you about."

She breathed loud enough for him to hear. "Okay."

Obviously not a chore she welcomed.

"Would you rather I do it?" he asked.

She hesitated. "Yes, but it'd take more time to tell you where everything is than it will for me to look things up. I have to dig in a box for the old check records. I'll do it."

Amy called back during her lunch period. "Okay," she said. "It took a while to find it, but here it is. Dad donated the $150,000 to the New Age Christian mission on June 15th, three years ago. His investment in the Art for the Ages syndicate is also dated June 15th, the same year. I have a certificate for that investment. I couldn't find a check he'd written for the art syndicate investment. He might have had a personal account at that time, but I don't recall that he did. I don't know how he paid for it."

Jake gave that news a "Hmm."

She continued, "The other two donations were made by checks on the same dates the following years."

"Trust account checks?"

"Yes."

"No envelope with the syndicate certificate?"

"No. He might have given the certificate to me. I seem to recall that he did. What do you make of it?" she asked.

"I'd say the donation and the investment were linked. Both had the same date. That would explain his 'profit' quip to you. The profit he expected was to come from the investment. The fact that there was apparently no check written for the investment is curious. I think he got the investment in exchange for his donation and the two promised donations. In effect, he donated $450,000 and received a $350,000 investment in exchange."

"What? He got a tax deduction AND an investment?"

"That's what it looks like. Over a three year period, the $450,000 in donations could have saved him around $225,000 in taxes, assuming he was in the fifty percent tax bracket. That was like money in his pocket over a three year period."

"What about the $350,000 investment?"

"Knowing Nate as I did, I expect he somehow knew about the Art for the Ages syndicate and negotiated. He'd donate the $450,000 in exchange for a free investment in the Art of the Ages syndicate. Not a bad deal for him. He saves, say, $225,000 from the donations and gets a free $350,000 investment with yield potential of twenty percent."

"That sounds just like Dad."

"His 'profit' quip makes sense now. From his $450,000 donations of hard cash, he'd not only save $225,000 in taxes but also get a free $350,000 investment that would yield twenty percent."

"That must have been what Dad was talking about."

"The problem is, he's received no return on the investment to date. I think he was wondering when the money would start coming in and asked Bradley to do some snooping around. He ended up dead."

"Well, Warren says it takes a few years to fund each syndicate."

"I'd forgotten. I don't suppose Warren donated to the mission?"

"Not that he's said."

"Nate must have done some negotiating and got his in exchange for his donations to Rasmussen's New Age Christian mission."

"Do you think Dad was killed because of that?"

"I don't know. However, knowing Nate as I did, I expect he would have pushed and probed until he got a specific date as to when *his* money would start coming in. If the art thing is on the up and up—Warren vouches for them—Nate might have been considered a pest, but no legitimate organization puts a contract out on a pest. However, if the art investments are a sham—Warren says millions are involved—Nate's pushing and probing might have made someone nervous enough to stop him."

"Warren vouches for the Art syndicates. He even asked if I wanted to put money in. I didn't. I'm still building a practice. I need all my spare cash as a cushion."

"In that case, it could be that the hit-and-run was just, as the police suspect, a joyrider."

She asked, "What do you plan to do now?"

"That is the big question. I'm not comfortable trying to link your dad's death to the attack on me and Sister Brigit's death. They just don't fit together well. A little, but the lawyer in me isn't satisfied. I wouldn't want to go to court with what I have so far. And, Bradley's another lose end I can't connect."

"A real puzzle," she said.

Suddenly remembering, he said, "Add to the puzzle how somebody knew about Wagner's old car with the key inside."

"Well, you're still on my payroll. Keep at it. Let's play tennis. I'll ask Warren when he's available. I'm going home. The rest of this day is mine and Warren's."

Her offer to play was good news to him. *She must have forgiven me for that kiss. Or, maybe she enjoyed it as much as I did. Until I know for sure, I'll recite my Satan mantra when I'm around her.*

* * * *

He visited with Bessie that afternoon then spent some time thinking about what he could say at the Sister's funeral service the next morning. He made notes from his Bible.

* * * *

The cemetery was filled with mourners. The only sounds were from cars on a street a couple of blocks away and the rustling of clothes as people walked toward the tented burial site. Birds sang in the trees and bushes that surrounded the site as if it were an ordinary day. People talked in hushed whispers.

Jake and Bessie stood with those who had gathered close enough to the gravesite to hear the service and to respond when the priest asked for testimonials. Jake wore his working suit with a tie. Bessie was in her black dress.

When the priest spoke and extolled Sister Brigit's virtues, his voice was the only sound in the cemetary. It was as though all creatures stopped to listen.

After the priest, Jake spoke. "I speak for Bessie and all the men at Sunrise House, where Sister Brigit made regular visits to minister to us. The Bible says that the dead will be alive in Jesus Christ. It gives me comfort to know that our dear Sister is with Jesus on this day and is alive. She has no heartaches and no tears. She is with the Savior and will enjoy eternal life. The death of her mortal body was simply the door through which she passed to gain entry into God's heavenly realm. I wish she was here, but knowing that she is happy makes it easier for me to accept her loss. She is with the Lord."

Bessie and others close said, "Amen."

As he stepped back, he saw Rasmussen staring at him. *I hadn't thought about him. He may have recognized my voice. It can't be helped. What's done can't be undone. Walter will be getting another letter or maybe I will.*

Rasmussen stepped forward and gave a prayer about how Sister Brigit was in heaven sitting at the right hand of the Lord, smiling down on us. He ended by saying, "Death is swallowed up in victory. Oh death, where is your victory? Oh death, where is your sting? Death sent a saint to be with our Lord. We know he must have had need of her there. We pray that we will be able to overcome our loss. Amen."

More "amens" from those closest.

Bessie stepped forward and said, "I know this is not the place to say angry things or wish vengeance on anybody, but I can't help it. I'm a sinner, unlike Sister Brigit, and I ask that the Lord strike dead all those who had a part in Sister Brigit's death. May they burn in hell for the rest of their days."

The priest reached out and touched her shoulder tenderly. He said something so softly Jake couldn't pick it up.

* * * *

After letting Bessie off at the half-way house, Jake went to the McGuire's to do some researching. He had an idea he wanted to pursue. As it often did when he practiced law, without being under the influence, his subconscious had spoken to him.

Using the Internet, he ran a name check on Rasmussen. Not surprisingly, he found out mostly what he already knew. The man was born and raised in Iowa. His parents were working people and had a small farm. He graduated from a small teacher's college and went to sales, eventually selling drugs for a pharmaceutical distributor until he became a preacher. Ordained, the web site reported, after studying in South Africa at the Theological Institute of Johannesburg.

Most of the more recent sites reported on the services he had held as part of the New Age Christian mission. There were dozens of those. Some with quotes from his sermons; a few with questions raised by people in attendance, usually media representatives. He had hoped for reports beyond his mission work. The photos he'd seen on the wall of the hilltop home suggested that Rasmussen was socially active in circles broader than religious ones.

On Stern, there was nothing by way of a bio. A few, as part of a Rasmussen site, quoted him in his capacity as financial manager of Rasmussen's mission. Jake had hoped to find his law school and something about him. He called the State Bar and was told that Stern did not show up as an attorney admitted to the California bar.

Next, Jake did a name search on Eli Reid, the owner of the house where Rasmussen was staying. Supposedly Rasmussen's friend. He did a little better than he'd done with Stern.

Reid was a small time character actor with a few film credits. No movies Jake had ever seen or was likely to ever seen and none that carried any acclaim.

"So, how'd he end up with an estate worth probably a couple of million? He must have gotten some roles the Internet isn't picking up. Maybe he inherited money."

He called the Screen Actors Guild and asked for information about Reid, claiming he was with a small theater group in San Diego looking for a good character actor. The lady who answered was very nice. She said, "Eric Reid is inactive at the moment so he's not taking roles. I would refer you to his agent, but I know his agent has long since retired. Do you want me to refer you to another agency that represents a number of character actors? I'm sure they can find someone for you."

"I was looking for a picture ... to help us. Is it possible you could send one?"

"I don't see how his picture could do you any good since Mr. Reid is not available to help you, but even if he were, we don't send out photos. You could talk to his agent but, as I said, he has been retired for years."

She gave him the agent's name with the admonition that he wasn't likely to get very far with it.

Jake found the agent's phone number and called him. The man sounded ancient, hoarse and coughing every other breath. Jake gave him his "small theater group" story.

"I haven't heard from Eli in years. He never really made it," the man said. "I don't even have an address for him. He and Tammy had an apartment in Hollywood. Nice couple. Not anymore. I don't know where they went."

When asked about a photo, the man said, "I don't have one. I live in a small condo and I threw away all my files when I retired. Sorry I can't be more help. It's time for my medicine."

He hung up before Jake could ask any further questions.

Well, where is Eli Reid? He is letting Eric Rasmussen live in his house, so where is he living? Hmm, Eli Reid and Eric Rasmussen. Same initials. I wonder.

He did an Internet search for the Theological Institute of Johannesburg and found it! A surprise. He went to their website and sent a "contact" request.

At least that checks out. I don't want to get ahead of myself, he thought. *Maybe Rasmussen is legitimate. Maybe Reid is touring with a play group, doing small theater productions.*

He revisited the Reid websites and wrote down the movies in which he'd had a bit part. Then, he turned on the McGuire's television and recalling how to do it, accessed movie rentals and typed in the first name on his list, the latest. It wasn't available. He tried the next. It was available—black and white—but Jake didn't have a card to rent the thing. However, the site did offer "trailers." He clicked on trailers. There were three. The first two were no help. The third however, showed a face he thought he recognized. It didn't have a beard and it was only one for a second or two, but it looked remarkably like a younger ... Brother Rasmussen. The clincher was the guitar he strummed. Of even greater assurance, as far as Jake was concerned, he was playing the role of a minister in a small Mid-western town.

"How about that!"

He had hit pay dirt. He still had to wait for a reply from the Theological Institute of Johannesburg to be certain, but it certainly looked like the Brother was playing a role.

That find called for a celebration. A beer? Indeed, a beer would be just the thing, but he was afraid of even thinking about a beer. He owed that much to Sister Brigit. Instead, he brewed another pot of coffee.

"Wonder what time it is in Johannesburg?"

He checked his email. There was a message. His email to the Institute could not be delivered to the address given. *Email addresses get changed all the time and web sites aren't always upgraded, especially if they're no longer active. It could be the school is closed.*

Where did that leave him? Maybe Rasmussen was an ordained minister or maybe he wasn't. His name was not Rasmussen. That much was clear, but did it make him a crook?

He sighed. "Not a crime to impersonate a preacher. A lie, to be sure. Likewise it's not a crime to lie about one's background. People do it all the time. Some end up in disgrace, but few are prosecuted. It will certainly ruin him; maybe even ruin the mission he preaches about."

He paused for a sip of coffee.

"The guy does a great job. Well, he is an actor. Eli Reid is playing a role and apparently making money; enough to afford a luxury home. Those pictures I saw must have been from movie parties."

He sent Amy an email with the news and asked permission to call South Africa. For good measure, he sent the same news to Demarco.

He had another idea he could try to nail things down.

Chapter

21

He checked the *La Jolla Light* for Rasmussen's next service. It was at a non-denominational church in Pacific Beach the following Saturday afternoon. Refreshments promised.

When Bessie saw him reading the story and asked if he intended going. She wouldn't mind hearing Rasmussen's sermon if Jake didn't mind her coming along.

"I am going, as it turns out and I need someone to help me with a problem. You'd be perfect. Would you do it?" he asked.

"What do I have to do?"

He told her. She was skeptical or cautious or reluctant; maybe all three. Jake couldn't tell for sure from the way she shook her head when he explained.

"You'll be okay. Nothing to it."

With her head still shaking no, she said, "Easy for you to say. I'll do it, but it's not something I want to do. I'm doing it for you, Jake."

"I appreciate that and I thank you. You'll be glad you did," Jake said to reassure her. He walked her through what he wanted her to do. After a couple of times, she appeared to be comfortable with it.

Demarco called later that day to get more on Jake's latest discovery. "You've been busy," he said. "So, you think the Brother is a fraud."

"It looks like it, but I still haven't heard back from the Theological Institute where he claims to have been ordained."

"What if he isn't an ordained preacher? Lots of preachers running around with no credentials ... other than the Bible they thump."

"I know, but why use a false name?"

"You think he is. You saw an old movie and wanted to find Rasmussen. I think you call that jumping to a conclusion, counselor. You used to jump all over us for doing just that."

"He played a guitar in the movie and he played a preacher. There are too many coincidences for me to ignore."

"All kidding aside, I kind of agree with you. But, there's not much we can do about it. No crime has been committed. If you're thinking about the McGuire killings, protecting a false identify is not much of a motive."

Jake agreed. "There may be more to protect than a false identity. Nate gave Rasmussen's mission $450,000. He got back an investment of $350,000 in a syndicate called, Art for the Ages, free. A huge tax write off and a free investment. Suppose Nate was snooping around asking when his "free" investment would begin paying dividends. That could be enough to motivate murder if the syndicate never intended to pay dividends."

"You're saying they'd collect investors' money and stall until they've collected enough to close shop and disappear?"

"Something like that. Usually some people get dividends in the interim."

"Well, Christian Detective, when you get some real evidence of that, let me know and I'll put you with some of my friends who love a good fraud."

"I'm on the trail. I'll let you know."

"I'm just curious, but how do you—if you do—link all that stuff you've been telling me to Sister Brigit's murder? Just asking." Jake imagined him grinning as he said it.

"Yeah. I hear that cynicism. I don't link it. I've been too busy tracking Rasmussen down to even try."

"Let me know when you find out. So far, we have the McGuires as a hit-and-run. Sister Brigit as a homicide committed in the act of burglary."

"And, Bradley, do you have that as a homicide committed by a trick or treat witch."

Demarco laughed. "If you say so."

Amy called. She and Warren wanted to play tennis that night with dinner afterwards. A place in town with great crab cakes if that was okay with Jake.

"That's fine with me. I like crab cakes."

"We'll talk about what you discovered at dinner, if that's okay. I'm running behind right now."

It was okay. He'd meet them at the Beach and Tennis Club at six. Warren would arrange a fourth.

He didn't know how much longer he'd be able to refrain from having beer with dinner, but was resolved to stay alcohol free until he was reinstated as an attorney.

* * * *

Jake's partner was the older guy he'd partnered with the last time they played. Calvin was his name. They lost two sets 6-2, 6-4. Warren was on his game. He and Amy were able to take the net and control the games. Calvin was having an off night and Jake wasn't strong enough to pick up the slack. In the second set, he was able to lob them back enough to get them out of their rhythm but it was too little, too late.

Calvin passed on dinner so it was Jake, Warren and Amy at a small seafood place off Prospect. They had wine but he stuck with coffee.

As soon as the waiter left with their orders, Amy asked, "Now, tell me about Rasmussen. You think he's a fraud? Goodness! You read about such things, but you never expect to know about them personally."

Jake explained what he'd discovered about Eli Reid, the actor, with an estate north of Escondido. He talked about what he still needed to nail down his suspicions that Reid and Rasmussen were one and the same. "I'd like to call South Africa to verify whether Rasmussen or Reid got a degree in Theology from the Institute there."

"Sure. Go ahead and call. Use the phone at the house. I'm curious too," Amy said.

"What will that get you?" Warren asked.

"In effect, that's what my friend on the police force asked. I'm not sure yet. However, it makes me suspicious that Rasmussen might be the tip of a much bigger fraud."

"Are you suggesting the New Age Christian mission might be a sham?" Warren asked.

They discussed that possibility until the drink orders arrived.

Jake, summarizing what had been discussed said, "I'm not sure of anything at the moment, but Sister Brigit had been prodding one of Rasmussen's people, a guy by the name of Metefara about an Archbishop in CAR. That's what the Sister calls the Central African Republic. If I assume the mission is a sham, and is raking in tons of money, I can see how the people counting that money, might get worried if somebody threatens it."

"Wow, Jake, you have one active imagination. I don't know the people involved, but I've read about them and from all accounts, they do good works all over the world. Certainly Nate must have felt that way or he wouldn't have donated like he did," Warren added.

"I don't think Nate cared one way or the other about the mission. I think what he cared about was his tax deduction and the fact that he received, apparently free of any contribution, a $350,000 stake in an art syndicate. You had to pay for yours, didn't you?"

"Why, yes. I paid."

Amy put her hand over her mouth. Her face took on a shocked look. "If the mission is a scam, do you think the art syndicate is also a scam?"

"I haven't gotten that far, but I'd have to say at this point, it's definitely a possibility."

"I know doctors who are getting dividends on their investments in the art syndicates, Jake. Be careful what you say." Warren cautioned.

Amy ignored Warren's comment and said, "Do you think that's why Dad and Mom were killed? To keep them from discovering ..."

"I know that's the logical jump," Jake said, "but I don't really have anything to back it up."

Warren looked at Amy and said, "That's right sweetheart, Jake's just letting his imagination run free based on the fact that some guy may be preaching without a license. When you boil it all down, that's it, isn't it Jake?"

"That's right."

"See Amy. Don't let yourself get upset."

She nodded toward Warren and touched his hand, adding a smile as she did.

Their crab cakes—they were served on a common platter—came and the food more or less interrupted the conversation. What there was came between bites and drinks.

All agreed that the crab cakes were excellent.

At the end of Jake's continued speculation about Rasmussen, Warren said, "It seems to me that all you've actually determined so far is that he's preaching without a license. From what I've heard, he's good at it and the people who show up for his sermons have high praise for him." He shrugged and added. "The man's an entertainer."

"I agree. He's very good and you're right. That's all I have so far," Jake said.

"Also, Jake, there may be a logical explanation about his theological degree," Warren continued. "Indeed, he may even have one. Not only that, Eli Reid may be the friend Rasmussen says he is." He looked at Amy and said, "I'm sorry this business has upset you, sweetheart. But, as you can see, there may be nothing to be upset about."

Jake didn't exactly agree, but he wasn't sorry that Amy's concerns had been assuaged by her fiancé. There was no need for her to be upset. And, as Warren had pointed out, there could be a reasonable explanation for everything without any sinister undertones.

"Changing the subject," Jake said, "now and then, I detect an English accent, Warren. Are you from England?"

"You might very well ask," Warren said with a big smile. "I was born in London. Went to med-school there but immigrated here ten years ago. I was working at the hospital where Amy was interning. That's how we met. I've found a home here. And, someone I love." He put his arm around Amy's shoulders and gave her a big hug. She smiled and kissed his cheek.

"How about you?" Warren asked. "Where'd you go to law school?"

"USC."

"Southern Cal. I'm impressed. I've heard it's a great school."

"It is," Jake said. The man was beginning to annoy him. First he didn't like the way he downplayed Jake's theories and secondly he didn't like the way he swooned all over Amy.

"Well then, you should be able to handle yourself if that LA firm gets after you again."

"I'm sure I will."

"What are you going to do next?" Amy asked. "I still want you to find out who killed Mom and Dad."

Warren interrupted before Jake could speak saying, "Honey, don't you think we should let Jake get on with his life? And, we can get on with ours. We can't change things. Maybe we'll rest easier if we let the police finish the investigation. Every time anybody brings it up, it upsets you. And, it upsets me when I see you upset."

"Thank you Warren. You have helped me deal with my grief. I appreciate it more than I can say, but I still want Jake to dog it out. Maybe there is nothing he can find. Maybe I'm wasting my money, but I want closure and I won't get it until I know."

Jake responded before Warren could speak. "I will call the Institute where Rasmussen was supposedly ordained. I'll let you know what I find out. After that, I'll see."

"I think that's a fair way to end it, Jake. Good fellow. Follow that lead and wrap it up. Smart thinking."

Jake was thinking with more than a bit of cynicism, *I didn't say I would wrap it up, old man. I don't intend wrapping it up until I've finished. Like Yogi Berra said, it ain't over till it's over.*

Instead, he said, "I appreciate your support, Amy … and yours Warren."

With dinner finished, they walked to their cars. Warren said, "Good work Jake. Keep us posted. Great game tonight. You had me worried."

"It didn't show," Jake said.

Amy stopped and gave Jake a hug with a kiss on the cheek. She whispered, "Keep at it."

Jake nodded a goodbye.

He was back at the half-way house well before Minnie Sue's attention span for missing inmates had been reached.

Sleep came easily, even with the decaf coffee but, he awoke at three with a thought. *The LA firm! I don't remember telling Warren about the firm threatening me. Did I tell Amy? I don't think I did. It wasn't that big a deal to me.*

The implications of that, kept him awake for another hour.

He rushed through breakfast, helped Bessie clean up and drove to the McGuire's to check his sent emails. He read each one carefully. None said anything about being threatened by anybody.

"That's not the first time he brought it up," he said, recalling their prior conversations.

Would he have a link with the firm? Doctors do retain law firms — their insurance carriers anyway — to handle their malpractice claims. If he has been sued, he might have a link with the firm and my name might have come up. I don't believe it.

He shrugged it off and called the Internet number for the Theological Institute of Johannesburg.

The phone rang a number of times. No one answered and no message machine picked up. He hung up and called a number of churches in Johannesburg to ask what they knew about the Institute. He got about the same answer from everyone he talked to. No one had heard of it.

Finally, he called the American Embassy and asked for someone who could give him information about Johannesburg. A young lady came on the phone.

Jake said, "I hope you can help me." He told her he was an attorney defending a murder charge against a client whom he believed was innocent. The main witness against him was a preacher who claimed to have been ordained by the Theological Institute of Johannesburg.

"I think the man is a fraud and may very well be responsible for the death of the man my client is accused of murdering. I can't find anything about the Institute from anybody and I've spent the morning calling. I wonder if you could check them out. My client's life is hanging on what you can find out."

"Talk about being handed a hot potato," she said. "I'm responsible for a man's life! I don't know if I can help you or not. I've been here for six years. I haven't heard of the Institute but, tell you what. Let me ask around. I'll call you back." She took the McGuire's number and promised to call back within the hour.

"Thank you," Jake said. "Court is in recess for now. Anything you can find will help."

He hung up and waited. More coffee. If sloshing was an indicator, he decided he might be addicted.

He waited. Finally, thirty minutes later, the phone rang. It had to be the embassy!

"Hello," he said. "Do you have news?"

"Some. I don't know what to make of it. I've checked around. As far as anybody knows, the Institute was never active. It has an address and a web site with a phone number but no offices and no personnel. I don't think your preacher could have been ordained there. As far as anybody around here knows, it's just a name."

Jake asked her to fax him her conclusions. She was somewhat reluctant, but Jake convinced her it would not get her or the embassy into trouble. Minutes later, Nate's fax machine pushed out a single sheet of paper summarizing what he'd been told.

"Rasmussen did not study religion in South Africa. I wonder if he's ever been there?"

The next day was Saturday. Rasmussen was holding a service at a church in Pacific Beach.

* * * *

He drove to the service in his old Chevy. Bessie sat in the passenger seat, looking very nervous.

"Don't you worry," Jake tried to reassure her. "I'll tell you when. Just do what we practiced. Nothing will happen to you. Trust me."

"If I didn't trust you, I wouldn't be here. This is the hardest thing I've ever been asked to do, Jake."

He parked. They went inside the church. Jake stood out of sight behind her, near the door he figured Rasmussen would enter. They waited.

Fifteen minutes later they heard a commotion outside, the door opened. In came Rasmussen's four apostles, clad in their freshly pressed green and whites. Seconds later, Rasmussen appeared, dressed in white, guitar handing around his shoulders, wearing a smile. He waved. A murmur swept through the crowd.

As he passed in front of Bessie, Jake whispered, "Now."

Bessie stepped forward and said, loudly, "Well, glory be! If it isn't Eli Reid. Mr. Reid, I've seen your movie three times. *Love and the Bible*. I just love it. It's been an inspiration to me."

Rasmussen stopped dead in his tracks, like he'd just run into a brick wall. He hesitated, as if unsure about what to do. Finally, and probably against his better judgment, Jake supposed, he turned to see who had called out. And, there was Bessie shoving a pad and pen at him. "Can you sign for me? My grandchildren will be so pleased to know that I've met you in person."

Still flustered, Rasmussen glanced right and left. Satisfied that no one had heard Bessie, he regained his composure, gave his Preacher Rasmussen smile and said, "Madam, I wish I had been in that movie, 'cause I'd love to sign your pad, but it wouldn't be right. But, I'm glad you've—"

Jake stepped forward, snapped Rasmussen's picture with his camera and in his downtrodden best said, "Howdy Brother. Good to see you again."

Rasmussen starred at him with such spite and hate, Jake felt like he'd just looked a spitting cobra in the eye. "You ... you trespassed ..." he said, spun around and continued to the lectern which had been set up for him, waving his arms at the assembled congregation, smiling, strumming his guitar to the tune being hummed by his happy apostles.

Jake took Bessie by the arm and let her out. "Wait here," he said at the front of the church. "I have one more thing I need to do."

She let go a big sigh of relief and walked toward Jake's car, obviously relieved that her part was over.

He took his camera and sought out Stern. He and Metefara were giving an interview to a television reporter near the door Rasmussen had entered a minute earlier. Metefara was saying, "We are much ... giving much help to *Medecins Sans Frontieres* ... that is Doctors without Borders ... I forget. It is French. We help the medical center near Zemio."

When the reporter interrupted for a question and got their attentions, Jake edged close and snapped pictures of both. At the second click, Stern half turned, but Jake had melted away by then.

"All in all," he told Bessie when they were underway, "it was a good day."

"I would have liked to stay for the sermon," she said. "Brother Rasmussen is a wonderful preacher, no matter what you say."

Jake laughed. "Next time."

He figured he'd get a letter from the law firm, but maybe not. Surely, *he recognized me at Sister Brigit's funeral service and had me pegged as the trespasser. Why hasn't that LA firm sent me a letter?*

Chapter

22

Later, Stern and Rasmussen met at a condo Stern rented while in San Diego to discuss that very thing.

Rasmussen told him in a tone that left no doubt about his concerns. "I tell you the guy is onto me. He had that woman at the half-way house call me by my real name. I also saw him at the nun's burial. He spoke. He's the same guy who barged in on me and Tammy at the house. I know it. I tell you Alan, he's trouble."

"Calm down! Okay. Back off. What does he know? What could he possibly know? He suspects you are Eli Reid. Actors use stage names? So what? No crime. Okay. NO CRIME! Understand? No crime. He's not going to find out anything from South Africa. We've closed that down. He may think he knows something but that's all he'll have. You won't be charged with a crime for what he thinks he knows. Okay?"

"Okay. I think. I don't like the fact that the nun was killed. He's a lawyer. You know how they are. Somebody gets killed and the person they suspect of anything is automatically the one they go after for everything."

"I'm a lawyer," Stern said.

"I know. So, I've had some experience with them."

Stern scoffed. "He can speculate all he wants. The nun was killed, as I understand it, by burglars. You were home at the time. Tammy is your alibi. Don't sweat it."

"Can't you do something about him?" Rasmussen asked. "The guy just keeps coming. Can't you have the firm get a restraining order or something? Just stop him. He upsets me."

"You're a nervous Nellie, Eli." Stern sighed slightly. "I'll ask if we have enough to nail the guy. We can probably put together a couple of affidavits, enough to get a temporary restraining order pending a hearing to show cause why it shouldn't be made permanent. I have a bit of a problem with that."

"I don't," Rasmussen said.

"You wouldn't. Let me educate you. I did some checking on Carson. Before he became a drunk, he was one of the best attorneys, if not the best, in San Diego. And, from the way he tried to pin me down and the way he trapped you, I'd say he's making a comeback."

"I could have told you that."

"Right, but you didn't," Stern said with a poke at Rasmussen's chest. "Now, I'll tell you something you couldn't tell me. What if Carson alerts the media about the court hearing to restrain him? All this stuff he's been hammering away at gets put in the public record. You're not who you say you are. You live in a big house, not an RV. Nobody can verify if you are a minister or not. Suppose you're asked the question by the judge. Perjury comes to mind. Carson will likely try to talk about the "profit" he was questioning me about. Our attorney will successfully object. In fact, he'll be objecting to everything, but that won't stop the press from hearing it … and reporting it. Just what do you think it'll do to our donations if people start wondering whether we're for real?"

Rasmussen looked down. "They might dry up, I imagine."

"You imagine! Ha. You'll be back looking for bit parts. The publicity might do you some good."

"Yeah. I see what you're driving at."

"I'm hoping Carson will spin himself out of questions," Stern said.

"If he doesn't?"

"One step at a time, preacher. One step at a time. I have something I want to try. It should work. I'll let you know. In the meantime, don't get your bowls in an uproar."

"I really don't like that crude talk, Stern."

"I picked it up when I was in Louisiana. It's cultural. I kind of like it."

Chapter

23

Jake had some thinking to do. Of course, he should email Amy about what he and Bessie had done. She was paying him, after all. But, she would probably discuss it with Warren. That bothered him.

Before doing anything, his thoughts turned back to Sister Brigit. He still didn't have a motive for her death, but he was getting a thought or two about it. He went back to the Internet and found what he was looking for.

He emailed Demarco the details about what he and Bessie had done. The last paragraph of his email said, "I have an idea about how to find out if Rasmussen's mission is legitimate or a sham. Are you game? You'll have to be involved."

Thus far, Jake had surmised, he was lukewarm to the investigation, but to be fair, fraud and deception, even murder weren't his responsibility. He was in traffic and all things related and, as he'd told Jake a couple of times during their lunches, if he steps on toes, his performance reviews suffer.

He also emailed Amy the details of what he and Bessie had done. He had something he wanted her to do, but didn't want to put it in an email in case Warren read it. Instead, he asked if she could have breakfast with him.

Her email came back first, thanking him for the report and applauding his efforts. "Yes, I'd love to have breakfast. How about tomorrow? Warren is subbing in Ocean Beach and will be away early. Phillip is back with another proposal I'd like your opinion on."

They'd meet at seven at a breakfast place down from the old post office.

He put together a package for her including things he wanted her to do. "Wonder what Phillip has come up with this time?" It occurred to him that perhaps he should report the cooking club deception to Demarco. Let him take some credit for stumbling onto it. On second thought, maybe he'd just forget it. Although the woman had planned to defraud Phillip, she hadn't actually done it. Questions of proof seemed murky. *The DA would probably not want to waste his time with it"*

If he did nothing, the woman might perpetuate fraud on some other unsuspecting soul. That bothered him, but he wasn't the world's policeman.

He had turned the coffeemaker on when he walked in so it was ready. He punched the buttons and waited for the brown liquid to fill a mug. He drank it black. In between sips, he did another Internet search on the New Age Christian mission, specifically its work in Africa. All he found were newspaper reports issued by the mission.

The McGuires subscribed to a music channel which Jake elected to use. Beethoven's Violin Concerto was playing. It had been a long time since he'd heard it. It relaxed him.

Demarco finally called. "What's this bull about how *we* might find out what Rasmussen's doing in Africa? I'm in traffic, remember, a mere peon who depends on defrocked attorneys for free *hamburger* lunches. I have a request in to transfer to major crimes, but it's rotting in somebody's in-basket. That doesn't qualify me to work on what I think, might be a scam, or fraud by any other name."

"You've been investigating it already. Didn't you check the ownership of that estate north of Escondido?"

"That was a favor! Don't give me that legal double talk. So, what is this thing *we* might do?" He laughed. "I'm not saying I will do it, but it sounds intriguing."

"I thought it would get your attention. I don't see you staying in traffic the rest of your life."

"I won't. I'll be looking for work as a security guard if you hang around much longer."

Jake walked him through what he wanted him to do.

"You gotta be kiddin' me! *There's no way in hell I would do that?* There's no way I could do that! Absolutely no way." From the way his voice was cutting in and out, he knew Demarco was shaking his head back and forth vigorously as he talked.

Jake went over it again. Having had some experience convincing people, he knew the second time through anything complicated made it sound simpler. That time, he broke it into smaller steps.

He could see Demarco still shaking his head.

"Slow down. Okay. Listen a minute. I'd be right there with you, listening and prompting. If you get stuck, all you have to do is ask for a second to think or something. I'm sure you can come up with a stall to give me time to get you over a hurdle."

"What about the phone charges? My boss looks at every phone bill. We get docked if we make personal phone calls."

"You're not telling me you don't make personal calls," Jake said.

"Sure, we just label 'em investigation enquiries. But what you're proposing wouldn't fly. No way would I even try it. I'd be out of here in a minute," Demarco said.

"I wasn't saying do it there."

"Where then?"

Jake told him they'd use Nate's phone. He was fairly certain Amy would approve and the phone had a speaker so he could listen in and make comments when necessary.

"Afterward, there's a great taco place in La Jolla. Good chips and salsa."

"I could report you for trying to bribe me," Demarco said.

"But think of all the free lunches you'll be giving up."

"Let me think about it. I wouldn't feel comfortable doing it, frankly. BSing is not my bag. I leave that for the lawyers … even ex-lawyers. Maybe what I'd be willing to do is sit in a chair and let you make the call, claiming to be a police detective. If the stuff ever hits the fan, I'll just deny any involvement," Demarco said.

"You wouldn't do that to a buddy would you? A Christian Detective?"

"I wouldn't hesitate. I have a family. They come first."

"Okay. I'll let you know," Jake said, ending the conversation.

* * * *

At his old firm's offices, now the Walter Hoffman firm, he logged onto a service to which they subscribed and searched the data bases for every name associated with the New Age Christian mission, including Alan Stern. The data bases provided much more extensive information than could be found on the Internet.

Stern graduated as an accountant and lawyer from Tulane University in New Orleans, La. He was not admitted to practice law in any jurisdiction but had qualified as a CPA in Louisiana. Before becoming the financial director of the New Age Christian mission, he served as financial advisor for two televangelists, one of which shut down after he'd moved on. "Questionable practices" the report said. The second televangelist was still preaching the gospel on television, healing the sick and lame on late-night Sunday television, tape delayed.

For Reid, the data base showed his old film credits then nothing. No word on any tours or any other work. The only address listed was the estate north of Escondido, CA. Though Jake hardly needed convincing, that make it pretty clear that Rasmussen and Reid were one and the same.

The report on Rasmussen showed the same data Jake had found on the Internet. However, the information about Rasmussen's birth place and parents "could not be verified."

"Likely means it was planted by somebody," Jake mumbled to himself.

The mission itself had addresses and phone numbers for every state. He called a couple of numbers and got the same recorded message about the mission's schedule of services. The caller was offered the option of leaving a message but was cautioned that there may be delays in getting an answer. A number was also given for donations.

"Probably no delays on that line."

He called it and it picked up on the first ring. "Hello," a cheerful young lady answered. "May I have your name and address and how much you want to donate?"

Jake almost laughed. "I don't want to donate. I regularly donate. I want to speak to Mr. Stern. Alan Stern." He didn't figure to get through, but thought it was worth a try.

"Mr. Stern? I don't know a Mr. Stern. I just answer the phones and take down information." Phones ringing with voices answering in the background confirmed that. It was like a PBS fund raiser.

"Let me speak to your supervisor."

"Her name isn't Stern either. I don't exactly know how to reach her, sir."

Jake thanked her.

Having been frustrated with that venture, he returned to his data base report. It reported mission activities in a number of countries over the years, with the caveat that no attempts had been made to verify any of those activities.

He finished up and dropped by Walter's office before he left.

"Jake. Good to see you. Have we been keeping you busy?"

"Actually not very. I think your office manager is mad at me," Jake said.

"Hmm. I'll talk to him. He gets moody. Something set him off the other day."

Jake didn't have to wonder what that was.

"By the way," Walter continued. "I got a call from Amy McGuire. She says you have done a remarkable job for her. She is very pleased and offered her affidavit that you have completely recovered. Bessie Melton reported to the court administrator that you've been drink free as far as she could tell since December. The administrator sent me a note that in another month you should ask to be reinstated."

"That's good news."

"For me too. I've put a note on my calendar to file a petition to do just that. I'll ask that you be reinstated on the basis of affidavits, Amy McGuire's and Bessie Melton's. I'll file one as well. The judge might accept it without negative blood tests. I'll let you know. Also, I'm sure he'll want to see you, ask direct questions, before approving anything. His administrator said as much," Walter said.

"Okay by me. I haven't had a beer since December. Actually, it sounds like a cliché but in some sense, I am a born-again Christian. Not really, but I've relied on the Bible to get me through some tough times. Sister Brigit of the Catholic Church also helped, not to mention you guys with the work and Amy McGuire. I call it a team effort."

"By the way, from what Amy tells me, you're still investigating the McGuire's deaths. Are you finding anything?"

"I'm not sure. I'm finding some things, but I can't be certain it ties into their deaths. I'm in a lot of muddy water."

"Let me know will you. There's still the possibility that the estate or the heirs can file law suits against whoever ran them down," Walter said with an optimistic tone.

Jake acknowledged that and left. He called Bessie to see if she needed help with the evening dinner. Apparently not, so he drove to the McGuire's home, for no reason other than he felt comfortable there. At one time, he had owned a nice home, nothing as grand as that one, but nice. Drinking and womanizing cost him that and everything else he'd accumulated. Just to be comfortable again was a feeling he never thought he'd experience again. He thought of Jen. Her image in his thoughts was followed by Amy's.

He admitted his feelings for Amy. "That's stupid!" he said out loud, kicking himself mentally for letting his thoughts torture him like they were. Still, he couldn't shake free. The conflict sent him to the refrigerator. He grabbed a bottle of beer and popped the lid before realizing what he was doing. The smell hit him. It smelled good! He lifted the bottle, and took a sip.

"Wait!" he called out as if talking to another person. He spit the sip into the sink. "Don't be a fool." Walter's words echoed in his thoughts. He recited his mantra and reluctantly poured the rest of the beer down the drain. He broke out in a sweat as he did. Twice, he stopped pouring. Twice more, he recited his mantra. "Satan get thee behind me!"

Staring at the upturned bottle, he said, "Lord help me. Please." The image of Sister Brigit flashed in his mind. That gave him the courage to finish emptying the bottle. He breathed a big sigh of relief. Another bullet dodged. Each time, he felt stronger, like he might win his fight against the crutch of a drink to get him past frustrations and conflicts. He forced himself to acknowledge that frustrations and conflicts are part of life. "I just have to anticipate them." He resolved to do that.

Chapter

24

In the morning, he drove his Chevy to meet Amy for breakfast. He was excited about seeing her. He cursed himself, but let it pass. It was okay, he decided, to like her. He just didn't have to let it become a cause. She was nice and pleasant and he enjoyed being around her. *No big deal. I don't have to go on a weeklong binge because she belongs to somebody else.*

She stood on the sidewalk in front of the café, dressed in her office clothes, a gray wool worsted jacket and skirt with a white blouse. When he drew near, she greeted him with a hug and kiss on the cheek. He held her close and looked into her blue eyes without thinking.

"Is that your fifteen degrees look?" she asked with a wink and a smile.

That brought him back from where his thoughts had drifted holding her close.

"I have to plead guilty. Your eyes mesmerized me. You have magic, Amy." He stepped back, a little embarrassed getting caught like that.

"In my medical opinion, the distance is closer to twenty degrees," she said.

The smell of bacon on the café's griddle lay like a warm blanket on the sidewalk where they stood. Jake took a deep breath and smiled with satisfaction. The smell of bacon got to him every time, that and the pretty woman which stood in front of him.

He reached out with both hands and touched her shoulders. "I don't mind waiting an extra five degrees for a taste of heaven."

She stood on her tip toes and kissed him on the lips. "Was it worth waiting for?"

"Well, I'm in heaven now." He wrapped his arms around her for a big hug.

He escorted her inside. They were lucky to find a free table. The café was usually crowded with morning patrons. They ordered coffee and the breakfast special, bacon and eggs.

"I thought you might have been offended by my indiscretion," Jake said, referring to the time he'd kissed her on the tennis court.

She shook her head. "Hardly. I could tell it meant something to you. Your eyes were a dead giveaway. I would have been disappointed if you hadn't made a move. Warren and I are not married. I don't know if we ever will be. He's been pressing since Mom and Dad died, but I'm not ready."

"He seems devoted," Jake said.

"Uh huh. I suppose. I'm stronger than I was when Warren and I first met. Then, I was a quivering mass of uncertainty wondering what to do next. He popped up with a calming bedside manner that charmed the heck out of me. I thought it was love, but now, I'm not so sure. Now and then when I catch him looking at me, I think he may be far away. Like he's not really there. It's disconcerting."

"Thanks for telling me. That makes me feel better. I'd like to be part of your life."

"You already are. Have been since the first time I saw you looking at me, the first time your eyes practically looked me straight to bed."

"That obvious?"

"Yep." Her eyes twinkled, he thought.

Coffee was poured.

"So, enough small talk. What did you want to talk about that you couldn't put in the email?"

He summarized what he'd sent in them email, then added, "If I assume Sister Brigit was murdered because of something she was doing and not because of a burglary, I smell the possibility of a massive scam, the New Age Christian mission. Obviously, I could be dead wrong, but having discovered that Rasmussen is a fake strengthens my assumption."

"I can see how you would. Do you think Dad was taken in? Could he have discovered the same thing?"

"Certainly, that's the logical jump, but I can't find anyway to make it. He never said anything to you, did he?"

She shook her head.

Their breakfast plates came with a happy smile by the waitress, like she was thrilled to be serving them. "Born for her job," Jake said.

They dug in.

Jake repeated his question. "Your dad never raised any questions about the mission, did he?"

"I was trying to remember. I don't think he did. If he was concerned, he never said."

"I know he had Bradley request a brochure from the Art syndicate. That was only days before Bradley was killed. I don't see how that request—I don't doubt Nate was snooping— would have triggered, in effect three deaths. I will ask Cynthia Berger if she recalled anything."

"No telling what she could recall. You could have said that in the email. In fact, most of what you said was implied."

"Yeah. I guess it was. Well, this is what I had in mind. Are you familiar with the Doctors without Borders program?"

"Some. It was started in France decades ago. I think it's in practically all the undeveloped countries. Doctors volunteer to help. I've thought about it myself, but since I'm a one-person office, there's no way I could abandon my patients like that."

A thought occurred to Jake. "Does Warren substitute for you?"

"No, oddly enough. Occasionally I've had a need, medical conference and the like, but he says he'd rather keep our relationship personal, not clouded by professional requirements. I doubt he could accept the fact that I'd be telling him what to do. Why?"

"I have no idea. The question just popped into my mind. The reason I asked about the program, is this: the Doctors without Borders organization is active in the Central African Republic. Since you're a doctor, I think you could make enquiries about the activities of Rasmussen's New Age Christian mission over there. In one of his sermons, he and his on-site director, a guy by the name of Metefara, went on at some lengths about the work and sacrifices the mission has made bringing aid to the program."

"You want me to call the … and ask?"

"Yes." He slid the New York phone number across the table to her. "You'll have to call their New York headquarters and find out how to reach their headquarters in the CAR. They may have more than one, but I assume they'll have one central contact location."

"What do I say?"

"That's where it gets a bit tricky. I'd prefer asking a direct question about the mission, but sometimes when you do that, it spooks the person you're asking and they suddenly forget everything they know. Whereas if you nibble at it, they're more likely to tell you what you need to know."

"So, I'm willing. How do I … nibble, as you put it?"

"On that sheet of paper with the New York phone number is an outline of how I'd go about it"

She picked up the paper and read through it quickly.

"It seems simple enough. I wouldn't be able to do it at the office, too busy and too many interruptions. Probably the best place would be at Mom and Dad's place. Put them on the speaker so you could listen in … scribble questions for me."

"When can we do it?"

"I can call New York right away. I don't know the time difference between California and the Central African Republic."

"I think they're nine hours ahead of us. So, seven o'clock here would be four in the afternoon."

She looked at her watch. It was a few minutes after eight. "Probably pushing it to call now. How about if I meet you at the house in the morning at six thirty?"

"Perfect. I'll get there a little early and do breakfast."

"Continental is fine. I don't usually eat this much." She gestured at her plate.

Jake asked, "You said Phillip was coming at you again. What's he up to now?"

"Some guy wants him to open a franchise cooking club store in La Jolla with plans to open more stores periodically in other upscale cities, Santa Barbara, for example, Palm Desert, places like that."

"How much money is he asking for?"

"He wants me to, in effect, set up a reserve of five million to be drawn against over the next three years."

"And, I suppose he wants it yesterday?"

"That's right."

"How long has he been working at the place your mother found for him?"

"Less than a year. He's complaining about it. He wants to quit because they don't know what they're doing."

"Less than a year. I don't know anything about the business so I'm reluctant to say much. However, just going on instinct, I agree with Nate. He should work there long enough to learn the business. Less than a year, in my opinion, is not enough time to learn the business. Besides, the guy with the big ideas is probably charging a big up-front fee for all sorts of recommendations and promises which, when you sort through them, are nothing. Usually the promises are for his best efforts which mean nothing. Just another phony operator out for a quick buck."

"You're right. The guy wants two hundred thousand up front and more later to develop a two year program for him. I tried to tell Phillip he sounds like a quick buck crook. He blew up and called me a bitch. Then, he said you're behind it."

"Maybe I am. What the guy will do is give Phillip a colored brochure with graphs and charts showing growth and profits as he adds stores. He'll get a commercial broker to scout out new locations for Phillip. Phillip can do that himself. The guy will also contract with someone to prepare a business plan for Phillip. Phillip can also do that himself or he can ask the SBA to help. Actually his bank probably has a commercial loan officer who'd be happy to help. Phillip probably knows enough now to have a list of suppliers for a cooking store. If not, once the word gets out that he's opening a store, they'll find him."

"I'll tell him that but I don't think he'll listen. He says I block everything he wants to do."

"Why don't I meet with him? See if he'll listen to me. I can tell him about incorporating and make some marketing suggestions, *at no charge*. Maybe he can bring the guy who's pushing for a big fee with him."

She'd pass the suggestion on but wasn't optimistic. "I'll see you in the morning at Mom and Dad's house."

* * * *

Jake called Demarco and asked him to drive to the McGuire's home at ten. It'd be eight in the Central African Republic. He figured the Red Cross people would still be in their offices. He doubted they stopped working for very long, considering the dire responsibilities they faced.

Demarco promised to be there and was waiting at the gate when Jake rolled up.

"What took you so long?" Demarco asked.

"You probably just got here," Jake replied.

"Yep."

They went inside.

Jake called the Red Cross number for Bangui and put the call on the speaker so Demarco could hear. He'd tracked the number down using Internet leads.

A woman answered. Jake thought he picked up her name, "Gabrielle Ansel" followed by something he didn't understand—that sounded French—followed by "… Bangassou."

He said, "I'm afraid I don't speak … French." He hoped it was French.

"I'm sorry," the voice said. "I'm so accustomed to speaking French, I forget. My name is Gabrielle Ansel, I'm a staff member of our headquarters here. How can I help you?"

Jake explained his problem. He was an investigating detective with the San Diego, California, USA police department investigating a series of murders. "We think a Doctor Aga Mertefara might have been a witness. We were told that Dr. Metefara works with an aid organization called the New Age Christian mission that is active in the CAR. He was here in San Diego briefly and may have talked to our suspect. We desperately need to interview Dr. Metefara. If he can identify the man responsible, we may be able to prevent another murder. The man is a serial killer who preys on young women. We've tried to reach Dr. Metefara, but so far we've been unsuccessful. None of the numbers we've been given have been helpful."

Jake heard the woman breath loudly. "I don't think I can help you, Officer. Our Bangui headquarters has received faxes from … Mr. Metefara. They were passed on to all our aid facilities. He has never identified himself as a doctor. Perhaps he is but in the correspondence I've been given, he always signs as Aga Metefara without any prefix"

"At least you know him?" Jake was somewhat disappointed. He had tentatively assumed Metefara had never been to the CAR.

"Actually I don't. As I said, our Bangui headquarters got a fax some months ago indicating the New Age Mission was bringing in food and medical supplies with manpower and materials to build multipurpose buildings. They were going to train people to fix things, that sort of program. Very welcome and needed here," she said.

"That's more or less what Dr. Metefara talked about when he was here. He told the television people they were in and around the city of Obo and Zemio in the northeastern part of the Central African Republic," Jake said.

"I haven't heard that they were in either place. A second fax said they had been delayed because the pilots would not fly over rebel held territories. Later another fax was received saying they were going to truck in the relief. That was followed by a fax saying their convoy had been hijacked by rebels. That's the last thing we've heard. As far as I know, the New Age Mission has never made it to the CAR."

"Have you checked with other areas where the Red Cross has operating centers?"

"I didn't. If they've been here, they've come in secret, worked in secret and departed in secret."

Jake said, "I'm sorry. Not only for your disappointment, but also for ours. I'll try something else."

"I wish I could have been of more assistance to you. If I hear anything, would you like for me to call?"

Jake said he would.

After hanging up, he looked at Demarco and said, "It's beginning to look like somebody's using smoke and mirrors. Scooping up the money and finding ways not to spend it."

"Yep. Lots of wiggling, but no movement," Demarco said.

"I have one more bit of investigating to do in the morning. If it still looks like the New Age mission is playing games, maybe you should discuss it with the DA."

"I'd like a little more substance to go on, Jake. Before I make a fool of myself going to the DA. I think you've discovered enough to create suspicions, but would you say you have any real evidence of a scam yet?"

"I'd say it's close. Circumstantial, but piling up. However, I agree. If the DA questioned Rasmussen, or Reid, assuming that's his real name, he could wiggle off the hook by saying they're still trying to get a shipment into the country."

"My thinking too. Tell you what. I think they're scamming but I'll wait until you have a little more to go on before I start yelling about the sky falling."

Jake had to agree.

"I'll let you know what happens tomorrow," he told Demarco as he stood to leave.

On his way to the front door, Demarco turned and said, "By the way, your old buddy Wags called. He said he'd talked to one of our compliance officers. I assume that was you."

Jake nodded.

"Anyway, he called to say he remembered talking to his dentist's receptionist about leaving the keys in his old car. He thinks maybe he told the dentist too, but isn't sure the dentist heard him over all the noise he was making. The dentist's office is in PB."

"I assume you checked them out."

"We did. Nothing extensive, but so far as we could tell, neither the receptionist nor the dentist ever heard of or ever had anything to do with the McGuires. Wags promised to keep in touch."

"Yeah. Next, he'll remember telling his vet. I don't know if you noticed, but he has pets."

"You mean all that hair floating around when you sit down? No, I didn't notice."

"Ha ha."

Jake bought lunch.

Chapter

25

After lunch, Jake decided to play another card. He drove to San Diego to visit Cynthia at her office. It was in one of those modern high rises like his old firm occupied, with a view over the harbor. The real estate firm she worked for occupied the eleventh floor.

Jake told the receptionist he had an appointment with "Cynthia." She directed him to her cubical, an interior one without a view but nevertheless impressive considering the reputation of the brokerage firm she worked for.

"Hi," he said. "I was in the neighborhood. Thought I'd drop by."

She smiled, stood and offered her hand which he accepted. "Have a seat," she said with a gesture at the chair beside her desk.

"My guess is that you have more questions."

"You're right. How about this? If you and Larson aren't busy tonight, how about if I buy dinner at the noodle café?"

She shrugged. "Sure. Why Larson? I don't think he's been up to anything."

"I'm trying to eliminate people from my list. He's on it but I don't think he belongs. However, it's part of the way I do business. I eyeball people I have doubts about. I'm not always right, but I have a decent average."

"Well. I doubt he's doing anything. He's trying to change. I'd appreciate it if you didn't upset him."

"I'll try."

They decided on six o'clock.

* * * *

Jake was waiting in front of the café when Cynthia rolled up in her sports coupe. Larson was in the passenger seat. They got out and hurried across the drive to meet him. Larson looked somewhat subdued, Jake observed. *An improvement over the last time we met.*

They ordered and sat in a booth to wait for the food to arrive. Jake, taking a chance, ordered sake. He and Cynthia had had it before without adverse consequences. If he felt himself liking it, he vowed silently to push it away and hoped he could.

He poured for the three of them in the small little cups that came with the ceramic bottle. They touched cups but nobody smiled, and nobody said anything. It was as though they were all waiting for something to happen.

Jake decided to move things along. "Okay, Larson, Cynthia says you're trying to put your past behind. I hope you are. You'll live longer and be happier."

Larson looked into his cup, gave a little shrug and said, "Yeah. Cyn took me to church. I don't believe in all that crap, but it made some sense what her pastor was saying. He said the love of money was the root of all evil. I could get into that. That's what got me in trouble in the first place."

Cynthia said, "I'm proud of Larson for turning over a new leaf. He's had a hard time getting work, but some people are willing to take a chance and give him a few hours here and there."

"Is that true?" Jake asked.

He bobbed his head up and down, slowly. "The Bible says a thief should do labor ... honest work with his hands and share what I make with people in need. That's what I'm trying to do. The church is helping me find work."

"Very commendable. I was in somewhat the same position. It has taken me a while to get myself straight so I agree with Cynthia. You should be proud of yourself."

"Cyn said you still have a bone to pick with me. Go ahead and pick. I'm not going to jump up and make a fool of myself tonight."

Their noodle bowls came, steaming hot, with the little soup spoons and chopsticks. Jake asked for a fork since he'd never mastered the wooden things. Cynthia and Larson didn't have a problem with them and twirled them up easily. .

Larson looked at Jake, waiting for him to ask his questions.

Jake obliged. "I want to know why you sicced those two overgrown thugs on me. Jer and his buddy. They tried to kill me and I didn't like it." Jake looked him straight in the eyes when he said it.

Larson's face went blank. He actually dropped his chopsticks on the table. "What?" He began shaking his head.

As far as Jake was concerned, Larson had passed the test.

"I ... I don't know a Jer. I didn't sic anybody on you. I swear."

Cynthia said, with anger in her words, "He didn't Jake! I told you he didn't. I'm surprised you're pushing it!"

"Actually, I didn't think he had, but I wanted to make sure. Somebody did. Okay. I'm convinced it wasn't you, Larson. I'm glad it wasn't. I'm glad you're trying to put your past behind you, Larson. I'm doing the same thing so I know what you're going through." Jake stuck out his hand. Larson took it.

"Thank you," he said. "I appreciate what you said."

"Talk to your preacher when you have questions," Jake said. "He may not have all the answers, but he'll be able to help."

Larson picked up his chopsticks and resumed eating, clearly relieved that Jake had accepted his story. Jake had witnessed many people lie and he was certain Larson wasn't. That meant it somehow had to be the doings of the New Age Christians and he was beginning to suspect why.

They finished eating. Half the ceramic urn of sake was left.

Near the end, Jake pulled out an envelope of photos he'd taken and laid them on the table. He slid the one of Rasmussen toward Cynthia and asked, "Did this guy ever come around Nate's office?"

She picked it up and studied it and began shaking her head. "Not that I can recall. I think I would have remembered him. He's not the kind of guy you can forget."

"I had wondered if he might have been the money broker, you told me about."

"No, that's the money broker," she touched Stern's photo, the one Jake had taken the day he and Bessie confronted Rasmussen. It was in the stack he had in the envelope.

"Alan Stern," Jake said. "He's the money broker?"

"No doubt in my mind. He was a slick looking guy; always well dressed, and never a hair out of place. He never smiled or said hello to me. He just pushed open Nate's office door and barged in unannounced. He was the money guy. Nate never liked him much, but put up with him because he brought Nate money partners. And, that made Nate lots of money."

"Did they ever argue or shout at each other?"

"The last time they met, after Nate decided to retire, they shouted. They guy stormed out and Nate came out laughing. He told me, 'The guy's a sore loser.' That was about it. Nate didn't seem concerned. He always felt things would work out in his favor. They usually did."

Alan Stern, the money man. The implications were more than Jake could absorb just then. He thanked her.

He doubted he'd ever see her again. From the look on her face, she didn't like Jake putting Larson on the spot about the knife attack.

Did Stern have Nate and Jen killed over money differences? Samuels said if they were going to be killed because of the partnerships, the time for that would have been before the negotiations. What did Demarco say? They wouldn't have tried to make it look like an accident. They'd have imported a couple of guys from the east to put a couple of slugs in Nate's head.

Plus there was the "key in the car" thing. No hit men would have worried about that. They knew how to steal a car. Why take a chance on an old clunker?

* * * *

The next morning, Jake hurried to the McGuire's home and put together something continental for Amy. He borrowed some fruit from the half-way house along with some whole wheat bread. He'd toast bread for butter and jam and slice fruit. With coffee, that should qualify as a continental breakfast.

Amy showed up on time. They shared the breakfast with coffee and went into Nate's office to make the phone call Jake hoped would end any doubts he had about the New Age Christian mission.

Amy dialed the Doctors without Borders number in New York and said, "I'm Dr. McGuire." A man answered and she followed the script prepared for her by Jake.

She said it was urgent that she get into contact with Aga Metefara of the New Age Christian mission working in the Central African Republic. "We do their medical work, when they're in town. We got the results back on their physicals and when we called their hotel, they'd checked out. So far we haven't been able to find them. Aga said they had been working with the Doctors without Borders in a makeshift medical facility near Zemio."

The man said, "We do have a camp there."

"The hotel said they'd received an emergency call and I suspect it was from their mission in the CAR. I need to talk to them about their results and wondered if you had a number for your facility at Zemio? That's probably where they went."

"It's possible. There's a lot of unrest in that area. Let me see if I can find a number." There was a delay as the man apparently searched for a number.

Seconds later, he came back on the phone and said, "Okay. Call Doctor Reynolds." He gave her two numbers. "They work all the time so if you don't get someone the first time, call again."

She thanked him and dialed the number he'd given. After four rings, someone picked up. "Doctor Reynolds," he said. "Make it quick. I have new patients being unloaded. Another ambush."

Amy told him the story she just given the New York headquarters.

He said, "Aga Metefara? I've never heard of him. The New Age ... whatever you said has never been around here as far as I know. Maybe someplace else, but not here. Lord knows we can use all the help we can get so I'd remember if anybody brought aid. I'm sorry, Doctor McGuire. No one by that name has been here since I've been here and I've been on site for eighteen months. Sorry now, I have to go."

Amy looked at Jake. "Well you heard. Looks like Metefara and Rasmussen have been lying about providing aid in the CAR."

"That's consistent with what I found out yesterday." He summarized what he and Demarco had found out from their earlier call to the Red Cross.

"At least they'd heard of them."

"They slipped up with the Doctors without Borders. They should have faxed them something. Better still, they should not have been specific about what they had done. If they'd said they were going to do it or in the process of doing something, we wouldn't have anything. By going on record as having done it, I think they've admitted to fraud. I'll talk to Demarco. He's in traffic, but wants to move up. He'll tell his boss and they'll likely go to the DA. I'll let you know what happens."

"Well, what a morning. First a wonderful continental breakfast and then some Sherlock Holmes sleuthing."

"You did a great job. Well done," Jake said.

She gave him a quick kiss. "Hope you don't mind."

"Are you kidding? I loved it. I'd stand in line for them."

"Nothing serious," she said. "I just feel close to you."

"We have a common goal. Finding out who killed your parents."

She shook her head without saying anything. He could tell the memory caused her to tear up.

"Sorry."

She shook her head again. "It's okay."

"If you don't mind, can you keep what we learned confidential for a while?"

"You mean, don't tell Warren?"

Jake nodded. "I didn't want to mention it, but somehow he knew that an LA firm had been threatening me. I don't recall mentioning it to you or him. So, I wonder how he knew."

"I might have forgotten, but I don't think you told me. If I didn't know, how would he know?"

"I have no idea unless he has some connections with Rasmussen's mission. I don't suppose you've ever heard of Alan Stern."

"No."

"He's the mission's financial advisor. And, interestingly enough, he also arranged money packages for Nate."

Her eyes widened. "He did?"

"That's right. So, somehow there was a link running from the mission to Stern's money sources. There was some acrimony between Nate and his partners during the final negotiations, but they all seemed to be satisfied with the final agreements. So, it doesn't jump up and say anyone of them had anything to do with Nate's death, but the suggestion won't go away."

She gasped at the thought.

"Until I have a better handle on it, if I ever got one, I'd just as soon not spread the word around. That includes Warren."

"I hate keeping anything from him. We're engaged, even if maybe it's gone stale at the moment."

"It may be important," Jake said.

She grimaced. "Not a good way to build a relationship, but I'll do it for now. Let me know if you find out anything else."

He promised.

After she'd left for her office, he prepared a report of her telephone call to Doctor Reynolds at the Doctors without Borders facility in Zemio. In the report he talked about Nate's $450,000 contribution to the New Age Christian mission and the apparent "gift" of a $350,000 interest in an Art for the Ages syndicate. Plus the fact that he had yet to receive income from the investment. To complete the story, he did say that one other investor said income should not be expected for a number of years. He hated to do that since it more or less gutted the inference that the syndicate might not be what it seemed, but he also hated not to give a complete picture.

He faxed a copy to Demarco with a suggestion that he and his supervisor call the DA. To cover himself, he also faxed a copy to Walter.

He'd wait to hear from Demarco before doing anything else. If the DA wanted to proceed, he was out of it. If not, he'd have to come up with some way to push the peg up a notch.

Chapter

26

Jake spent the rest of the morning helping Bessie and wondering when Demarco would call back. Walter did call.

"Hard to believe," he said. "You're suggesting these guys are working a scam. I know you haven't broadcast it."

"No. I don't like being sued any more than you do. Accusing somebody of fraud might just trigger a litigious response."

"Big time. You might as well file Bankruptcy without filing a response. What are you going to do with what you were told? I'm sure you know, your report is mostly heresy."

"I do, but it's pretty suggestive and persuasive."

"I don't disagree as a layman. As a lawyer, I'm cautious."

"Well, I've passed it on to the guy I've been working with on Nate and Jen's hit-and-run. He's in traffic, but I figure he'd want the glory so I'll let him carry the ball for now. I think the DA will have to investigate, heresy notwithstanding."

"I assume he will. He'll be calling you and Amy. Keep me informed. You may need an attorney before it's all over. Or, if the implications of what you're saying are true, you may need a bodyguard."

Jake agreed. "I can't comfortably tie Nate and Jen's murders to the mission scam, but I'm pretty comfortable linking Sister Brigit's murder and the attack on me to them. Lots of money involved."

"Enough to motivate murder if somebody threatened its flow."

That gave Jake another idea but he'd wait on it until he'd heard from Demarco. If the DA took over, all he had to do was sit on the sidelines and watch the show.

* * * *

It was late afternoon before Demarco called. "My department head went to the DA with your report and all the rest of the stuff I had in my file."

"And?"

"The DA is impressed. He thinks you may be onto something. His problem is—he's a very careful guy and keeps one eye on reelection—it's mostly hearsay. He's going to the mayor with it. Let the mayor make the call. The mission has apparently spread enough political money around to make people—politicians—reluctant to throw stones. If the mayor says investigate, he'll put together a task force. If not, he'll probably let it simmer until you come up with something he can't ignore."

"Like another body and Rasmussen standing over it with a smoking gun?" Jake asked with more than a touch of sarcasm.

"Probably."

Jake scoffed. "That's crap. There's enough in my report to justify bringing Stern and Rasmussen, aka Reid, in for questioning. Also that guy Metefara if they can find him."

"I happen to agree with you, but I'm just a lowly traffic cop. And, you're not much higher on the totem pole than I am at the moment."

"And, I haven't contributed to anybody's reelection."

"You said it, not me."

"I think you did."

"I'll deny it," Demarco joked.

"Okay. I'll go to plan B."

"Which is?"

"I haven't worked it out yet, but I'll let you know," Jake said.

"Bear in mind all I do is write traffic tickets, man speed traps and investigate accidents. Otherwise, I just drink coffee with super cops who investigate homicides and other major crimes."

"Crap," Jake said after hanging up. "Politicians are more interested in not making waves than doing their jobs."

He poured himself a cup of Bessie's coffee and sat down to drink it. Bessie passed and seeing him in deep thought asked, "How are you doing Jake? Having troubles?"

He brought her up to date with what he'd been discovering in particular the possibility that the New Age Christian mission might be a sham.

"I can't believe Brother Rasmussen would be part of anything like that, even if he isn't a regular preacher. I embarrassed the poor man. I don't know how I could have done that. I wouldn't have for anybody but you. You must be mistaken about him somehow. He's fine man, a Christian, God-fearing man. I love the man."

"Apparently you are not alone. I'll admit he's a fine speaker but the facts can't be ignored," Jake said.

With a doubting shake of her head, Bessie said, "I contributed every extra penny I had to help the poor people in Africa get on their feet. Doctor McGuire just didn't talk to the right people."

Jake raised his eyebrows. Rasmussen had made a conversion that even the facts couldn't overcome. "I wish I could say you might be right, but I know you aren't. I wouldn't count on your donations getting to Africa."

She began shaking her head before he'd finished.

Seeing he was getting nowhere, he said, "Maybe we were mistaken."

From the look on her face, he could tell she was relieved. He imagined the mayor and DA had similar reactions, theirs prompted more by campaign contributions than benevolent feelings.

What the heck am I doing? Sticking my nose out for people who are already convinced.

I'm doing it for Jen, he reminded himself. *And, now, I'm doing it for Amy.* That thought made it easier to forget the beer he'd been thinking about. He poured himself another cup of coffee and sat down to consider what he was going to do next.

Two cups later with one bathroom interruption, he had an idea. It wasn't one he liked, but it was the only one he'd had that might move the peg. He felt like he was in a criminal trial on the prosecution's side, searching for evidence that'd prove someone guilty beyond a reasonable doubt.

He pulled out the *La Jolla Light* to see when Rasmussen was holding his next service. He had been having one or two a week. The *Light* reported that this week's service would be on Saturday afternoon in Rancho Santa Fe at a meeting hall. It was being sponsored by a number of churches so as to be non-denominational in spirit.

At five thirty, his phone rang. It was Amy.

"I had to call, Jake. I know I said I wouldn't, but I had to ask Warren about what you said. How he knew about that LA firm threatening you. We are either honest with each other or we don't have a relationship. Lately I've not been so sure."

He wished she hadn't done it, but he couldn't change it so he asked, "I understand. You are practically married. You should be able to trust each other by now. So, what'd he say?"

"It seemed to take him aback at first, but he put his hands on my shoulders, looked me in the eyes, smiled the way he does and said, 'Sweetheart, I don't know where I came by that information. I simply don't remember, but somebody told me. I'd have sworn it was you. Are you sure it wasn't?' I wasn't sure. Is it possible you told me offhand and just forgot it?"

Jake wasn't sure either. So much had happened. It was possible he had, even though he didn't remember. It would have been unusual for him to tell her something that wouldn't have meant anything to her, but possible.

But, he said, "Amy. I think I could pass a lie detector test that I didn't, but who knows? Maybe I did and just forgot."

"He swore that he knew of no lawyer anywhere who was threatening you."

No doubt the son of a gun turned on the charm, Jake thought.

"I'm relieved for your sake," Jake said even though he wasn't. "I'll stumble on a bit. See what else I can find out, then, I'll consider closing my file." He related his conversation with Demarco, how the DA was shifting the responsibility to the mayor and how political contributions might cloud their judgments.

"That's not right," she said. "How could they make public decisions on that basis?"

Jake agreed, but told her that was the reality of our politically based system of justice.

"Warren's taking me out to dinner," she said.

"Enjoy," Jake told her.

He'd go to Rasmussen's Saturday service in Rancho Santa Fe and make a nuisance of himself. That was his plan, his last resort plan.

* * * *

He showed up a few minutes early with his camera just in case he saw anything interesting. It was a large parking lot, but he'd have expected that in Rancho Santa Fe where wealth and all its trappings seemed to reside. And, no one of importance wanted to be hampered by a lack of parking spaces or by tiny things one had to shoehorn into.

Rasmussen's old RV hadn't arrived. He'd be a little late to let build the excitement stirring the crowd's anticipation. A couple of vans were parked near the door into the tile covered building.

"The apostles," Jake said to himself. "Maybe Metefara as well. And, he's the one I want to speak to. Him and Stern." He expected Stern to show up with Rasmussen.

With a quick step, he hurried into the hall to locate Metefara who indeed was inside, talking with the four apostles. All were as happy as could be, laughing and joking. No Stern in sight.

"Aga Metefara," Jake called out, cheerfully, as he approached. He stuck out his hand with a big, Warren-smile.

The man blinked, obviously confused and wondering just who Jake was.

"Jake Carson," Jake said. "I'm with the *Spiritual Hands* magazine. My editor asked me to get a few words from you for our next edition. Can I have a few minutes?"

Metefara glanced around, searching for someone, probably Stern, Jake figured, to bail him out. Seeing no one, he put on a slight smile and said, "I can maybe say … give you comments … about our mission … you want the comments?"

"That's exactly what I do want and a picture." Jake touched the camera hanging around his neck. "Why not get the picture first." He pointed his camera and took a couple of photos.

Jake pulled a note pad out of his jacket pocket and said. "The pictures are out of the way, so now we can talk. Okay?"

"Yes. Okay," the black man said with a nervous edge to his words.

"First question. Your mission is active in the Central African Republic. Right?"

"This is correct."

"I believe you've said around Zemio and Obo. You've been helping the Doctors without Borders group. Providing aid. Right?"

Now Metefara began to fidget uncomfortably. "We provide aid in many parts of the CAR."

Jake flipped back through his note pad. "Ah. Here it is. You said your mission had installed a pump for the Red Cross at Obo and helped repair a generator for the Doctors group." Jake recited the date Metefara had said that during the mission's service at the Catholic Church.

"If you say. I don't recall."

The man's being deliberately obtuse, Jake thought. *Okay, I'll come at it from a different direction.* "Well, maybe I'd better … say, ask just where is your mission providing aid in the Central African Republic? What villages?"

Now, Metefara, sensing he was being put on the spot, nervously switched from one foot to another. Trapped, he finally said, "We are in Zemio and Bangui. Our convoy provides aid to refugee camps. We build churches people can use for shelter and for schools when fighting is over."

"Well, our readers will love to hear that!"

"What's this?" Stern's voice rang out. "We're not holding interviews until—" He stopped when he saw Jake.

"Jake Carson! You are not with the media." He looked at Metefara. "This man is a troublemaker. He is opposed to our mission and seeks to stop our programs. Always ask for credentials before talking to anybody."

He turned back to Jake and said. "I believe you were warned not to approach any member of our mission again. You have publically accused us of deception. I will be filing a criminal complaint against you. Criminal libel. You'll spend some time in jail, Mr. Carson. Please leave now or I will ask some of our staff members to escort you out."

"Jer and his friend, perhaps?"

That brought a frown to Stern's face but it quickly vanished. He turned and waved to two men standing by the door.

"I believe this is a public place, Stern. If your goons touch me, I'll charge them with assault and you with conspiracy. How's that going to look in the newspapers? Also, I'll tell them the New Age Christian mission has never been to the Central African Republic. Your man," He nodded in Metefara's direction. "just lied in his teeth."

Stern dismissed that saying, "More threats and lies. I'd have hardly expected that from an attorney, even one who has been disbarred for being a drunk. Our mission provides aid where it is needed. We don't always know which village or which aid group we give the aid to. We don't care. We only care about the people we help."

His glance at the four apostles who were watching with great interest, told Jake he was speaking for their benefit. *Can't have them knowing the truth, can we?*

Jake said, "We'll let the DA and the FBI make the final decision on that won't we?"

By then, the two men had walked over to stand beside Stern, waiting for orders.

He said, "Escort this man out. If he resists, drag him out. He's disrupting our meeting. He's making criminal accusations." He smiled at the apostles and added, "I'll need for you to sign affidavits. This man will be arrested and charged."

"Good," Jake said. "The television people and the newspapers have been alerted. They'll get a full report, with sworn statements, about the scam you are pulling. Do you want my address?"

"Get him out!" Stern said firmly. "Now!"

One man grabbed Jake's arm. Jake swatted it away. "That's an unauthorized touching, a battery. I'll be filing a charge against you. What is your name?"

The man looked at Stern, bewildered, waiting for further instructions. "Take him out."

Jake turned and walked away on his own. He paused and shouted back at Stern who was watching with his hands in his pockets. "You know the address, I think. It's the Sunrise House. Jer and his friend found it."

Those who had arrived early found it amusing. Jake thought with a laugh to himself, *probably think we're having some kind of bellum sacrum or holy war.*

His escorts stopped at the front door.

A cold beer would have tasted good just then, but he was pleased that it was not the overwhelming urge it was a few weeks before.

"I'm regaining control," he said as he drove along. He turned on his portable CD player. An old ABBA CD played. Gusto music. It was impossible to feel depressed when ABBA played.

However, some ominous thoughts began to creep into his mind. He checked his rearview mirror. No one was following.

He parked as close as possible to the halfway house, checked all his mirrors before turning off the key and getting out.

I'm getting spooked. Maybe paranoid. Relax.

As he thought that, he looked toward the house and saw Phillip and Billy sitting on the front porch. *What the heck! I guess Amy told them I would talk to them. Never a dull moment these days.*

As he bounded up the steps, he said, "Well, a surprise visit. What can I do for you gentlemen?"

Phillip snarled, "Amy says you're screwing up my plans again! Are you homophobic? Is that it?"

His buddy added a "yeah."

Jake walked close to where they sat, bent down a bit and said, "If you ever accuse me of anything again, I'm going to make you wish you'd never met me. Understood? For your tiny little brain, I'll say this. I'm not homophobic. I'm a lawyer, or was. Lawyers don't have prejudices except against non-paying clients. We look at problems, not individuals. We don't care what you are, what color or religion. We only care about your problem and whether we can solve it. Do you understand that?"

Phillip shook his head nervously. "But, you're screwing up my deal! I finally get somebody who can help me and you tell Amy he's a scam artist."

"I didn't exactly say that. What I said was, he was offering you services you could get for yourself without paying anything. And, I told her I'd tell you how."

He jumped up. "Yeah, so you can make it so hard, I'll give up. Is that your plan? You and Amy are hand in glove! You don't want me to succeed!" He screamed the last. Billy jumped up and stood next to him.

He screamed too. "I know your type. You sound so glib, but under it all, you're a sneak. You don't want Phillip to have what's his. He's entitled to half the money you and Amy are trying to hide. That's it, isn't it! You turn Phillip down and take his money!"

Phillip swung at Jake, a big roundhouse right. Jake saw it coming and ducked. It brushed the back of his head. While he was bent over, Billy tried to uppercut him with his right hand but Jake was rising up, so it barely grazed his shoulder.

By then, Jake was swinging. He doubled Phillip over with a punch in the stomach. And, he pulled that punch back and rammed Billy in the stomach with his elbow. With both men doubled over, he pushed Phillip's shoulders and sent him tumbling into the yard. He grabbed Billy's shirt and threw him into the yard on top of Phillip.

"I'll get you!" Phillip screamed.

"You're dead!" Billy shouted. "Dead meat!"

Phillip said something over his shoulder but Jake couldn't make it out. They stalked off to their red truck parked across the street and drove away.

Bessie opened the door. "Dinner is about ready, Jake. Unless you have more cleaning up to do." She grinned and gestured across the street at the departing truck. "A Dale Carnegie you're not."

"I read the book," Jake said of Carnegie's *How to Win Friends and Influence People*. "I became a lawyer instead."

Chapter
27

Amy sent Jake a text message the next day. *Guess what? Dad's trust received a check for $15,000 this morning with a letter from the Art syndicate. Call me.*

He texted back. *Will call at noon.*

She replied. *Better. Meet me at Starbucks at noon.*

Will do.

* * * *

Jake saw her drive up and ordered two cappuccinos; his wet. She liked hers dry. While he waited for the chipper young girl to make the foam, he grabbed a table ahead of one of the college kids who used the Starbucks wireless to do homework.

Amy approached him with arms outstretched for a hug.

"I could get used to this," Jake said. "Makes me feel loved."

She laughed.

"Jake," the server called out. Jake hurried to get their coffees.

"How much time do you have?" he asked.

"Thirty minutes. I have an annual exam scheduled at one and I need to call in prescriptions before that."

They sipped the foam at the tops of their cups.

"Okay then. With time of the essence," Jake said, "tell me about Nate's check."

"The letter promised more at mid-year, more or less. Checks are issued near the end of June following the close of an exhibition. The tour began with two exhibitions in Spain, the last in Madrid, two in Portugal and one in Rome at the end of the year. It is now moving to Venice."

"Not bad."

"That's what Warren said. He got a check for $1,500 but he doesn't have much invested in his syndicate."

"I had been thinking the syndicates were a kind of pyramid scheme, tied to the New Age Christian mission scam, but this makes me rethink that theory. I wonder … would you mind asking Warren if he knows any other doctors who subscribed to his syndicate. If he does, would he mind calling them to see if they also got checks?"

She'd do it.

He let out a little chuckle.

"What?" she asked.

"I just remembered something I read in the Bible Rasmussen gave me. Let he who is without sin cast the first stone. I guess I'm in no position to cast the first stone. When I'm with you, I have to confess that I have sinful thoughts."

She blushed, but to cover it picked up her coffee and drank it down. She breathed and said, "You shouldn't say such things."

"I apologize."

"I should have added, in public." she said with a mischievous little smile.

Her little smile brought back memories. Jen had the same mischievous smile with her quips.

He finished his coffee. His thoughts were torn between the young woman at the table with him, wishing she were his fiancée, wishing he had a right to even have a fiancée and the task at hand, the New Age Christian missions and its tie in to the Art for the Ages syndicates, if any. And, it was beginning to look like there wasn't one.

Whereas he'd been thinking Warren might be part of what the heck was going on, it appeared that he'd been totally wrong.

"Somehow I may have missed something," he said.

"I know. I had the same thought. I know what we heard when we called the CAR. Doctor Reynolds hadn't seen anyone from the New Age mission."

"Frankly, I don't know where to take this thing. If the DA doesn't want to investigate based on what I've told the police, I may have to drop it."

"Does that mean you'll quit investigating who ran down Mom and Dad?"

Jake shrugged. "That has kind of been on the back burner anyway. I had hoped to tie that to the other investigation but now it looks like that one is a dead end. I may have to start over."

"Hmm," she said. "What if—"

"I was thinking the same thing," Jake said.

"What if they sent the checks to throw you off? They must know you're working for me. They'd know I'd tell you about the checks."

"Yes. The checks at the very least would buy them insurance time to figure out what to do. And, if they got lucky, maybe I'd go away."

"Great minds and all that," she said.

"I'll have another look," Jake said. "I'll go back to the drawing board and see what I can come up with."

Before they left, she asked if he'd have time for tennis later in the week.

He'd be delighted.

She wasn't sure Warren would be able to make it.

"Too bad," he said with a conspiratorial grin.

* * * *

He called Demarco from the McGuire's. "Any word from the mayor's office?"

"My boss says he is having lunch with the financial director of the New Age mission."

"Alan Stern. Like the song says, he could pour water on a drowning man. That won't get him anything but a free lunch."

"The mayor thinks he can see into a man's soul over a dinner table. That's what he says. So, he'll look into the director's soul, the Stern guy, and know whether he's a crook or not." Demarco said with tone that was obviously tongue in cheek.

"So, that lead is dead," Jake said. "Stern will tell him that with all the civil unrest in the CAR, it is impossible for his mission to know every aid group they help."

"Yep. Looks like it's dead. Got any other bright ideas?"

"I could start calling every art gallery in Spain and Portugal and Rome and ask if they'd had any African art exhibits recently."

"What would you tell them? The San Diego police department is tracing stolen African art? Don't ask me to be your co-conspirator."

"I'm not going to do that just yet. I think it's a good idea, but I have another idea we can try."

"Bull. Forget that *we* stuff. I've been dodging bullets ever since you turned up on my doorstep. No more. Find somebody else's career to ruin. I've got work to do."

"You should at least hear me out."

He heard Demarco's sigh at the other end of the line. "I know I'm not going to like it, but go ahead. Which side of the Bible are you on? The guy upstairs or that guy with a tail that ruins lives?"

"Sometimes I wonder."

"Tell me before I involuntarily hang up. Self-protection is instinctive."

Jake outlined what he wanted to do. Demarco said no, blustered about how stupid it was and how illegal it was. But, he said, "It's not a bad idea, Jake. You'd take the lead so if anything went wrong; it'd be your non-career that'd be blown."

"All I'll need is a little help from you," Jake said.

Demarco agreed. "I'm thinking a good security job is what I'll end up with. What's that mantra you recite when you're tempted to do something you know damn well is wrong?"

"Get thee behind me, Satan."

"Thanks. If you don't mind, I'll be reciting that every time I see you coming."

"This will work. You won't be sorry," Jake said.

"I already am."

* * * *

He checked in with Bessie to see if she had any chores for him. "Not really, Jake. A couple of volunteers will be coming over to help with the laundry. That's always a chore."

"Where's the *Light*?" Jake asked.

She told him. "By the way," she said, "I must be losing my mind. A guy came by here a while ago. Let his card." She disappeared around the corner but returned within seconds holding a card.

"Here." She handed it to him. "He said he had a job for you."

Jake frowned. "What kind of job?"

"He didn't say. Told me to ask you to call. Nice looking man. Dressed in a suit. All business. Drove a new car."

Jake was puzzled. He looked at the card. It said, "Western Explorations." The name on the card was, "Richard Todd, Field Agent."

"A job?" Jake said. "Hmm." Two surprises in one day. Coincidence? *I am becoming paranoid.*

"I'll call the guy later. First I want to see where Rasmussen's holding his next service."

"I know that. It was on the television. It'll be in Oceanside this Saturday morning with refreshments and entertainment afterwards. A local choir group will sing after the service."

"Are you going?"

She sighed. "I'd like to but with the stunt we pulled, I'm too embarrassed to even think about it. Don't get me wrong. I was glad to help, but I don't know if I can face Brother Rasmussen ever again."

"Why don't you go if you enjoy his sermons that much? He won't ever see you in the crowd."

"You think?"

"I'm positive. There'll be so many people there, no one will notice you."

"Thank you for encouraging me. You don't have anything planned for it, do you?" She asked suspiciously.

"I won't be within miles of Oceanside."

He could see the relief wash over her face.

She went on about her business, getting ready for the volunteers. Jake looked at the card again.

He shrugged and called the number. "Nothing ventured, nothing gained." Besides, he was curious.

Todd picked up on the first ring. "Todd here."

"Jake Carson. You left your card at the half-way house where I'm staying."

"Oh yes. Mr. Carson. I may have a job for you. I got your name, second hand, from the San Diego police department. They said you were a good investigator and my company needs one."

"What kind of job do you have?"

"Tell you what, why don't we meet at Hennessey's for lunch. I'm told they have a good soup and salad menu. I try to eat light when I'm on the road. I'll explain the job to you over lunch. Okay?" he said.

"When?" Jake asked.

"I'm nearby so how about ... fifteen minutes?"

"I'll be there." Without time to change into his suit, Jake went in the worn khakis and the old suede jacket he'd slipped into that morning. It wouldn't impress anyone, but if they'd decided he was the man for the job, impressions weren't what they were looking for.

* * * *

To Jake's amazement, there was a parking place in front of the restaurant. He had never been inside the place but had heard the food was excellent and the atmosphere, Irish décor, entertaining. He assumed the man in a dark brown suit standing in front and looking back and forth was Richard Todd.

He walked toward him and when close said, "Richard Todd, I presume."

The man smiled and shoved out his hand. "And you must be Jake Carson."

After a meaningless exchange about how beautiful La Jolla was and the weather, Jake followed him inside where they were seated in an atrium room. Indeed, the walls were decorated with colorful scenes from Ireland.

They ordered. Todd asked for a beer with his soup and sandwich; tomato bisque and half a BLT. Jake was tempted to get a beer with his and figured he could handle one, but elected not to try. He took tea instead.

Todd began. "I understand that you're also a lawyer."

Jake nodded. No need to go into details at that point, he decided.

"Well, what I'm going to tell you is confidential. Is that okay?" Jake agreed.

"My company drills for oil and natural gas."

He talked about his company's history, where they'd drilled, that sort of thing.

"Right now, our seismology has identified some decent sized pools northwest of Santa Fe, New Mexico. Our problem is getting authorization to drill. One family owned most of the land, a thousand acres, and the drilling rights. Over the years, they've drifted away and we can't find most of them. We want you to find them and have them sign agreements authorizing us to drill. We pay royalties of course once we start pumping."

"I don't know anything about oil and gas."

"You don't have to. I know all there is to know about drilling for oil and gas. All you need to know is how to find people. Investigate. It's what you do! Just find the heirs for us and get them to sign. It's worth $20,000. We'll give you a retainer of $5,000, with all expenses paid. How about it?"

"When did you want me to start? I'm on an assignment right now."

He turned his head with a shrug. "Well, I want you to start yesterday. We are ready to drill. You'll stay in Santa Fe. The La Fonda. We'll have a car waiting for you at the Albuquerque airport. Everything you need to know is in this folder." He slid a manila folder across the table toward Jake.

"You meet Mr. Begaye at the Ohkay Owngeh Pueblo Cultural Center. The map is in the folder. He'll have the forms you need to get signed, in Navajo and English."

"I'll need to notify my ... other clients. Can I let you know tomorrow?'

He shook his head. "I'm scheduled for a plane this evening. You'll have to let me know today. If you can't do it, I have to find somebody else. There's a guy in Albuquerque, part Native American, who also comes highly recommended."

Jake sighed. "I'll let you know by six today."

"I can do that. Call me."

Todd picked up the check.

Jake drove to the McGuire's home to think about what to do. Obviously $20,000 was more money than he'd made in a long time. And, all he had to do was ask questions and drive around looking for people who'd drifted, some off the reservation. Usually relatives knew where to look.

"Unbelievable!" he said. "Unbelievable!"

Right. Unbelievable. When it looks too good to be true, maybe it isn't.

He spent the next hour and a half trying to track down a telephone number for the Okhay Owngeh Pueblo Cultural Center. Finally, he found a number and called.

"Ohkay Owngeh Cultural Center," a woman said.

Jake introduced himself as an attorney and said, "I'm trying to locate a Mr. Begaye. I was told he comes in to the Cultural Center from time to time. Can you tell me how to get in touch with him?"

Silence. "Mr. Begaye? Are you sure about the name? There was a Fletcher Begaye around here some years ago, but he's long dead. I don't think he had any relatives. Could you be mistaken?"

"I could. Let me check my source. Thank you."

He hung up. "Well, if the guy I'm supposed to meet is dead, I doubt any of the other names I'm supposed to find are any more real. It was too good to be true. First Amy gets a check. That was a pleasant surprise. Now, I get an offer for a job that is unbelievable. Somebody wants me off the trail."

He wondered who might meet him at the Cultural Center and where they might take him for his first interview. *Most likely down an isolated canyon. Nobody would ever hear from me again.*

He called Todd and told him he was not going to take the job.

"Hard to believe, Mr. Carson. Is it the money? I can bump the retainer a bit if that would help. I report to the Director of the Board. He's anxious to get started. I'm sure he'd let me put another $5,000 on the table."

"No. I've decided. By the way, Mr. Begaye is dead."

"What! You gotta be kidding. I just talked with him last week."

The guy is playing his hand like he has a winner, Jake thought.

"Well then, you have special powers. The answer is still no."

"You may wish you had taken the job. I don't think you'll get that kind of offer again."

"I suspect you're right."

Jake called Demarco and told him about the lunch and the too-good-to-be-true offer.

"Why can't I get offers like that?" Demarco asked.

"My thinking is, I wouldn't collect any more than the retainer and that would have covered my funeral expenses if they ever found my body."

"You're kidding me!" Demarco said.

"No. I think it was an attempt to get me out of town. That's the good side of it. The bad side is, it was the first step not only to getting me out of town, but making sure I'd never return. These guys are good. They know what they're doing and they don't want any interference. They make smoke and mirrors look like Deception 101."

"Scary."

"So, how are you doing with what we discussed this morning?" Jake asked.

"I'm still working on it. I'll get it done by Friday. I'm going in disguise."

"Chicken."

"With what you've been saying, I think it shows good sense. I'll see you Friday," Demarco said.

"I hope I'm still around then," Jake said.

"What's that supposed to mean?"

"I mean they may resort to Plan B," Jake said.

"They?"

"The New Age Mission bunch or the Art for the Ages bunch. And, maybe they're one and the same."

"You're guessing, right?" Demarco asked.

"Yeah. Kind of," Jake said.

"Watch your back."

Chapter

28

Demarco called that evening. "The mayor had his lunch. Ate with Stern, Rasmussen and Metefara. All of 'em showed up. His Honor was very pleased with the work the New Age Christian mission has been doing. He told the DA who told my boss, 'Don't let some booze-soaked attorney stampede you into interfering with the good works these people have been doing.' My boss told me to not to bring it up again. I think he got his butt chewed some by the DA."

"Politics as usual," Jake said. "Well, we go to Plan B. Tomorrow. Are you ready?"

"Hell no! I'm not ready. Sure I've got the stuff you asked about, but I'm not ready. You're asking me to commit a crime, Jake. Maybe a crime. I think it is a crime! I'm not going to say a word and I'm wearing dark glasses. How could I ever let myself get talked into doing something as stupid as this?"

Jake answered, "Because you want to see justice done as much as I do. You know they're crooks. We just have to prove it beyond a reasonable doubt. Tomorrow we take a big step in that direction."

"I'm hoping something happens. Maybe you'll get sick or something. Maybe you'll have a lucid interval and decide not to do it."

Jake laughed. "You've been going to those legal seminars again."

"It's required. We get points for every one we attend," Demarco said.

"Let's meet here at eight."

Before hanging up, Demarco said, with a laugh, "Wags called again. He remembered another person he told about leaving the keys in his car. You had already guessed. It was his Vet, well the staff in the front office. I had my guy call out there. They didn't

245

know the McGuires. I don't think they had anything to do with the hit-and-run. Wags promised to keep thinking. I almost told him to forget it."

"Yeah. I know what you mean."

Amy also called. She and Warren wanted to play tennis at the Beach and Tennis Club on Sunday morning; breakfast first. My partner would be the old guy.

Jake didn't sleep much that night. His thoughts were on Plan B, all the things that could go wrong.

Murphy's Law, he thought. *If it can go wrong, it will go wrong. Just once, I'd like a break.*

He swallowed his pride and said a little prayer.

Bessie got him up early. It was bacon and eggs day. The eggs would be scrambled. They were easier to do that frying each egg. He was on serving duty, but he'd be finished before eight.

"I can tell you're doing something. You have that look on your face. I pray you'll not get into trouble. I know you think you're doing the right thing, but I have prayed for you and Brother Rasmussen."

He thanked her. "I need all the help I can get, Bessie. Before it's over, I think Rasmussen … or Reid, will need your prayers and then some."

She walked away distressed at the suggestion.

At five till, he was dressed and waiting for Demarco on the sidewalk. He pulled up and got out holding a bag containing the items Jake had requested. Demarco had a mustache and dark glasses.

"What is that?" Jake asked, laughing.

"It's what's going to keep me employed when this thing we're about to do hits the fan. It's never gonna work, you know? I can only hope we can escape before the cops show up."

"There's a name for you in the Bible?"

"Oh yeah. What's that? The sacrificial lamb?"

"No. Doubting Thomas. You have to feel the wounds before you believe."

"That's what I'm afraid of, feeling wounds. Mine."

"Come on." Jake motioned for him to come inside where they could complete their preparation for what Jake had called Plan B.

* * * *

Jake drove to his look out spot to spy on Rasmussen's house with Nate's binoculars. A car and a van were parked in front. Soon, people began pouring out the front door. The first to come out were the apostles in green and white. On their heels were Stern and Metefara and the driver of the RV. They were followed by Rasmussen who paused long enough to kiss his wife goodbye.

Minutes later, the RV backed out of its shaded parking spot and rolled down the hill.

"They're on their way to Oceanside," Jake told Demarco who had been nervously pushing at his mustache to make sure it was securely in place.

"Can you see out of those glasses, James? They seem awfully dark."

"They're okay. I borrowed them from an evidence bag. All I'm going to do is grunt anyway. I don't have to see anything but the door out."

Jake also wore glasses. They were kind that turned dark in the sunlight but lightened up when inside.

"Okay," Jake said. "Let's go."

Demarco cursed.

Jake parked where he had before near the gate. He tore the no trespassing sign off again and threw it across the road into the bushes. He and Demarco squeezed through the gap between the gate and the fence and hurried up the hill.

Jake pushed the doorbell.

Tammy answered. She really didn't recognize Jake in his suit and glasses and certainly not Demarco whom she'd never seen.

Jake said, "We're FBI, Ms. Reid." He flashed the fake badge Demarco had dummied up for him. "I'm Special Agent George Broome." He handed her a card which, Demarco assured him, resembled something an FBI agent would hand out. "This is Special Agent, Ronald Adams." Demarco didn't offer a card, but flashed his fake ID instead.

A stunned look covered her face which had blanched white.

"May we come in?"

She hesitated, so Jake strolled in.

"May we sit?"

Still in shock, she gestured toward the living room.

In passing, Jake said pointing, "I like these old pictures of you and Mr. Reid. Doing the Hollywood scene. I suppose that was a disappointment, Eli not making it big."

She nodded.

Jake and Demarco sat down. Jake set his brief case on the carpet next to him. "Please sit," he asked the woman.

She numbly did as he directed and sat with her hands protectively in her lap.

"You probably wonder why we're here."

She shook her head yes.

"I'll tell you. The FBI and the SEC have been investigating your husband's New Age Christian mission and the phony Art for the Ages investment scam for a number of years. The FBI and the SEC are about to file charges against Mr. Reid, aka, Rasmussen, Mr. Stern and Mr. Metefara for fraud, selling investments without a permit. They will serve a long prison term."

Her hand went over her mouth.

"You may also be charged. That's why we're here."

"I don't know anything about what's been going on. I'm never in the room when they discuss their affairs. I don't know what you're talking about."

"That's fine, Mrs. Reid. I understand. We think you do know some things. You know that your husband was approached by Mr. Stern and offered money to act as a preacher for the New Age Christian front. You know that he was offered this house and a good salary for preaching sermons. You know he is not an ordained minister and has never been out of the country. Isn't that true?"

"Mr. Stern said it was not illegal for Eli to preach. Eli does not collect any money. He just says what Mr. Stern tells him. Mr. Metefara is the only one who says he's been to Africa for the Mission. Eli only repeats what Mr. Metefara tells him … about what the mission is doing. There's no crime in that, is there?"

"That's called conspiracy to commit fraud. Mr. Reid knows what's going on, as do you, even though you might not make direct representations."

She was shaking her head all the time Jake was talking.

"You are a co-conspirator. Probably get 5 years in a minimum security prison."

She gasped.

"We do have a problem however. That's the main reason we came to see you. A nun, Sister Brigit, was murdered. We think Mr. Stern ordered her killed because she was about to uncover the fraud being perpetrated in the Central African Republic. That crime is much more serious than fraud. Even co-conspirators get hard time for murder."

"I ... we ... didn't know anything about that! We didn't. Eli had nothing to do with anybody being killed. He's a good man. He's a good preacher. It's his calling. He loves it. He was good at it in the movies. He just never got a break," she said.

"Until Mr. Stern came along and offered him the role of a lifetime. Right?"

"Uh, yes. Eli has loved it. He calls it his salvation. He knows the Bible. He studied it when he was in Hollywood. How can he be charged? He's just an employee. He does a job and gets paid."

"He can be charged because he knows there are no missions to Africa or to anywhere else. He has said nothing. He is a co-conspirator, as are you. I know Mr. Reid has told you everything," Jake said.

"He doesn't want to know. Mr. Stern doesn't tell him much. Just where to go. Mr. Stern does everything."

"He's the Wizard of Oz. Is that what you're saying? The guy who pulls the strings," Jake said.

"Uh huh," she said.

"When did you find out about the murdered nun?" Jake asked.

"I read about it in the paper. Eli said he knew her. He went to her funeral."

"Did you hear Mr. Reid or Mr. Stern talk about Nate and Jeanette McGuire?"

She looked puzzled. "McGuire? No, we've never talked about them."

"How about Aaron Bradley? Has your husband or Mr. Stern mentioned him?" Jake asked.

"No. I've never heard the name."

Jake stood. "Ms. Reid, I'm going to ask you not to discuss this meeting with anybody other than your husband. If he's interested in making a deal, maybe we can work something out so he won't have to spend much time in jail. You'll be able to enjoy this beautiful estate." Jake waved an arm about.

She nodded nervously.

"I'll ask you. Are you willing to testify to what you've just told us? It could get you a reduced sentence."

"I will say my husband knew nothing of what's been going on. He may have guessed about what Mr. Stern and Metefara have been doing, but we haven't done anything wrong. Eli preaches and he does a good job. I'll testify to that."

"Will you also testify to the fact that your husband read a letter he says came from Prince Charles. That letter was also a fake. We checked it out. And, your husband knows it was a fake."

She stammered and searched for words. Jake knew he'd nailed her. "Uh, Eli … well, we were given the letter by Mr. Stern. Eli says it was likely written by Mr. Stern. Eli just said what the letter said, not that the Prince had sent it."

Jake thanked her. He and Demarco left. On his way out, Jake fortuitously picked up the card he'd given her where she'd left it on a table in the entry hall.

When they were back in Jake's car, Jake said, "What say ye now, Thomas? Still doubting?"

Demarco felt relaxed enough to say, "No, I don't doubt. It was a good plan. I never thought it would work, but I guess you were right. I'm not sure what we found out that we didn't already know or suspect though. Except that now, we kind of have a witness. Bradley was killed by a crazed Halloween nut and the McGuires were run down by a joyrider. Sister Brigit was, as you suspect, likely killed to cover up Rasmussen's fraud in Africa. I should say Stern's. I believe the woman. Did you?"

"Yes."

"Do you think she'll keep quiet?" Demarco asked.

"Would your wife?" Jake asked.

"No."

"That's your answer. Even if Rasmussen reports to Stern, which I expect him to do, it's going to be a nervous time for them. They'll know somebody's closing in."

"Won't they suspect you?" Demarco asked.

"Probably. In fact, most likely. They won't know my accomplice however. That's gotta worry them."

"You mean, if they get rid of you, they still have your accomplice to worry about?" Demarco asked.

"Yep," Jake said.

"They may decide to start with you and let your accomplice show himself later. I'll sleep very well thinking about that," Demarco said.

"A man like you, Demarco? You let little worries like that roll off you like water rolls off a duck's back."

"Yeah! That's me all right. Well, if bad comes to worst, we have everything she said on tape," Demarco said, patting the tape recorder around his waist. "I have absolutely no doubt none of it can be used in evidence."

"I agree but we've proved that the New Age Christian mission is a fraud. Even though it can't be used in evidence, it is pretty persuasive, even to a mayor and a DA worried about reelection," Jake said.

"Yeah. Who's going to play it for them? Not me, that's for sure. And, I don't know you. Don't use my name either." He ripped off his mustache. "I'm glad to get rid of that thing. It's been itching the heck out of me."

"I don't know how we'll get it to the DA. I'll figure something out. It won't involve you," Jake said.

Jake dropped Demarco off at his car and drove back to his lookout spot to see what would happen when Rasmussen and his entourage returned from Oceanside. He had to wait almost an hour.

They all poured in through the front door. Jake couldn't see if Tammy welcomed them in or not. A few milled about in the back yard with glasses of what Jake assumed was wine. The post-service meeting only lasted thirty minutes. They all left. None seemed unduly nervous or anxious.

"So, Tammy didn't say anything," Jake said to himself. "But, I bet she is now."

And, she was.

* * * *

"Two FBI guys were here Eli," she told her husband who had taken a beer and sat down.

"What!" he shouted and leaped to his feet, spilling beer over him in the process. "FBI! What the hell for?"

"They know about you. They know you're not Rasmussen. They know you're preaching for Stern and that you are not ordained. They say no aid has been going to Africa. And, they know that letter you wave around during your services, the one from Prince Charles, is a fake."

"My God! Did ... did they say anything about ... arresting anybody ... me?"

"They talked about charging you ... and me as a co-conspirator ... with fraud. They know about the Art for the Ages thing Stern is doing."

"What did you tell them? God, I pray you didn't tell them we knew anything about anything?"

"I told them you worked for Stern and didn't ask questions and didn't know anything. I told them if I had to testify, that's what I'd say."

"That's not too bad. They'll still charge us ... me for sure. Maybe not you. I'll say you didn't know anything."

"They kind of hinted that if we cooperated, our jail time would be less. They also asked about that dead nun. I heard you and Stern talk about it."

"You didn't hear anything! You understand? Nothing! I don't know anything about it. Stern says burglars did it. I believe him. I went to her funeral because I liked her. She was a good woman."

"She had been asking questions, the FBI guy said. Questions that would expose the mission. That's why she was killed the agent said."

"What was his name?"

"He left a card." She turned to get it from the table in the hallway. "Not here. He must have picked it up. Strange that he didn't leave it. I guess he didn't want anybody else to see it. Like Stern."

"Yeah." Rasmussen grew quiet. "I have to do some thinking, Tammy."

A few minutes later, he said, "I think I have to tell Stern. If they're closing in, he should know. Maybe he can pull strings. He seems to know everybody."

"You think he can get us out of this mess?"

"I pray to God he can. I'd better go see him. This is not the kind of thing I want to discuss over the phone. Besides, the FBI might have a bug on our phone."

* * * *

Rasmussen knocked on the door of Stern's condo along the harbor. Stern opened the door. "What are you doing here?"

"We've got trouble. Real trouble."

"Come in and tell me what you think we have."

Rasmussen proceeded to tell Stern about the two FBI agents who visited his house and interrogated his wife. He glossed over what she said about how little they knew, but told him enough so that Stern got the idea that she had pointed at him.

"She should have kept her mouth shut. That's why I've never let her come to any of your services. She doesn't know when to keep quiet," Stern said.

He sighed, went to the kitchen and poured himself a glass of wine. "Want one?" Stern asked Rasmussen.

"No. I don't want one. I want to know what we're going to do to get out of this. Can we get out of it? I expect the FBI to knock down your door any second," Rasmussen said.

"Stay calm, Eli. Look at the facts hard. Let me make a few calls."

He picked up his phone and called the Art for the Ages number, identified himself, and asked, "Have you had any strange or enquiring calls lately. Say the past 6 months," Stern said.

The woman told him the only calls she'd had except for one were from people who had been referred. "And, I checked all referrals before giving out brochures or any information."

Stern told her to hold a minute while he pulled up a file on his lap top. He read names and dollar amounts to her. "Are those the names you have on your list?"

She took a few seconds to compare. "Yes."

"Those are okay. What about the one call without a referral?"

"I told you about that one. Jake Carson. He said Nate McGuire had referred him, but when I checked I saw that Mr. McGuire was dead so I didn't send him anything."

He thanked her.

"Anything wrong?" she asked.

"No, just doing a little bookkeeping."

"If you think anything's going wrong, you'll let me know won't you? I don't want to be here when people show up with a court order," she said.

"You'll be the first to know, but don't worry. Everything is okay." Stern hung up.

"Maybe to you, it's okay," Rasmussen said. "I don't think everything is okay."

"Calm down. I'm not sure the FBI called on Tammy. It doesn't smell right. Nobody's been snooping around. Just that one guy, Jake Carson. I got a picture of him coming out of Hennessey's with Todd. I'll get a print so we can show it to Tammy."

"Carson?"

"Yeah. I thought I had a way to get rid of him. I offered him money for a job in New Mexico but he turned it down. I think he got suspicious."

"Was he ever coming back?"

"No."

"I didn't think so. Not after Sister Brigit. You shouldn't have killed the poor woman."

"I notice you don't mind getting your check every month. She was about to blow that to hell. Unfortunately, we still have to deal with Carson or he could do the same thing."

Rasmussen rubbed his beard. "You think he's the guy who claimed to be the FBI? Suppose he's been undercover FBI or San Diego police?"

"No way. He's a drunk, disbarred lawyer. I've confirmed that. Besides, we would have had a clue from our dinner with the mayor and the DA. Let's show Tammy Carson's picture. If it's the same guy who claimed to be FBI, we're okay. Don't panic until you're sure the sky is falling, Eli. Stay cool. I'll bring the photo out in the morning."

Chapter
29

"That may be the man," Tammy said when Stern showed her the picture. "It could be. The guy who was here wore a suit and glasses so I can't be sure. Do you have one of the other guy?"

"I'd guess it's the same guy, Jake Carson." He cursed. "It stands to reason. Isn't anybody honest these days?" Stern asked with a sly grin on his face.

Rasmussen turned toward him with a shocked look on his face. "Coming from you, that's like the pot calling the kettle black."

"Just joking Eli. Just joking. Learn to be cool. We just got some good news. I'm happy. Now I know who's causing us trouble."

"Do you have one of the other guy?" Tammy asked.

"No," Stern said, "It might have been some bum from the halfway house. Don't worry about it. I may want you to sign affidavit."

"I'm not putting my neck in a noose for you," Tammy said. "I'll say they look similar. For all I know the guy was an FBI agent. Sure acted like it."

"That's stupid. That's why you're living off my welfare. I feed you! Don't forget it!"

His tone shocked both of them. Tammy stepped back with a gasp.

Stern wagged a finger in their faces. "Now, listen to me! Both of you. You'll do as you're told or I'll foreclose on you. You and Eli will be living in that old RV he brags to people about."

"A sword cuts two ways, Alan," Rasmussen said. "I—"

"Don't threaten me, preacher man or you'll be back in Hollywood begging for stand-in slots."

"I'm just saying ..."

"Well, don't. You bore me."

Rasmussen sighed. He patted his wife's shoulder in resignation and said, "Okay. What do we do now? My thinking is, it's time to fold our tent."

"What?" Stern said. "Run for cover at the first sound of thunder? No wonder you never made it big. I just have to figure a way to neutralize Carson. That's all. I'll let you know."

"Just don't let me know too much," Rasmussen said.

Stern laughed. "I imagine if I looked, there'd be a yellow streak down your back, Eli. What does the Bible say about cowards?"

"Why are you afraid, ye of little faith? But, Jesus stood and calmed the seas and the winds for his disciples. Are you Jesus, Stern? Can you calm things?"

"As far as you're concerned, consider it done." Stern laughed.

Stern turned to Tammy and said without a smile on his face. "Next time anybody comes around asking questions, keep your mouth shut! Ye of little faith. Got it! You may have talked Eli out of a job." He poked her in the chest with his index finger.

She stepped back.

Rasmussen pushed between them. "Don't talk to my wife like that. Okay? And don't poke her with your finger."

Stern stepped back and wagged a finger at both. "I own both of you. Keep your mouths shut. Talk only when I tell you to. Eli, that means you preach at sermons. Tammy you never talk to anyone."

Stern left. He had thinking to do.

* * * *

Sunday morning, Jake had breakfast with Amy and Warren. His partner would meet them on the court.

They exchanged the usual meaningless talk while they waited for breakfast, the weather, how they slept, and the movies they might see.

Jake told them about his run-in with Phillip and Billy. "Have you had any feedback?" he asked Amy.

"He called and complained that I was trying to make him fail. He wanted to know when the estate would be settled. He says he's getting a lawyer to make sure he gets what's coming to him. I may have to give him something."

"Trade for the house," Warren said. "He'll trade. He's desperate."

"Yeah," Jake said. "Desperate to fail."

"I may do what Warren says, offer him money if he agrees to release any claim on the house."

"Kind of shortsighted, if you ask me, to procrastinate. Offer him the exchange now!" Warren said.

Amy looked at Jake and said, "Warren's in a bad mood. He didn't sleep well last night. Got a late call … from a patient."

Warren forced a smile. "Yeah. Some guy with a problem. I don't know how he got my number. I don't encourage calls. That's why I do *locum tenens*. I couldn't get back to sleep. I'm right about the house though."

He turned toward Jake and asked, "How about you? Anything exciting happening to you?"

Well, well. I bet he already knows. "Funny you should ask. I got an offer to do some investigating for an oil company in New Mexico. $20,000 plus expenses for one month's work."

"When do you start?" Warren asked as if there should be no hesitation about acceptance.

"I turned them down. I didn't think I'd ever be able to do the work." That was a double entendre. What he thought was, he wouldn't live long enough to do any work.

"You turned down $20,000! That's hard to believe."

"Actually I probably could have negotiated it up to thirty. They were anxious."

"You may wish you had taken it."

I can understand how you might say that. "Right now, I doubt it. However, you could be right. Who knows what might turn up?"

"Do you think it had anything to do with the New Age Christian mission you've been checking out?" Amy asked.

"Yes. I think it was a way to get me out of town. I suspect I would never have returned from New Mexico."

She gasped. "You mean they'd kill you?"

"That's what I figured."

"How in the world did you come up with that?" Warren asked. "Didn't they have credentials?"

"Credentials can be faked." *Don't I know it?*

Breakfast came. They ate it and after an after breakfast cup of coffee, they headed for the court. Jake's partner was already on the court, warming up.

Warren's game was a little off; something he blamed on his lack of sleep. Jake played a point or two better and he and his partner took the first set 7-5 on a rare double fault by Warren. The second set went to a tie breaker which Jake and his partner won when Warren's backhand sailed long.

From the glum look in his face, Jake knew he was upset at having lost. He did the usual, congratulating Jake and his partner, making excuses to Amy about his poor play.

Before they left, Warren looked at Jake and said, "You turned down $20,000 for a month's work because you suspected somebody's credentials. You should have asked for the money up-front. I would have."

"Next time, maybe I should bring you in to negotiate for me," Jake said, hoping it didn't sound as patronizing as he knew it was.

Amy hugged Jake goodbye. "Call me next week. I'd like to get an update on everything. Be careful." She squeezed his arms and smiled.

He watched them drive away. *Be careful, she'd said. Not a bad thought. If I were Stern, I'd have figured out that the FBI agents were fake. He could browbeat Tammy in to swearing I was one of them.*

So, what would I do if I were Stern? I'm pretty sure he had the same thoughts when he learned about Sister Brigit's efforts to contact the Archbishop in the CAR. And, look what happened to her. So, being careful is exactly what I'd better do.

His problem was not knowing when being careful would help. Stern's goons could show up any time. He couldn't ask for police protection. No one had actually threatened him.

That was a time when a cold beer would have hit the spot. He thought about getting one. *Nate's refrigerator is full of good beers. I could drink one. One wouldn't faze me. I drank sake without a problem and I don't have to meet anybody today. I'm sure I could handle one.*

He drove to the McGuire's home and was about to open the gate, but stopped when he saw Amy's car parked in front. Since she and Warren had come in her car, he assumed she was inside with him. He kept driving.

The distraction helped him forget about having a beer. He went to Sunrise House and parked in the alley after checking for strange cars or odd people standing around. He entered the house at the rear.

"Bessie," he asked. "What do you need for me to do?"

His grandmother once told him, "An idle mind is the devil's workshop." Lately he'd come to believe that so he tried to stay busy.

Bessie put him to work vacuuming.

When he had finished, he had a cup of coffee with her and talked. "I don't want to worry you, Bessie, but somebody might try to kill me. I don't know when or exactly how, but I wanted you to know."

"My goodness! Are you sure? Does it have anything to do with what I did for you?"

"Yes. And a lot of other things I've been doing to smoke out Sister Brigit's killers and Nate and Jeanette's."

"Do you think they'll come in here and start shooting? My God. I pray that they won't."

"I do too, but I thought you ought to be warned."

"My, my, my. I don't know what I should do. I trust you. If you say somebody might try to kill you, they probably will."

"Nothing is for certain, but there's a strong possibility that I'm right."

"I could take some time off but the person who took my place might be killed. I don't know what to do, Jake."

"Nobody will be trying to kill you. Just be on your guard and stay out of sight if anybody comes calling for me. However, I don't mind if you call the police if somebody starts shooting."

"I will."

"Later today, I will type up a report of everything I know and suspect. I also have a tape recording which, in part, corroborates what I suspect has been happening. Rasmussen is a crook."

She opened her mouth to protest, but he cut it off with a wave of his hand. "I know what you think, but that whole New Age Christian Mission if a sham. I have proof. That's why somebody might be gunning for me. I'll write it up. Take it home with you. You don't have to read it unless something happens to me. In that case take it to the DA. Maybe he'll have enough guts to do something about it."

"Don't let anything happen to you, Jake," she said. "You're a fine man and you've overcome your problem. That took a lot of doing."

"With your help and lots of others," he said and patted her shoulder with his hand.

He drove back to the McGuire's home to type his report. Amy's car was gone so he had the place to himself.

After he'd finished, he put it in an envelope with the tape of his conversation with Tammy Reid. Fortunately, Demarco had not turned the recorder on until they were in the living room. So there was no mention of a second "agent" on the tape. Nothing that would implicate Demarco in the deception.

Back at the half-way house, he gave it to Bessie. Again, he had parked in the alley, out of sight and walked in through the back. A quick look out the front windows didn't reveal anybody watching the house.

Bessie walked up behind him and said, "You're worried."

"I am."

"Do you have a gun?"

"No. I wish I did but I don't know if it'd help or not."

"My late husband had one. A revolver. Six shooter, he called it. He said we needed a gun in the house in case anybody tried to break in. You want to borrow it for a few days?"

"Thank you Bessie. I think that might be a good idea."

She'd bring it the next morning.

* * * *

Demarco called late the next morning. "Thought I'd call to see if you would answer," he said.

"I'm still here," Jake said.

"The DA got a call from Eric Rasmussen complaining that two men impersonating FBI agents trespassed on his property and verbally abused his wife. He's coming down today to file a report. He told the DA that he suspects you, Jake Carson."

"Sounds serious."

"Off the record—I have that kind of relationship with my boss—I told him what you'd done. Not us, but you. How you taped a conversation with Rasmussen's aka Reid's wife and how she admitted that the whole thing might be a sham."

"What'd he say? Send out an arrest squad ... for me? That's the way my luck's been running."

"No. He understands off the record. He was intrigued. He thinks they're likely running some kind of scam. He says you should go to the press. Let those media jackals get after them. If you get them interested, they'll yap at Rasmussen's heels until they bring him down."

"That's a good idea. They don't need proof beyond a reasonable doubt. When they see a good story, they stay with it. I'll tell you something no one else knows, James. I once had an affair with Jeannette McGuire. It was when I was spiraling down to my ultimate state of being an enemy of the state. Actually, I loved Jen. That's what I called her. So, when I found out she was killed, I pushed to get this job. I wanted to find out who did it. I owed her that much. So, I'm reluctant to turn it over to the press just yet. I may go that way but for now, I want to finish it myself."

"But the McGuires were killed by a hit-and-run joyrider. This thing with Rasmussen is totally different, as is Sister Brigit's murder."

"I know, but when I started, my psyche lumped them together."

"Maybe you should have a word with your psyche. One thing I want to tell you. Wags called again and left me a message. He said he told the nurse who gave him a flu shot about his car. My guy checked 'em out. No one ever heard of or has ever had anything to do with the McGuires. Wags said he'd keep thinking."

"Commendable. Anyway, as screwed up as my reasoning is, I want to stay with Rasmussen a bit longer before I throw in the towel and dump it into the press's lap."

"It may be your funeral. If those guys killed Sister Brigit, what makes you think they won't come after you?"

"My housemother loaned me her late husband's thirty eight revolver with six extra bullets."

"I hope you live long enough to reload."

Jake did too.

Talking about Jen with Demarco stirred his feelings for Amy. He called and asked if she could have a cappuccino with him at lunch.

"I'd love it," she said.

They met at Starbucks.

* * * *

"How you found out anything?" she asked. She was in her office attire, a conservative dark suit and light gray blouse. He wore his usual, khakis and dark brown jacket.

"Not really." He told her how Demarco's boss suggested that he turn the thing over to the press. "Let them feast on it. It's the kind of story they love to get their teeth into."

"Sounds like a good idea to me."

"It is, but I want to keep it a little longer. I put a fire under the pot. I want to see it boil."

"Just don't let it boil over."

"I'll try. How's Warren?"

"He's pushing me to make a deal with Phillip about the house. I think he wants it for … us."

"I got that impression the first time we all met."

"You did! I never did. I guess from an objective point of view, you could see things I couldn't."

"I just got that impression."

"You may be right. He's been acting odd lately. It seems like he's totally distracted. It wouldn't take much for me to tell him to move out."

"I can't say that would make me unhappy."

"Are … are you saying … Are you saying you want to have an affair with me?"

"Not an affair."

She blushed crimson.

"Does that turn you off?"

She looked up and gave him a genuine smile. "No. I've had the same thoughts myself. That's why I blushed. It was like you've been reading my mind."

"It's a good thing you haven't been reading mine. I haven't said anything because ... well, you're engaged and I'm totally without portfolio. That means no money and no real way to make money."

She nodded and said, "Warren says he wants to get married, but I'm not sure he wants to for the right reasons. I'm not sure he really loves me. Not the way, I think you do."

That hit Jake between the eyes. "You have been reading my mind."

"Oh Jake, I don't have to read your mind. It's obvious. The way you look at me. The way you touch my arms and hands. The tenderness in your voice when you talk to me. You don't have to come right out and say it for me to know."

"I do love you, Amy. It started as a flashback to your mother, but it spread over to you and has haunted my thoughts ever since. Day and night. I have no right to, but I do and always will."

She put her hand over his. "I think I love you, Jake. I love to be around you. I know that. Don't apologize for your feelings. You have a right to have feelings."

He cupped her hand between his and looked into her eyes. "That'll give me a reason to push on. A reason to stay clean of drink. I think I could stand a beer or glass of wine these days without stumbling back into my black hole, but I want to be sure so I'm disciplining myself to drink nothing but coffee ... and a tiny cup of sake now and then. I know I can handle that."

"When you've finished what you're doing, we'll talk more."

His insides fluttered when she said that.

They finished their cappuccinos and walked to their cars. At hers, she turned and kissed him full on the lips, looking him in the eyes as she did. He held her close and kissed her again.

And, when she drove away, he whispered, "I thank you Lord for leading me along the right path. I have a reason to live."

But, would he live? That was the question in the back of his mind.

Chapter

30

Late afternoon after dinner, Jake sat on the front porch of the halfway house and watched traffic. He saw nothing suspicious. He was about to go in when Amy called, very distressed. "I just got off the phone with Phillip. I think he's flipped out. He quit his job. Maybe he was fired. I wouldn't doubt it, but he says he quit. He said you were conspiring with me to make him a failure. He screamed at me."

"It'll pass. He probably did get fired and he called you to blame somebody for his failure. People like Phillip never take responsibility for what they do wrong. Always blame somebody else. That way, they never mature."

"I don't know Jake. He was talking out of his head. Saying things like 'Dad knew I wasn't a failure. He knew. It's just you and that guy who slept with Mom. You think I'm a failure. Every time I come up with something that makes sense, the two of you knock me down. You are out to get me. Billy is upset too. We're not going to take it, Amy. We don't have to. Half of Dad's money is mine! Me and Billy mean to have it.' He hung up on me. I'm worried he might do something. He can't get into this building, but I don't know if you have any protection or not."

"I've had, I think, three run-in's with Phillip and his shadow and they've turned tail and run every time. They're all bite and no bark. I'll be on my guard, but I don't think you have to worry. Thanks, though, for warning me."

That call gave him something else to think about. He had been worried about Stern making a move. *Now, Amy thinks Phillip and Billy are cooking something up. I doubt it but stuff happens.*

Bessie came out to water the plants in the front yard. One of the other inmates had been assigned that chore, but he managed to duck out.

"You want me to do it?" Jake called out to her.

"No. Now and then, I like to get out of the house. I'm going home after this, anyway."

Cars went past. None looked sinister. Then, along came the red truck that belonged to Phillip or Billy. Billy was driving. When he saw Jake on the front porch, he gave him the finger. He pulled to a stop along the curb and got out.

He walked around the truck to the sidewalk and made a motion with his arms, daring Jake to meet him.

Jake could scarcely believe what he was seeing. Billy was beefier than Phillip and about Jake's height, but he had never struck Jake as having the guts to take him on face to face. *Maybe he's been taking martial arts lessons. I wonder where he left Phillip.*

Jake jumped off the porch and walked toward him. If he wanted to fight, Jake was in the mood.

"You've crapped on me 'n Phillip the last time. I'm gonna teach you some manners." He gestured again with his arms. His hands were straight, his arms outstretched, in some kind of martial arts readiness. He held no weapon, no knife or gun but Jake was nevertheless wary as he closed the distance between them. Something wasn't right. Where was Phillip?

Bessie, who had gone around the side of the house to get the hose hadn't noticed Jake leave the porch. She turned on the water and began her chore.

Billy walked toward Jake, slowly, deliberately. His arms moved about slowly as if ready to strike. "You're gonna get it now. You won't push us around after this."

"Well, let's not waste time." Jake raised his arms, preparing to do battle. Billy bounced on the balls of his feet, like he was readying himself for something. Jake wanted Billy to make the first move to avoid a charge that he'd attacked him. *Maybe that's his angle.*

He moved half a step closer to encourage him. As he did, he heard a commotion behind him. It was Bessie calling. "Watch out!" At the same time, he felt the splash of cold water on his back. He turned to see Phillip swinging a bat at him and missing because Bessie was spraying him in the face with cold water.

Without hesitation, Jake charged into Phillip, knocking him flat and sending the bat flying into the yard of the half-way house for Bessie to pick up.

Jake turned to see Billy turning tail once more, running to the truck. He did a U-turn in the street and swerved close enough for Phillip to dive into the truck's bed. Its tires screeched as it roared away.

"Are you okay?" Bessie asked. "I didn't see him until he was right on you."

"Good thing you were holding that hose or I would have been dead," Jake said.

"Should I call the police?"

"Ah, well, I'm not sure … Tell you what. I'll call my old buddy Demarco. Something just clicked in my head." He wanted to get out of his wet clothes, but figured calling Demarco took precedence.

Bessie quit watering and rolled up the hose. She had had enough excitement for one day. She was going home.

In the meantime, Jake had Demarco on the line. "James, old buddy, I think I have some information that might be useful to you."

"Is this a pretext for another favor? I just got home. My wife is putting dinner on the table. I don't want to talk. Okay?"

"I think I know who killed Bradley."

Finally all that talk from Phillip about how Nate knew he could handle responsibilities and how he was sure Nate was going to change his will made some sense. He had heard his dad complaining about Bradley and took it on himself to get rid of Bradley as a way of currying his dad's favor. Nate's comment to Cynthia about the boy coming up with some crazy things to convince him he had balls hadn't meant anything when Cynthia told him, but just then, it made a lot of sense.

"Okay. I'm listening."

Jake related what had just happened.

"You should have him arrested. But, what does that have to do with Bradley's murder?"

"Remember how Bradley was killed. The witch hit him from behind with a bat. Leopards never change their stripes. Phillip's sister says he's a tight wad. Never throws anything away. Why don't you get your buddies in homicide to get a search warrant, based on my affidavit, and search Phillips condo? If the witch's costume isn't there, have a look at his storage locker. Most condos have one someplace."

Jake gave him Phillip's condo address. Walter had told him where Phillip lived right after Nate and Jen were killed.

A warm shower felt good. He threw his wet clothes in Bessie's washer.

* * * *

Using the warrant issued based on Bessie's and Jake's affidavits, the police searched Phillip's condo. They didn't find the witch's costume there, but as Jake had suggested, found it in Phillip's storage room. He was arrested and charged with murder.

Jake had called Amy ahead of time. Until he told her about Bradley, she was in favor of counseling and a sizable loan. Once she heard that he probably had killed Bradley because Nate was having a dispute with the man, she gave in and told Jake to go ahead. She did hire the best criminal lawyer in town. Jake had no doubt that before the trial was over, the lawyer would make it look like Bradley had provoked the incident. Maybe Phillip would get off with very little, if any, jail time depending on how well his lawyer bonded with the jury.

Phillip was out on bail almost immediately and Jake went on alert for another ambush.

Demarco took full credit for solving the case, though he did give Jake a credit. His request for a transfer into the major crimes unit suddenly attracted attention.

The DA sent an investigator out to interview Jake about "impersonating" an FBI agent.

Jake vigorously denied it and even with Tammy's positive identification of Jake as the perpetrator, nothing happened. Jake caulked it up to a case where the Rasmussens didn't want to press charges because all they wanted to do, at Stern's request, was to throw a scare into him.

That hadn't worked. Jake was still on the prowl.

Amy called Jake to play tennis. That was for Warren's benefit. Actually, she wanted to enjoy a quiet dinner with Jake at the Marine Room.

** * *

"Warren is insisting that we get married," she told Jake. "He wants to settle up with Phillip. Give him some money or something. He says bargain with Phillip so we keep Mon and Dad's house. He figures Phillip is vulnerable now and can be dealt with."

"That's probably true. What did you tell him?"

"What do you think? I don't want to marry him. I've decided. I want to marry you. I guess I shouldn't have said that. The man's supposed to propose first."

"I have proposed to you hundreds of time between ten at night and six in the morning ever since the first time I looked into your eyes, Amy. I'll do if formally now. Amy, will you marry me? I don't have a pot or a window to throw anything out of, but I want to marry you with every fiber of my body and my soul. I love you. I feel like I have always loved you. I want to spend the rest of my life with you."

"Thank you, Jake. I think I needed to hear that. I love you too. I'll help get you reinstated. Once you can practice again, you won't have to feel ashamed about not being able to provide. As a practical matter, I make enough for both of us, but I know that a man, a responsible man, wants to be able to support his family." She smiled. "Besides, I expect us to grow in numbers."

"Count on it."

"Phillip has called a couple of times. It's amazing how contrite he is these days. Now that I'm paying his attorney."

Jake laughed. "Just so he stays away from me."

"I think he will. He hasn't mentioned your name."

"I had wondered if he might have run Nate and Jeannette down, but decided he didn't. Wagner called Demarco with his last recollection. It seems he told his mother and father about leaving the keys in his old car. Demarco didn't bother to interview them"

"Have you heard anything more from Rasmussen and his bunch? What's it been, a couple of weeks?"

"I think they're content to let the DA put a scare into me. Impersonating an FBI agent is a serious crime. If I make any more noises, they might move on that. They're crooks and running a pyramid scheme that'd make Madoff's look like child's play. But, without some proof or somebody willing to undertake an aggressive investigation, I might just as well be howling in the wind."

"That's frightening to think about."

"It is. I'm going to make more noise however. Right now, I'm thinking about visiting the local media to see if I can generate some interest in the story."

"I'd rather you just forget it. It's not your job. You tried. Now it's time for you to work on getting reinstated and getting back to the practice of law. It's safer."

"You're probably right. But, I'd like to see what a reporter thinks about it. I'll just show him or her some of the smoke to get a reaction. Maybe their publisher will have enough guts or· interest to pursue it. I agree with you however. My main priority is to get reinstated. I'll sleep on it."

"You're very bright, Jake. Be careful about what you say to anybody. People get sued for less. I'd hate to see you get reinstated and spend the next five years fighting a lawsuit."

"I don't disagree with that. I'd rather spend the next five years building a family with you."

"Me too. That'd be more fun."

They enjoyed dinner. The food was good, but mostly they enjoyed being together.

The next day, Jake went to see Walter to ask him if he would file a petition to have him reinstated to practice law.

Walter said, "I've already talked to the judge about it. He said, if what I've told him is true, plus the positive reports he's been getting from the court administrator, he would have no trouble reinstating you. What he'd like is to have dinner with you one night to discuss it informally."

"That's fine with me. Depending on where we go, he may have to pick up the tab."

Walter laughed. "We have an account at the University Club. Go there and put it on the firm's tab."

Jake thanked him. "I'm always free. Have your secretary make the appointment and let me know."

* * * *

Jake wrestled with his conscience that night. Should he go to the press with the story or sit on it to see what might happen? The best plan, he finally decided, was to have dinner with the judge, convince him he was on the wagon for good and start rebuilding his practice. It excited him to think about getting back to some real work. Beer had leveled him. He felt relief to be free of its addiction. And, he offered thanks to the Lord for standing with him in his fight. "I couldn't have done it without you, Lord," he whispered in a prayer before falling asleep. He also thanked Sister Brigit for her help.

He'd keep the Rasmussen problem on the back burner for a couple more days. *See if my subconscious tells me anything,* he thought. Sister Brigit weighed heavily in his thoughts, but so did Amy.

After breakfast, Bessie took him aside and said, "I've seen black cars come by here. I couldn't see inside because the windows were dark, but I've never seen them before."

"I'll be on the lookout. Did they slow down?'

"They did. Ever so slightly."

"May be nothing. Somebody looking to buy a house or something. But, thank you for watching. I'll be on my guard. How about people who live on the street? Could it be them?"

"No. the people who live in the big houses are absentee owners. They come out here when it gets too cold or hot where they live. And, they drive Mercedes or BMWs. These cars had out of state tags."

"Hmm." He had taken wearing his old coat continuously. Its pockets were deep enough to hold the revolver Bessie had loaned him.

Chapter

31

On most afternoons, Jake sat on the porch, read the afternoon paper and watched the street. He'd rather see the intruders he was certain to come before they saw him. If they wanted to shoot, he had a plan. He'd hit the porch floor behind a wooden table and fire back. That would be better than having somebody sneak up on him. He almost welcomed it. *Get it over with.*

Then, one afternoon, a car he had not seen before pulled against the curb in front of the house. It did not have tinted windows so he could see Tammy sitting in the passenger's side.

"What the heck?" he said. As he stood, he saw Rasmussen get out of the driver's side and approach the house. His hands held nothing, Jake noted. He wore street clothes with a dark jacket, not his usual white.

Rasmussen saw Jake on the porch, gave him a nod, no smile, no indication that it was a social visit. Jake would have been surprised if it had been. He wondered what did bring Rasmussen to see him and was wary. He looked up and down the street, apprehensive, but saw no strange cars.

Rasmussen said, "Carson, I want to talk."

Jake motioned for him to sit. "Talk."

"I don't like you. I want you to know that. Tammy despises you. I want you to know that."

"Well, I like people who like me. It follows that if you don't like me, I sure as heck don't like you. That may be from the bible."

"A paraphrase from Proverbs." Rasmussen took a seat. "I'm here because I want to make a deal. Are you undercover FBI?"

"No."

He grimaced. "Stern said you weren't. Tammy thought maybe you were. Stern figured it out. That you were the one who came to the house. Maybe we can do business. Maybe we can't. I'd hoped you were FBI."

"I have connections with the San Diego police department. High level." He was thinking of Demarco's boss.

Rasmussen breathed loudly. "It'll have to do." He looked back at the front door, nervously. "I think Stern is planning to kill you. Your threat to go to the press with your investigation sent him into orbit."

Jake wondered how he came by that information. He'd talked to Demarco about it. Demarco must have talked to his boss and who knows who else. He'd also told Amy. Did she tell Warren?

Rasmussen continued. "Last night Stern and some guys he meets with now and then, met at the house. Tammy and I went to bed, but I left the door open and listened. I couldn't hear everything, but from what I heard, I got the drift that you had to go." He again looked back at the front door. This time with a nervous frown. "Say, do you mind if we walked while we talked. I don't like somebody overhearing what I'm saying. You aren't living with the most reputable of people here."

He stood without waiting for Jake to answer. Jake again looked up and down the street. It smacked of a setup, but he could see nothing strange anywhere so he followed the man onto the sidewalk. They walked away from where he'd parked. Tammy rolled down her window and looked back.

"Tammy and I want a deal," Rasmussen said. "We don't know everything that's been going on, first hand, but we know things aren't legit with the mission. It's like you told Tammy. It's a scam. A few dollars get spent here and there, but most stay with Stern. The same with the Art for the Ages thing. It's all a scam."

"You'll tell that to the DA?"

He nodded. About that time, a car with tinted windows rolled past and pulled to the curb behind them. A man got out of the passenger side, dressed in dark clothes. In his hand was an automatic. He was about as tall as Jake, but beefier, like he spent a lot of time in a weight room. *Jer*, Jake thought.

"Preacher man," he called out, gesturing with the automatic. "Step out of the way or you'll end up like Carson."

Rasmussen looked at Jake then at the guy with the gun. He said, "I didn't … I—"

Another man got out of a car parked on the other side of the street, similarly dressed, also weight room build. He had a blackjack in his hand. And, in front of them, suddenly appeared a third man, dressed in dark clothes, like the other two and waving a billy club.

Jake didn't have to guess what they had in mind. The one guy would keep the automatic on him while the other two beat him to a pulp and if he tried to run, he'd be shot. There was no way out. Jake's hand made a slight move toward his jacket pocket and Bessie's revolver. He would not go quietly.

They'll have to work for it.

"Step away, preacher," the man repeated with more gesturing. He'd moved closer. The other two guys had also closed the distance between them, moving fast.

Jake sensed that Rasmussen was edging away and eased his hand closer to the revolver.

He told Rasmussen, "It's time for you to put up or shut up Rasmussen. The Bible says be strong and courageous. Help the ones in need. Right now, I'm the one with a need."

Rasmussen glanced at Jake, then at the three men approaching them. He said, "Okay. Let's take 'em on, Brother."

In one motion, Rasmussen swirled around, whipped off his jacket coat and swung it at the man with the gun, sending him back a step. That gave Jake time to get the revolver out of his jacket pocket. By that time, the other two men were on them, swinging their weapons. Jake squeezed off one shot at the man with the automatic but was off balanced and missed. The man, that had ducked away from Rasmussen's jacket, steadied himself and waited for a clear shot.

Rasmussen, a big man, was lashing out with lefts and right, making contact with the face of the man who was clubbing him with his truncheon. Soon, Rasmussen was bleeding from both eyebrows and his right arm hung limp from a blow. Still, he kept swinging, as did Jake.

Jake, a little more at ease in a fight, had managed to dodge most of the blows but not all. His head had begun to throb. The angry man in front of him, hadn't fared so well either. Both his eyes were almost closed and filled with blood, making it difficult for him to see where to aim his blows.

The man stumbled back, wiping at his eyes. "Shoot him," he said. "Shoot!"

By that time, Rasmussen was on his knees, stunned and unable to do more than balance himself on his knuckles. The man facing Rasmussen, having heard his cohort shout "shoot," backed off to give Jer a clear shot.

Jer was about to do just that, when Tammy, who had gotten out of the car, flew into him, knocking him sideways. The man's shot caught Rasmussen in the shoulder. He rolled over and fired again. That bullet grazed Tammy's head and sent her reeling sideways.

That was all the time Jake needed. He had his revolver in his hand. When Jer's automatic began its sweep back toward him, he fired. His bullet caught Jer in the chest and knocked him backward. The automatic flew out of his hand. Jer didn't move.

The other two guys turned to run. Jake shouted. "Stop or I'll kill you."

They stopped.

"On your knees," he ordered them. They did as he said.

He got his phone out of his pocket and dialed 911. It wasn't necessary. Bessie was running toward them. "I've called the police, Jake."

Minutes later, San Diego's finest were on the scene trying to sort out the good guys from the bad ones. They had no trouble believing Jake and Bessie. Rasmussen was in no condition to say anything and Tammy wasn't in much better shape. The ambulance took them to the hospital.

Jer didn't need an ambulance. He was dead. The other two attackers were hauled away in a police van.

Jake took stock of his physical condition. He had lumps and bruises all over his body; cuts on his head and face from the man's club but nothing was broken.

The police had offered to take him in the ambulance with Rasmussen and Tammy, but Bessie said she'd take care of him.

As soon as he could, Jake called Demarco and told him what had happened. "Get the fraud squad to send somebody to the hospital to interview Rasmussen, actually Reid, and his wife Tammy. They are ready to blow the whistle on Stern and his scam. You can tell your boss to call the DA and let him know how you helped solved the case. It's going to turn out to be one of the biggest pyramid schemes this country has ever seen."

* * * *

Stern was on a plane to Russia before he could be arrested. Jer's failure to call had alerted him. He was apprehended as he changed planes at Heathrow Airport in London and was being held for extradition.

The two men, Barney and Whitey, arrested at the scene blamed Jer for everything. "We were only hired for the Carson job." They claimed to know nothing about any other murders.

Jer was dead after all and couldn't deny anything. They swore they didn't know Stern or Rasmussen. The woman in Vegas who transacted business for the Art for the Ages scam testified that Stern had met with Jerry Verucchi a number of times when he was in town. She identified the dead man as Verucchi.

The police assumed Stern had hired someone else to make the McGuire's deaths look like an accident of some sort after he began to wonder about the return on his investment. Without a witness to link Stern to Brigit, the DA didn't think there was enough evidence to charge Stern with her murder.

Unfortunately for Stern, when Whitey had to face a long sentence for being an accessory to murder, he suddenly wanted to bargain. In exchange for a reduced sentence, he remembered being present when Verucchi and Stern talked about the failed attack on Sister Brigit. He overheard Stern tell Verucchi to try again. The DA added murder as a charge against Stern.

Rasmussen and Tammy recovered and agreed to testify against Stern on the fraud charges. In exchange, both were offered immunity.

"I heard both were released," Amy told Jake during their noon time coffee rendezvous.

"Rasmussen, well Reid, told me—we had a brief chat—he was buying a tent to hold tent revivals around the county. Tammy said a Hollywood agent had called about a part. The publicity helped him."

"Well, you said he was good," Amy said.

"He was. Stern knew what he was doing when he hired him. It's ironic, in a way," Jake said. "There I was, wallowing in self-pity and depression and I happened to stumble by Rasmussen preaching on the beach. It turned out that he was a phony, but his words were real and became my watchword as I struggled to overcome my weakness. In his own way, he did some good."

"I'm glad he did," Amy said as she leaned over and kissed him on the cheek.

* * * *

Jake had dinner with the judge who told him afterward that he could resume practicing law at any time. He had just wanted to make sure. Jake hung out his shingle the next day. He got a considerable amount of publicity when the scams were revealed. In fact, he was given credit for having dogged it out when others were reluctant to do anything about it.

He immediately began getting phone calls from scammed investors. They wanted their money back and Jake was ready to oblige. He filled a class action suit and went to work.

Walter and his former partners welcomed him back into the fold ... as a senior partner. He turned them down.

* * * *

Amy told him she'd kicked Warren out. While he never admitted to knowing Stern, she was certain that he did. Certainly, somebody had alerted Stern that Jake was about to go to the press with the story about Stern's scams. It had to be Warren. Amy had told him what Jake had said about giving it to the press. The attack on Jake came after that.

He was charged with conspiracy to commit fraud in the Art for the Ages scheme. A number of doctors said Warren recommended that they put money into Art for the Ages. He claimed he was a victim just like they were. It was determined that Warren had dropped out of the medical school he was attending in London. He was considered bright and a great tennis player. The DA was reluctant to take the case to trial.

Amy said, "He fooled a lot of people with his charm, including me. I think that was the real reason he never opened an office. He was afraid the officials would find out he was a fraud."

"This whole thing has smoke and mirrors. Nobody was real," Jake said.

"He's called me a couple of time, charming as he can be. He wanted us to get back together but I've told him to forget it. What are your plans?"

"I'm knee deep in the class action suit. It may take years to resolve that. I'm hiring two junior attorneys and some paralegals to help. Stern hid money everywhere. We're finding most of it. After that, who knows?"

"The newspaper stories have lauded your efforts. You should be pleased. You're a hero," she said.

"It has been a long time since I had much to be pleased about. Most of all, I'm pleased that we're getting married. I hold my breath that you don't change your mind."

"I will never change your mind, Jake. Somehow it just seems right ... what we have between us."

"Phillip might not agree. How is he doing? I haven't heard from him lately. Since the judge let him off with a probation. I think he got off light, but his attorney did a great job. His claim that Bradley made a slur about his sexual preference did the trick with the jury," Jake said.

"He's in counseling. I don't think I told you," Amy said. "If his doctor says he can handle it, I'll arrange for the trust to loan him some money to start a business. He can cook. I'll say that about him. If he can get someone with a cool head to actually run the business, I think he can make it."

"The assault charges against Billy were dropped," Jake said. "I expect he'll want to help. I don't know what he can do, though."

She coughed. "I'm sorry. I've been treating people for the flu. I tell everybody to get a flu shot, but not all of them do. They end up with the flu and I have to treat them. I hope I don't catch it."

Something flashed into Jakes consciousness. "Flu shots! Wait a minute. Let me ask you something. Do you remember the morning Nate and Jeannette were killed?"

"I'm not likely to ever forget it."

"What was Warren doing?"

"He was up before me. He said he had to go out for something. Cream for his coffee, I think. Why do you ask."

"Let me make a call and I'll tell you."

He dialed Demarco's number. After an exchange of hellos and well wishes, Jake asked, "Do you remember one of Wags calls? The one where he'd told a nurse about leaving the keys in his car?"

He did.

"Well, can you check the doctor's office to see if Warren Meyer was substituting in his office? I'm betting that he did. If so, check to see if the nurse told Meyer about Wags' keys."

He'd do it.

Amy was shocked speechless. "You can't actually think Warren killed Mom and Dad?"

"It makes sense."

Demarco called back the next day. Warren had substituted at the doctor's office and the nurse had told him about Wags habit of leaving the keys in his car. It would have been a simple matter for Warren to look up Wagner's address and take the car. Witnesses saw a man wearing a baseball cap and a sheep skin coat the morning the McGuires were killed. He was taking off his gloves as he jogged past their home, after leaving Wags' car. They thought it odd that a man in a coat would be jogging.

Amy told the police that Warren often wore an old baseball cap to protect his face from the sun and that he owned a pair of gloves. And, he owned a sheep skin coat.

Warren was arrested again and that time was charged with murder. His attorney picked up on the fact that the DA was keenly interested in the bigger fraud, began negotiating. Warren would be a witness against Stern in exchange for a light sentence on the charge of murder. More negotiating ensued with his attorney attacking the witness's credibility. Finally, it was agreed that Warren would receive a ten year sentence for the murder in exchange for his testimony against Stern.

It turned out that Warren steered doctors to Stern in exchange for a fee and an investment in the Art for the Ages syndicates. He also alerted Stern that Nate needed money.

Jake took Jen's picture out of his wallet and looked at it one last time before putting it away. "I thank you Lord," he said, "for letting me balance my books with her."

The End